IRON FANG: GRIM

MC SHIFTER ROMANCE
VERA FOXX

FOXX FANTASY PUBLISHING

First paperback edition: March 2023

Book design by: Etheric Designs

Publisher: **Foxx Fantasy Publishing LLC**

Editing by: Cissell Ink

CONTENTS

DEAR READERS

Please read the following trigger warnings and other important information regarding this book.

This book contains:

Dominate male.

Submissive female: This does not mean she is weak and fragile.

Sex Trafficking.

PTSD.

Blood, gore, torture.

Detailed consensual sex scenes.

Knotting.

Breeding Kink.

Primal Kinks.

Obsessive MMC.

Strong Language.

Memories of past rape, but written in passing. No details.

PROLOGUE

Grim

The gavel rang in my ears, the same gavel that made my wolf salivate. It was the only sound that would get my wolf to move anymore. That gavel meant an impending mission from the acting alpha.

Each time the gavel hit the pulpit in the abandoned church, the howls and snarls began. Our brothers' growls would drive my wolf's lust for blood that much greater. This church across the street from the Iron Fang bar had been our meeting place since Locke bought the land on this side of town, and it fully represented what we thought of our prior beliefs.

Dead and dying.

My claws elongated, scratching the pew in front of me. The shifters here were all so damn happy to find a place to rest their weary souls, but not me.

This was a dead end. This was where all rogues went when they had nowhere else to turn. The rogues weren't necessarily evil, but they weren't good, either. We were the gray. We were the in-between. The shifters that didn't belong out in the forest, eating dead carcasses, because we had lost ourselves and were mostly known as rabids. We were the rogues transitioning, and that meant we didn't belong in a pack, tribe, or pride.

We were all the misfits that no one wanted, especially our mates.

The gavel hit the wooden pulpit again, making me cringe. I dared not let others see the squint in my eyes as my wolf amped up our hearing to listen to the latest task. These tasks, these missions, as Locke liked to say, were to keep us busy. To ease our troubled animals, since no mate was coming to calm us.

Because they abandoned us.

The shifters all sat in neat little rows, some drinking cans of human alcohol that barely touched the minds they wanted to fog. We all still healed quickly, just not as fast as if we were in a formal pack.

"Settle down." Locke set the gavel down more gently this time, his eyes darting toward me.

The hushed understanding Locke gave me stirred my wolf. My wolf didn't trust anyone, and he barely trusted Locke because, at one time, he trusted *her*. And look where that got me.

Locke was different, though; we had an understanding. Promises that if things went wrong, we would be there for one other. We had each other's backs.

"We've got a hit on a warehouse," Locke said. The shifters in the room slapped their hands together, some howling, others growling at the impending blood that would be shed. That was our favorite—to let our frustration and aggression out—even if it was in our human forms.

Once you go rogue, controlling your animal without an acting alpha was difficult. We had to keep our animals inside, never letting them see the sun. It was to protect not only each other but any humans around. If an animal burst through its human side, which it inevitably would, they would be uncontrollable, and they would really go rogue, or rabid as we now called them.

Once you went rabid, there was no going back, and actions were taken to see to it you never saw the sun again.

You were put out of your misery, put down, the proper euthanization, anyway you wanted to call it. There had been a few. The bear that I put down several years ago had to have been the worst. The fight in him was strong, and it took three of us to pin him until I slit his neck with my knife.

Feeling the heat of the bodies surrounding me made me snarl; the shifters backed away, scooting down the torn padded seat. I wasn't far from going rabid; it had been far too long keeping my wolf inside. My wolf was so deprived of touch, compassion, and interaction with anyone that he had shut down completely. There was no speaking to my wolf. My wolf was a pure animal now, with no way to bring him back to the light.

"This came in just this morning, a note stating there are both humans and shifters in a warehouse by the loading docks on Ocean Ave."

Once Locke and I moved here and slowly gathered other rogues like us, we began getting letters. All were anonymous, with a circle around measuring scales of judgment. On one end laid a feather, and on the other sat coins. We continued to get the same letter over and over, speaking of women needing help with exact coordinates to their locations.

Locke took it upon himself to gather a group, and we all set out to see if that first letter could be true.

That one dark night changed everything for us once we realized what we were meant to do. For the rest of our brief lives before we went rabid, we were to rescue and protect the innocent because no one had looked out for us.

That was the night we all took a vote; Locke became our acting alpha. We continued to receive letters and worked on the tasks given to us because what else were we supposed to do? We all lived in this small human town we had officially taken over. We tried to live ordinary lives amongst humans. But even the humans knew we were dangerous and stayed away.

It was for the best. They all needed to stay the hell away from us.

Especially me.

The cops were afraid of us; they let us do what we pleased as long as we didn't cause issues. In reality, we kept the streets cleaner; we didn't put up with anybody's shit.

We were the black knights of the town. The humans would never know what good deeds we'd accomplished.

The gavel hit once again. My mind had already zoned out too many times today for my liking. My time was fading fast. The wolf inside shifted our deep blue eyes to his black. Locke put a hand on my shoulder, which made my wolf stiffen. He grabbed his wrist. A resounding crack sounded as we twisted it. Locke swore, pulling himself from our grip.

"Easy there," Locke murmured.

The crowd of shifters departed with the heavy thumps of their thick leather boots. Sizzle, one of my brothers, tipped his head in recognition.

"Are you up for it tonight?" Locke asked me.

I slapped my hand on my thigh and squeezed my hands against the leather gloves that covered my knuckles. They were riddled with scars even before I was cast out from my pack.

Nodding in silence, I stood up, pulling on my cut.

I hung my head, following Locke out the door. The wolf skull with crossbones stared back at me from his cut. The haunting eyes looked straight into my empty soul—the soul that would always be empty.

Bikes lined up outside the church, everyone revving the loud engines of their hogs. Not being able to feel the wind in our fur or scales had reduced us to the thrill of fast motorcycle rides. Anything to get a high, anything to get our animals some sort of freedom that they couldn't have any other way.

Gritting my teeth, my wolf surfaced far too close, wanting to break free from the skin where I forced him to stay. He let out a deadly howl that echoed down the line of shifters on their bikes. They howled in return, many taking bets on how many lives I would take tonight. Because I was the worst of them all. I was the one the enemies hid from when they saw me coming.

They see me as Grim, the Grim Reaper of the Iron Fang MC.

The official enforcer.

I had a sick fascination with blood; I liked to bathe in the red liquid that splattered onto my skin. Each cut with a claw, a knife, or a fang had me tingling with anticipation. My favorite was taking my time and forcing them to feel the same pain I felt, which made me itch to get to our mission faster.

We may save women from evil fates, but it was really saving me, letting me push my tormented soul toward something else. Let the enemy feel the pain I felt because there would be a time when I wouldn't be able to do even that.

No, instead, I would die a mateless shifter and sink into the abyss of hell with no one to remember me. I would join the rest of the dead that I had murdered and fight with them throughout eternity. I would do it because there was no redemption for me. There were no second chances to find the other half of my soul. Each day I could fucking destroy someone trying to hurt someone else's happiness would be a fucking gift.

I straddled my hog, revving the engine. The vibrations of the powerful motor between my legs made me sit more comfortably as my wolf settled.

Locke stood next to me, pulling on his gloves. None of us wore our brain buckets, not caring if we slammed our skulls into the hard asphalt. Really, it might be better that way, better than watching from the inside of your mind as your brothers ripped your animal to pieces.

The wind moved through my shoulder-length hair and caught my beard.

I sighed heavily, feeling the rays of the sunset rest on my face.

Feeling Locke's stares, my brother gave me a thumbs up. The gavel rang in my head again as I rubbed my temple fervently. My vision shook for a moment, but once the engine revved, I pushed the accelerator forward, leaving the broken church behind.

We passed the bar; its neon lights lit up the shadows of the alleyway. Humans that we had saved from previous lives looked out the windows as we passed by.

We protected our own. That was all that mattered now. The rogues of the Iron Fang would be our own pack, even if it wasn't recognized in the supernatural world.

I heard the gavel in my head again. The echoes ran through my body, opening files of memories I didn't want to remember.

My bike wobbled, and I almost lost my balance. Locke grabbed hold of the handle to help steady it.

Again, the gavel rang, slamming those memories away. My heart felt lighter for once, the hammering in my head ceasing. Locke's curious gaze made me nod as we pulled closer to the docks.

We parked our bikes five blocks away, and shifters reached into their satchels, pulling out guns, bags of magical knockout powder, knives, and iron cuffs.

We weren't sure what we would face this night, but one thing stood out to me more than ever as my wolf tried to push through my walls to end me: *The Moon Goddess was a cruel, heartless bitch.*

CHAPTER ONE

Grim

Locke threw out his hand signals. The four groups of our brothers scattered in various directions. Some went around the back, making sure doors were covered and no one could leave. Another team was led by Hawke. He was an ex-guard with great stealth capabilities who also come in particularly handy with his sniper rifle. He led his team across the street to set up scopes.

My group, which comprised Locke, Sizzle, and other members, stormed through the front gates, so to speak.

Locke had his Glock hidden in his side holster, along with other fun items he liked to carry. He was like a damn arsenal. Other members carried the basics but still looked up to their leader in awe. Which was all fine and shit for their human parts.

But their wolves would never fully submit.

I ran my finger over the machete on my right hip. I hated guns and felt like the fight should be within arm's length instead of being a coward and shooting damned bullets like humans. But now we couldn't use our animals, so some of us, in part, felt only human.

I didn't.

We all still healed, still bled, the scars remained, and the desire of our wolves to follow an alpha was stifling. But it wasn't the same, not when our leader couldn't rely on his wolf's alpha authority.

No matter how much Locke believed he was in charge, he wasn't. A rabid wolf wouldn't submit.

The pad of my thumb flicked my serrated knife on my belt. Blood ran down the cold silver, dripping onto my thigh.

Locke did his signature strut, his shoulders pulled back confidently as he approached the teller-like window of an old-fashioned movie theater. The men behind me chuckled. Pushing each other like this was some game. To them, it was. Our lives were technically already over; we were just waiting for the "game over" to cross our eyes and send us into the next life.

The surrounding area was obviously glammered by a spell. To the human eye, it would look like a run-down warehouse, the lights flickering where the light bulbs were dying, the wind blowing a loose board away from the windows. But it was more.

There was a tiny gold coin in the middle of the building that blasted the glamour within a certain radius. It could be seen within and outside of the glamour spell. No human would look for such a small coin, but if they did, they would be opened to a whole new world.

At times, when magic wasn't the strongest, the coin would flicker like a television that was on its last leg.

But humans didn't pay much attention to that. They believed what they saw and were none the wiser. They didn't believe in magic like the fairy tales they were told. If they only looked, they would see what was right in front of them was another world. A world where their nightmares could easily come true.

We walked forward, and the glam flickered, unable to work on the supernatural. It was too weak.

The glamor glimmered again, revealing a winter fae. His pale white skin and the frost on his brows twinkled in the small candle that lit his box. The window fell away, but he didn't look up. He continued to manicure his claws.

"Name and coin." The blasé attitude made Locke stop his chuckle of amusement and grow stone cold.

"We are actually here for payment." As the fae glanced up, his frosted eyes widened, while Locke grabbed the manicured hand and cuffed him with iron. The fae's winter-like appearance dulled, turning slate gray, his head falling to the table.

Reaching over the table, Locke pulled on the switch, a buzzer sounding to open the door to the left. "Let's get to work," he smirked, pulling out a satchel of dust.

The group behind us didn't wait. They walked into the dark halls of the beating bass of music. They waved their hands and moved their bodies with the beat. Blood was going to be shed, and we were ready.

The lights glinted twice at the entryway, letting us know Switch had already dismantled the cameras inside. Hoods were thrown off, and growls of approval rang through the black-light-lit hallway.

This was indeed a warehouse. The walls were mostly bare with only support beams, large overhanging headlights, and open tunnels for airways.

As we split through the crowd, the bass thumped, rattling our bodies. The stage was filled with some vampire wanna-be band. Fae women threw their undergarments onto the stage, and small orgies stayed hidden in the corners.

I did a double take when a human joining in on the fun caught my eye. *Humans weren't allowed to know of supernaturals, so why the hell was he here?*

He wore a business suit and smoked a cigar while two scantily clad she-wolves hung onto him. Surely, they were releasing their musk to tempt the poor bastard so they could steal his wallet.

Then I saw it, a small bag of black powder with sparkles of gold inside. *Fae Dust.*

Fae dust, in small amounts, could get supernaturals a high they couldn't get from human drugs.

The she-wolf pulled it out of her pocket, sliding it into the human's hand. He passed over some cash, not so subtle, I might add, and pushed it in her bra, letting his hand linger there.

Locke's eyebrow raised at my inattentiveness, not seeing the spectacle I'd just witnessed. I shook my head, following him through the crowd.

That was something we would have to deal with later.

Finding the stairs, far away from the enormous party, five of us climbed the wooden planks to nowhere. The darkness enveloped us as we trudged upward. Our sight had declined considerably since we had lost our animals, but it was just enough to see ahead of us.

The hallway was not guarded. It was too easy to get up here. We would have to work fast.

Locke reached for the first door, hoping to find a prisoner of some sort until an alarm sounded with just his touch. Red lights that lined the hall lit up brightly, and the music on the main floor stopped.

Locke forced the door open. We stood behind our leader, looking into a red-lit room with a desk and a fake backdrop nailed to the wall. The only thing real was the bed behind her and the desk that held a computer and camera staring straight at her.

The female's head turned, her bouncing curls hitting her perfectly made-up face. Before she could scream for us to stop, her body lifted from the chair.

"Shit," Locke cursed.

A fae had abruptly appeared from nowhere, pulling her forehead back and slitting her throat straight across her tanned neck.

"NO!" Locke sprang into the room to catch the fae.

Women in the distant rooms cried and shouted for help, and with each passing second, more and more of their screams faded away.

My wolf forced our hearing abilities to increase at the wrong moment—the screams pierced my ears.

As Locke jumped through the air to catch the autumn fae, the fae jumped into a hole beside the body.

"We got portal skippers!" Locke yelled. Screams turned into gurgles and choking. Our team shoved doors open, not moving fast enough. This one fae was portal skipping so quickly, we hardly had time to open the doors to save the dying women.

Men growled, roaring in frustration as they broke down doors. Their animals were outraged. For the first time, we were failing our mission.

Locke pulled out vials of magic, throwing potions and dusts into doors to dissolve them from the frames. Once he ran out, he began blowing entire holes into the walls, but none of it was fast enough.

Twenty-some doors, and with the five men we had, we still could not get in fast enough. It was all a worthless endeavor. The fae that was portal skipping hopped into each room, ruining them one by one.

If we could save just one.

I snarled.

The men in the halls stood back, putting their backs on the walls while I ran down the hallway. My wolf caught a scent that both intrigued and enraged him, but fuck, I couldn't understand what he was doing.

The jacket I wore fell from my body. The knives clanged together on my utility belt as I ran. Reaching in my pocket to grab my brass knuckles, I dashed around the corner to find another set of doors. I heard only one heart beating from the other side of the last door.

Ignoring the yells of my brothers and Locke screaming for me to wait, I forced it open with a shoulder in one blow. I stumbled, my scarred face looking up to find the autumn fae just coming out of a portal.

Not blinking, I jumped, landing on the fucker's body. He screamed out, trying to pull an iron dagger from his thigh.

I ripped it from his hand and raked his body from nose to navel with my claws. His screams resonated in the room, and the desk holding the computer and webcam fell to the floor. The desk lamp threw our shadows up on the wall.

My wolf surged forward. I felt the fury to kill. Losing control, not considering we needed this fae to question, my wolf lengthened our fangs, ripping out the lightly colored orange skin of his neck. The fae no longer moved, but that didn't mean we were finished. My claws ran over the fae's eyes, pulling them out one by one. It continued as I watched from the inside.

I stayed in the shadows of my mind, disgusted that I was not strong enough to force my wolf back. Was it my strength or was it my will that was not strong enough? I had no will to fight him, no reason to keep living. Maybe this would be the nail in my coffin to rid me of this nightmare that I now lived.

Once my wolf was finished, the entire room was sprayed with blood, my clothes were soaked, and trails of crimson ran down my bearded face. My heavy breathing slowed as I looked up at my brothers in the doorway.

Fear shone in their eyes. Locke tightened his fists, but his shoulders slumped as he looked me over. I knew that look; it was a look he gave when the last man went rabid.

My breathing slowed; Locke entered the room along with Sizzle. Sizzle mouthed if I was alright, but we knew the answer to that damned question.

"We have little time," Locke muttered to the room. "We got no leads on this and no one to question."

"Party is cleared out, looks like no one was ever here. Switch texted and said no one left the building either." Karma added. "Only thing left are the bodies." The heavily breathing men behind him all looked at each other, all disappointed in our failed mission.

"Must have portal skipped." Locke kneeled to the floor, glancing over at the fae.

"Looks like a webcam call girl thing?" Karma kicked the camera on the floor.

Sizzle pulled up the laptop, looking at the webpage. "Yeah, they do things for money, private chats, do some private entertainment." Sizzle continued to scroll on the page. "Making plenty of money, too."

"Is that legal?" Karma looked at the fake backdrop. The bed was once pristine, with a white comforter and big fluffy pillows in bright colors.

" 'Course it's legal," Sizzle argued. "But I doubt these shifters were doing it because they wanted to. Not the way they were brutally murdered to keep their mouths shut." That had been consistent. Every one of these women were shifters, not one fae female.

Fae and shifters weren't the best friends, but there was a mutual under-standing between both our species. Did this mean that a race war could be on the horizon?

I hung my head low, staring at the lifeless body shredded beyond recog-nition. I rubbed my pant leg to get rid of the blood on my fingers. A whimper came from under the bed. No one else noticed, but my wolf did.

My body stiffened, now listening to a beating heart. The whole fucking point of coming into this room was to save someone. Anyone.

Locke continued to talk to the others, coming up with a plan to get out of here and see if we could find a control room for the cameras that hung in every corner of these fake scenes, in addition to the computer cameras.

I moved, my wolf pushing me to do something for once besides killing, to see where the noise came from. My boots stuck to the bloody floor, making a terrible sticking, squelching sound until I reached the bed.

Sizzle smacked Locke in the chest to shut his mouth as they watched me intently.

I rested my knee on the floor, pulling up the tarnished blanket. Staring back at me with two caramel-colored eyes was a human woman, her shaking body curled in the fetal position, gripping a pillow for dear life. She gasped at seeing my appearance.

Of course, she would find me frightening. I was a scary fucker.

Blood dripped down my skin, my ugly mug hovering right in front of her face. I knew I had to back away, but my damn wolf pushed for something else. My wolf pushed harder for it than for killing the fae fucker that now laid in hunks of meat. I reached out, but she flinched away.

For the first time in a long time, I talked to my wolf. The disconnection between us faded. I wanted to talk some sense into him.

"She's scared. Can't you see that?" A whimper, a fucking whimper, chimed in my head. I paused, taking control of my hand and backing away.

"There's someone under there," Locke hissed, his hand went to my shoulder. "Want me to take this?"

Did I want him to take this opportunity to coax this little human out? My wolf growled in protest. Shaking my head, I stayed in front of the caramel-eyed woman as my wolf purred in my chest.

Fucking shit.

What was wrong with me?

"Come," I said.

The shuffling of footsteps around the room stopped. Locke gasped like a drama queen. Gazes bore into my back. I reached out my hand toward those beautiful, deep caramel eyes.

Her gaze lingered on my bloodied hand, the drying blood cracking around my knuckles. I went to pull away again, but her icy hand took my shaky one.

CHAPTER TWO

Journey

He reached out his hand. It was still covered in blood.

The crimson, wet substance was drying and cracking on his hands while around his wrist it dripped onto the plywood floor. I watched one trail of crimson slowly curve around his wrist, making a plopping sound as it hit the floor. Blinking harshly, I looked upward at the bearded man who'd dared to look under the bed.

It was funny. Usually monsters hide under the bed, but I spent most of my time under one as I grew up. I'd rather deal with those monsters instead of the ones that walked in the light.

I gulped, feeling the tension in the room. There were more of them now. Many pairs of feet could be seen from beneath the lace of the comforter. Most looked like steel-toed boots, black with chains hanging from their ankles. They clanged together, ringing in memories of the past. Which I should not in the slightest be worried about because I had a new nightmare coming.

There always was.

This beast of a man waiting for me saved my life. Whether for good intentions or not, I wasn't sure. I knew that Aedar was going to kill me. I heard the screams of the other women down the hall. They'd been here for a lot longer. They never said a word to me or each other. It wasn't allowed, the talking, the whispering. We stayed in our respective rooms but couldn't even sleep on the beds.

The beds were for "show" to make it look like we lived in some glamourous bedroom on our own somewhere. That we were doing this willingly of our own accord to make money and make the men or women on the other side happy.

It made me sick.

Luckily, I had only been here a few months. The other girls obviously were here much longer because their rigid beauty routines were down to the letter.

After I was taught how to apply my makeup and do my hair in a prim, proper, innocent way, I had to do it fast. I was anything but.

I grew up in a strict religious town. There was no make-up to play with as a little girl. I lived on the bare minimum, but I was expected to look beautiful once I came here. I was ugly by Aedar's standards. He told me I was nothing unless I put the hideous mask on every night. That I should be thankful he'd taken me in, but he hadn't sung that tune when he bought me.

He was downright giddy when he handed over the gold coins to the villains that kept me prior.

Gold coins. Who pays with gold anymore?

One would wonder why none of us fought back. We only saw Aedar and one other, who kept his face hidden. He was a tall, well over six feet, and wore a ski mask. You did not want him showing up.

One girl barely hung on to dear life as he flogged her with a paddle with "bad girl" written across it. The worst part was that her ass would be beet red. It was just enough pain for the night while she sat smiling into the screen. She had to "show her audience" what a naughty girl she was, and how her dominant had to spank her.

Of course, these nasty people would come up with something like that. I hadn't been paddled. I wasn't sure why they had been more lenient with me. They commented how I bruised easily, and they couldn't risk me being unable to work. They punished me in other ways. Like by not feeding me or not letting me sleep, or even worse, coming in during a video chat and letting the viewers decide what they should do to me.

That had been the worst. And all of it had to be done with an innocent smile.

My rescuer, who had saved me from certain death, still sat patiently, holding out his hand. He wasn't budging, and I wasn't in the mood for any other sort of punishment that I might have to endure, so I took his hand.

Despite it being dirty, it was warm, but the electrical shock was unexpected. He drew his hand back, his knee giving way and dropping to the floor. My heart raced, watching those deep blue eyes widen for a moment until it was back to his usual glare.

"Grim, what's wrong?" The soothing voice that spoke earlier to him tried to grab his wrist, but he pulled away harshly. My hero, now known as Grim, reached out his hand again, and I took it.

The gruffness of his face, which wasn't at all unpleasant, had me study him further. He was covered with leather, still sticky with the remnants of blood. As much as I wanted to shy away, I let him pull me from under the bed.

Aedar was everything Grim wasn't. Aedar looked angelic, beautiful, with sharp features and clothing that clung to his slim, muscular figure like a glove.

Grim was the most rugged of all the men in the room. The rest of the men had a five-o'clock shadow or clean-shaven faces. No blood on them at all. They all stared at me. I wasn't sure if it was for lust or shock that I was still alive after hearing all those other women scream, but it made me uneasy.

I bit my cheek, remembering what I was wearing. Of course, they would gaze at me with lust because I was half naked, wearing a stupid kitten costume with fuzzy ears and a tail.

Letting go of Grim, I wrapped my arms around my body and hid my face in shame.

"Aight, easy there." The one who had spoken to Grim earlier came closer. Grim snarled, causing me to jump in surprise and fall back onto the bed.

"We aren't here to hurt you. We came to rescue everyone here, but—" his voice trailed off, and I shook my head.

Yeah, they really were gone. Part of me hoped they would still be alright, but who was I kidding? None of us knew each other. We didn't hold any sort of prisoner bonds of friendship. As sad as it was, all those women dying may have been a blessing. They no longer had to suffer in this hellhole. We had food and water, but the internet humiliation was worse than where I was staying before.

I was a drugged up then, hardly remembering what was done to my body. It was for the best, but the ache in my body afterwards always made me cry in shame.

Grim set his eyes in a vile stare at his comrades. His lip curled, showing his teeth, setting off another warning growl. My cheeks flushed, and my stomach flipped. It was guttural, possessive. And even with my fear washing over me like a rushing waterfall, I found it comforting in a strange way.

Grim swiftly pulled off his leather vest, jacket, and black shirt. He was stripping his clothes off right in front of everyone. I went to crawl further away, for fear of what he was doing.

This was it. This is where it ended. He was going to rape me, defile what little dignity I had left in front of all these people—but he didn't.

He pushed his black shirt into my hand. I clutched it in my shaky hands while he redressed.

"Right." Grim's friend gazed at Grim warily, clearing his throat. "We were sent here to rescue everyone, but you're all that's left. Can you tell us what you *know*?" His voice trailed off.

I cocked my head at the note in his voice at the last word.

What was there to know? We were forced cam girls, hidden away in some building. What else was I supposed to know?

I stood there shaking, unable to form words.

"See anything suspicious, something almost like *fantasy*?"

My mouth dropped, and I hugged the shirt close to me until Grim pulled it away and motioned for me to lift my arms. He delicately dropped it over my body, and the tension in my shoulders loosened.

That was nice of him.

"Um," my voice cracked, holding the hem of my shirt. "F-fantasy?" Grim stayed beside me, his body moving closer. His gaze never left my face; I could feel the heat of his stare on my cheek.

"Yeah, like seeing things you wouldn't normally see?" His men shifted their feet on the other side of the room. "Hey, look at me. No one will hurt you, none of us. I know it seems contradictory to how we look, but we wouldn't harm a woman."

"Sorry, that's a little hard to believe when most of the men in my life want something. Regardless of how they look," I said.

Grim growled again.

I flinched. I needed to keep my mouth shut.

The man frowned. I felt Grim's body heat on my arm. The heat was enough to warm me all over, but I stiffened anyway. Any touch was just...unbearable right now. Too many bodies, too many eyes, it was all overwhelming..

"I'm Locke. We are Iron Fang, a club that helps people in trouble. We are going to take you home. Just have to ask you a few other questions, and you can be on your way. Do you have some family you want me to contact?"

Ha. Family.

"No," I mumbled. "I don't have any family."

Locke pursed his lips, crossing his arms. "That so?"

I glared back at him. What the hell was wrong with him?

"Yeah, no family. I'll be fine on my own. Thanks for saving me, I think." Maybe it would have been better to have died with the others.

I hung my head, looking at the trail of blood. I had almost forgotten the whole reason Grim had barged into the room.

Aedar had mysteriously appeared behind me. I was in the middle of a call when I saw him looming in the corner with a menacing look in his eye. Then all hell broke loose when Grim barged in and beat him to a bloody pulp. I thought I was next.

My eyes continued to trail the floor beside the now broken computer. Hunks of flesh that were once attached to a body lay littered near the door. There was no more Aedar, just a pile of bones and meat. It was a scene so obscene I gagged at the sight.

Now, Grim, who just killed Aedar, stood beside me. His breath fanned my neck, as he made sure I didn't run.

Should I be standing so close to this killer? He'd just violently murdered...slaughtered a person in front of me. He didn't flinch, didn't second guess himself, and he could very well do the same to me.

"You alright?" Locke stepped closer. Grim pulled me back into his chest like Locke wasn't to be trusted.

Were any of them to be trusted?

The metallic smell of blood wafted toward me as Locke came closer. My hand went to my nose. I shook my head until I felt lightheaded.

Grim grunted deeply, shaking his head. He lifted me up into his arms and covered my eyes with his large hand. I felt him tighten his grip until I lay against his bloody jacket.

Was it sick and wrong that I felt safe at this moment? He freaking killed a man. No, he mauled him to death, and I was cuddled up to him. It was a feeling I shouldn't have, feeling safe, but I couldn't help but sigh into the enormous chest.

I had lost all my senses. I was giving up, giving in to the demise that was set before me. If I could just have this five minutes of someone holding me close, maybe I could take that and remember it for the rest of my life.

It would give me hope that at least one person on this earth cared.

So, I was taking it. I sighed deeply into his bare chest.

"Get away," Grim murmured lowly.

Locke stood back, his hands pulling back in surrender.

"That is the most I've ever heard Grim talk. Does anyone have a camera? I gotta record this shit," the other man snickered. My fingers gripped the vest underneath Grim's jacket, glancing at the various patches.

"Let's get her out of here. We can ask more questions later. Switch has all the info we need, and some cops are pulling in at the front. Let's go around back." Locke went straight through the crowd, and the men parted, following behind. Grim grunted in reply, following closely.

As we left the warehouse, it differed from how I remembered. It was worn and dirty, with hardly any walls, and the rooms that held all the women were now blasted open. Some doors hung off hinges, giving me the perfect glimpses of lifeless bodies on the floor.

I whimpered—those poor women.

Grim pulled me closer as I tried to roll up into a ball. I should feel repulsed by this man holding me so close to his body, but I felt more at ease as each passing moment went by. He'd killed one man that was the bane of my existence, but that didn't mean I should trust him.

Locke was certain that they were going to let me go. But as we trailed through the frosty night air and traveled five blocks away from the warehouse, I realized I wasn't being let go soon.

Rows and rows of bikes parked in a perfect line. So, this was an MC club then? Only a few of them put on their helmets. They started their engines and drove off with the loud sounds of their motors announcing their departure..

Oh, my god, was I going to ride this thing?

Grim set me on the motorcycle. It was large. Definitely could travel long distances, yet small enough to go wicked fast. He had a bag on the side, which he opened and handed me a helmet. I stared at it, glancing back up at those haunted blue eyes.

"She can ride with me," Locke mentioned as he kicked the kickstand up. "Whatever makes you more comfortable." Locke shared a knowing look at Grim, who only shook his head.

Locke raised a brow to question, but Grim nodded him away. We were the last bike since it took me a moment to settle the straps. He climbed on the bike. His legs were so thick that they tightened his dark leather chaps as he sat.

Grim reached over, pulling one of my arms and guided me to sit behind him. He took one of my hands and wrapped it around his body and gestured for the other hand to follow.

He was like a tree trunk; my arms could hardly go around the wall of steel.

The bike rumbled, and I lifted my legs, but it wasn't just the rumbling of the bike I felt. His back had a constant purr-like vibration coming from it. My breath stopped, trying to feel the gentle vibrations until he revved the engine and I could no longer feel it.

I gripped ahold of him tighter, and he took off quickly, traveling into the dark, cool night. Goosebumps rose on my legs as we forged ahead.

"Name?" He yelled over his shoulder. His voice wasn't as strangled as when he told me to come out from under the bed. This time, it was much smoother, less animalistic.

"Journey," I replied in a normal voice, not expecting him to hear. But somehow I think he heard because he didn't ask again.

CHAPTER THREE

Grim

We pulled up outside the bar. Humans stumbled out, tripping over themselves after the last call for shots. Two a.m. came fast for these low lifes that had no one to go home to.

Locke shouted to them, pulling some up off the sidewalk. Vomit ran down the curb while they steadied themselves to stand. The last taxi drove up, coming by to pick up the last lot of them. Three piled in one taxi, and Locke shut the door with a slam, waving for the car to go.

The other lagging humans staggered down the street, humming a tune or punching the brick walls of the joint. The girls must have had a handful tonight if the customers didn't want to leave.

"I've got Delilah coming, she's going to take her," Hawke stuck his phone back in his pocket. "She has a spare room in her apartment with the rest of her kind. She'll get her settled."

Delilah was Hawke's distraction. Nothing more, he said. But I saw the way he looked at her. He was infatuated with the human. He always brushed her hair back and whispered things in her ear. She was one of the many humans we'd saved. She had no family or friends to speak of. Locke let her stay in one of the apartment buildings he owned to give her a chance to start over.

The constant flirting between the two sickened me. But we all deserved to keep our minds busy instead of concentrating on our loneliness.

"No," I grunted. Journey slid off my bike, my shirt covering her ass just enough, but her poor legs were cold. Goosebumps rose on her skin, her legs pushed together to try and retain what little bit of warmth she had left.

Locke leaned on his bike, lighting a cig.

"She can't stay here with us, Grim. You know the rules." He flicked the cig from his mouth and stomped on it.

Hell, I knew she couldn't stay, but I didn't want to part with her either. Not until I figured out why my wolf was all up in a huff about her. He had his eyes on her from the very start, and the jolt of electricity under the bed made me question what it could be.

Humans weren't allowed to go into the living quarters of the bar. We had rooms for prospects that wanted to join and for members. They were wolves mostly, and Locke stayed in there with all of them. It was their own space, their own unofficial pack, to sate their animals need for company. It was a place to let their wolves growl and howl and not worry about showing too much animal to anyone outside the club.

I didn't sleep there much. There were two studio apartments above the tattoo parlor that Sizzle owned. I work with him, and he offered for me to stay there if I felt more comfortable being alone instead of at the bar. I was afraid I would go rabid and the fewer souls around the better.

Maybe my wolf was regressing far faster than everyone else because I stayed alone and away from other wolves.

"I can do a background check on her, then you can decide where you wanna put her," Switch said, coming from the bar. He wore a dark tee with a gamer logo. He was reclusive too, but Locke needed him to stay in the headquarters so he was at the pack's disposal.

"We don't know her name, yet." Locke threw the cig out and walked up beside Journey.

I stepped forward, chest to chest with my supposed brother. Locke wouldn't hurt a woman, but my wolf would not let him lay a hand on her.

Locke stepped back, looking me up and down again. He assessed me, seeing if I was in the right state of mind. I obviously wasn't. Hell, I'd lost control back there. Locke was ready to put me out of my misery; he knew I was suffering. But no one wants to see their close friend dying, and he was hopeful I would last longer. Hell, I had lasted a long time without going rabid.

After the years of being ready to die, I wasn't anymore.

I had to show him that I wasn't going to hurt this poor woman. I would never. I'd fight my wolf tooth and nail on that one.

"What's your name, sweetheart?" Locke asked, ignoring me.

Journey continued to hold herself despite the cold. Her knees shook, and her lip trembled. Her makeup was smudged and dried to her cheeks, but she didn't cry. Not one tear ran down her cheek as she stood before a bunch of men that looked down at her wondering how she'd survived it all.

"Journey," she mumbled. "Journey Smith."

Switch scoffed in the background.

"Journey's your real name? I don't reckon I'd find many Journeys but Smiths are a dime a dozen," Switch stated.

Locke ground his teeth, his full attention on her. I could hear her heart, listening for an offbeat that could measure a lie. We all knew she had a family when she said she didn't. The lie was obvious. But now we needed to know who she was and if her family might be looking for her.

There was one question, however, Journey technically didn't answer the question we really needed to know—if she'd seen anything out of the ordinary, like magic—because that would add a whole new mess of problems.

"Yeah, it's my real name."

Switch continued to ask her questions, writing them down on a small notepad. I continued to assess her, watching how she talked and how she moved her body. I wanted to memorize it all, but I wasn't sure why.

Surely, I wasn't developing feelings for the human woman I'd just rescued. I'd rescued far too many of them, and not once had I given any woman a second look. This one, though... The moment her caramel eyes looked up at me, there was something.

My damn wolf howled. He howled in excitement for the first time in a long while. He wasn't some mindless beast anymore; I could feel his feelings, an emotional connection. It was the first time since—

Shit.

"Alright, I'll see what I can do." Switch nodded to Locke and took off back to his den and left Journey with Locke and me.

Locke cleared his throat and nodded to the other side of the bikes for me to follow. I stopped halfway over, making sure she wouldn't run. Then again, where would she run to?

"Brother, what's wrong? You got the brothers eyes on you." Part of the crew was over by the bar entrance, watching the scene unfold. The nosey bastards. I knew some were waiting to see if I would come home at all, that I'd have to be taken out because I'd officially gone rabid. But now they saw me with this girl who'd ridden in on my bike. "You ain't going to kill this woman are you?"

I growled, my eyes blazing at the group until they scattered.

Running his hand through his hair, Locke snorted. "This is the first time I've seen you have an opinion on something, though." He smirked. "Here's the thing." He pointed at me. "I can't leave you alone with her because of your 'situation.' I can't have anything happen to this human. We can't afford for the Royal Council to look our way, thinking we're breaking any of their laws."

Fuck the Council.

They let the fae run rampant, let souls reject their mates without consequence, and let the supernaturals go rogue as long as they were kicked out of Elysian. The realm and the counsel wouldn't bat an eyelash if someone was killed on the other side, especially around some rogues. As long as we didn't make a spectacle and no humans found out about the existence of the realm or magical entities, the council didn't give a flying fuck.

We all fucking hated the council, but they had left us alone. They didn't send their guards to complete the job. Just threw us to the humans and said, "don't fuck shit up for the rest of us." That was our "blessing" to live another day.

"I'll watch him." Sizzle's bright blonde hair and the scar decorating his neck glistened in the light from the bar. His dark eyebrows were a terrible contrast to his hair, but dragons were supposed to be flashy with their looks. "We live in the same building, in case you forgot." Sizzle barked a laugh. "He won't hurt her. I've never seen him glance at a woman his way. Maybe he just needs to get laid, and his wolf will calm down."

I growled. Journey would not be like that. She wasn't some whore. Besides, supernaturals were not to lie with a human. They couldn't handle our animalistic qualities in bed.

"Easy man." Sizzle patted my shoulder. He blew a small flame from his mouth, lighting another cig for Locke. "I was just kidding. I'll let Hawke know she'll stay at our place. Delilah has some clothes at her apartment that Hawke is picking up."

My eyes never left Journey as they talked. Her gaze floated over the street, her constantly moving eyes made me wonder how long she had been on her own.

Because I knew what being alone was like.

"Okay." Locke sighed. "I trust you, Grim. Please call me if it gets to be too much, and I can take her to Delilah's."

The apartments were a few blocks from the bar. It was basically a large dormitory with human employees, more of those we'd saved who had nowhere else to go.

The humans were grateful and had been honest in their work. With Switch's background checks and their oath of secrecy about what happened in the club, they'd made our lives a bit more bearable.

They were still blissfully unaware of what we all were, though. And it would have to remain that way to keep them safe.

Journey would be okay to live among the humans. It was fully guarded by cameras and other security measures, but I didn't like the idea of her being far from me.

If she went to that apartment building, I would end up climbing the fire escape to make sure she was sleeping. And I was fucking tired; I didn't need the extra work.

If she came home with me, I'd rest easier and keep my damn wolf in check. Yeah, that was it. Keeping her close to me would be better...for my wolf.

Locke was still talking, but it all sounded like whiny pussy whispers compared to the growls I heard inside my head. I stepped over to Journey and grabbed her arm and began leading her down the street.

"W-wait." She tried to pull back, but I continued to walk.

Locke laughed in the background and slapped someone on the back.

"Where am I going?" she yelled and tried to pull away from me. My wolf, dissatisfied with her reluctance, turned her around and threw her over our shoulder. She squealed.

Sizzle shook his head as he ran beside us and slapped me on the arm. "Dude, man, you can't do this." He looked around, waiting for one of the brothers to come out and argue.

Journey continued to wiggle, but her screams stopped when we reached the back side of the tattoo shop.

Fumbling with the keys, I set her down. Her face was red, and her hair was tousled from hanging over my shoulder. She grunted, pushing her hair away, and gave me a scowl. No one had scowled at me before, but hers was fucking adorable—an angry little kitten with claws.

"You can't do that, and why am I here? I thought I was going to stay with some other women," she asked worriedly. Her fierceness died, and the scared undertone in her voice caused my wolf to pace.

She shouldn't be scared, not with us.

But what do I expect after throwing her over my shoulder?

"You'll be safer here," Sizzle said off-handedly. "Think about it. You were the last one alive from that warehouse, and there were cameras. They are going to know you're still alive. Setting you up with a bunch of women is going to put them in danger, too."

Fuck, I didn't think about that.

"So Grim and I, I'm Sizzle by the way." He winked. "Are gonna watch you until we can ask you more questions tomorrow." Sizzle pushed the heavy metal door in. It groaned as she looked into the darkness. Biting her lip, she stood behind me. She at least considered me as a shield despite the fear radiating from her.

Once we climbed the worn, wooden stairs up to the apartments, Sizzle unlocked his door. "Well, night. Let me know if you need anything."

Journey's eyes widened. "Wait! Where do I stay?" I pulled on her arm and led her to my door, pushing it open with my shoulder.

"Oh, um." She stumbled until I trapped her with my arms. Those caramel eyes caught mine again, and we stood holding each other until Sizzle screamed out profanities as he cursed his toe for finding the corner of a table.

Journey jumped, breaking the eye contact I was enjoying far too much. I wanted to fucking kill Sizzle right now, but since he'd vouched for me to get Journey over here, I owed him. I hated owing people.

"Well." She pulled at the hem of the black shirt. She jumped as someone pounded on the door, falling back into my arms.

Maybe it wasn't so bad she was jumpy.

Fuck, what am I doing?

"It's Hawke. Brought the clothes." I heard the thump when he dropped a bag on the other side of the door and his footsteps retreated. He was probably pissed he couldn't hang out with his girl. Fuck him then.

Opening the door, I picked up the bag and locked the door promptly. Journey had stepped further into the empty studio apartment to look around. It wasn't much, a couch, a bed, a place to eat, and one bathroom, but it would do. Stripping off my jacket and vest, I stood there with a bare chest, showing the scars and tattoos I used to cover them. Throwing the dirty clothes on the kitchen table, I turned to see Journey's mouth hanging open.

"You won't to do anything to me, will you?" Her voice trembled.

Fuck.

I shook my head, waving my hands out in front of me. "No, never." It came out softer than I thought possible.

Journey stood, her ass leaning against the couch. I pointed to the bathroom and led her to it, bringing the bag of clothes with us. Pointing to the towels and the soap, I stepped away to give her enough space.

She stood wide-eyed, looking at me instead of the bathroom I was showing her. I tried to speak, and explain where everything was, but pointing was the only action I could give her.

I wasn't used to talking, let alone softly. She would have to figure out what my actions and grunts meant for herself.

I fought with my wolf to bring her closer to me, to feel the heat of her skin. It didn't help in the slightest that her eyes never left my body. She watched me curiously while I tried to show her everything she could need.

I stepped out, backing away slowly like she was a small animal I didn't want to spook with any sharp movements.

My wolf sat in the background, watching her intently. His fucking tail was wagging—so happy she was here. Hell, I was too, it felt so damn foreign. It reminded me of once when I was happy.

And I haven't felt that in a long fucking time.

I closed the bathroom door, and we simultaneously let out sighs we didn't know we'd been holding. I leaned on the door, my sweaty, bloodied body sliding down until my ass hit the dirty floor. Moving my hands to my face, I rubbed the dried blood into my cheeks. Some flaked off, getting in my eye.

What in the hell was I doing?

Why the sudden urge to protect this woman? I've protected many, making sure they had a safe roof over their head and food in their bellies. But that was that, and that was all I could give them.

This woman, this scared woman who went through gods knew what had burrowed herself into my wolf.

And he would not let her go so easily.

CHAPTER FOUR

Journey

I stared in shock as the door closed.

Grim was a strange man, or should I say neanderthal, because he threw me over his shoulder like I was a rag doll. Part of me wanted to laugh. The thrill of my stomach being hoisted up so fast made my head spin, and I forgot that I was being dragged off by some overly muscular biker.

I hadn't laughed in, I don't know, years? Not unless you counted the on-screen acting job. Those private chats could earn a large sum for my owners. Being flirty and smiley was part of the job. I shuddered, recalling all the dirty things I had to do. Some didn't want to do anything but talk, but those were few and far between.

And They were just lonely, like me.

Except they talked to me of their own free will to fill their loneliness with the companionship of some cam girl paid to care. I was there because I had to be.

I tightly gripped the bag of clothing Grim gave me. He'd done an elaborate show of where I could find things in his bathroom. The towels, the shampoo, and the likes, but I wasn't paying attention to that. I could have easily figured things out on my own in such a small bathroom.

All I could concentrate on was him. He growled at his friends when they wanted me to go with the women to their apartment. He refused to let me go, and I couldn't help but wonder why.

It was a way for me to get out of his hair, for him to not care about me anymore because he looked like someone that didn't want to get their hands dirty by caring for someone else.

Surely, I would have been safer there, and hell, the bikers had kept their word so far. They weren't using me, playing with me, or trying to pass me off to others.

But no, the gruff and hard to read biker forced me to stay in a studio apartment with one bed, a couch, a coffee table, and a kitchen table. It was small, the perfect bachelor pad, and surprisingly clean for a man of his, um...caliber.

My back hit the door as I slid down and hugged my knees. God, what was happening to me? One thing after another, and now I was almost free, I could taste it.

Once I answered Locke's questions, maybe they would let me go.

The radiating heat from the other side of the door made me question if I wanted to leave, however. As odd as it sounded, the guy who'd rescued me still felt that duty to ensure I was alright, which I found comforting.

Never thought a man could do that. Make me feel safe. Women either, I mean, that was what got me into this whole mess. Women were just the brains of the operation, while the men followed like little puppies to do their bidding.

I slapped the bathroom floor with my hand in frustration and rubbed my itchy eyes with the other. I pulled my hand back, the fake eyelashes falling into my palm.

Right, shower and get this over with.

The door didn't lock, so my shower had to be quick. The false sense of security was there, swirling around me. He could change at any moment and be just another man trying to get in my pants. That was just how the world worked.

After the quick shower, I pulled on an oversized sweatshirt; it covered me down to my hips while the black leggings held me tight.

This was the most clothes I'd worn in years. It felt so good to have clothes that warmed my body instead of a thin sheet on a cold floor in nothing but a bralette and lace panties.

I cracked the door open and steam rolled out of the bathroom and into the main room. Grim sat at the kitchen table, his eyes watching like a predator.

"Thank you." I held onto the bag with my dirty kitten outfit. The chair scraped across the floor, making a loud screech, and I jumped in surprise as he stood in front of me.

Wow, he's fast.

He held out his hand. It was tanned, dark, riddled with light-colored scars and scrapes except for the finger tattoos across his knuckles. He knew I was looking at him as much as he looked at me.

He took this time to examine me up close, too. I didn't find his stare lustful or intimidating. For a mysterious reason, I felt drawn to him. Like a moth to a flame.

Maybe it was because he was my rescuer, the one looking out for me. I could paint him as my dark knight because that was what I really wanted.

He leaned in, his hands reaching for the bag, but he was so close I could smell the hint of leather and motor oil on his body. Not to mention the sweat and blood that was stuck to his skin.

He took a giant whiff of my scent, which I'm sure smelled of nothing but antibacterial soap after I scrubbed my body raw. When he backed away, he closed his eyes, purring in his chest. It was a strange sound to come from a man of his caliber.

He wasn't built to be soft and comforting. He was a wild animal.

Grim took the bag and tossed it into his open trash can and walked to the lone bed near the window. My gut churned, looking at the window.

I hated windows. I rather enjoyed the room I'd stayed in last because there were no windows to worry about. No one could crawl into the room, and I could keep my attention fixed on the door.

Not this time. I had to watch the window, the door, and Grim, too.

Grim pulled down the sheets, which looked really clean. Cleaner and nicer than I'd ever had.

I didn't remember the last time I slept in the bed. Sleeping on beds was a no at my last prison. We had to sleep on the floor next to it—we weren't afforded such a luxury.

But this was one bed, and there were two people.

"I can sleep on the floor. I'm used to it," I muttered. "You've done a lot for me already."

Grim grunted, shaking his head, and nodded to the bed again. The soft mattress beckoned me with its suppleness.

Sleeping in a bed would be so lovely.

But what will he do once I'm in it?

Not arguing, because what was the point? He could lift me and put me there if he wanted. I crawled into it. The warmth of the hoodie and my covered legs made me sigh.

So warm.

Grim leaned over, and I sunk further into the mattress while my body tensed. I waited for him to do something, but he didn't. Grim lifted the blankets at the end of the bed and tucked them around my body, making a perfect little nest of warmth.

He just tucked me into bed. Like I was a child.

I waited for him to climb into the bed. He only did his manly grunt of approval and backed away.

I shuffled in the blankets, squirming so he would have space because he'd planted me firmly in the middle. If he was going to be in here too, he needed room. But he let out a growly "Stay" and continued to back away.

He turned from me, rummaging through the small bureau, and grabbed his clothes. He took steady steps to the bathroom, looking at me longingly. He didn't follow his order with a threat, like what I was used to. Not that I would leave right now. This was the first time I'd felt this warm in a long while.

Then he closed the door, but only enough so a crack was left open.

The shower turned on, and my tense body relaxed. My mind whirled around me as I rubbed my eyes with the heels of my palms. It was so late in the night, there was no point in sleeping because sunrise was around the corner.

Sunrise.

When was the last time I remembered what a sunrise looked like? I couldn't remember how the golden light of the sun reacted to the green blades of the grass? I wanted to feel the tree leaves brushing my cheek like I had as a child. I smiled at that, it could very well become a reality. I could almost see myself touching the bark of the tree, reaching higher into the branches for the butterflies that might hide inside.

Free, I was almost free.

I wasn't sure what I would do with myself once I left here. Whenever my freedom finally came, it would be difficult to start over, but I was determined to succeed. I didn't have any educational background. I would have to start from the ground up. Maybe get a local waitress job in town.

I hoped the people who kept me as a web cam girl wouldn't look for little ol' me. I knew nothing of their operations, and only the masked man was still alive. Once he caught wind of what happened, he would be on his way to Mexico after being raided by a bunch of large, crazy bikers.

I was so deep in my thoughts, I didn't see Grim step out of the bathroom. His body glistened in the low light, water trailing down his chest. There was something unusual in his eyes that captured me.

His soul looked so shattered. I couldn't ask myself why I knew that, but it was. Maybe that was why he talked so little, too worried he would give himself away and show how broken he was.

Grim sat on the couch, his forearms resting on his knees. The sofa was unbelievably small for a man his size.

Grim's shoulders alone were double the width of the bottom cushion.

"I can sleep there." I pointed. "I'm smaller. You won't be comfortable," I tried to reason.

Grim gave me a nonverbal grunt and turned his body so he could watch me from where he slept.

Yeah, because I'm going to sleep now.

My gaze didn't wander far from him, either. Even with the comfort of knowing he'd saved me, I still stayed on the cautious side. I didn't want to sleep, worried he would come closer, and I wouldn't know.

My body was very aware of where he was, however. His stares were not heated with the lust and desire I'd seen before. His gaze was soft, gentle. There was a look on his face I couldn't decipher. When he was near his friends, it was cold and unforgiving. But when he looked at me, the hardened lines softened, and his rigid stance relaxed.

Instead of my mind telling me to worry, to stay awake and watch him to make sure he wouldn't touch me, my heart flipped in my chest.

Trust him. I could hear my heart whisper.

"Sleep," he commanded.

My eyes drooped once or twice. The calm hum in his throat lulled me deeper. I rolled onto my stomach, fists gripping the pillow beneath me. "Sleep," he said again, adjusting himself on the couch.

Instead of fighting my mind, I listened to my heart and obeyed. Finally, my eyes drooped after an exhausting night.

My night was filled with nightmares of my past.

I would wake to see Grim still sleeping on his side on the couch, only to fall asleep again. He stayed there until the sun just barely came over the horizon when a rattle at the door jolted him awake. His bare feet hit the floor with a thud, and he looked over at me.

He was always looking at me. Checking on me.

He sighed, his nose flaring. I didn't know you could angrily walk to the door, but he certainly did.

"What?" he ground out. Sizzle stood on the other side with a white plastic bag in his hand, holding it up to eye level.

"Food," he smirked, walking in the door, and set it on the counter.

I retreated to the further side of the bed, next to the wall, shielding my body with my knees.

Being more than exhausted had rattled my senses. I didn't want to trust anyone, or anybody. My body shook, the wave of unease hovering over me.

"Sleep on the couch?" Sizzle cocked an eyebrow at Grim. He gazed steadily at Grim while he pulled white food boxes from the bag.

Grim grunted, opening the white food boxes.

"How'd she do last night?" Sizzle leaned on the counter, watching Grim make the plate. Again, they talked like I was the deaf person in the room.

"Nightmares," he mumbled. Sizzle stood up, crossing his arms. He inspected Grim and put a hand to his forehead.

Grim slapped his hand away.

"I'm checking to see if you're sick because of all this word vomiting you're doing," he chuckled. Grim glared, pulling a plate away and heading toward me. "Meeting at the church at noon," Sizzle said without looking back.

Grim kneeled in front of the bed. The distance between us didn't feel right, but I didn't have the guts to come any closer. All the tiredness, the adrenaline from the night before, when I felt like I could talk to him, was gone. I was back to my scared self, worried about being used all over again.

"Eat." His voice was soft. The stark difference from talking to his friend warmed me.

His patience with me was far greater than anyone I had ever met. Beckoning me with those eyes, I scooted my body over, falling in love with the scent of carbs.

Biscuits, gravy, eggs, and bacon laid on the Styrofoam plate. My mouth salivated. I didn't remember if I'd ever seen so much food on a single plate.

The fork in Grim's hand was given to me, and I took it shakily. When was the last time I ate like a real person with a food utensil?

Pushing the thought away, I gently grabbed the plate, grazing Grim's fingertips. The same jolt we felt last night appeared, but he didn't pull away. Instead, he grabbed my wrist and pulled me closer to him, luring me into him with food.

The fork dropped, and I whimpered at the loss. How pathetic was I? Couldn't even hold a fork.

My body shook, my stomach churning in protest that he was taking the food out of my shaking hands. I needed it back, but protesting was something I could not do. He could hit me, smack me, use me.

Grim let out a frustrated breath. My heart stopped as he let go, lowering his gaze. He tapped the plate with his index finger while he stabbed pieces of food with a fork with the other.

I obediently sat on my knees and watched. Then he leaned forward and held the plate closer to me so nothing would fall onto the bed.

Like a frightened animal, I kept my eyes trained on him. Grim held the forkful of food closer to my mouth for me to eat. I reached to pull the fork away from him, but he shook his head, nudging it closer to my mouth.

If I wasn't starving, I would have laughed at him. But, I was starving. I didn't even remember the last time I ate a full meal. My captures wanted us skinny and to look like the perfect doll.

Grim nudged it forward again, his tension fading. The pleading look in his eyes entrapped me. So I did what I never thought I would do. I parted my lips and let him feed me the first bite.

"MINE."

CHAPTER FIVE

Grim

Journey didn't know my wolf was pestering me. She didn't know that my animal was grazing the surface of my mind, ready to unleash his animalistic qualities in my human form. This was the most he had stirred in my mind besides when it was time to kill something.

Her lips wrapped around the fork. I watched in awe as she pulled it from her mouth.

When was the last time she had eaten?

"Calm," I repeated to my wolf. My wolf snarled, but even then, I had to push him farther down so she wouldn't hear his growls of protest.

Feeding a female was an intimate act among wolves. It wasn't done lightly and was usually reserved for their intended mates. My wolf felt a reaction toward Journey. To feed her, become more intimate with her. But she couldn't possibly be my mate. I already had my chance, and she'd chosen another—a chosen mate over the stronger bond we could have had together.

My gut churned at the painful memory, but hearing the gentle hum as Journey continued to eat soothed me. I had provided for her, filled her belly, and made her a temporary nest.

I liked it far too much.

Journey finished her plate, keeping the sheet around her like a frightened animal. I didn't like it. Not one bit of me did.

She feared me. We would have to overcome that. But another thought pounding my brain was what Journey was to my wolf. His feelings were clear—he wanted her. I could feel the animal stir, pawing at my head, begging. I could almost shift through the last conversations we had before we were rejected.

He was coming alive again.

Could it possibly be he was returning to me? Ready to establish a connection again? It was unheard of for a rogue to come back.

If our mate rejected us and mated with another, the leftover soul rotted, meaning me and the rest of my brothers. There were no chosen mates for the broken soul.

"Thank you," her soft voice said. She had become a different person this morning, not the spunky girl I carried to my apartment who was not afraid to ask questions.

Before I could start a conversation with her, Sizzle opened the door. I growled, causing Journey to jump and scurry back to the wall on the other side of the bed. Sizzle glanced down at the plate in my hand and the fork ready to feed another bite to Journey.

His eyes widened, glancing from her to me.

Sizzle was nauseatingly attractive to the females that roamed the bar. He stayed away from the bar unless it was absolutely necessary, hiding in Saturated Ink to stay away from the seductive glances. I wasn't sure of his story. Most of us didn't know anyone's stories except those we'd grown extremely close to. Sizzle had an aversion to women and refused to tattoo any female.

Journey watched him intently. Her body didn't get aroused at the sight of him, but my wolf thought it would be best to keep him away.

"What?" I growled, the veins in my forearms pulsed, and my grip tightened on the Styrofoam plate.

"Did you?" He pointed to the plate and to her but shook his head. "Pres wants us at the church. Bring the girl." He didn't look at her again, his lips pressing into a thin line, and walked out the door.

Journey and I walked side by side, our arms brushing from time to time. At least she didn't pull away because my wolf wouldn't have it. He wanted her close. Wanted to bury our nose in her skin, smell that floral hint that had become stronger. I was unsure if my chest hurt because of indigestion or heartburn, but I knew one thing it couldn't be. A bond.

There were no second chances, no matter how magnificent she smelled to us.

As dead set as I was in believing she wasn't a female we could keep, my wolf snarled again with distaste. He liked her; he never wanted anyone.

I guess that counted for something. But what was that something?

Her skin was naturally pale without the pounds of makeup that decorated her face when we found her. Her eyes were far brighter without the painted lids, and her pink lips much more innocent than the seductive red.

She kept her slender body warm by covering it with large clothing. The occasional shiver ran through her, and it made me come closer to her. So far, I was the only one she trusted, and I would keep it that way.

I grunted, trying not to look at her. My gaze was heated as I looked at her. My wolf wanted her.

Surely she could feel my stares. I diverted my attention back to the broken sidewalk, the worn-down buildings, and the weeds that crawled up the storm drains as we walked closer to the church.

Locke thought it was a beautiful tragedy to pick an old church as the center of the Iron Fang. Once the church had been filled with human sinners begging for redemption, now it was stuffed with those who had no souls to save.

Locke bought out the previous owners with what money he had. We started from the ground up, giving us enough money for supplies for the businesses around the three blocks where we all stayed.

We were set with an apartment complex, tattoo parlor, bar, mechanic, garage, and bodyguard services. Set enough for us to live comfortably until our animals finally arranged for us to leave this world alone.

The old church was left unchanged. It wasn't repaired like the rest of that small part of town where we congregated. The cross that hung over the front door had lost a nail, so it dangled upside down, swinging in the wind.

Old stained glass, dusty and filled with cracks, slowly deteriorated. Locke wanted us to keep it this way, a reminder that the only savior of the world was us. We were on our own.

No one believed in the Moon Goddess anymore. That ship had sailed long ago. We'd burned a wolf skull into the wood of the pulpit. That was what we were. Nothing but empty vessels that used to house our souls.

Today's meeting would be held in the bishop's office. The round table was meant only for Locke's closest brothers—me, Sizzle, Hawke, Switch, and Beretta, the only female anyone trusted. She was a black panther shifter with a crazy obsession with guns. The small gun shop and arsenal she ran for the club proved most helpful.

She was one of the only ones that didn't deserve to be here. Her mate had died in front of her when the alpha male of her tribe sought to take her as his chosen female. She fled her pride so the alpha wouldn't force a claim. But with her mate gone, her soul started to die as well. That was not to say that she hurt any less than the rest of us who had been rejected by our mates.

Journey stiffened when we strolled into the room. It was filled with old books, papers, and dust-covered busts of saints the humans either worshipped or prayed to. We never paid much attention to what they believed in.

Locke sat at the far end of the table. His smile brightened when we appeared. He was the least dangerous-looking male in the room with that damn smile, yet people feared him. Maybe it was because of that playful exterior that he liked to show to the enemies to lull them into feeling more comfortable. But I damned well knew why he smiled.

He was a fucking lunatic to those who crossed him.

"Come in." He beckoned for Journey to sit down. She looked at me for guidance.

My wolf purred in excitement that she would trust us before Locke, because no one ever trusted us, not entirely.

I nodded, bending to reach her ear. "It's alright. I'm here." Her breath let out slowly, as she sat in the slightly padded chair.

I stood behind her chair, crossing my arms, glaring at anyone that looked her way. They all cowered, shifting their bodies toward Locke.

Locke raised an eyebrow again, his signature look since last night. He had questions, fuck, I had questions, but one thing was certain—my wolf wouldn't let anyone harm Journey, not that they would.

That would defy the pledge we all took when coming here—to save the weak.

My wolf snarled at the thought of someone touching her. I could feel his rusty red hair stiffen, prowling around the small window where he would one day come forward to shift. And I knew I would not have the strength to hold him back.

"We are just going to ask some questions, Journey, and then you will be free to go," Locke said.

I lifted my lip, showing a fang.

Locke ignored me, his eyes still on Journey.

She shifted in her seat and nodded, folding her arms over the large black sweatshirt. "Okay," she muttered.

"And I need you to be honest. We will know. Switch over here"—Locke tilted his head to him—"will know. We've done a background check, but I want your side of the story."

Journey said nothing. Her body slipped lower in the seat, and her heart raced. The claws on my fingers, which grew longer and thicker than they had in years, gripped the chair, splitting the wood.

Sizzle, who sat beside Journey, raised an eyebrow, signaling Locke.

In understanding, Locke sat back in his chair, putting his hands on the table. "Right, so do you have family, Journey?"

"Yes," her answer was short.

"And do they know you're missing?" he pried.

"They don't want me." My claws raked across my leather jacket. "They're the reason why I was in the situation I was in," she muttered.

"Can you elaborate?" Locke leaned on the table.

"I can, but I won't," she snapped. Breathing ceased in the room. No one told Locke "no."

It didn't matter if he looked carefree. He was deadly, like me.

"You asked if I had family yesterday. Technically by blood, I do. They are not my family, though." Her teeth ground together.

I placed my hand on her shoulder, and the tension in her in her body relaxed.

"Fair enough," Locke backed off, his fingers thumping the table. "This last person you were sold to, do you know who they are? Their name?"

Journey shook her head. "Just that Aedar was my 'boss.' He trained me, told me what I needed to do, and I did it. If we didn't follow his orders, then a man in a black ski mask came in, and then you were in trouble."

Beretta shifted her feet, the growl in her throat becoming too loud for her panther, and Locke glared at her in reprimand.

"Do you need to leave?" Locke asked.

Beretta shook her head, bowing her head in submission. Journey locked eyes with Beretta, but she only winked in return.

I moved my other hand to her open shoulder, my thumbs rubbing her back and neck. Journey slumped her shoulders in defeat. Her head hung impossibly lower, and her cheeks displayed a deep shade of red.

"Working with Aedar, I had to perform in front of a group of chatters. Each day I prepared myself, as well as the others. We put on makeup, dressed in revealing clothes. Taught what to say, how to act." She licked her lips.

"Then we flirted until we could get them into a chat room. That was when they 'asked' us to perform certain tasks. Mostly removing clothes, touching...ourselves." She closed her eyes, tightening them. "We had to use implements, dildos, or fingers to get ourselves off. Had to say their name as we came."

I saw red. I wanted to bring Aedar back to life and kill him all over again.

As the group looked at her, she gulped. Her face was aflame. I wanted nothing more than to take her discomfort away from her. But we had to find out more about these stolen shifters, and it sounded like they were experimenting with humans.

"And how did you come into this call-girl facility? Where were you before?" Locke asked.

"I was blindfolded from my previous...place," she gulped. "Shoved in a van with my hands and feet bound. I didn't know if it was night or day. When we arrived, they injected me in the neck, and when I woke up, I was in the same room you all found me in. I couldn't really tell you how many days I was there. Often, I felt like I was in a fog with some of the things I did. I just counted the training or work cycles they gave me." She let out her breath, balling her fists into her knit pants.

"They taught me things to please the customers on the other side of the screen. Basic cam girl stuff that I didn't know about. The worst was when Aedar would be in the room, telling me what to do to myself. When I couldn't see the other person on the other side of the screen, I could pretend they weren't there. But Aedar liked to watch the girls, sometimes doing things in the corner while we performed. That was the hardest."

A growl left my throat when I smelled her salty tear fall down her cheek. She hung her head in shame, not watching the others in the room.

My brothers and sister were not disgusted with Journey. They were disgusted by the evil monsters who forced these innocent women to perform as cam girls. No one should have their choices taken away, forced into an industry they didn't want to be a part of.

She wiped away the tear with the base of her palm, her heart pounding in her chest.

"Sometimes, if they offered to pay enough, there would be meetings. I was drugged though, so usually I don't remember."

"Oh fuck." Hawke ran his hair through his mohawk. "Don't let the girl say any more than she has to. This is fucking terrible!"

Journey's lips pursed, her eyes not meeting anyone's gaze. Locke raised his hand, silencing the room.

I knew that look, he wanted to probe further, ask her deeper questions like if she knew where she was taken, or if the customers came to her. If she saw anything fantasy, like if she knew of our kind.

I snarled. I couldn't hold back any longer. My wolf was drawn to her. Journey gave him life, gave him meaning to survive. Slowly, he was pushing through, becoming different from what he was. No longer the rabid animal, but the wolf that shared a body with a man.

I pulled Journey's chair away from the table. My brothers stood up with my quick movements, fearing that I had lost myself. They drew weapons from their belts. Beretta already had her Glock in her hand, pointing it straight at me. The red dot danced across my chest.

I pulled Journey to my body and sat down on the chair where she sat. My body encompassed her as I settled her on my lap as I tried to keep the stares away from her. She gasped, but I held her tighter in my embrace.

My wolf needed her touch, to hold her. He was howling at me, growling because old wounds were being ripped open again for this poor woman who had already endured much in her time.

My purr heightened, rumbling into the back of her body. She melted into me, her fingers gripping my jacket.

Fucking heaven.

"Don't hurt him," Journey mumbled. That was all she could say because I had her too tight against my chest.

"He saved me. I owe him everything."

My fangs lengthened, elongating longer than they had in years. My wolf was still uncontrollable and most of all, unpredictable. And somehow, he had pulled down the barriers I'd kept up for years and showed his displeasure, warning our brothers to stay back.

My brothers did not stand down until Locke lowered his hand slowly and touched the table. "Were you taken to one of these clients? Did you see their faces? Maybe we could—"

I cut off Locke abruptly. "SILENCE!"

The room shuddered.

Journey gripped my jacket. My wolf stood up in all his glory, radiating more power than I'd felt since our prime as a warrior. My vision sharpened, my smell heightened, and my strength made Journey feel like nothing but a feather in our arms. The desire to keep her safe, to protect her from anyone, even if that meant I denied my close brother, trumped all. I would not have her become more upset.

"You don't have a right to ask her that," I barked.

"You can't make her decisions for her, Grim," Locke curtly said. "She needs to be with her own kind, get a new life, start over."

There was a hidden message behind those words—that she needed to stay away from the club, stay away from me.

But we could hire her as a second hand, give her the apartment with the rest of the human women we protected, but I would have to stay away like the rest of the shifters had to with the humans.

I'd seen how Hawke looked at the one girl, that longing. I didn't want the hope. I wanted Journey. It took enough pushing from my wolf to see it. I wasn't about to give her up. I wouldn't let her leave me, leave the umbrella of my safety. I needed her and she needed me.

My wolf stepped forward, slow and steady. He inched into the window of my mind, that small window where he could take over. For the first time in fifteen years, I let him peer outside, giving him the reins on our body.

He opened our mouth and let out a thunderous roar.

CHAPTER SIX

Journey

Grim clung to me with determination and such possessiveness.

The members of the club looked anxiously at each other while Grim's muscular arms wrapped around me. He took his calloused hand and rubbed my cheek, coaxing it to rest on his chest. The smell of his old vest filled my nose. The wild musky smell made me breathe effortlessly as he shuffled around, kicking the chair behind us while having us stand on the once carpeted floor.

The chair broke against the wall. There was no mistaking it. The splinters of wood hit the back of his leather pants. His thick boots thumped as he came closer to the table, and his body leaned over it with me in his arms.

This room was strange to begin with. It reminded me of my days attending a religious preparatory school and being sent to the office to be reprimanded.

I wasn't the best-behaved child because of my ADHD, but I wasn't the worst either. I was a mover, a child that couldn't concentrate on one thing for more than a few minutes at a time. It got to where my parents didn't know what to do with me, and any sort of drug was out of the question.

The devil or some demon possessed me. What could they do with a child with problems?

Ship me off when I was fifteen, that's what.

Grim's breathing grew thick. A wild, woodsy scent poured from his pores. It was intoxicating, almost like an aphrodisiac of calmness dripping all over me. I melted into his body, feeling safer than I had ever felt in my entire life.

I had been so scared most of my life. Men wanted nothing but to use women, but Grim had not touched me in any vile way. He held a possessive and protecting nature I never saw in other men who declared they were there to help. I'd only known Grim for less than twelve hours, but my subconscious continued to whisper to trust him. He was gentle to me at least, kinder than anyone I'd ever known.

He was a gentle soul—to me at least.

I breathed in relief thanks to this unfamiliar smell. My wariness of being in danger was long gone, while the beating of Grim's heart filled me with warmth. A feeling I had never experienced.

And in some crazy way, I wanted to revel in it.

"He scented her," Sizzle whispered.

His eyes were as wide as the rest of them as they opened their mouths in shock. Collective gasps and chairs screeching across the floor as they backed away sounded in the silence. I tried to move my head, but he gripped me tighter, rumbling deep inside his chest.

Fear. That is what I should have felt, but the constant smell of wood, forest, and pine all intermingled with one another. I rubbed my face against his chest again, feeling an inexpressible feeling of safety.

"Easy now," Locke soothed.

Grim didn't falter, his stance firm.

"Journey, can you reassure him we won't do anything he doesn't like?

We are just here to help you."

My breath hitched. The idea that Grim felt the need to protect me made me stiffen.

"We promise, Journey. Please help us out," Locke pleaded.

I couldn't move my head. Grim held me so tight I couldn't if I wanted to.

Wait, does that mean I didn't want to move?

"Okay." I breathed in his scent again. "Grim?"

He growled.

Holy shit, he freaking growled. He was a beast.

Well, he did rip Aedar to pieces. It shouldn't surprise me.

"Grim? I don't think your friends want to hurt you."

My head moved slightly against his chest. The bikers in my peripheral were crouching, looking like animals ready to pounce.

"I'm protecting you," his velvet voice called to me. Grim buried his nose on the top of my head, taking slow tantalizing breaths.

"Me??" I asked, flabbergasted. No one had ever protected me in all the years I'd been alive. "Why would you do that? I'm no one special."

The men in the room faded away. They became empty faces of the void. The loneliness I felt soon joined them when he whispered into my ear, "You are mine to protect."

Holy crap. You just met me.

Grim relaxed, my fingers still tangled in his vest. His grip loosened, and he set me down.

Hell, he was cradling me like a baby.

"I'm in charge of her now," he announced.

"He can't." Sizzle jolted from his seat. "He will put the entire club in danger. He can't be allowed to do this! For what? Some quick lay?"

Grim let me go, then jumped over the table so quickly I barely saw it.

The woman in the corner dashed to my side, holding her arm out to keep me from interfering. She had a tall, muscular build. Her beautiful, dark skin looked like velvet under the light as she looked back at me.

She had feline-like eyes, gold and beautiful. Her lip curled at one end when her gaze met mine.

Things were not right, even if this was a biker gang.

Grim pinned Sizzle to the floor on his back. I cringed, hearing the cracking of bone so I turned my head. I could hear the continued beats of fists to face. I raised my shoulders to my ears.

"You're scaring her," Locke said as he remained in his seat while Grim's punches slowed. Grim's thick breathing echoed into the quiet room. Sizzle spat out blood.

"Sizzle, not everything is about a fuck," Locke deadpanned. "You get to sit in the confinement room on the member floor while you heal. Have Bones look at him. Make sure this hothead heals properly," Locke ordered Hawke and Switch as they picked Sizzle up by his shoulders.

"Oh, my god." My body shook as I gazed at the trauma.

Sizzle didn't look the same. His blonde hair and pretty face had been brutally beat out of place. Blood, so much blood, I should be used to that by now. Grim growled at Sizzle until Switch and Hawke dragged him out the door.

"Let it be a warning," Grim declared to the room. He took three long strides toward me.

My mind wanted me to back away from this biker. He was damned dangerous, and now he'd staked some sort of claim on me. I didn't hate the idea, though. There was an undeniable, strange, gravitational force pulling me towards him.

It felt good to be protected, to be in his arms. He had saved me physically from that hellhole, and now he defended me when I grew upset.

"I–" I began, only for him to pull me to his side and tug me out the door.

My head jerked back, watching the faces of his friends staring at his back in shock.

Grim stayed silent, weaving me through the old church building. Not one of the other bikers came out of the office to stop him. No one challenged him even when our feet stepped outside of the worn-down church and into the brisk air.

"W-what just happened?" I squeaked when he pulled me into his embrace, carrying me like a damsel in distress. "What are you doing? Y-you can't do this!"

Of course, my body did the opposite of what I wanted, and I instantly wrapped my arms around his neck.

Oh, hell.

I wanted to fear him and scream from the highest mountain tops that this was not okay. That I was not to be pushed around from one owner to another, that I was my own person. I didn't want anyone to own me, to keep me.

Yet the idea of being completely alone didn't feel good either. I had always been alone, and I was tired of it.

But I was not his to protect. I was just another woman they'd saved, but now it seemed like I'd landed myself in another predicament.

I trusted Grim. The tiniest part of me liked that he stood up for me and took me away when I felt uncomfortable.

But my heart knew what could happen when you placed too much faith in those that tried to act as if they wanted to help you. They crushed it. They sold you to the highest bidder and acted like you were dead.

Would Grim be like that? Crush me? Break what little of me was left?

One lone figure walked out of the church behind us. Locke pulled out a cigarette, taking a drag from it until he had inhaled half the stick. His strides were long, heading straight towards us. I opened my mouth, but Grim and his caveman tendencies grunted in disapproval as he continued to walk further away.

Grim laid me on the bed once we made it back to his apartment. He wrapped a blanket around my shivering body as he sat beside me. He gazed at me with such tenderness. I couldn't believe I was staring up at the same man that had beat up his friend just minutes ago.

Trust him.

That same little voice whispered in my ears. To trust him, to give him a chance. But could I truly give him a chance with a past like mine? Could I fully trust him despite all his noble actions in the past twenty-four hours?

Blood, already drying thanks to the harsh afternoon wind, stained his face.

I had been rescued from hell on earth because all these bikers had saved me from those evil men that exploited me. But I hadn't been freed, and I was unsure if I was happy or sad about it. Where would I have gone if Grim had let me walk out of that church alone today?

I stiffened, smelling the remnants of a cigarette.

"A word, Grim?" Locke flicked the butt on the other side of the open door.

Grim's jaw tightened. Glancing down at me, he gave me a look that told me to stay. I nodded slightly because where the hell would I go? I had nowhere, and Grim seemed to be on my side.

For now.

Grim strode to the door, taking off his jacket and vest and leaving them on one of the two kitchen chairs. He stood in the doorway, turning to see me sitting on the other side of the room. He nodded his head, toward me and shut the door keeping me separated from their private conversation.

What the hell was happening?

I could easily be trading one bad life for another. Now I was a prisoner stuck in a studio apartment with a man who claimed me as his. Who really says "mine" anyway?

A neanderthal.

But he was my neanderthal.

What the hell!?

I shook my head. With Grim right on the other side of the door, it ate at me. Why did I care? Why did I miss it when he didn't have his arm around me? He was everything I despised. A man. A man could easily overpower you physically, and Grim seemed to be the worst of them all.

He'd killed people and beat up his friend.

He was rugged. Tattoos covered his body. His forearms were as big as my damn thighs, for heaven's sake. I had seen men like him on the other side of the camera, shamelessly showing things I never needed to see and then watching me.

I trembled.

That was a time I couldn't go back to—rid it from my mind and never bring it up again.

But it isn't that simple now, is it?

Grim was unusual. He was the strong and silent type. When he spoke, people listened, and everyone, except for Sizzle, took that seriously. They were all going to leave me alone, but because he said, "mine?" And what was that word they used? Scented? Is that some biker gang slang word for putting the claim on me?

I wrung my hands between my legs. The tick in my eye had returned, which was surprising since it hadn't happened yesterday. It would tick, tick, tick, throughout the cam girl calls, but they weren't paying much attention to my face.

It drove my mother crazy. She would try to slap it out of me some days, but I couldn't help it. That's when she thought the demon would rise from inside me, telling me to do something awful to her and the rest of the family.

With shaky steps, I walked across the room to the door. With each step closer, my tick subsided. I pressed my ear to the barrier that held Grim on the other side.

I was sneaky, and I shouldn't be, but I needed to know what was going to happen to me. Was Locke going to get rid of me now? Even with Grim putting some claim on me? Would I want to leave given the opportunity?

Because I'm not sure if I would. Not when a huge biker was taking extra steps to protect the weak woman with nowhere to go.

CHAPTER SEVEN

Grim

I shut the door, and the click echoed through my head as I was about to face off with the acting alpha. Not once had I ever defied Locke. Today was the first. The hint of disappointment in his eyes when I slammed Sizzle to the floor was clear enough when he didn't dare leave his seat.

"I know you don't like to, but you need to talk to me, Grim." Locke flicked another half lit cig to the floor, stomping it out.

The black leather rubbed around his ankles like a second skin. He was on his second pack, and it was barely two. It was a bad sign, meaning there was another letter or trouble brewing.

"But I need to know why you scented her, a human." His face went soft. "Is it because you're almost gone, brother?"

The pity in his eyes only angered me. How dare he think I wouldn't have control of *that* at least? Scenting was downright deliberate. A shifter had to open their soul and let their animal out in the most vulnerable ways. We have human sides, but we were mainly animals. It allowed my scent to seep out of my pores and intertwine with my mate's own unique smell. My wolf had claimed her as his.

Mine.

That scent poured onto Journey.

She was mine, and there was no stopping it. Even a brisk shower wouldn't eliminate the smell. It was powerful, only to be used on a mate. Scenting was an act I had only dreamed of, a practice I never experienced with a mate that rejected me so long ago. Instead, I gave my first scenting to Journey.

Because she was *mine.*

"I did it purposefully," I growled.

Locke's eyes widened, his hand rubbing his forehead. Pulling out a lighter, he flipped it around in his fingers, lighting and relighting the flame. The pacing and the mumbling to himself made me anxious.

"She is mine, Locke," I spoke to him as a friend rather than my alpha. His head whipped to me, his forearms tightening, causing the pine tree tattoos to ripple with a warning.

"You can't, and you know why. I can't ignore this. I know you are coming close to being rabid, but—"

I reached out, taking the lighter and chucking it down the stairwell. I pushed Locke hard enough to the wall to make him hit the back of his head. My nose flared and sweat beaded on my brow. My claws lengthened, scraping old scars around his neck.

Just under an hour ago, my wolf had spoken for the first time in a long time. His consciousness was building back inside my mind. No longer did I feel the ocean of emptiness in my head. My wolf had come home from years at sea, and he brought Journey with him.

Journey, my wolf, and I were all I needed now, and I wouldn't give either of them up.

"My wolf says it must be so," I huffed, letting go of his cut. The badges displayed on his cut unfolded gently from my harsh fingers.

Locke was right. This shouldn't happen. To have a human living with you every hour of the day, they were going to see things. They would slowly figure out who we were, that we weren't normal. The growling, purring, rutting, nesting, the things that make a shifter, would make a human afraid.

Humans didn't know who we are. At least they weren't supposed to. If they knew, a potent memory spell was cast on them. It was so powerful they could forget who they were as a person. Which was better? A spell to have them forget not only us but who they were? Or death? Most of the time, death was chosen.

Humans were skittish. They couldn't handle or fathom the idea that they weren't the only sentient beings on this Earth. If only they knew how big this world really was... If they knew about us, they would either try to experiment on us or kill what they didn't understand.

Most supernaturals wanted peace, and when the Royal Council convened, they created a treaty to prevent other humans from learning about us. Showing who you were to a human meant death for you and the human as well.

Humans had become obsessed over the recent years, watching and imagining what it would be like to see a supernatural. Talk of letting the supernatural world become known by the humans was discussed. Many wanted to come out of hiding, since now humans were becoming more welcoming of the idea.

What will happen now that a wolf was mated to a human?

"Grim, I'm speaking to you as my brother," he sighed, pulling down his cut to straighten the wrinkles. "If *they* found out, it would be over for her and you. If someone saw you two together, like *that.* And what is this, anyway? You just like her?" He raised his eyebrow "I dare not say what Sizzle said, but is it something to do with your rut coming in?"

I snarled, my wolf flashing his black eyes then back to my own. "Never.

She is more than just rutting company." My heart thumped in my chest.

She was more. Journey was so much more. She was more than a possession, a thing, a toy for my wolf to play with and discard for later.

Journey was...my mate.

I pursed my lips, my fangs lengthening at the thought of having to give up Journey. I had a chance, my former mate rejected us for another, someone more robust, faster, better. My wolf growled out, forcing those thoughts of inadequacy from my lips.

I would be the best damn wolf for her.

"Journey is our mate," my wolf growled out. Locke stepped back, leaning his back against the wall.

"Holy shit, Grim," he panted. "No fucking way, no, no, no!" He pulled at his hair, pacing up and down the hallway. "No damn way!

My ears perked at the light breathing on the other side of the door. There was no denying what I heard. My wolf was growing stronger by the minute, having Journey near us. I could hear the faint beating of her heart, how her ear grazed the old wooden door, her fingertips gently tickling the wood beneath them.

I put my finger to my lips to silence him. Locke was still in a state of shock. So, I put my hand on the door. I could feel her warmth, the heat of her breath. Why had I not entirely accepted it when our fingers let out the jolt of surprise last night? It was time wasted, time that I could have been spending with her.

"What the fuck are we going to do? If this gets out?" Locke rubbed his hands up and down his face. "I'll take care of it." His hands shook. "Without a doubt, yeah? She's your... your?" he whispered as he lit another cig.

My lip curled into a smile. I had a chance at being happy for once in my life. She brought the wolf back to me. She brought me from the brink of losing myself, and she didn't even know.

"Oh fuck, she is." He pulled his hair and turned his back to me to walk back down the stairs. "Wait." He turned around, the cig dancing on his lips. "If she is—" He pointed to me and the door. "Then does that mean—" He pointed back to himself, then his finger swayed to the open window towards the bar.

Fuck if I knew. I just knew I had a second chance. If the others did, I wasn't sure. I just knew I had one thing I never thought I would have.

A second chance.

"I'll take care of it, yeah—" Locke muttered. "We don't tell anyone, not yet. Can't cause a stir in the club, you hear?" He wagged his finger at me. "We can't let this get out in the open yet. Not until we figure something out about the Royal Council, because if they knew. Fuck, if they find out..."

Locke had never lost his cool in all years I'd known him, and he was breaking at the seams. I held in a growl, shaking my head and keeping my hand firmly planted on the door. Journey had backed away, the heat dissipating.

"They won't know," I gritted my teeth. "We are just a bunch of rogues, anyway. Who are they to care?"

Locke shook his head. "Just keep it quiet. She can live here, obviously. Can't separate you two."

No, he can't, not when she was mine.

"Word is out you scented her. Everyone will stay away. I'll just tell them you have an urge to protect her as your last effort to keep sane. That alright with you until I figure it out?"

I nodded, holding out my hand in agreement.

I wasn't a complete prick. Keeping the rest of the brothers safe was a priority for me. I'd do my best to keep my hands to myself in public, if she would even let me touch her.

Locke was a suitable substitute alpha president for the club. He was fair and honorable, always had been since I'd known him. He simply better not impede my mate.

"Need money?" He walked from down the stairs.

I had so much money saved up from doing tats for out-of-towners and Switch setting up a social media page. I had plenty of clients. I could take care of my mate no problem. I was her provider now.

"I'm fine."

Locke ran back up the stairs. He put his arms around me, patting me on the back. "I'm so glad you're gonna be alright."

Little did people know how close of a relationship Locke and I had. Behind closed doors, I swear the gods mixed us up at birth, and we were supposed to be blood brothers. Spirit brothers are closer, I suppose.

"Thanks," I said patting him equally hard on the back. His head nodded to the door.

"Go get your girl. Let me know if you need anything. I'll leave you alone for a few days." He winked.

Before he strolled away, I gripped his arm. "Yesterday, at the club. I saw—"

"Already on it. Human with a bunch of she-wolves and fae powder? You wound me if you thought I wouldn't know." Locke held his hand to his chest, rubbing it as if it hurt.

Playfully, I punched his shoulder and headed to the door with my mate on the other side.

My mate.

Opening the door, I found her sitting on the hard-seated chair by the table. Her arms are wrapped around her legs, staring at me like a frightened mouse. Her hair was up in a messy bun, her caramel eyes staring back at me. She shook, her eyes batting erratically.

"What's wrong?" My wolf pushed to reveal himself, to show how strong and dependable we were to keep her safe.

She did not need to fear us. Others needed to fear for their safety when anyone stepped near her. Not another moment of worry should cross her path. I was her protector. I was her mate.

"You were gone a while. Everything okay?" she asked.

My smile curled. I sauntered over, my boots tapping the floor, until I kneeled before her.

Her body shifted away from me.

"Do I scare you?" Journey looked me up and down carefully. My body was still covered in one of my brother's blood. "I can--" I stepped away, but to my surprise, she held out her hand for me to stop.

"No, no, you don't scare me." Her head dropped between her knees.

"Then what worries you? Ailes you?"

The wrinkle between her eyebrows creased the skin. She smacked her nude lips and blew out a breath.

"I'm scared to be alone," she whispered.

I put my hand out, palm facing upwards. A silent request for her hand. She placed the cool fingers in mine, and I squeezed them tight. Warmth engulfed us both, and I swore I heard her breath hitch.

Could humans feel the bond too?

"You won't be alone again," I promised.

CHAPTER EIGHT

Journey

*Y*ou won't be alone anymore, it echoed through my soul as he stepped away, pulling me with him.

"I don't understand what's going on," I said as he led me to the couch. Despite it being old, it held my body upright as my back sank into the cushion.

My body no longer tense, I stared up into his eyes. They were such a dark blue when I first saw them, so guarded and hidden from the night when he peered under the bed. Now they were lighter, almost a light navy.

He claimed me in front of his friends, his protective stance and hitting his best friend who lived across the hallway was proof enough.

"Not alone, not anymore." He stood up and went to the fridge, pulling out bottles of water.

It was mostly empty, no food to be seen. A true bachelor, probably ordered in or went to that bar I saw last night.

Most men weren't one to plan and take care of themselves, and Grim was certainly far from caring what people thought of his home.

So, what makes me think he could look after me?

I glanced around the room, the bed I'd made still sat undisturbed. The afternoon sun's rays highlighted the dust particles that littered the air.

Grim ran his hand through the messy hair on top of his head. The sides were buzzed short, and his beard was now trimmed neater than it had been last night.

His appearance already looked less feral. The usual scowl had softened considerably since returning from speaking with Locke.

Now his body moved freely instead of the with the rigidity of earlier. Something had changed, and I wasn't sure what. The lightness in the surrounding air buoyed my spirits higher than what they should be, and that was worrisome.

Since he claimed me, what would he do to me now?

He was my rescuer, my protector, but now he was also my captor. If I left, what would he do?

"Protecting you," his voice rasped. "You're a witness." Grim rubbed his throat.

"But I didn't see anything." I tried to compel him to listen. "I only saw that strange man and barely talked to the other women. Surely they wouldn't care. Just let me go, and I'll—"

Grim growled, stepping towards me. "I'm protecting you. You're mine," he whispered under his breath.

I knew the last part wasn't meant for me to hear, but I couldn't help but shudder.

I was his? As in meaning his to protect only, right?

Grim's leather boots clicked across the wooden floor of his apartment. The leather on his feet stretched, in the quieted room. It was an erotic noise that should have frightened me with his dominating presence, but instead it gave me an adrenaline rush of excitement I wasn't sure of. It was erotic the way his pants pulled around his thick legs, the material of his clothes tight on his body. It was clothing meant for riding, but the allure of it made me grip my thighs. I pulled my legs up onto the couch and hugged them tightly.

I was finding him dangerously attractive.

Grim pulled out his phone. He scrolled through the screen, tapping and scrolling until he grunted in satisfaction.

"I could just stay hidden, go to that apartment where all the girls down the street live." My voice became hopeful, but the tinge of regret at the thought of leaving still beat in my heart. Grim had done enough for me already, and I didn't deserve any more of his kindness.

He may be utterly rugged and handsome in his own way, but he wouldn't want some broken women in his apartment mooching off the things he didn't have, eating food I couldn't pay for or using borrowed clothes.

I needed a job, a life, and to move on. I could get started easily with the help of Locke. Earn my keep, and once I had enough, move far, far away.

Grim stomped up to me, holding out his hand for me to take. I gulped, putting my hand in his as that funny electric shock jolted me back to the present. He led me back to the door and down the stairs.

Despite the upstairs apartments looking more on the worn side, the downstairs was a stark contrast to the building. It was immaculately clean and crisp, with lines perfectly straight and walls decorated in beautiful skull and tribal patterns. A large skull was placed in front of the window, the same skull that adorned the outside of the old, tattered church.

The four stations were filled with chairs, equipment, and mirrors. Ink lined the shelves. Each one was separated by a partition for privacy.

"Tattoo parlor," Grim stated the obvious, as if I might not know what this place was.

He flipped on the lights. The walls were painted in a deep red as opposed to the black I thought they were, and they were covered with rustic décor.

Grim led me to a large desk with scattered papers and an old computer.

Grim typed on the keyboard, putting in his log in information. He pulled out a stool that sat out of sight, and his eyes guided me to sit.

"I'll stand," I murmured. Not seeing a chair for Grim, but he sighed, sitting on the stool and pulling me onto his lap. I squeaked,; his arm wrapping around my waist as I glanced at the computer screen.

Grim didn't hide the information that was displayed. It was a large schedule filled with names of clients and appointments. Each one had a "send notification of cancellation" in each box. Grim clicked three clients he had for the day, as well as Sizzle's, and canceled them.

"Wait," I said too loudly.

Grim stopped scrolling, his face next to my cheek. The heat of his breath made me lose myself, the aromatic scent of pine and forest calming me instead of frightening me.

"D-don't cancel because of me. I can sit here in the back while you work." Grim grunted and continued with his tasks. I shook my head, not understanding why he would send a client away.

"Don't work without Sizzle," he muttered and continued with his tasks.

The scattered designs of papers on the desk displayed wolves howling at the moon, dragons, lions, panthers, and even fairy-type creatures. They were all so beautiful in their own unique way—many wasting away to skeletons, some emerging through soil or fire.

"Did you draw these?" My fingers trailed over the red wolf staring back at me. It had black eyes, its maw in a snarl. Grim nodded as he watched me finger each drawing "They are all so beautiful. You're so talented."

Grim hummed, still typing on the computer with one hand.

"I drew them, yes," he said.

"Like this one?" I pointed at the red wolf that called to me.

It was a photograph of the final draft on someone's chest. Bright red from the continuous needle picking, the colors stood out starkly against the pale skin. The client's body was riddled with scars, and the wolf took the entirety of this man's chest. The fur looked like Grim's hair, and dare I say the shape of the eyes, even looked similar.

"My design," he muttered. "Sizzle tatted me."

My eyes widened, realizing the muscular back I was ogling was Grim's. My face flushed, and I let go of the photograph.

How could I have missed such a beautiful piece of art on his body?

Oh, maybe because you were scared out of your mind yesterday to really look at his ink?

"H-he did an excellent job," I muttered, still looking at the wolf staring back at me.

He pulled me in closer to his chest. My tense body relaxed again when I heard a rumbling in his chest. It wasn't an anger driven growl of frustration from my constant questions; it was a constant purring noise that relaxed me further.

My face heated, feeling the blood rush to my cheeks at how much I enjoyed his touch. It was crazy, right? To feel this strange feeling of wanting to be touched after so many years of the idea of anyone touching me? But I wanted it. I wanted a tender touch—not a forceful unwanted one.

It was different with him, and I wasn't sure how.

It was an invisible force, a pull, that I couldn't deny. The question was, did Grim feel it, too? Or was it the pure obligation to take care of me because he was the one who found me?

I pursed my lips, not liking that idea, but what was I to say?

I'd never had a proper relationship. I wouldn't know how to act in one. I was taken from my home at fifteen years old to go work on some crusty old man's farm until the day I turned eighteen. That old farmer must have felt guilty about sending me away at fifteen because he wasn't supposed to keep me.

It was just a stop where they abandoned all the lone girls that had no homes. But when my birthday came around, he loaded me up like cattle for slaughter, and I was sent to be a sex worker.

As much as I hated the old man and his wife, I enjoyed working with my hands. To work the land and tend to the animals. I had a warm place to sleep and enough food to keep my belly satisfied after a long day in the sun. Those were the happiest days of my childhood, despite it being such hard manual labor.

I moved my head so I could stare up at Grim's bearded face, his eyes were already set on me. Like memorizing every line of my face, the curve of my cheek, and the flush of my skin. The trance was set, and I wasn't about to break it. His eyes had a hold on me, those eyes that also grabbed at the deepest part of me, the vulnerable parts, the parts that were never meant to be seen. I blinked, slowly turning my face only for his rough, calloused fingers to bring my chin back into view.

If only he could really see the problems that lay beneath.

"Um," I whispered, feeling the sensual hold around my waist. The vibrations of his chest grew deeper, and I felt them between my legs. My eyes closed, feeling the deep vibrations of his body. Could men really make such a noise? Or was it just Grim?

It was a euphoric feeling I had never encountered in all my years. I welcomed it as I felt his vibration rush through me. My body surged, my arousal heightening like it never had before. I'd seen many asshole men in my life, some supposedly handsome, but none of them made my body buzz with need like Grim did.

My face reddened further. His stare searched my eyes in the deepest parts of my soul.

Grim's vibrations ceased, his eyes flashing from his navy blue to black.

I blinked several times, making sure I saw nothing amiss, only to see him shutting off the lights to his right.

The wolf in the photo, I swear, was howling at me at the ridiculousness that I was creating in my mind. I shook my head, trying to realize that I had finally gone crazy.

He picked me up like I was a newborn baby and carried me back up the stairs. As he held me close to him and opened the door, he didn't even wince when his elbow abruptly hit the corner of the bed.

He laid me on the bed and stepped away. I missed his touch; I wasn't ready for him to let go, but my mind reeled with other thoughts.

I didn't know him, didn't really know his intentions. I had to remind myself of that.

My body wanted him, but my mind was a jumbled mess. I had to stay away. He could be another predator, even though he had treated me better than everyone else had.

"Rest," he commanded. "Stay."

He stepped back to the door, my eyes watching his every move until his hand reached the handle. Looking back, he nodded again, then opened the door just enough and slid through.

CHAPTER NINE

Grim

Humans didn't realize the arousal that they emit from their bodies. From the outside, her facial expressions remained calm, almost too un-lifelike. She was an excellent actress in that regard. Possibly from the many years of having to please whoever held her as a prisoner.

Who will all eventually die a slow and painful death.

When she sat on my lap, I held her close, keeping her body next to mine. It helped my wolf's demanding voice fade, but then it stirred something else entirely—my cock.

Since becoming rogue and almost rabid, the liveliness of my cock had dwindled as the years went on. The animalistic part of my body had taken over and disregarded anything to do with procreating because my wolf deemed us unworthy.

Hell, I deemed us unworthy.

For a time, I could sate myself, taking care of my problems on my own when I went into a rut. Only a few times had another female rogue needed help with their heat, and I was happy to oblige when my rut seemed to coincide with it.

Now I regretted those moments.

If I had known I was to be given a second chance, I would have saved my cock for her.

But right now, the combination of her closeness, her arousal, and my wolf scenting her had stirred my body back to life. I was healing and with that, my cock stirred to knot inside her.

Leaving Journey in my room, I barged into Sizzle's apartment. It remained unlocked, the lock long since broken, but no one dared to break in any door on this side of town. I pushed his bathroom door open and fumbled through the enormous amounts of lube in his medicine cabinets.

For a dragon who lived a celibate life, he worked out his hand. I muddled through, finding the most basic shit I could find. My hand fumbled, my cock pressed hard against the inside of my jeans. It was painful. Every second that passed, I thought it might explode from the pressure against the rough fabric. A knot was forming at the base, my grimace reflecting in the mirror.

Grunting, I ripped my belt from the loops, unbuttoning my pants. My cock stayed swollen, red, and inflamed. Fuck, I don't remember the last time it had ever been this hard, this painful. Gripping it with my right hand, I squeezed the base, pouring lube on top of my slow and steady strokes.

The smooth, hardened shaft felt slick in my hand. The area where I'd had a Jacob's ladder piercing done when my cock become permanently flaccid tingled with extra sensation.

It hadn't been this hard since I had I got it pierced. I had hoped it would stir my body to feel something, anything, but that was all for nothing. Now, it was hard for *her*, my second chance at a new life.

I growled, leaning against the wall.

My face gazed at the mirror, my wolf growling at me to have Journey take care of this. To have her hand graze over the thick shaft, her tiny hands would barely be able to reach around it.

Fuck, she was too delicate for this, too fragile to handle the beast my wolf was becoming. It wasn't possible. We couldn't claim her, not yet.

My wolf flashed images in my mind of Journey in the outfit we'd found her in—a tight bodice of black spandex, the fabric caressing her in all the right places. Despite being too skinny thanks to years of deprivation, she was perfection.

I groaned far too loudly at the thought of the swell of her breasts, her slim waist, and her rounded ass. Those caramel-colored eyes beckoned me to draw closer to her, to graze my lips over her until I slowly claimed every part of her body. First, her forehead, lips, and down her neck. Then, The swell of her breasts until she let me undress her.

My wolf howled, creating images of her mouth around my cock. I squeezed tighter, the image of my hand grabbing the back of her head to sink her deeper.

I tightened my hold on her hair, her mouth hummed into me. My wolf panted, begging for her to suck us dry.

Journey's golden orbs dove into my soul as soon as I saw my cock disappear into her mouth once more. One of her hands massaged my heavy balls, the other holding my hips as I continued to fuck her mouth.

Groaning, my hand fisted my cock until the knot swelled inside my hand. Gripping tighter, my claws ripped into the counter as my release coated my hand. My release was plentiful, but my cock swelled again.

Shit.

My rut was coming and having Journey in the same apartment as me would be damned impossible. I couldn't take her, I'd scare her. We didn't know each other at all, yet my wolf seemed to think we knew her just enough.

But if her arousal meant anything, she at least found me attractive.

My crooked smile widened. She thought I was attractive. In her eyes, I was attractive. My chest swelled and pride filled me. Her arousal was for me.

The wolf inside me dared to roll his eyes like I was some wide-eyed fool. I was, fuck, after being told we were not handsome enough, strong enough, fast enough, of course I wouldn't believe I was attractive enough for a female. Our first mate rejected us, but so far, Journey hadn't.

But she didn't know what I was yet.

Shaking the thought away, my wolf brought more images, forbidden images of Journey to my mind. From behind, the front, hell, all over the kitchen table, and my cock continued to spray my seed all over Sizzle's small bathroom.

Someone banged on the other side of the bathroom door, and I halted. My hand was covered in the sticky substance; I grunted in disapproval. I would need to take care of myself at least two more times before I could face her. Walking back to her with an enormous erection was not a great way to establish a relationship with her.

"What?" I growled.

The banging on the other side of the door ceased and Hawke's voice came to my ears. "I've got all the stuff you ordered. It's sitting outside your door," he mentioned. "I tried knocking on your door, but all I could smell was your girl."

I growled, not liking the distaste in his voice. "Mine," I growled, wiping my hand away. "She's mine," I opened the door.

His hands were raised in surrender, his gaze now turning to my barely covered cock. "Oh, shit." He ran his fingers through his hair. "You're rutting? I mean, that's great. It's been a few years since you had one, right? You're getting...better?

I nodded, pulling my jeans up and threading my belt through the loops.

Many would find the bodily functions of another man grotesque, but we were not men or humans. We were animals.

We all visited Bones, the club doc, frequently. It was mandatory for all the rogues to receive regular checkups. Especially those who would go rabid soon. I was at the top of the list.

Symptoms were posted throughout the clubhouse's private quarters—what to look for and what to expect when one lost their rut and their ability to harden and grow a knot. The list included brothers who had lost theirs. It was damned emasculating, but it was there to let the brothers know we would succumb to the rabid stage.

Once my name appeared on the list, the inner circle thought I was done for.

My wolf had been silent for years, but other club members surpassed me and went rabid before I did. Maybe my wolf had something to hang on to. The hope that another female could be called our own kept us hanging onto life a while longer.

Because I survived, I'd come this far.

"How can that happen? Is she? Holy fuck, is she like? Are you getting better because of *that* girl?" He looked to the distance, out the window in longing.

"Mouth shut." I buttoned my pants. "Still don't know." Hawke let out a nervous laugh, his hand running over his beard.

"I... Wow."

I pulled Hawke away from the bathroom, gripping his neck, and pushing him to the wall. "Shut up," I growled. "No speaking."

Hawk nodded in understanding. His back straightened, and he crossed his arm over his chest in respect.

"Right, I understand." He pulled his cut away from his neck. "It's just that this is big. Is that why Locke is acting funny? Around the women folk? Watching us all interact with the humans that work in the bar?"

Locke was going to get himself in trouble if he didn't stop being obvious.

"Is she your mate, Grim? Your second chance? Does that mean? Really?" His enthusiasm was insufferable, but he was in the inner circle. I grunted in agreement, and he laid his head back on the wall.

"Fuck, damn." He cursed, running his hand through his hair. "I wish…"

I knew what he was going to say before he said it. He wanted that human girl, Delilah. He dared not touch her, worried that his own selfish desires would get the better of him. Hawke was fond of her. Often times he had to leave the bar when jealousy overtook him. She was a friendly, pure soul that welcomed everyone with her kindness. He couldn't force her to quit her job so men wouldn't stare at her or seek her favor. Because he couldn't claim her. Not a human, not when he was subject to becoming rabid in the future.

She wasn't his, she was human. There wasn't a bond.

"How did it go? Did your wolf just claim her? Just scent her on his own?"

I groaned, feeling my cock swell again. As excited as he was, as many other brothers would be, this was delicate, especially with a human and the potential for the Royal Council to get wind of the situation.

"Animal spoke to me." I walked back to the bathroom door. My fingers already unbuttoned my pants, my cock springing free as I rubbed along my knotted shaft. "Claimed her, scented her all on his own."

When finding a mate, the human side could find their mate extremely attractive but the animal inside a shifter was the one who made the official claim. The human side was able to reject a mate however—just like I was rejected—but their animal would forever be sore with their human side.

Now that we were rogues, we had lost most of our ability to smell, but my eyes appreciated Journey's appearance. She was attractive, and the first moment I saw her I wanted her close.

And then, her touch. I wanted more of it.

The thought it could just be lust had never been the issue. I couldn't get my cock to rise just looking at her then. A magnetic bond pulled me to her, and now that my wolf had claimed her, there was no going back. Not that I ever wanted to.

"Go," I grunted.

I shut the door hastily to finish my first round of rutting. My cock would be sore and inflamed and there was nothing I could do. Gritting my teeth, fisting myself, another pounding of the door made me yell for them to leave.

"Locke's on his way, he's got something to help." I heard through the door.

It could have been hours that had gone by. My raging dick wasn't letting up. It was getting worse, and my wolf continued to argue with me to take Journey, to make her ours.

The bathroom door bashed open, revealing a disturbed Locke shoving his hand in his cut to reveal a red bag.

"Rutting root," he said. He pushed me away from the sink, my cock still hanging free as he poured water over the red substance. It turned to paste as he rubbed it with his palms. He looked to me, to my cock, and back to his hand.

"You gotta stick it on your dick," he raised a brow. "And I love you like a brother, but I can't do that shit."

I growled, rinsing my hand before I wiped away most of the paste from his hand and coated my cock. The blood rushing to my groin ceased, and the burning, the knot, all faded away. My breathing became shallow, my back hitting the wall, while I covered myself with my jeans.

"Thanks," I said, relieved. "Fuck."

CHAPTER TEN

Journey

My eye twitched, doing that annoying dance it did before my body shuts down.

I don't remember the last time I had been left in a room alone, with no expectations given to me. I usually had a job, something to do—put on some make-up, clean the room, or some other idiotic chore.

I stood in the middle of the room, my body swaying, feeling the itch on my feet. My untreated ADHD didn't bother me much over the years, but now it had settled inside since I was now idle. I'd never had anything to do. On top of it all, was he coming back? Grim had left without a word, and now I was on my own.

I could leave. I looked longingly at the door. Pick the old, rusty lock, walk down the stairs and into the wide abandoned-looking street. Sure, his friends were out there, but there were other people out there, too. It was late afternoon, if I was lucky, I could get out of this section of town without anyone even paying attention to me if I took the alleyways.

My breath caught, hearing the knock at the door.

Grim wouldn't knock. He would just come in.

Then who could it possibly be?

My eye twitched again. I sat down on the old wooden chair as the door clicked open and a petite brunette popped her head in the door. Her cheeks were rosy, and her white teeth and pretty smile lit up the room. "Hi, I heard you needed some things, so I thought I would stop by."

This woman didn't have the same authority oozing from her as the woman in the meeting hours before. She was much smaller, sweeter, and didn't look like she would harm a fly.

I thought about the woman who I used to call mother. The same woman that would be so sweet to others but looked at me like I was trash behind closed doors. She sold me to that farmer. That old coot would then in turn sell me again for a higher price. But while I was there, he saw that he needed extra help.

"It's okay." The woman padded into the room, setting bags of groceries by the door.

She spoke to me like I was a frightened animal, her hands laying close to the side of her body. "I'm just here to help. Hawke said you needed some clothes, and the girls back at the apartment all pitched in to give you some until Grim gets you settled." She smiled. "It's kind of weird he didn't put you with us, but I can see how you are shaking. You don't take kindly to new people."

New people? Don't take kindly to much of anyone.

"T-thank y-ou." I fiddled with my fingers. "I'm just not used to trusting people," I whispered. "Usually, people want something."

The woman frowned, stepping through the door and shutting it. The gentle push along with the draft resulted in a slammed door, and my body jumped from my seat in surprise.

She winced.

"Sorry, these old buildings do that. Do you mind if I sit?" The couch was the only thing between us, but she posed no threat, at least that I saw.

The piles of bags of food and clothes sat there in the corner, but I was too worried someone else would come through the door.

"Hawke will come in and take care of the food and clothes. He's talking to Grim." The woman had read my mind. "Hey, I'm Delilah." She waved shyly. "I heard your name is Journey, is that right?"

I nodded in reply, gulping while I fidgeted with my fingers. My leg bounced, part of my nervousness and part of my need to move.

Where was Grim?

"Listen, uh, if you want to move with us to the apartment, you can. We all kind of have our demons," she chuckled. "I came into town with bare feet, a backpack, and no money to my name, and these crazy bikers put me up in that apartment down the street, and now I've got a job, a roof over my head, and a full stomach. They aren't bad people." She leaned forward. "Even if they can be a bit scary looking."

I chuckled at the twinkle in her eye. Smiling, she leaned back on her part of the couch. "There is more stuff coming, but Hawke wanted me to bring stuff over as it came so you'll be comfortable. He's talking to Grim, now."

I bit my lip, thanking her again. My breath quickened and my hands shook while I played with my hair. Hell, why was I so nervous? She was being nice, just a pleasant woman trying to make me feel welcome, and I couldn't even carry a conversation.

I'm more messed up than I thought.

"It's crazy, Grim ordered new bedding, pillows, curtains like he is dressing up the entire apartment," she said, astonished. She frowned, watching my body shake. "The men folk around here don't do that. Usually, their places are bare. Several of the women started a cleaning business and at least sweep through the apartments not connected to the bar. They won't let us go back there. Must be secret club stuff," she whispered the last part, giggling.

I gave a modest smile, trying to accept her attempt to make me feel more at ease.

"Men around here don't like a personal touch. They are all bare like this," Delilah rambled. "The only apartment they haven't cleaned is Sizzle's, though. He hates women, but take no offense to that," she added. "Some girl must have put a foul taste in his mouth, or he's extremely gay and bitter about it."

I giggled, covering my mouth.

"There, she does laugh!" Delilah cooed. "Seriously though, these men are good people. Just don't get romantically involved or catch the feelings for these guys." She gulped. "Because they aren't into us like that. I'm not entirely sure if they are all into each other or just don't have hearts," she trailed off.

She cleared her throat, the door opened, and Hawke sauntered in. He grabbed more bags that sat by the door and dropped them on the counter.

He had empty holsters on either side of his hips, a knife in his boot, and cuffs tucked into his belt. His short mohawk gave him a cold-blooded killer vibe, but that wasn't what Delilah saw.

She looked at him like he hung the moon.

Hawke's leather boots clomped on the floor. You could hear the leather move with him around his ankles. He glanced around the room until he met Delilah's face. His stony face warmed, seeing her smile back at him.

Were they a thing?

Maybe not since she just said not to get romantically involved with these guys.

"Come on, Dede, we need to go." His voice was far softer than I would have thought. He nodded his head to the door, and she stood to leave.

"Are you sure she can't come to stay with us? She needs to be around some women and not just Grim, even if he is good people." The tiredness in her voice appeared, and she gestured toward me. "She would be far more comfortable than being with a man alone in this apartment, especially after…"

"Dede, that's enough," Hawke said sternly. His face went stiff as both of us flinched. Groaning, which sounded more like growling, he stepped away, putting his hands up.

"This is the way things are. She is safer here with Grim. She's under his protection until further notice," he said patiently.

"Let me just give her a quick hug. Everyone likes hugs, right?" Delilah stepped over, but Hawke pulled on Delilah's hand, pulling her away.

"Don't touch her," he warned.

"But why not? The poor thing needs coddling, don't you, Journey?"

Tears came to my eyes, but Hawke pulled her away.

"You can't touch her right now."

We both cocked our heads. There was no room left for her to ask questions while he pulled her away.

"Will you come visit?" I asked.

It was nice having another woman around, one that seemed to like me. I wasn't sure if it was because of an ulterior motive, but her words were sweet. There wasn't an evil glint in her eye or awkward movements like she was hiding something.

"Of course."

"Dede, you can't promise that. Now, come," he barked.

My mouth was left hanging open as she walked to the door. His hand went to her lower back, leading her out. She didn't question, didn't bother to argue. Hawke gave me one last look, as he led her out. Before he shut the door, Hawke pushed his head back in.

"Everything is going to be all right. You are safe here, little one." He nodded, and I flinched again as the door shut.

How was I safe if I wasn't allowed to be around anyone?

The banging next door grew louder. The door groaned, and it slammed at the last minute. The knot in my stomach grew. I didn't want to be alone, but I didn't want to know what was happening in the apartment next door.

Was it Sizzle? I thought they'd locked him up.

The banging lessened, and heavy footsteps approached the only door in or out of the room. I scurried away, hearing voices on the other side, and slipped into the one closet this apartment had. It was small, just large enough for me to slip into and gently close the door. Growling and scuffling came from the other side, and a bark of laughter sounded.

I kept the door shut, not wanting to see who it was.

I used to be so wild, so free, scared of nothing and no one, but look what I had become—hiding in a closet from people that had yet to hurt me. But what if they did? Hit me where it hurt, crushing what little self-preservation I had left? What if that little bit of hope that these people were friendly was all a ploy to get me to do something for them?

What about the girls living in an apartment complex a few blocks away? Had they actually saved them or were they using them for labor? It could all be a lie. All of this could be a lie. Doubt encircled me, closing in on the dark closet.

Muffled noises and words of panic filled the other side of the door.

"I'm safe, I'm safe," I whispered, rocking myself into a ball. How many times had I told myself that lie? How many times had the mantra been drilled into me, but I never was okay?

Because nothing was ever okay, lies were part of my life, and I would always have trouble trusting people. No one really cared about other people. That was just not how the world worked.

"Journey!" A yell came through the closet door as soon as he opened it. I didn't look up, but I knew who it was.

His enormous arms gathered around me. He kept me in the tightened ball I'd created for myself and took me away from the closet. He didn't yell at me, didn't scream, didn't ask where I was. Grim gently pulled me to his lap as he sat on the couch. One hand petted my hair, and the other rubbed up and down my back.

"She's going into shock," Locke muttered under his breath.

He pulled out his phone and left the room to make a phone call. Shudders wracked my body, sweat beading on my forehead.

"Relax," Grim's rugged voice called to me. "I'm here." Those words shouldn't have brought me comfort. They should've terrified me. He was a big guy, a guy I knew nothing about, but the soothing words relaxed me as I melted into him.

"Good, keep breathing." His beard tickled my forehead, and I unwound my legs slowly from the ball I'd hid myself in.

The door slammed open, hitting the wall, and I curled back, wincing at the sound.

"Locke," Grim growled.

The growl and purr in his throat made me bury my face in his chest. God, he smelled so good, so nice. It was a drug. It was a smell I found so comforting. I never expected it to calm me like it did. To feel comfortable with a man, to feel safe was not a feeling I was familiar with. I couldn't remember the last time I felt like that, to feel the touch of another person who didn't want something sexual or to hurt me.

"Bones is coming," Locke whispered.

Locke's voice was soft, just like Hawke's when he spoke to me and Delilah, when she wasn't disobeying. Maybe there was a softness to these men, and maybe something more.

But don't fall for them. Don't fall for him.

If Delilah was telling the truth, then I shouldn't get invested. That was hard when the only person who had stuck up for me was holding me in his arms, treating me like precious cargo, and taking every movement he made into account to make sure I wasn't startled.

God, my brain hurt.

"Hurt?" Grim grumbled, the heat of his breath tickling my ear.

By body ached, the longing to be touched and a bit of something else. It was the same as earlier, the wanting to be closer. Wanting to be with him more than just him holding me.

A giant Grim blanket.

To have him lying on top of me, shielding me from the world, making me feel safe. It felt just so right.

Grim groaned, and I squirmed. "Easy," he rubbed my back soothingly. "Stay."

The command was there, the stillness holding onto me as I let my head rest on his shoulder. My body slumped, but his grip never wavered. He held me close as the deep purr in his chest lulled me to sleep.

CHAPTER ELEVEN

Grim

I growled, watching her eyes flutter closed. My body stiffened, feeling Locke behind me. "Back away," I grunted and relaxed at his fleeting footsteps and his hands out in surrender.

Journey's dark hair was wet with sweat, and her body, once trembling, now lay limp in my arms.

Tucking her closer to my chest, my wolf purred deeper, causing her to grip my chest with her tiny hand.

"Is she all right?" Locke kept his voice low, knowing my wolf was close to the surface.

I had yet to shift now that my wolf was speaking to me—more like ordering me to keep our mate safe. I had no damn clue what was happening.

"I don't know," I said, strain in my voice. "She went to sleep after I grabbed her."

Journey's body was curled in the fetal position, her stomach touching mine. I kept her head under my chin, feeling the gentle pants of her breathing. "She's breathing. That's all that matters."

Locke ran his hand through his hair, cursing under his breath. He pulled out his lighter, flicking it on and off. The constant clicking would normally bother me. The click, click, click, and his swearing didn't matter anymore. My eyes had locked onto my mate, memorizing every detail of her face. I couldn't look at her longer than a few seconds at a time while she was awake, fearing she would shy away, and my wolf couldn't handle it.

She had tiny freckles sprinkled over her cheeks, and her eyelashes were dark and thick. Her body was still too thin, but she was gorgeous nonetheless, and she was mine.

All damned mine. Lifting one of her hands, I could see pale scars on her knuckles. I frowned, wondering what it could be until the knock at the door. Locke jumped to open it.

"Bones." Locke nodded, plastering the uncaring visage onto his tanned face. He walked Bones, our club doctor, over, and Bones kneeled on the floor.

"Damn, you got your wolf back," he muttered quietly. "Did you know about this?" Bones pointed to me, his eyes lingering on my mate.

I snarled as he looked at her face for far too long, and he stood back. "Hold on," he snapped his fingers. "Are the rumors true, then? His wolf has some attachment to this girl?"

"There are rumors?" Locke cursed. "No one should be talking about this."

"Doesn't help when you look at every woman coming into the bar, Locke," I interrupted. "Even Hawke figured it out, and he can be dense with social interactions."

"Fuck," he whispered. He pulled out his lighter again, flicking it on and off.

"So, is she your mate? Truly?" Bones kneeled in front of me again, using two fingers to take Journey's limp arm. He glanced at his clock, measuring her heartbeat.

"Mine," my wolf surfaced, growling at the question. Bones nodded, pulling out his bag and taking out a stethoscope.

"Yours, old, friend. She's yours. I'm just checking her health. Nothing more," he said to pacify my wolf. "I need to listen to her heart. I must put this on her chest."

My wolf snatched the probe and laid it in between her breasts. Bones said nothing as he listened, except for when he asked me to move it to various parts of her body.

"She has pneumonia, if it was my guess," he muttered. "I don't have an x-ray machine, but her breathing is labored. How did she come into your hands? Where did she come from?"

I ignored the question, letting Locke explain where we found her at the club. I rose from the couch, not wanting to let Journey go, but if she was to sleep comfortably, the nest is where she should go.

I laid her down reluctantly, her hand latched onto my shirt not letting go. My lips twitched as I gently prodded her fingers away. A dull moan left her as I put several pillows behind her head.

"Yes, keep her elevated, if possible. It will help her breath better." Bones clicked his pen and wrote notes. "I've got to take some blood. Make sure she doesn't have any underlying diseases since she came from that...place," he spat.

I had forced away the thoughts of any other shifter or human touching her, but there was a high probability she was forced to perform acts she didn't want to. She had been sold into a business that trafficked young women, and paying for a virgin would cost a pretty penny.

"Easy Grim," Locke approached.

My breathing grew haggard, my wolf wanting to release himself into his animal form.

"Easy man, she's safe now. You can go after all the bastards that ever hurt her." Locke patted my shoulder, but I turned away.

My wolf paced at Journey laying on the mattress alone. I sat down on the old mattress and pulled her into my arms, where she would always stay.

She was so small, so tiny, and she had gone through things no woman should have to go through.

"Possessive bastard, isn't he?" Bones winked at me. I showed my fangs as he rolled his eyes.

"Right, I'll get some blood for the tests. I'd like a full work-up on her when she's feeling better. Most likely, she's gone into shock, Grim. She's been on her own, trying to protect herself for who knows how long, and now that you have come along and saved her, along with a bond pulling you to her, she knows she will be safe with you. She may not understand it, but I think it's there. Especially since her body relaxed quickly, and she fell asleep in your arms."

"You think so?" Locke looked hopeful. "Think that humans can feel it?"

"Why else would she have relaxed so easily when she was shaking in fear before he touched her? Is she skittish around others?"

"Yeah, she is," Locke answered. "She wasn't afraid to snap at Grim the other night when he threw her over his shoulder. No one snaps at Grim."

Bones hummed, a smile playing on his lips.

"We may have hope, then. If Grim, a wolf that was due to go rabid any day, can do a hundred and eight degree change, then I'm sure we all have something to look forward to if time is on our side," Bones sighed. "At least that is what we can hope."

"Hope for all of us," Locke said. He smiled.

I couldn't help but reciprocate as I held Journey close to me, her face buried in my chest. My wolf purred contentedly as she grabbed my shirt again to hold me close.

Bones sniffed, coming closer to me. "What is that smell on you, Grim?" Lock coughed into his fist, and Bones backed away.

I growled a warning, knowing exactly what he was referring to.

"My nose isn't what it used to be, but I swear I smell rutting root?" Bones cocked an eyebrow. "Locke!"

Locke puffed up his chest, prepared to go on the offensive, ready to take Bones out the door. Bones stood his ground, looking at me then back to Locke.

"Do you know the repercussions of using that shit? Especially without the advice of a doctor?"

Locke pulled a bag from his cut. "I did what I had to. He hasn't rutted in years, and now he has a mate to take care of. He can't let her know yet what he is. She's fucking terrified. What else was I supposed to do when my second is fucking his hand in the other room while his mate has a panic attack?"

Bones sighed audibly, his hands gripping and releasing into fists. His eyebrows furrowed, slowly softening as he took in my hold of my mate. "It's just that," he groaned. "Your rut will be twice as bad the second go around, Grim. You won't be able to keep your hands off her. No one will be able to go near her, and you very well might scare the shit out of her if your wolf takes over."

Locke cleared his throat, uncomfortable at the new information.

"Grim, I didn't know." Locke shook his head. "I was just trying to help."

I shook my head, running my fingers through Journey's hair.

"She will know who I am next time it happens." My lips touched her forehead. "I will make our den. There's time to prepare her."

"And what if she isn't ready?" Bones asked worriedly. "You wouldn't force her, would you?"

"Never," I growled.

The deep vibrations in my chest rattled the floor. A whimper left Journey's lips, and my wolf instantly stopped.

"I will keep her locked up in the apartment with me. I'll do what I have to and make sure she is never afraid. Even if I have to lock myself in the bathroom to take care of it."

"That would take an obscene amount of self-control, Grim," Bones said.

"I'd do it, for her."

"I'll see if I can find anything to hold off your next rut, or at least something to ease the potency," Bones said and took notes again while I continued to watch my mate sleep.

By the time Locke and Bones left, I had Journey sleeping with her body slightly raised on the bed. My first job was to make the apartment more livable. I had no reason to dress up my dwelling. I never thought I would have a mate.

Now that she was here, I had every reason to ensure her home was comfortable. I reached for the bags of food I had ordered, and I put them in the proper cabinet and refrigerator. Most of the food I would have to cook on my own, but I didn't find that to be a problem.

The club might see me as an enormous wolf with enough muscle to take on even an Alpha like Locke, hell, even overpower him, but I hadn't always been this way. I was born from a long line of omegas, thus I started life on the bottom of the pack's totem pole.

At a young age, I was deemed too weak to seek warrior training at ten. Instead, I learned how to clean the pack house and do small menial jobs throughout the pack territory. That could be collecting trash to take to the human quarries or collecting firewood and setting them out on wolves' doorsteps for their own homes. One of the primary jobs that my family inherited was cooking.

It was considered a low-level job, cooking and cleaning the kitchen, but my parents enjoyed it. They had full range of the kitchen, along with my siblings, to feed over a hundred wolves each day for three meals. My parents always hummed a tune, smiling at each other as mates would do.

I had grown up intending to find my mate, to love her just as my father loved my mother. I prayed to the goddess however, for a special request, and the request was for me to become strong enough to protect my mate.

More than likely, my mate would be an omega. If my mate was higher than an omega, then she would very well forget me and find another wolf that could take care of her. I had seen it too many times in my pack, often ignoring the goddess's pairing.

I didn't want that to happen to me.

My father was lucky that my mother was also of low status. However, many times my mother and father were picked on because of their lack of strength. And they lacked the drive to become something stronger.

That led to my mother crying because of the bullying, and my father could do nothing about it. He didn't have the training, the drive to do something more until it was too late. He now had too many chores and too many pups to feed. I never wanted to see myself in that position. I would never let my mate cry because of cruel words or any physicality from other wolves. So, began my training on my own.

It was unheard of to move up the ranks in a pack, but that didn't stop me. Once my chores were completed, I would run to the training fields. I lifted weights. I ran. I howled. Day by day, I grew more muscular than I ever could imagine, pushing myself to be something stronger.

The Alpha took notice. His long strides followed me into the rain one winter as I pushed myself by lifting tires and throwing weighted balls from one end of the field to the other. I was nearly eighteen, almost old enough to find my mate. I knew I had a short amount of time, and once my mate saw me, she would not see me as a helpless omega. I didn't care if she was one. All I cared about was being worthy of her and able to protect her.

"I'm impressed," the Alpha barked into the rain. "Even my warriors refused to practice today, and here you are, an omega lifting weights my Gammas could not hold."

I stood up straighter, watching him stride toward me.

It was then I realized my muscles almost matched those of my Alpha, but I kept the happiness tucked away inside.

"I want to be more, Alpha. I want to protect the pack, protect my future mate." The Alpha grinned, putting his hand on my shoulder.

"I believe that. Why don't we test you further?"

A groan came from the bed, knocking me out of my reminiscing. I made chicken parmesan in the oven with garlic bread and salad. Journey coughed, and my wolf forced himself to bolt to the other side of the room to help her up.

Her doe eyes looked up at me, blinking away the streaming tears. "I'm sorry," her voice rasped. "I'm not sure what happened."

"Shock," I stated plainly. She nodded, gripping hold of my hand. "What happened? Why were you in the closet?"

Journey gulped, her hand shaking again. I took her hand and laid it on my chest as I sat down, which seemed to calm her.

"I was alone, and I heard banging. I got scared." She blushed. "I think it reminded me of the night before you saved me."

I hummed, pulling her head into my chest. I purred, and her tense body relaxed again.

"You are safe now; I won't leave."

Locke had given me as much time as I needed to help my mate, to show her I would keep her safe and to let her know she was mine.

CHAPTER TWELVE

Journey

I didn't know what was happening. This strange calmness came to my body as he hummed in his chest. My mind rushed through all the scenarios of what could go wrong from one moment and the next. The hum silenced it all.

I tried to pull away, but his grip tightened.

"You need to rest," he said.

I shook my head and tugged again. He let out a frustrated huff.

I sat up on my knees, taking in the new look of the apartment. The once-bare walls and floors were covered with rugs, thick curtains, and even a cover for the couch. Baskets of fruit and vegetables sat in the kitchen on sparkling clean counters.

The only way I knew this was the same apartment was the bed that I had slept in. The same duvet, along with the two pillows that were meant for his head and mine.

Taking in the room, he cleared his throat, standing. "Come, I have food." He held out his hand for me to take, and my questions outnumbered my answers.

He led me to the brand-new kitchen table made of light pine-colored wood with two white chairs. The old table had been small and beat up. I stared at it, along with the prepared food.—some sort of breaded chicken with noodles and a red sauce.

Grim pulled out the chair, nodding to it, and I sat down. My heart raced and his hand landed on my shoulder.

"Everything is alright, Journey. I'm going to take care of you."

He lifted his hand, and I immediately missed the warmth as he sat on the other side of the table.

Dishes were left on the counter, no plastic bags or plastic forks were being used. It was all brand-new cutlery. The cabinets had been wiped down, removing the grease and grime.

"W-what happened?" I couldn't speak, couldn't even say a simple "thank you" to the poor biker who had made the radical transformation to his home.

"You were in shock, you fell asleep. We had a doctor check you."

I touched my face, and then I pulled up my sleeve to see a band aid on my arm.

"They took blood," he said.

My face paled, and I pushed away from the table.

"Shh, it's all right. They only took a small amount. To make sure you didn't have any infections."

Skimming his colossal form, I sat puzzled. I really didn't understand any of this.

"W-what do you all want with me?" I gripped the hoodie with my shaky hand. "I don't know what's going on. Am I staying here forever? A-are you all going to use me?" My voice cracked, and I accidentally inhaled a bit of the spit that had collected in the back of my throat.

It threw me into a coughing fit, and I covered my mouth with my hand. It was hard to breathe, hard to take a deep breath.

"Easy." Grim pushed his chair back. The deep sound of the chair scraping over the floor startled me further until he kneeled beside me. "Here, take this."

In his hand, he held up a device in the shape of an "L" and pushed down on the circular end. "Breathe in." My coughing continued until I obeyed, figuring I couldn't be worse off than this.

Slowly, my lungs cleared, and my breath came in more even pants.

"You are sick," he grunted, capping the device. "Pneumonia. I'm going to get you better."

Grim moved his chair closer to me, taking my plate and cutting up the large piece of chicken breast. He took the fork, speared the breaded chicken, and held it to my lips.

"I-I can do it." I went to grab the fork from him, but he took it away.

"You are weak. I will take care of you," he stated.

Alright then, mister caveman.

That is exactly what he was. Short and to the point with his words, but he meant everything he said. Not arguing, I let him feed me. Using the same fork, he fed himself from his plate while I chewed.

Why did I like that so much? That he ate from the same utensil? It was like he didn't see me as dirty.

"Did you make this?" I inquired. He simply nodded and fed me more. I shook my head, using the napkin to wipe my face. And then he frowned.

"You need to eat more," he commanded, pushing another bite to my lips.

"I'm not used to eating this much. I'll get sick if I eat more."

He grunted again, taking the piece for himself.

I've always had an aversion to beards, but he wore it quite well. Grim was ruggedly handsome. It was clean, as was the rest of his body. He must have showered and trimmed his hair because he could very well be on an outdoorsmen magazine.

"I'll feed you smaller meals throughout the day. You need your strength." Putting his fork on the plate, he took them to the kitchen sink to clean the dishes.

A man cleaning the dishes. Hell hath frozen over.

I leaned my arm over the chair and stared at him while he put the dishes in a drying rack. He dried his hands and leaned on the kitchen sink with his muscular forearms and sighed.

"You know," I interrupted his thought. "You never told me why I'm here. Will you all use me? Or let me go?"

His brows turned downward in anger. "We would never use you, Journey."

My name rolled off his tongue sweetly despite the angered words before it.

"Never. We don't do that." Grim stepped closer to me and I backed up into the chair.

"Shit," he pulled at the hair on his head. "I didn't mean to scare—"

"—You didn't," I replied. "For some reason, I don't think you would hurt me. It's just, I don't know your intentions, the intentions of your club." I looked away toward the window that was now covered by thick curtains to block out the sun.

It was obviously night. The twinkling of the stars lit up the night sky in the gap between curtains. How long had it been since I stared up at those stars? To see the moon?

"No one does something good for nothing," I said bitterly. "There is no kindness left in this world. Before I came into the life of sex, drugs, and gambling, I thought someone was helping me out of the kindness of his heart. But in the end, he was just fetching a better price. How do I know that you and your club won't do the same? You treat me nice now, but soon you'll get bored or fed up with me. Whatever game you all are playing now, just cut the crap because I can't take it anymore. Just tell me how it is. Are you going to sell me off? Get me comfortable that I want to stay, and then make me a slave for your bar?" I half yelled.

My cough came back as soon as I raised my voice. I continued to cough, my eyes watering at the sensation of not being able to breathe.

Grim set his warm hand on my back, while he placed the other hand on my chest. He pushed my hunched body upwards, helping me sit up straight.

"Calm," was all he whispered. The humming in his chest got louder until my coughing slowed.

He picked me up from the chair and took me to the freshly cleaned couch. He took a throw blanket from the arm and wrapped it around my body, then cradled my head against his chest.

I concentrated on his humming, my cough ceased, and his hand brushed my hair away while I stared into my lap.

"There are no motives other than to get you better, for me to see you well," he whispered. "I understand you can't trust me or the club."

I sniffed, trying to keep the cough away.

"I will prove to you that we're trustworthy—that I'm trustworthy. But I must tell you, you are worth something."

I tilted my head upward, staring into his eyes.

His eyes held a deeper, darker story. I could see pain behind them, but also a longing for hope. Getting lost inside his eyes, a dark shadow ran through looking like the shape of an animal running. It passed through his eyes several times before he closed them.

"You are worth more to me than you will ever know. More than any dollar amount, more than any bike or precious gem." His eyes opened again, beaming at me with warmth.

"What?" I whispered.

"Journey, I'm going to keep you safe. I swear it on my life. I can't tell you why, yet, but I'm asking you to just take the small amount of faith you have left...and give it to me."

That was certainly a lot to ask.

Grim rose from the couch, not letting me answer, and led me to the bathroom, which was as changed as the rest of the apartment—cleaned floors, hand towels hanging, and even an array of soaps and shampoos cluttering the small shower. I picked up one bottle; it smelled of cherry blossoms and vanilla. Pretty sure it was meant for me since Grim smelled like nothing but man and bike.

It was going to be hard to trust him.

I stepped into the shower and let the hot water stream over my body. I had grown far too thin. My collar bones gave my shoulders a sharp edge, and my pale skin looked unhealthy. My hair was thin, much thinner than it was when I lived with my parents, where at least I had a full belly and an abundance of nutrients. Little did I know even that had ulterior motives.

Make me plump and sweet, easy to steal.

I took the white towel and wrapped it around me. It was lush and thick. I enjoyed its warmth. Did he throw the thing in a dryer before putting it in here?

I shivered, my cold skin rubbing against the thickness of the towel. I raised it to my nose and deeply inhaled the smell of detergent; I began coughing yet again. The coughs grew harder, and I gasped for breath until the door hinges cracked and in burst Grim with wild eyes, panting. He'd removed his shirt. He had a large wolf tattooed across his chest, with more running down his arms. I stared at his chest, the muscles rippling as he breathed heavily.

Why hadn't I noticed his tattoos yesterday?

"What?!" I screamed.

Grim pulled me to his embrace, rubbing my back, and pulled out the medicine from his pocket, helping me inhale it again. Once again, my lungs opened up, and I slumped into him.

"T-thanks." Gripping the towel tighter, I tried to back away, but he held me close.

The warmth of his body, his scent, it drove me mad.

"Um, I'm naked." My body betrayed me—my nipples were hardening, and I pushed my legs together.

The warmth of his chest against my cheek made me long for something I had never wanted. The touch of another man.

There was something when our skin made contact—an instant warmth and calm each time he touched me. I felt normal, better than normal. I was safe; I was home. That had to be crazy though, right? No one could feel this sort of feeling, especially with a man like this. He was dangerous, flying off the handle with his best friend and knocking him square in the face.

But he did it to defend my honor.

Now I'm defending him.

He cleared his throat and nodded, stepping away. "Sorry," he apologized and stepped out of the bathroom, closing the door that hung from only one hinge.

Once dressed, I stepped out in trepidation, my bare feet touching the large carpet rugs that now covered the entire apartment. It didn't look messy or cluttered. It was a beautiful mixture of textures and softness. Like a large den of a mansion home that resided in the basement.

Warmth, safety. He had done everything to make me feel comfortable.

It was more than anyone else had given me.

He strolled up behind me, he put his hand on my lower back. He wore a tight black muscle shirt and better looking pajama bottoms. A hint of disappointment hit me at the sight of him covered. I quickly sobered when he handed me two pills and a glass of water.

"Antibiotics for your sickness. I have the bottles if you wish to see that they came from the pharmacy." The nervousness in his voice made me smile.

"No, I trust you." I took the medicine from his hands.

His muscular shoulders relaxed and, dare I say, I saw a smile under that beard. As quickly as it came, it disappeared, and he lead me to the newly made bed.

A thick, deep red comforter laid on top. The bed was pushed up against the wall and blankets and pillows covered the perimeter, encasing the bed in a nest-like state leaving a small opening for me to climb in. More blankets were set up at the foot of the bed.

The window didn't look as scary as it had before. It was covered with a thick curtain that kept the sun out. Even though it was fabric keeping me from the outside, it made me feel safe no one could see in.

"Do you not like it?" Grim put his arm around me.

I should shake it off to keep any man's touch away, but I liked it too much.

"It's wonderful," I sniffed. "You should sleep in it tonight. I can sleep on the couch." I pointed to the new-looking love seat.

Grim shook his head, guiding me to the bed. Pulling the blankets away, he covered me up like a child.

"But it's too small for you. I would fit just fine on it," I gently argued.

He kept quiet and reached under the bed, pulling out a cot to fit his enormous frame. It was already made with a pillow and sheets to cover him.

He would sleep so close to me. I could just reach out and touch him if I wanted.

"Who are you?" I whispered. "Am I in a dream?" I felt the tears forming, but I held them back.

This guy didn't need some weeping mess, but somehow, he already knew what I was feeling. He cupped my face, both of his large, calloused hands rubbing my soft cheek. His thumbs wiped away the treacherous tears that ran down my gaunt face.

"I'm your protector, your guardian. Never again will you feel afraid and alone."

CHAPTER THIRTEEN

Grim

The roars of the bikes caught my ear. They were far, maybe miles away, but the familiar sputter from Locke's bike let me know it was my brothers returning to the club. The bar was quiet, too quiet for a Friday night. That only meant one thing—another letter.

Locke called and said that the same off-white letter with its usual branding sat on his desk this morning. It was yet another clue to find the fuckers that had been bringing in not just supernatural women but humans as well.

Someone was playing in the human world, bringing in women of the weaker species because they knew they weren't as strong. Since we found the mayor at a supernatural hub, and no one cared he was there, he must have been a frequent visitor. Who was keeping their mouth shut about this human? Were there more?

As Journey slept, Locke kept me informed of what Switch had found out about the mayor. It was hard to keep my growls repressed hearing about what an idiot he was betraying his own species.

Mayor Stockton's previous slogan for his election campaign was, "Cleaning up the town." Meaning, putting those who were homeless in shelters, finding them jobs and housing. He was praised and quickly re-elected for his new ideas. But where did these people go? Even the battered women's home was empty with no documentation of where they went after they were sent away.

Switch did his digging and quickly realized the relationship between the fae.

Mayor Stockton was supplying humans from both homeless shelters and battered women homes to help fuel the fae's dirty work. With Mayor Stockton getting rid of his problems and handing them to the fae, he was taking the extra profits from not funding those branches and putting the money straight into his pocket.

Thank fuck for Switch. If it wasn't for his ability to hack into the mayor's private computer, we would still be lost. Because right now, this fae community were like ghosts.

For the Mayor's silence, it was believed he was given Fae Dust. It was a drug which would give a high without the hangover human drugs could give. Fae Dust was a hot commodity in the supernatural world. For witches, it gave an added boost to spell casting. For shifters, a surge of strength. For humans, they got an unexplainable euphoric high. Whether he used it for himself or to drug helpless women or men into his bed was the question.

The dust was odorless, tasteless, and left no signs of usage in a human's body. The perfect drug for him to use while in office.

My cell buzzed in my pocket. I reached for my side, keeping Journey tucked close to my body. She had been in a coma-like state for days.

She woke up enough for me to lead her to the bathroom to relieve herself and get food into her. My mate had been fighting off a high fever that panicked my wolf. We did the best we could, giving her medication and soothing her with a cool cloth.. Unfortunately, it had become too much and had become too difficult for us to manage on our own, so we had to have Bones intervene.

My cell buzzed again. I growled, pulling it from my sweats. Journey groaned, her body seeking and reaching for me to stay. The multiple nightmares while she slept were too much for me to bear. I did the only thing I could think of, and that was to curl my body around hers. Hold her close and with the bond we shared, it was only then that she settled.

My wolf purred, satisfied with her body understanding the bond, but I knew once her mind was clear of the fever, we would have to start again with her trust.

"What?" I muttered into the phone, trying not to disturb her.

"How's Journey doing?" Locke asked with a clipped voice. That could only mean one thing when he gets in one of his moods. He'd brought someone back, and he needed answers. Me being an unofficial executioner and interrogator meant I would have to be present.

"Fever is breaking. She's sweating out the sickness," I mumbled.

"Fuck, I don't want to take you away from her, but I need your help. We caught a fae that helps run the operation. There are more women, Grim. More human women like Journey in these damned cam girl centers."

"Shit." I scratched my forehead.

"Can you control your wolf, leave her and help us out just for a few hours? I'll bring in trusted brothers to hold down your apartment. You should be back before she wakes." Growling low, my wolf paced inside my head.

Leaving her would be difficult. My wolf was unsettled with our mate being sick, and we had yet to knot and mark her.

"An hour." I leaked my scent on the nest. Pulling blankets and pillows around her, she snuggled in deeper, deeply breathing in my musk.

"Sizzle is still on probation, but he's next door, too. He's happy for you man, knowing that this is real."

I grunted, ending the call, and got dressed.

I took one more look at my mate. Only the top of her head could be seen poking through the blankets. I kissed her forehead. Her fever had indeed broken, a small sheen of sweat glistening on her skin.

Getting Journey better was the priority, but my wolf had grown more territorial now that I had set up our home, our den, and the nest that we laid in. My scent coated the apartment. Having another male enter the apartment would be suicidal. My wolf, becoming stronger every day, would kill even the closest of friends, even Locke.

"I'll wait until they get here." Sizzle crossed his arms, leaning on his door. "So, it's true. Your apartment reeks."

My jaw ticked, fist tightening.

"Hey man." Sizzle held up his hands in defense. "I couldn't be sure if it was just a rut gone wrong or not. I was looking out for you and the girl."

He was. Sizzle didn't care about feelings and was an even worse communicator I didn't know why the hell he put up much of a fuss, but he knew I would have felt like shit if I had done something to hurt the woman I had claimed. I've always had respect for my work partner; I'd forgiven him the moment I fucking punched him in the face.

"Protect my den," was all I muttered, stomping down the uneven steps.

I headed across the street and stepped into the bar. It was filled with club members and humans who liked to think they were bad-ass bikers. I scoffed, continuing to the back until Delilah stepped in front of me.

"Is she all right, Grim?" Delilah had a sweet innocence about her, but she had been through some shit. It still haunted her to this day.

For once, I didn't feel like pushing her away. Journey would need friends once this was over, and Delilah was the only one I trusted out of all the females that had been rescued.

"She's healing," I stated simply.

Delilah smiled, nodding.

"That's great. If there is ever a time I can talk to her, I'd like that. We might have some things in common."

Her hesitation hovered in her voice, and I relaxed. I didn't want her to be afraid of me, but I was sure Hawke had warned her to stay away.

"When she is well."

Delilah took my short answer and skipped away. Shaking my head, I pushed the saloon doors to the back and trudged to the door that would lead me deeper into the prison underneath the bar.

The bar's music was deafening, and the walls were thick. No screams would penetrate the boards and layers of cement that encased our torture chamber. High-pitched screams permeated the wooden boards, the vibrations shaking the glass beer bottles lining the basement shelves.

Another slap echoed throughout the dank basement, as chuckles from our inner circle jeered for Locke to continue.

"Ah, there he is, the man of the hour." Locke's sadistic smile showed his white canines as he waved his hand at the stairwell.

Locke had always had a sliver of crazy embedded in him. When his wolf was still at the surface, you could see the tick beneath the surface. It often made me wonder if he'd truly killed his mate and lover instead of them just rejecting him.

"You see here." Locke walked toward me. He wrapped his arm around my broad shoulders, guiding me forward. I bent over to see the fae. He was a winter fae. His dark clothes made for a bright contrast to the shimmer that usually adorned his cheeks.

"N-no." The fae's voice shook. "The Grim Reaper."

Locke's whole body twitched , his eyes wild with hysteria.

"Oh, you know him?" Locke bent over, patting my back. "Yes, yes, this is the Grim Reaper."

"We thought he was dead. He had to be. He's lived too long without a…"

Growls ripped across the room. My brothers gripped the knives and guns holstered at their waists. My gaze caught each one. Slow nods of approval fell my way, my shoulders relaxed.

"They know, dear brother," Locke casually mentioned.

"You've given them hope." Locke cleared his throat, and he pushed the fae back with his hand wrapped around his throat. "And now the fun really begins!" he cackled. "Now, I need you to tell me, where is the next party?" He wagged his finger in the cold fae's nose.

Lock had rendered the fae's powers useless by dusting him with iron. Snow sparkled from between his eyes, trying to render an ice gaze. Grunting, the fae shook his head.

I growled, stepping away, and pulled out my bag from underneath the table they'd set up for me. The room was filled with brothers that had been here the longest—all whispering and watching, waiting for the typical show I brought down upon the scum of the supernatural world.

I wanted to keep this short, however. I had a mate to get back to.

I pulled out a neatly wrapped rag and slung it onto the table. Various knives and tools of different sizes waited for me there. I pulled the metal plyers, clinking them together several times before approaching. The fae curled his fingernails beneath his palm, shaking his head.

"I can't tell you! They'll kill me!"

"Funny, that's what we are going to do to you," Locke drawled, stepping away while I gripped the tied arm against the chair. "We can make it less painful, however, if you talk."

My thumb claw pierced his skin. He screamed, his frosted hair melting as I pulled each nail slowly from his right hand. The blue pointed claws clinked into a silver tin I left on his lap.

Blood dripped to the floor, his screams dwindling as he became used to the pain. I picked up one nail, handing it to Locke.

"Huh, guess they are naturally blue, huh, Grim?"

I shook my head, trying to hold my grin while I gripped the other hand.

Screams of protest shot into my ear, my wolf holding in the grimace as we pulled again. As we finished, I pulled the hot iron from the stove nearby. Wolves shuddered, watching me press the iron to each of his raw fingertips.

"Fuck!!! Just kill me!!" he yelled.

But I hadn't gotten to the good part yet.

My wolf howled in laughter.

It felt good to see his pain, pain that was nothing compared to what my Journey had gone through. She had been through hell and back, and I didn't know the details as of yet, but I would know soon. Killing this piece of trash that trafficked women was just the tip of the iceberg. I planned on killing every single one of the bastards that were part of the operation.

"Will you speak now?" The fae could only nod, a smirk coming to Locke's lips. "Where is the next party?"

"A warehouse in Clarks," he breathed. "It's unmarked. It's next to a boat rental company that uses it for part storage. It's small, but they have some witches using expanding spells this time."

Expanding spells to make the inside larger. A great deal of magic would have to be used to procure something like that. "Is there Fae Dust being used to accomplish that?"

The fae squirmed in his seat. My hand came down on his shoulder, claws sinking into his shoulder.

"YES!" he cried, trying to rip away from my grasp.

"What about the cam girls? Are there more?"

The fae gritted his teeth, the light blue appearance turning into a sickly gray. "You mean cam girls with benefits?" he grunted, watching the deep blue blood run down his bare torso. "Come on, give me a clean death, no more pain," he begged.

Locke waved me off.

"Supernaturals watch the cam girls, find one they like. Sometimes even at the party. Then they pay a price for a few hours," he gasped.

Gripping my fist tightly, my breath grew uneven. Journey had been a cam girl and very well could have been used.

My wolf snarled.

"They are getting rid of the shifters and other supernaturals, only wanting to use humans. You know, cause they can't fight back. Plus, they are easier to... dispose of if they are too broken to work."

Sweat beaded on my forehead, my wolf squeezing through the window of my mind. Fury slipped into my veins, my heart beating so strongly I felt it flutter on my cut.

Blinding rage filled my vision, my wolf running toward the light of my eyes. My shirt ripped, my muscles expanding quickly. Taking off my cut, I threw it to the floor.

My jeans became tight, so I pulled them down as quickly as I could and slung them across the room. Arguments on how to deal with me ensued, and my face morphed into the maw I had not seen in ages.

I smiled, feeling the pain rip through my body. The burn, the freedom to feel my wolf that had been caged inside my body for so many years. It was like coming home, feeling my body doing what it was supposed to do all along.

Hair sprouted from my skin, and bones cracked and rearranged. Locke stood frozen, only backing up when the last crack of my spine was put in place. I shook my deep, rusty fur from side to side, and I padded on my paws across the familiar concrete floor.

Claws clicked on the hard surface as I stared down at my furred body. I had missed this. The animal inside me had been released, all because I had my mate in my den. My second chance, my everything, and I would be sure not to let her go.

My lips curled, snarling at the fae strapped to the chair. His eyes widened in fear as the room full of my brothers backed into the corners. "W-wait! You said a quick death. You said you wouldn't cause any more pain, please!"

Locke smirked until a wide, mischievous grin fell upon his face. "Brothers, there is hope for us." He licked his lips. "All you neigh sayers are eating your words now." He threw his head back with a laugh.

My wolf snapped his head back to the fae—an outlet to let our anger rage. This was only one fae in a horde filled with many like him who preyed upon the weak. My wolf pawed forward, taking a sweet and calculated step toward him.

"Hey, man, please." He shook. My lips lifted, showing my fangs, until I sunk my teeth into his ankle. Roars of cheers erupted as I shook the fae's ankle. The yells were so loud, all the sound that left the fae's mouth fell on deaf ears.

The chair was pushed back, his head hitting the floor. Piece by piece, my wolf mauled each limb. Blood ran down the drain beneath his chair. My fur was drenched in blue blood. It pooled thickly on his chest before I went in for the final blow and snapped the bastard's neck.

CHAPTER FOURTEEN

Journey

I shifted in the blankets that enveloped me and opened my eyes and saw the tinkling of light filtered above my head. I stretched and found I was painfully sore from staying in bed for who knew how many days, but my lungs felt much better.

No matter how much I slept and rested, I never seemed to get enough. My body had completely shut down and took the safe haven of this apartment for granted. Which should have been weird that I would let my guard down, but with Grim here, that all seemed to fade away.

He literally nursed me back to health. He fed me and helped me to the bathroom. He was the perfect nurse. Grim was a far cry from looking like the typical nurse. The scruffiness of his beard and his muscular and heavily tattooed arms were quite comical when he dispensed my medicine.

A biker member who could be out drinking, riding, rescuing other women in distress and he was here with me. My heart heated. He picked me out of all the women. Well, I had hoped I was the only woman he cared for. The looks from his friends staring in disbelief confirmed it.

I blinked, looking over the giant fort of blankets and pillows. They were circled around me in a cocoon of softness. I don't think I had ever been this warm in my entire life. Usually, I was given sheets or nothing at all, and it was a welcome warmth I couldn't explain. They smelled like a home should—comfort with a hint of pine and the outdoors.

I lifted my head over the padded mountain, I could see Grim in the kitchen. His shirt was off, his hair pulled back in a ponytail. His body was covered in sweat. He wore light colored jeans that hung low on his hips. Grim was obviously not wearing any underwear and my shameful body reacted when it really shouldn't have.

How could a man be so ruggedly sexy?

Nothing like the suited, clean-cut men I had been with while working. He was something different. He was wild and free. He didn't look like he was a part of this town, but instead he looked like he belonged in a cabin in the forest. Yet he'd stayed here and made a home out of the dingy apartment that had hardly looked lived in.

I was drawn to him, but my mind's hesitance told me not to get close. It was still too early to know him, to understand what his friends and his club wanted of me. Surely, they weren't doing this for the sake of my safety without wanting something in return?

A low growl, one that an animal would make, rang from his side of the room. My head dipped back into the pillows, only letting my eyes wander just above the fluff. It sounded again, and Grim lowered his head and pulled back with a grunt.

I blinked, hearing a slap of something wet hit the counter. My eyes widened. The slap was a piece of raw steak. Grim's sharp jaw moved up and down, chewing, as blood dripped from his mouth as he moved down the kitchen, grabbing a towel.

He was eating raw meat.

Grim wiped his hands, and I looked at his nails. They looked longer, darker. I continued to blink, rubbing my eyes, watching him stare down at them, only for them to be nude and short.

Do I still have a fever?

I rubbed my head, waiting to feel the heat, but it wasn't there. Surely, I hadn't seen what I thought I had?

"Journey?" he asked.

I squeaked, lowering my head back into the pillows only to feel Grim's presence hover over me.

"Hi." I waved my hand shyly.

Hell, why should I be shy? The man had almost seen me pee. The man wouldn't even leave the bathroom, stood at the door with his arms crossed grumbling like I was inconveniencing him because I didn't want him to watch me pee.

Shy bladder is a thing, and he wasn't buying it. Luckily, he turned on the sink, and I could go without worrying about slipping a toot.

"Are you hungry?" His eyes flashed with something unrecognizable. The same rushing of a shadow across his eyes.

"Um, yeah. I am." He lowered his hand to me, not taking apart the pillow fort that surrounded me, and pulled me up into his arms and set me down gently on the heavily carpeted floor.

Grim led me to the table. He had a large bowl of what looked to be stew. He kept most of my meals light throughout my sickness. My stomach could barely keep anything down. A combination of being sick, tired, and having too small of a stomach made it hard to eat.

Without skipping a beat, he pulled me into his lap. I didn't flinch at the movement, but instead leaned into him while he put a napkin on my shirt.

I chuckled, which earned a lip curl in return.

"I think I'm well enough to feed myself now," I politely argued.

He grunted. I had noticed the different pitches of the series of grunts that left his throat. They meant something, and I was soon going to figure out what his grunts meant. From what I could tell, this grunt meant, "I know you can, but I'm going to do it, anyway."

Not wanting to argue, because this scene had become far too familiar, I let him feed me bite by bite. Of course, he fed himself in between, and the sharing of utensils caused me to blush.

"You won't be able to do it forever, you know?" Thoughts of leaving Grim struck me hard, but I had to prepare myself.

I wouldn't be able to stay in the safety of his apartment forever. If I was at risk of someone from the cam girl operation finding me, I would just bring trouble to him and his club. That is, if they were even looking for me. They may have thought I died along with the others.

"Can to," he muttered.

"Grim, I can't stay here forever. As much as you have done for me." My eye twitched in annoyance.

I felt the anxiety bubble from within. "I can't. I'll never be able to repay you for your kindness—for taking care of me."

I began scratching my arm, he put the spoon down and covered my hand with his.

"I-I'll put you and your friends in danger. And Delilah, she's so nice. I don't want those evil people to bother what you all have going on here with your friends."

"Do you not like it here?" His chest growled.

I bit my lip, staring into him. His dark eyes, intense but not frightening in the slightest made my insides clench. My body flipped a switch at the dark stare and the allure of something dangerous. I was extremely attracted to him.

I wanted him.

God, this was insane. I had been used as an object by men and women. Not once had I ever felt this. Was this what all people felt when they were turned on? Because I'd never had it, not once.

The more I told myself I had to leave, the more I wanted him. An unidentifiable pull coursed through me telling me to stay and not let him go.

"Don't lie to me, Journey." Grim's chest purred.

His finger pushed away my tangled hair. The heat of his breath traveled down my neck as his head drew closer.

Standing, I pushed myself away from him, backing away, and my legs hit the back of the couch behind my knees. I fell onto it, grabbing the pillow and holding it tight to my body. I couldn't think straight when I was near him.

He stood in his wrinkled jeans. His Adonis belt was a path straight to the enormous bulge in his pants. I wondered what it looked like? Was he big, like, all over? I've seen a few, but the way his package was bulging, I'm sure it would be bigger than any I'd ever seen.

My nipples tightened, the pillow the only protection to hide them from his peering eyes. Holy hell, I felt so much better after being sick. It was a whole new rush seeing him stalk toward me. One hand landed on the arm of the chair, the other beside my head as he bent over, giving me the perfect view of his rippling abs hovering over me.

Good. Gods. I'm going to get the couch wet.

I gulped.

"I...really like it here," I whispered. Not daring to speak any louder for fear my voice would crack.

"Then you will stay here with me," he purred. "I will keep you safe, clothe you, feed you. Isn't that what a female wants?" His chest vibrated. I could see the slight tremor in his chest.

Was it what every girl wanted?

Yeah, no, it wasn't. There were many women that wanted the freedom, the independence to do what they wanted. To go out into the world and make something of themselves, yet those women, they weren't me. I had been trapped for a long time, forced to do horrible things. Lived on the bare minimum, never knew when I would be fed, have a warm bed, if I would be alive the next day, never protected. Never loved.

Never feeling safe.

"I'm not sure every woman would want that," I muttered. I sunk lower into the seat. Grim lifted an eyebrow. "But I do like it with you only." And his eyes softened. "I don't know why. I should fear you, but I don't."

Instead, I'm horribly turned on.

"What do you feel, Journey?" Grim let go of the arm of the couch, sitting beside me. "And don't run away from me, because my primal side will chase you."

I choked on my spit.

"It sounds silly. I don't want to say." I gripped the pillow tighter. "This could be some sort of Stockholm syndrome or something. Maybe I'm not in my right head space." I shook my head.

Grim's gentle touch moved my jaw to face him. "I can tell you what I feel," his low voice said. "I feel an undeniable attraction, a pull to you, Journey. And I never felt this want, this need so strongly before. The thought of something harming you, taking you away from me—" His fists tightened until his knuckles popped so loud I thought they would break. "I would crush them into pieces to protect you."

Should be a red flag, but nope. Body liked it. Hell, I liked it.

"Tell me, what do you feel, Journey?" His forehead lowered, touching mine.

Both of our eyes closed, and that spark ignited inside me all over again.

The fear of being taken away, of being sold, of doing the horrible things I used to do left my mind. The only people here in this world were Grim and me.

"I feel it, too. Something strong pushing me toward you. That I'm supposed to stay here," I whispered.

He grinned. A full-on grin showing me his pearly white teeth and the canines that were too large for his face.

"But I'm a broken woman, Grim. I'm not whole like I once was," I said sadly.

"That doesn't matter to me." Grim pulled my body into his lap, putting my face into his neck. I smelled his wonderful scent that was just him. He rubbed my cheek with his thumb.

"Because I'm broken too, and with two broken pieces, we can make ourselves whole."

CHAPTER FIFTEEN

Journey

My heart tugged at my chest. The sweet aroma of his scent washed over me completely. It was a wave of heat that settled below my waist, and the tingling between my legs only grew greater. The low rumbling in his chest, the twitch in his body as he straightened, caught my attention while he shifted me off his lap.

"How can you be broken, too?" I asked incredulously.

Sure, he was quiet, more reserved than his friends. He had some scars from fights, and if the fight he had with Aedar was any indication, he could hold his own. He was confident, more so than I had ever been, and it would take years for me to become whomever I was truly meant to be.

"One day, I will tell you, as one day you will tell me what you have been through," he said, looking away. "You need to sleep for now, little one." I raised an eyebrow at the nickname.

I did not find myself small in the slightest; in fact, I was of average height. He was the one that was ridiculously tall.

But I liked the endearment.

When he left the couch, the aura of warmth left when he reached the kitchen, tapping a small canister, two pills clinking out into his large hand.

He opened the fridge for a bottle of water, and he twisted the cap gently and handed it to me. In one sip, the pills were gone, but he nodded his head for me to continue to finish downing the bottle.

I shrugged my shoulders, listening. He had taken care of me so far and taking care of myself for so long had been tiring. I fully accepted he wanted me safe, an irrational feeling after what I had been through with men using me, but I was at the end of my rope.

Before Grim, I had little will to live anymore.

But now I was here in this apartment, and for the first time in my life since I was a tiny child, I felt safe.

"These will help you sleep," his voice said with a strained rasp. He winced as he said it, and my hand went out to grab his.

"It hurts for you to talk for a long time?" I tilted my head in confusion.

"I haven't used my voice much, had nothing to say until you."

My heart damn near exploded. This pull that he had on me... The connection I had toward him was too strong to ignore. Leaning forward, I willingly wrapped my arms around his neck and hugged him. It was the first time I went to him instead of him hovering over me. He stilled, his hands away from my body like he didn't know what to do with them.

"You can hug me," I muttered over his shoulder. "I'm not afraid of you anymore."

With a heavy sigh, the tension in his shoulders left, and his arms wrapped around me.

"And you don't have to talk. I can figure things out."

He purred, his nose resting in the crook of my neck. The chill, the spark, ran down my arm, and my chest pushed further into his. I wanted to bury myself in him. Be wrapped up inside his warmth.

He pulled away against my wishes and cupped my cheek.

"You are not a prisoner here," he muttered. "But you can never leave me."

I chuckled at that, because I very well was a prisoner if I could never leave him. That didn't seem to bother me, however. I was accepting whatever this feeling was, not questioning it, not being afraid of it any longer.

I was tired of being afraid.

And for once, I enjoyed being wanted for just company and human contact.

After having a proper shower and a good teeth brushing, Grim laid down a set of clothes on the counter for me to wear and a pair of underwear fell on to the floor.

He picked them up and blushed, his tanned face beet red. I giggled watching him leave while I held the wet towel around my body.

He was at least used to seeing me in a towel. When I was sick, he barely let me leave his sight, but he always kept his gaze toward my face.

Grim wasn't being perverted; he kept his eyes downcast to give me privacy. He was the first guy that was honorable toward me. He was certainly different, and I wondered if he just wanted a companion to be with him.

My thoughts were out of control when Delilah once said that these men did not hold attraction to women. But Grim was giving me all the signs that he wanted me and the touches he gave me stirred a deep longing to want more.

I wanted him to...want me.

I've never been in a relationship—not that I wanted one through my late teens and early twenties. I was concentrating on surviving and survive I did. It was Grim's presence that gave me the peace I had always craved.

I sighed, taking the gown he presented to me. Instead of the yoga pants and sweatshirt, this was a loose-fitting gown that went to my knees. It was light blue with decorative white ruffles around the hem of the gown. It was gorgeous, something so pretty I could have imagined myself wearing it if I was a teenager and allowed such things.

I stepped out of the bathroom, Grim was already laying on the cot beside the bed. His shirt was off, his arms behind his head as he stared at the ceiling.

I crawled into the bed, which was still covered in large pillows that rounded the mattress. I didn't disturb them, remembering that Grim purposefully didn't move them when he took me out of the bed earlier. I crawled over the wall—it was work—and I tried to get settled. But it didn't feel right.

This, this just felt wrong.

I wiggled in the blankets, trying to wrap myself in a perfect cocoon but to no avail; I was getting nowhere. Rolling side to side, pushing the covers away, I sighed dramatically, lying face up, looking at the open ceiling of the rustic apartment.

"What's wrong?" Grim poked his head over the mountain of pillows.

"I can't sleep." I shrugged, still pulling blankets around me. I shouldn't want to feel wrapped up to the point where I couldn't escape. I didn't like small spaces. Too many times, I'd found myself in a cage or chained to a bed.

I groaned, throwing one pillow, and Grim opened his mouth, looking at me, the pillow now resting on the floor.

"Do you not like the nest?" His dark eyes widened, and his eyebrows hit the middle of his forehead.

"The what? The nest?"

He cleared his throat. "Bed, I mean the bed. Is it not comfortable?"

I hummed, frustrated. "I like the bed," I said, still thinking about the term "nest" he'd used. "It is comfortable, but I feel—" I tapped my forehead, my eye twitching.

Grim grumbled, his finger gently touching the side of my face, causing the annoying twitching to stop.

My body calmed as he touched my face, the back of his finger trailing down my cheek. I rolled over to face him, to feel the heat of his body. "That feels better," I said shyly.

Grim had tucked me in while I was sick. Maybe he could do it again? "Grim?"

He hummed, still watching me closely. His eyes flickered with amusement. And I swore I could see the same shadow running across them.

"Can you tuck me in, like how you did when I was sick?" His eyes fluttered, the shadow falling away from them. The gentle caress near my eye stopped, and he pulled his hand away.

"Are you sure?" He stood hesitantly at the side of the mountain of pillows. I lifted my body to lean on my elbow and glanced up to his hovering form.

"Why wouldn't I?" I questioned. "I felt comfortable. Whatever you did to make me sleep, I want that again."

Grim rubbed his hands down his sweatpants. His bare chest and that magnificent v-line that hid between the fabric made me dart away.

Grim cleared his throat again, crawling into the bed. My confusion turned to panic as he laid beside me and pulled me into his chest. My body didn't fight him, but my mind certainly was. He purposefully moved my head to his neck, my hand now resting on his muscular chest.

Holy hell.

His gentle thumb thrummed over my cheek, making me forget the bare chested biker god lying next to me.

He...did this when I was sick?

I sighed happily. This was what I was missing. It was the missing piece to this bed. I'd only known him for a short time, but I was falling for him. I couldn't understand it. I promised myself to stay away from any man if I ever escaped. Yet, here I was, growing attached to my rescuer.

Now I forwent that vow, I had given it up. Part of me hated doing it, the other part was blissfully happy. To feel protected, to feel wanted, for someone to take care of me because of me and not to get anything in return.

It had only been two weeks knowing him. I still should be wary, but my body was betraying me in all ways. It was too soon to give him my full trust, but I trusted him more than anyone else, even if he was strange.

"Thank you," I whispered into his chest. "For taking care of me. It was very selfless of you to do something like that."

Grim continued to brush my cheek. The purr from his chest grew until I fell into a blissful sleep.

Grim

She reached for me.

She wanted me to hold her.

It didn't matter that she didn't know the extent of how she slept when she was sick. That it wasn't a simple roll of the blankets to keep her safe. It was me. The bond that would have been shared with my first mate was now gifted to Journey. A much better, more suitable mate.

Journey's breath slowed, her heart evening out with my own. I drew my nose along the top of her head, taking in her scent. She smelled so good, so appetizing.

Journey was much more beautiful than my last mate. I gripped the sheets with my free hand, my claws piercing the pillow. "*Much more suitable,*" my wolf agreed. "*She is accepting us.*"

That was true. She was taking the bond seriously, even if she didn't know what it was. By the day, it would grow stronger, tighter. There would come a time when she couldn't be without me and I without her. The bond would be stretched so tight that we would have to consummate our bond, to tie us together so the invisible string could be loosened to allow us to be away from each other for some periods of time.

I was already pushing Journey too much by staying with her while she washed, while she used the toilet. Now that she was better, no longer sick with the haze of the fever, I wouldn't be able to do it unless I had a good reason.

Now that I had Journey, and she was slowly accepting me, I couldn't let her out of my sight. I couldn't let anyone change her mind about me. No other male would touch her, have her, be complete with her.

It would become difficult for my wolf and me when she finds out what we are—a vicious shifter animal. It was only a matter of time.

The greatest question was, would she accept it?

I know she saw me. She saw the blood dripping from my mouth when I ate the raw meat on the counter. My wolf craved it. He was starving after sleeping for so long. Our strength was returning, and no one in the club could defeat me, even in numbers.

My mouth salivated, thinking of eating more of the meat. My wolf hungered for it, but he also hungered for this. The touch, the heat of her skin on me. I wanted to lick every crevice of her body, to pour my scent into her cunt and keep her with me always.

Patience. I had to have a lot of it to continue this gentle claiming. Journey had been through much. She didn't have my scars, the signs of the outward torment I'd experienced. Hers was inward, inside her mind. She felt used and broken, but I would be sure she would no longer feel that way when she was with me.

The bond that we now shared was stronger than the one I'd shared with my first mate. If Journey rejected me, I would die for sure. I would go rabid, taking everything I could with me into the bowels of hell.

I may have told her she had a choice, that she could leave when we found out who was behind these clubs and cam girl operations. Unfortunately, she didn't have a choice. I would never let her go, never let her near the presence of another male until my knot, my teeth, had claimed her.

She was mine. Mine to take, hold, take care of, provide for and, most of all, love.

Love like my parents had with each other. Only this time, I was strong enough to keep the harsh world away from her. I would destroy all those that had harmed her. My wolf growled in agreement.

Mine, mine, mine.

My grip tightened around her, my fangs lengthening, wanting to sink into her neck.

Journey shifted, her leg entangling within mine. Her shift came with a breeze that wafted to my nose. Her arousal.

Fuck.

I had smelled her on the couch earlier. It smelled like sweetness with a tinge of spice that held my attention. Licking my lips, I dragged my finger down her neck, feeling her warm skin. My mate didn't move, didn't shy away from my touch, but longed for it. Her body firmly pressed up against me, craving me.

She wants me.

Even with all that she has been through.

Maybe it wouldn't be so long after all until I had her. Until then, I would slowly work my way into her heart like a human would for their partner. Give her what she wanted, take care of her, pamper her, love her. Rejection wasn't an option.

Curling up against her, my head resting on top of hers, I pulled the blankets over us. Burying us deep in the safety of our nest.

She said she liked it.

I hummed contentedly, my purring keeping her in a deep sleep until morning.

CHAPTER SIXTEEN

Grim

My wolf was busy through the night. His constant prodding of his nose to the side of my head kept me stirring constantly. It didn't help that my cock was placed between my mate's supple ass while she breathed tenderly against the pillow.

My body stayed around her all night, holding her in place. Keeping her safe in the nest I'd prepared.

My heart sailed, liking how she needed me, even if she didn't realize it. A bond that was meant for supernaturals and us alone had now been gifted to humans. She wouldn't understand the pull, the continued desire to be around me. It made my life much easier, not having to force myself upon her.

Because now, I knew I couldn't live without her. And I hope she felt the same way about me.

I saw the shoddy job the fae did trying to heal the wounds inflicted on her. Some were claw marks, others—prods that pierced the skin.

The fae were vain creatures, so they created magical creams to dilute scars, and they'd been used on Journey. Unfortunately, they didn't give her enough, so her scars were merely faded instead of erased.

But I could see the suffering she had endured. Yet she trusted me, believed in me, believed I would protect her.

I nuzzled into her neck, smelling her brightening chocolate colored hair. Each day her skin, her hair, her eyes grew more vibrant despite being sick. Our bond would heal not just her wounds, but her mind as well. I could feel my depression and the dark images of my previous mate fading faster by the day.

I couldn't help but drag my finger down her bare thigh. My warmth kept my mate from needing the blanket. My dark tattoos were a contrast against her milky white skin. Her body let out an involuntary shiver, her ass backing up toward me for more warmth. My wolf half purred, half growled, feeling her ass against my shaft. She wiggled, and my groan could not be suppressed.

Her thick lashes fluttered. Her hand rose from the mattress and settled on top of my hand, resting on her thigh. My heart stopped, hoping she wouldn't be angry with me, but all I heard was a contented sigh.

Journey's scent intensified, and my wolf prowled closer to the window that held him back. "Grim?" she said, her voice raspy from her long night's sleep. "Did I keep you awake?"

"No," I said louder than I intended. Her shiver, her heartbeat raced to the surface, pushing fiery blood to her core, her arousal surrounding me. My purrs turned to growls, my wolf prodding for me to make a move.

But she was precious; she was wounded. I didn't know the extent of what had happened to her, what vile things had been done to her. I couldn't scare her, couldn't let my beast and my hunger destroy her before I had her.

I moved her body, so she laid on her back. Her ass brushed my erection. I held in a groan, as her caramel eyes sparkled at me.

Gold and chocolate brown flecks sparkled in her eyes as the sunlight peeked through the curtains. My vision was entrapped by her. All reason disappeared. The primal, the dark roots of my being came to the surface. I hummed hungerly, unable to keep my hands away from her, and grabbed the back of her neck.

Journey gasped, feeling my fingertips on her neck, my claws lengthening, but not where she could see. Her heart jumped in her chest, my head dipping lower until my breath blew the small tendrils of hair that covered her lips away.

"I-" before I could ask for permission, her lips met mine. My eyes widened, but hers were already closed. Her arms wrapped around my neck, her hips pushing into my erection. After the initial shock, I wrapped my other arm around her lower back.

The soft petals of her lips parted, her breath escaping her to grab another gasp of air, but my selfish body betrayed her, and I slid my tongue into her mouth. I growled at her whimper. It fueled my fire. My body crushed hers, didn't even hover, pressing as much of myself against her as I could.

I needed her touch; I needed her so my wolf would not die inside me. The fire across our bodies intertwined, the inferno of passion delving deeper as our desires intensified.

Journey's fingers ran through my hair. Grabbing it at the scalp, she pushed our faces closer together while I massaged her gentle tongue with my own. I felt her warmth, her body heating with arousal. I pushed my erection further into her mound. I could feel her clit throb between our clothes, and I growled warningly while her hands scratched down my back and grabbed my ass.

Fuck.

It felt good to be wanted. My sexual escapades during ruts were passionless. My wolf only took, not wanting to give pleasure to whatever supernatural was willing to give. It was a fruitless endeavor on their part to gain anything. Whatever reason they gave themselves to my wolf was their own. They knew what they got into when a shifter had their rut.

Whatever their reasons, I didn't care.

Now, I wanted to please.

I cared to give my mate pleasure, for her to feel my erection against her. For her to know that this cock would never be placed into a worthless cunt ever again. It was hers, all of it was hers, and her pussy was mine. Never again would someone take from her, especially me. I would give her everything before I let myself, my wolf, indulge in our own pleasure.

She pushed at my shoulder, my wolf whimpering at the connection between our lips. Her heavy breath, her large gulp of air, made me curse under my breath. She could not hold her breath as long as me. She was still soft, so fragile.

"I'm–" I went to apologize, but she shook her head.

"Sorry," she coughed.

My hands clenched into fists. Selfish of me to take her kiss and not think of her illness. I was already messing up.

"No!" she rushed, her fingers skimming up my neck. My balls twitched, feeling the touch of her fingers going up my neck. "I liked it," she whispered. "I just had to breathe."

"I shouldn't have." I went to push away, but she frowned. I stopped and lowered myself back on her body, her leg wrapping around one of mine.

"You didn't want to kiss me?" her eyes went glassy, and I groaned in displeasure.

"No, I wanted it. I should have thought of your health. I pushed too hard–" The thought of hurting her, pushing her. Fuck, I was going to mess this up.

"I think it was I who leaned into you, Grim," she said shyly. "I've never kissed someone before. I just got excited." She bit her lip, her eyes darting away from me.

I flexed my fingers, taking two of them and moving her chin back so I could delve deeper into her eyes.

"Your first kiss?" I asked, confused.

With Journey's past I didn't think this would be possible. She was forced to do horrible things. Men touched her, took from her. The thought alone sent anger coursing through my veins. I wanted to destroy every single one of the bastards.

My wolf came into my mind with blind fury. His desire for blood, for vengeance, came to the forefront. My mate's head tilted in confusion.

I shook my head, pushing the hair from my face. I calmed myself. Right now, I needed to concentrate on her.

"I couldn't save a lot of myself," she whispered. My arms tightened around her body, my wolf whimpering at her broken voice. "I tried, I did," she sniffed. "I had to give up on that dream. If I couldn't save myself for someone I really wanted and cared about in one way, then I thought I could give them something I had control over."

My heart broke. My wolf curled around himself.

"So, I saved my first kiss." She shrugged her shoulders. "And I wanted to give it to you." She smiled.

She said it like it was the simplest thing. That there was no question who she wanted to give her first kiss to. I touched my lips, still feeling the warmth.

"To me?" I asked in shock.

"You act like it's so strange." She tickled my lips with her finger.

They were soft, not calloused like my own, and I relished in the soft touches she gave me. Like she, of all people, could hurt me. "I feel safe with you, Grim. I don't know why, but I do. I should run away from here, feel trapped and afraid." She licked her lips. "But I don't. Not when you are here."

I let out a breath, my head dipping lower until I kissed her again, unable to keep my body away from her any longer. The herbs I'd taken, the rutting root, would only last so long. My rut would come back twice as hard, and I couldn't scare her then. Before I could do much more, she had to know me. Soon, she would know I was different, that my anatomy wasn't the same as a human male.

I moaned into her lips, her fingers running through my hair again. I growled, pushing my cock into her core.

"Mmm," she hummed. My wolf prodded me again, his desires seeping into my hand, trailing beneath her nightgown.

I cupped her hip with my large hands, my cock pushing into her core again with gentle movements, feeling her clit against my shaft.

"That feels—" Her lips left mine for a fraction of a moment. "Good," she breathed.

"It's supposed to feel good," I said into her mouth. "I want to please you. I want to make you feel things you haven't before."

Because I damned well knew that no one took the time to worry and care about her. They took things. They worked on their own desires. This woman, my mate, would never deal with that treatment again.

"You've already accomplished that." Tears sprung into her eyes. "I feel safe."

Shaking my head, I removed my sweatpants. She stiffened, but I hushed her with a kiss on her neck. She leaned over nuzzling into my beard. "I will not take you. I won't do anything you don't want."

She swallowed, trusting me.

Fuck, she trusted me. Journey's underwear was wet from her arousal. My nose flared, taking in the sweet musk of her body. I pushed my cock against her core, feeling the heat and dampness between her legs. She whimpered, feeling my shaft rub against her clit as my erection grew impossibly harder.

Moaning, she gripped my shoulders. I gently thrust my hips against her clit, rubbing it in tender circles until she panted. Her thighs wrapped around me, my head dipping into the crook of her neck, gently sucking at her skin.

"Oh, this feels–" she trailed off, meeting my light thrusts with her hips against mine.

Don't fuck up.

I cupped her breast. They were not overly large, the right size for my hand while I pinched her nipple.

"Oh!" her arms pulled me closer into her neck, my teeth now grazing the skin and licking her future marking spot. My face was engulfed in her scent, my wolf nuzzling against it.

Her body shuddered, her back arching, letting me have the perfect view of her chest.

"Pull up your gown," I panted, still rotating my cock around her clit. Journey quickly obeyed, pulling it close to her neck. I was disappointed her neck was now covered, but now I got to behold something new—the perfect view of her breasts.

Dusty pink nipples greeted me, and my mouth salivated, watching her breasts rise and fall. I groaned watching her nipples harden under my gaze. "You are fucking beautiful, Journey."

Her nipples hardened more, and my mouth descended on the nub. Her back arched, and I pushed both of her arms above her head. I wanted full access, nothing holding me down, but my eyes darted to her face to check for distress.

There was none.

Her eyes trained on me, watching me as I slipped my tongue around her nipple and sucked roughly. I pulled it with my lips. Her eyes rolled to the back of her head. My cock throbbed with desire as it pulsed on her clit.

Precum already leaked through the front of my boxers. I grunted in satisfaction at her wetness surrounding my shaft and the sweet aroma.

"Yes, oh!" Her body shuddered. "I, what?" Her words garbled together, her eyes widening and softening as I now concentrated on rubbing her clit.

"Do you want this?" My face hovered over hers. "Do you want me to make you feel good?"

She whimpered, her body reacting in every way I wanted. A light sheen of sweat swept across her forehead, and her heels continued to push into my back.

"Y-yes," she said hesitantly. My wolf grunted, knowing she wasn't truly ready to take our knot, but we were happy she sought pleasure from our cock.

"Shh, just feel me," I cooed. "Feel my desire for you. For who you are, for who you are to me."

My cryptic words didn't faze her. Journey was becoming lost in the bond she wouldn't understand. Her body, her soul was becoming familiar with mine. The bond was strengthening, pulling us tight like a rubber band, ready to snap if we did not take this further. My wolf was ready to plant our seed, spurt it into her womb to permanently claim her.

"I'm climbing," she whimpered.

I hovered over her body, I wanted to watch her come undone, to see the fire in her eyes. "Please!"

I pushed my cock to the left. Her love for the circular rhythms of my shaft pushed her over the edge. The silent scream, the wetness on her lashes, made me fall over sooner than I planned. I pushed down my boxers, letting my come fall upon her stomach. My seed continued to spill. I grunted my release. The liquid that would soon be meant for her cunt fell on her body, slipping into her navel and across her stomach.

We both panted. I stuck my cock back inside my boxers, hiding the knot that was filling again. Lasting much longer without forcibly taking her would be difficult. However, the bond would make it easier. She wanted me as much as I wanted her.

Her half-hazed eyes lingered on my lips. I touched her lips again with mine. My heart soared at the gentle pleasure of her sighs.

Journey was mine and soon, she would hold my mark and my knot, and everyone in the club would know for certain that we all might have a second chance.

CHAPTER SEVENTEEN

Journey

I'm not sure what just happened.

My body took control of it all. It was as if I was watching from above. Grim's body hovered over me, and I felt the heat of his skin.

His come was now painted on my body. He watched it pool in my navel. His fingers brushed it, smearing it up my stomach and across my chest.

The pleasant vibrations from his chest soothed me. The cracked window brought in fresh, cold air, and it made my nipples harden once more.

I have never had someone come on me. Condoms were a must to protect the merchandise and to protect the customers. Customers knew we were passed around. I was extra grateful for the implant in my arm to keep me from getting pregnant. I was so drugged up some days, I couldn't tell if everyone followed the rules or not.

Pregnant merchandise meant worthless merchandise.

Grims heated eyes stared at the painting he was making with his fingers. I didn't feel at all repulsed by it, and part of me felt turned on and more in tune with him.

He wasn't disgusted by me, jumping up and pulling on his pants to leave. He was cradling me with his body, tracing his finger around the curve of my breast, memorizing every line.

"I'm sorry," his voice rasped, still painting swirls into my skin. "I got carried away."

I paused, thinking of what I could say. What could I say? That I didn't like it? Because that would have been a lie. I really loved it.

When he came, there was another spark, not the one I felt on our skin when we touched, but in his eyes. He pulled me in—a feeling I had never felt before in my life. A deep connection that I couldn't ignore no matter how much my mind was telling me to run away.

"Don't be," I reached out, pushing away his thick hair. It had fallen out of his braid and brushed his bearded cheek. "I'm not."

And I should be, because this man gave me my first orgasm, one I hadn't given myself. Not that I had had a real orgasm like that, ever. Usually, they were fake and well planned.

I wrapped my arms around his neck as he leaned in for a kiss. He leaned into me, not caring if he covered himself with his own arousal.

He really enjoyed kissing. Hell, I did too. It was a new concept to me, and he was fantastic at it. For a man so rough around the edges, wait, scratch that, he was rough all over. Grim was gentle and watched his hands and movements when he was around me like I was fragile.

He and I both knew I wasn't fragile. However I was beat up and broken, but he indulged me and wanted to take care of me for some reason. Like I was something so precious, he didn't want me to break. I liked it, and I was going to let it continue for as long as it lasted, because time was never certain, and he could tire of me easily. Most men did.

After showering, I dressed in a pair of dark wash skinny jeans and a white sweater. He brushed my hair meticulously. He didn't want me lifting a finger, and he had a hard time deciding whether to brush my hair or feed me. I snorted, watching how his eyes glanced between the brush and the fork. I shook my head playfully at his hard scowl.

Luckily, brushing my own hair lost out, and he fed me. That seemed more important to him than "grooming" me, as he put it.

Grooming, the bed he called a nest, and the meat he ate raw raised more questions. He was definitely different from other men. I couldn't put my finger on it. To the untrained eye, he looked like a biker, a mean one at that. Grim was the enforcer from what I gathered. The undeniable rage he held he kept inside him. Like another person or thing. This persona only came out when he was protecting me. I'd seen people get killed, even other cam girls, but the way Grim slaughtered Aedar with such force and rage, it was unworldly.

And yet I wasn't afraid.

He was wild, but gentle with me.

I was going to keep my mouth shut a little longer before I asked. I needed to figure out who he really was, where he came from. It would help me with how to approach the subject. I could be reading too much into it, but my gut was telling me otherwise. He could very well be from another country, and these were the words his family used, if he even had a family.

My shoulders slumped as we walked down the sidewalk. I really knew nothing about him, and I let him rub one out of me.

What the heck was wrong with me? Because I really liked it... I liked it too much.

I rubbed my chest, feeling an ache inside when the thought entered my mind about leaving him. He would eventually push me away, they all did. I shouldn't get attached. No one ever did. I was a quick fuck, and that was all I was.

But with him, it was different. He took care of me. No one had taken care of me my entire life. Not a parent, not a friend. And that was before I was truly broken, used.

My eye twitched, and I scratched my temple. Grim squeezed my hand as if he knew I was thinking too hard.

He stopped us in the middle of the sidewalk, and his thumb grazed over my eye. The twitching stopped, and I stared up at him gratefully.

"Don't think, feel." He rubbed his chest then grabbed my hand again.

Grim was a thinker, that was for sure. He paid attention to the little details, watching my every move, studying it. He took his thumb and put it between our laced fingers and rubbed my palm. I smiled as it tickled.

A smile, a genuine smile. Nothing faked or forced.

Grim pulled me along beside him and led me up to his bike. It was painted metallic black with white claw marks painted on the side.

Grim and the rest of the members shared a large garage at the back of the bar, dubbed the "Iron Fang Garage," just like their club's name. It wasn't just a shed, however. On the outside, it looked run down, planks missing and the roof in need of repair, but on the inside, it was the difference between night and day.

Bikes lined up in perfectly straight rows on a perfectly laid concrete floor. Tall shelves filled with oil, tools, and tires stood against the walls. A cash register was at the front. There was a car in the very back, lifted high as a man pulled parts from below.

Two men were working on a bike, clanging the different tools against the metal, and another man with a vest just like Grim's sprayed on a fresh coat of paint.

"Grim!" one of them waved with a wrench in his hand. "You goin' out?" Grim gave a curt nod, and the club member chuckled. His eyes lingered on both of us, looking at our hands, and the biggest grin split his face.

"Alright man, your hog is ready to go. Original plates are on," he spouted off before going back to his work.

"Original plates?" I asked while Grim grabbed a brand-new helmet off the back. It was jet black, except for the large picture on the back of the Iron Fang logo I saw on everyone's vests. Under it, it said, "Grim" in wild organic letters.

"Before every mission, we put on fakes," he said. "Can't risk anything coming back here. It's our safe place." He tapped the helmet with his finger before setting it on my head. He buckled the belt under my chin, tugging on it to make sure it was secure.

Grim guided me to his bike, helping me swing my leg over. It was really tall compared to my short legs. He hopped on without a care in the world.

He guided my arms around his waist.

"Don't you need a helmet? I took yours."

"Don't wear one," he grunted.

"But this has your name on it?" I pointed to the back of it.

He chuckled, turning on the bike and revving it. "I know," he smirked, putting on some shades, then set the tires squealing on the way out of the shed.

I squeezed my arms around his torso, feeling his body contract as he took a turn. I didn't know if I should lean into it or lean out as he moved the bike. The little bit of weight I had was nothing to his enormous frame and the ability to tilt the bike over.

Grim's bike gripped the road. We were going slowly for my sake. The air was clean, the road a deep black asphalt. The smell of fresh rain cleared my senses.

The thick forest that surrounded us, the wet moss, and the dampness in the air soothed my soul. I couldn't remember how long it had been since I had been outside this long. To feel the wind in my hair and the nature surrounding us was rejuvenating.

I grew up on the plains—a prairie house just outside of a small town. The church was the center of it, but the constant noise of tractors, the schoolhouse bells chiming, and the yelling of parents chasing children made it all too noisy.

This was heaven.

We drove for close to two hours before we stopped. At some point, we had turned around and were getting closer to town. It looked like a scenic spot meant for tourists to park and snap pictures. The parking lines were faded, moss and pine needles covered the white paint. This scenic spot was barely used, and the view before us was untouched by human hands.

The posts of a previous fence that kept tourists away from the edge were all but broken. The rails were rusted over and hidden by nature.

"We own this," Grim spoke. "Locke and me." He held out his hand, leading me to the edge.

Grim reached out with his hand, looking as if he was touching the mist that was settling on the conifer trees below.

My eye twitched, realizing how close we were to the edge.

Grim's hand landed on my lower back, pulling me closer to him. My eye twitched slower when his thumb traced across it.

"We love the outdoors, the forest, the wildlife. It's in our roots, it's who we are," he said to the wind. I tilted my head, his eyes still pinned to the forest before us.

"I hope to build a home down there soon. Where it's quiet, peaceful." He cleared his throat.

We stood in silence for a long time, my head resting against his body.

"W-when do you plan on doing it?" I asked. Because if he wanted to build a home, maybe my time was shorter than I thought.

"When you know all of me," he breathed. "When you know who I am, and I haven't scared you away. Not that I'm going to let you go anyway," he chuckled.

I cocked my head in confusion and opened my mouth but had difficulty letting any words go.

"Well, I already know you kill the bad guys. What more do you think would keep me away?" I chuckled, burying my cold nose into his vest.

"There's more," he casually mentioned, rubbing his hand up and down my back. "More to me, the club, and the world you think you know."

My smile fell, and his hand stopped rubbing my back.

Grim led me to a bench covered with moss and rot. He sat down on it without a care. It creaked, and he pulled me into his lap, so I didn't have to sit in the dirt.

"And I'm going to tell you my story, but I really want to hear yours first. I want to know what happened to you, no matter how angry it makes me. The only way I can do that is out here, Journey. To keep me calm, to keep the wild beast inside me from ripping apart everything in our den."

I blinked, long and slow.

"If I get up from this bench and leave you standing here, you don't move. You stay, I will protect you. Nothing in this forest would ever harm you, do you understand?" he muttered. "Can you do that for me, Journey?"

I couldn't say no to the pleading look. I was more concerned with why he would have to go into the forest. There wasn't much of my story to tell. He knew most of it from the first day I had stayed here. The nitty gritty I left out; surely, he wouldn't want to know it all.

"All of it?" I whispered.

"Everything," his chest growled. "From the first day you were taken to when I found you. I must know."

"I really don't want to," I brushed a tear away. "I want to forget it."

"And I will help you forget, Journey." His large hands cupped my cheek. "It is the job of a mate to do these things. I will avenge you, kill every worthless piece of shit that ever touched you. I will erase their existence from the earth as if they never existed."

I heaved in a breath at the intensity of his words.

A mate?

"W-what's a mate?" I asked.

His eyes relaxed, petting my hair. His nose went to my shoulder, taking slow tantalizing breaths in.

"It is what my people call someone who is meant to be theirs. Always."

CHAPTER EIGHTEEN

Grim

Journey shifted, the imposing wind drawing shivers from her body. I shrugged off my jacket and wrapped it around her shoulders. It engulfed her entire body.

I cursed myself for not packing something warmer for her.

We'd ridden for hours, and now the sun was close to setting. I'd never been around humans much, for long periods of time, anyway. Their bodies were more vulnerable to the cold, the heat, and of course, to harms of the flesh.

Humans were fragile creatures.

And now she was going to tell me just how fragile she really was.

Journey sighed, taking in a large breath to fill her lungs. My chest filled with pride watching her looking up at me, smiling. No one had ever fucking smiled at me like that.

Journey was beautiful and so strong. Stronger than any woman I had known. She'd been through shit, and she was still here, still alive. Her soul reached toward a pull she didn't understand.

I couldn't wait to show her the part of myself I had hidden from her, but I was also deathly afraid.

Would she be repulsed by who I was? I was not a man, but a beast, and the world that she knew was all a lie.

I held her closer, my nose grazing the side of her cheek, taking in her scent. She welcomed it, snuggling closer into my embrace.

We might have a chance.

My wolf purred. It was continuous now. He no longer felt vicious like when we first found her. He was so unsure what this human could really do to us. She could reject the bond, just like our first mate, and that might still be the case. Journey knew what it was like to be alone and vulnerable and maybe, just maybe, she would take pity on our soul.

My wolf and I had high hopes for the completion of our bond. She had laid in our arms willingly in our nest, she felt our shaft, and she was not repulsed by our advances, even with the torment of her past.

"Before you tell me your past, Journey, I want you to know something about these woods." My gaze landed over the tall pines of the forest.

They were always green and filled with creatures great and small. The bears that roamed here were amongst the largest animals, but certainly not the most dangerous. Other creatures lived there too.

Creatures that had thoughts, desires, and a thirst for blood. And they were not afraid of the humans finding them. For if they did, their lives would be ended quickly.

They were out in the open here. It was a small piece of earth without a veil of concealment.

There was a cruelty to this forest, but Journey had my scent on her. Any and all supernaturals would yield, knowing she belonged to me.

My wolf was almost fully healed and at full strength. I could hear the rush of blood running through my mate's veins. I could hear the small gulps of a fawn drinking from the brook. My strength had returned, and it would only grow stronger once Journey and I became one.

"While I am in this forest, no harm will come to you." I pushed a tendril of hair from her face. "No animal, no person, or creature will come to hurt you. Do you understand?"

She bit her lip, her body no longer shaking, but nodded in agreement. Her curiosity heightened as she opened her mouth to speak, but I interrupted.

"I may get angry," I growled. "I may want to throw or hit the shit out of something, but I would never do that to you. I will set you down, and I will deal with my anger."

Her caramel eyes twinkled. She moved her hand to cup mine and stroked it gently. "I understand," she said softly. "You may not like me anymore once I tell you about myself, though. You'll think I'm dirty." Her eye twitched.

I turned her chin toward me, my wolf growled in protest at her frivolous words. "I'll always want you. You did what you had to do to survive, Journey. To find me."

She nodded in agreement, but she didn't believe me. Journey was preparing herself in case I abandoned her, but I would prove to her I would always stay. To have her. My mate had a shitty life, and I was going to be sure to show her how precious she was.

First, by destroying every fucking person who had touched her.

"Okay." She rubbed her hands together. "This is going to be hard." She whispered to herself.

Journey's eye twitched, and she rubbed it away roughly, heaving a frustrated breath.

"Go slowly," I reassured her. "I want to hear it all. Your pain will be mine."

"I don't want you in pain, Grim. That's the last thing I would want."

"We will bear each other's pasts. We will rise from the ashes of those who pained us. I will watch the light leave their eyes. I will do it until I have avenged my mate." My mouth twitched in a malicious smile.

Journey's lips parted, staring at me in awe.

"I'll do it. You can't stop me. Anyone that dared to lay a hand on you, I will have Switch and Hawke hunt them down. I'll kill them with my bare hands. Pluck their eyes from their sockets for looking at your body, rip their fingers from their hands for touching your skin and," I chuckled darkly. "I'll cut off their dicks and shove it down their throats until they choke."

Journey's mouth hung open; her eyebrows furrowed in fascination.

"That's quite a picture you painted," she said. She reached up to the side of my face, tracing her fingers over a scar that my beard covered. "You would do that for me?"

"Yes," I said gruffly.

She nodded, satisfied with my answer.

"I won't stop you, then. I don't want it happening to anyone else. There were children, too, Grim. I... I don't want that happening to them most of all."

"It won't. I'll make sure of it," I promised.

The entire club would join. Journey was part of our family now. And you did not mess with anyone in the Iron Fang—human or supernatural, it didn't matter. Anyone trafficking innocent lives deserved the worst kind of death.

Journey sat up straight, her gaze reaching the farthest end of the forest. The mountains in the distance would soon be covered in snow on the most northern peaks by next month. My mate would need thicker clothes, and thicker blankets to cover her in the nest.

I would take care of her. My wolf agreed wholeheartedly and purred deep within my chest.

"I was always a mover," Journey interrupted my thoughts. "For as long as I could remember, I moved. I couldn't stay focused on one thing, and my mind would constantly wander. I had trouble in school, always behind my peers. Too busy dreaming of faraway places, pretending that fairy tales existed, and there were creatures in the forest I could talk to," she giggled.

Gods, how ironic?

"I had few friends. I grew up in a tiny religious town in Kansas. One church, one grocery store, nothing but farmland for miles. The entire school was kindergarten to twelfth grade. I was considered the 'trouble-maker.' No one wanted to be around sin, around someone who differed so vastly from them. So, I was ignored, sometimes bullied on the playground, which only increased my need to move." Journey scooted closer, putting her head on my shoulder.

"My parents told me I needed to shape up. I needed to act better. That a demon was trying to take over my body and that I had to fight it." Journey balled her hands into fists. "I went to church every Sunday like they wanted, sat in the front row, pinched my own thigh to keep myself still until there were bruises. But even that wasn't enough for me to pay attention. My body may have been still, but my mind wandered instead."

Journey looked over the valley while I stroked her hair.

"I didn't touch anybody, didn't make noise. And sometimes my eye would twitch. Kids would point it out during class. I'd get more notes home for disturbing the other kids. That would make mother so mad." Journey covered her mouth, rubbing it until her eye twitched again.

I squeezed her tight, rubbing my beard on the crown of her head.

"The school had enough one day. They didn't have enough resources to take care of a kid that couldn't recite the scriptures. The counselor that was doing an internship for his degree at a fancy college told them I need-ed some extra help because I had ADHD. No one listened to outsiders, though. Not in that town," she said bitterly. "God had supposedly cursed me."

She bit her lip. "I wasn't loud. I kept to myself and didn't bother any-body. The school told my parents they couldn't help me any longer, that I was a 'lost cause' and maybe the preacher could help with an 'exorcism.'" Journey curled her body against mine, her face buried in my chest.

"Does it happen when you get nervous?" I asked. My thumb rubbed across her twitching skin, and it instantly calmed.

"Yeah." She nodded. "It started after she slapped me one day after getting a note home from school for not doing my work. It's done it ever since."

Fuck.

I snarled, pulling her closer. Taking my thumb, I rubbed her cheek tenderly. She sighed, gripped my shirt, and smelled it deeply.

It sounded like she lived with a bunch of dumb fuck religious cunts.

"Keep going, baby."

"One night, my parents told me how they really felt. They never cared. I was too much work. I was such a disappointment and embarrassment. They wished they would have just aborted me, if they had done that they wouldn't have had to get married to each other." Journey wiped her nose with her sleeve.

"I was a mistake. I wasn't supposed to be here." Journey broke into a sob, and I held her until the sunset crested over the forest and the mountains. The golden light filtered through the trees. Sparkles of light reflecting on the dust made the area look like it was meant for the supernatural world and not of Earth.

I kissed her forehead until her sobs lightened. Her fingers played with my beard until she continued again.

"The pastor told my parents he could help them. Take care of the entire problem with me. Just give him a few days to get the paperwork in order." She clenched her hair with her fingers, pulling at the scalp. "I thought I was getting help for my ADHD." Journey shook her head.

"The next night, it was dark. There was no moon. I remember because I would watch it rise every night when my parents locked me in my room. I would watch it light up the sky, bringing light to the dark fields. The moon beams looked like they were playing with the deer that ran across those fields. They were so free, so alive. I wanted to feel that way, too."

I didn't think I could pull her any closer to my body, but I did. Her nose went into my neck, breathing in my scent. My wolf continued to let out low growls and purrs to comfort her.

"But that night instead of seeing the wildlife, there were only the small streetlamps and the artificial light coming from the houses. I was lying in bed, drifting to sleep when a man crawled in the window and covered my mouth with a cloth. I tried to get away." Journey's hand gripped tighter on my shirt. "I tried to get away, but the next thing I remembered was waking up in a clean bedroom. It had actual sheets, a bed, and a chair. I just had a mattress at my parents' house."

My parents fucking loved me. They fucking provided me with everything. I don't know what I would have done if I hadn't had their love and affection. I would have grown up damned lonely, but my mate had to suffer from the very beginning. All because she had a disorder that could be treated, and her parents did nothing to help her.

They fucking punished her. They should have loved her. Just like my parents loved me.

"Time passed; an old man came into my room. He said my parents paid someone to take me, to make it look like a kidnapping, and there was no hope for me to escape. He said my parents were putting on some fake tears right now and looking like the poor couple that lost their cursed child. I was to stay at this man's house until a van would come by and pick me up and take me to my next destination, but I think he felt sorry for me when

I told him I just wanted someone to love me."

The wind blew harshly. It came out of the blackness of the forest. Clouds rolled into the valley below us. The mist blocked the last of the light, and I clutched my mate to keep warm as the temperature dipped.

"The van never came," Journey added. "The man, he kept me, Jimmy kept me. He had me work manual labor. It was a farm, and he had tons of animals. Jimmy needed the extra help, and I was good at what I did. It kept me moving, kept me using my hands. My mind could stay on task." Journey lifted her hand to the sky, feeling the soft fog settling around us.

"I heard screams when I was locked in my room one night. Girls just like me screamed into the night to be let free and unmarked vans would pick them up the next morning. I met none of the girls and didn't know who they were. I was just glad it wasn't me. That's terrible to think, huh?"

"No, it isn't terrible." I petted her hair with my callused fingers. "It isn't terrible in the slightest, you were surviving. You did what you could to stay there, to be safe. He never touched you, did he?" I lifted my lip, ready to snarl, but I faked a cough instead.

"No, he didn't." She shook her head. "He treated me great—warm food, a nice bed, and clothes. But I must have messed up somewhere because one night my food must have been drugged. I remained in a drug-like state for who knows how long."

Journey's eyes drooped, keeping the side of her head to my chest. Her eyes blinked, heavy in thought.

"It was like dreams faded in and out." Her voice sounded hollow. "One moment a man would be on top of me, then in another, someone was feeding me food or drink. Then in another moment, I would lie in bed, unable to move. Until one day, the fog lifted, and I realized I had been drugged for a long while. My body was thin, bruises marred my skin. It hurt between my legs." She sobbed.

I picked up Journey and strode over to the cliff, clutching her to my chest and roared into the valley below. My wolf speeding far too quickly to the surface for me to refuse entry. Veins bulged out of my neck, my claws lengthening by the second.

Trying to shake the darkness and keep the beast inside me from surfacing, I shook my head. Journey gripped her fingers around the scruff of my collar, her body wincing at the noises I created.

I set her back down on the worn bench and stepped away, running both my hands through my hair. I wanted to hold her, comfort her, but I could not. I would not harm her or make her afraid of me.

My wolf howled inside me with a sad cry. He had not howled like that since our first mate broke our heart, our bond. His cry echoed through the depths of my soul.

My knees weakened, dropping into the dirt just five feet away from her. She held her tiny fists to her chest to hide herself.

"Keep going," I growled. "Tell me all of it."

"The place where I stayed had been infiltrated by a rival trafficking ring. This gang had many men, but they were slender in appearance but unbelievably strong," she continued.

I backed away, afraid I would shift.

"The drugs had barely worn off, so they kind of looked like elves, maybe a fairy with no wings and one had fangs like a vampire." She chuckled nervously.

"I thought they were saving us, but once the drugs had worn off, I realized they were just ordinary men looking for fresh meat for their own services. They only took me, saying I looked the least damaged." She chuckled darkly.

"For the longest time, I thought some higher power was out to get me because there was nothing I wanted more than to die right there and not go with them."

Hot breath seeped from my nose and into the air. The back of my neck was covered in fur. My fingers threaded through the braided mohawk Journey made earlier and I pulled at the strands.

"What else?" I growled at her. "What else happened? Names, I want names!"

She shook her head.

"I just know Aedar. He was my boss and told me how to work the cams and how to perform." She spat out the last word with disgust.

"Did you?" I stepped forward. "Did you have to meet these men in person?"

She gulped.

"A-few. Most of the time, I was drugged. Sometimes I can remember a face. I was actually grateful they drugged me. I didn't want to remember it. But I felt it afterwards." Journey lowered her head in shame. "I'm so dirty," she muttered.

"FUCK!" I yelled into the valley, my roar echoing back to hit me.

My urge to comfort her was powerful, but my control over my wolf was waning. The back of my shirt tore, and Journey stopped her sobbing to stare.

"A-are you okay?" She stood to come forward, but I held my hands out, shaking my head frantically.

"Sit!" I snarled, voice cracking into that of an animal. The hair on my face grew, my body trembling. I turned, running into the thick underbrush of the woods, pulling off my clothes.

"*Kill.*" My wolf echoed. I could no longer hold the rage back. I shifted in the underbrush beneath the pine branches.

CHAPTER NINETEEN

Journey

Instead of Grim embracing me after my confession, he sprinted into the woods. The area was now darker than when we arrived. Fog fell into the basin of the valley below us. The trees had grown in the darkness, and the moon in the distance climbed higher.

A chill ran through me, my hand rubbing up my arm until I felt the friction of the movement warm me.

Grim was outraged. More enraged than I had ever seen him. Not that I had been with him for long. Without his presence, the gloom surrounded me, and the darkness crept around the small clearing.

My heart yearned for something, pulled for Grim, maybe? A hollow in my chest grew bigger, the desperation to find him growing with every second.

"Grim?" I called out to the dark forest into which he fled. "Grim!" It echoed into the darkness.

My eye twitched, and an aggravated whimper left my lips.

Even if this forest was supposedly safe, I didn't feel it at all. The plains of the grasslands were familiar to me, not the tall trees. I could see for miles out of my tiny window. I'd never been in an environment like this, alone.

The howling of a distant animal and the breaking of branches came too close for comfort. I backed away, feeling the back of my knees hit the broken bench and collapsing onto it. I should run, I should stand up and run back to the road and hope that Grim would meet me there. Or perhaps a passing car would keep me company?

I shook my head, pulling the thick leather jacket closer around me. The musk of the forest smelled far cleaner than the surrounding environment and pacified me. It was Grim's smell bringing me what I needed.

It was the same smell that surrounded me when I was sick. It was a smell that I would embed in my memory, just like a favorite smell of a mother baking cookies for a child. It would become nostalgic as time went on.

"I've become a psycho, relying on my boyfriend? Is that what he is? I'm addicted to his scent? I'm losing it," I whispered, shivering.

My heavy, labored pants were the beginning of a panic attack. I could hear my heart beating in my head.

Until warmth surrounded me. My usual breathing pattern returned when I felt the warmth in my chest grow brighter. I didn't feel alone anymore; I didn't feel the emptiness, and that was because there was an enormous, heated body behind my back.

Eyes widening, I turned slowly, not to spook the person or animal behind me. Why I thought about keeping my voice silenced instead of screaming for someone, anyone, was beyond me. I was petrified with fear.

As I turned, deep coppery fur filled my vision. Whatever this was, it was close. I couldn't see the whole animal, but I could smell a musky scent that was all too familiar. My fear faded, and my curiosity climbed.

It smelled...like Grim.

Hand shaking, I reached out, petting the beast. He was everywhere, towering over me. It was far larger than I realized.

I took careful steps, drifting away and keeping my eyes on the animal in case it attacked. Not that it mattered. One swipe and I would be done for.

It was a wolf, one that could very well be the size of a large pony or a small horse. Its head was larger and thicker than any wolf I had ever seen on the plains of Kansas. I was certainly not in Kansas and was in a completely unfamiliar land, but this animal should not exist. It was too large, too wild; and the constant growl in its chest wasn't going away.

It gazed at me, unmoving, the sides of his body rising and falling as it breathed. Steam rose from his snout. Eyes, a deep shade of blue, regarded me inquisitively as it stayed on the other side of the bench.

"Hi?" My voice shook.

I knew the animal couldn't talk; I knew it wouldn't reply, but something told me to greet this creature instead of standing there looking like an idiot.

"Pretty thing, aren't you?" It relaxed. Picking up its enormous paws, it walked around the bend, and softly, carefully moved to where I stood. I was right in the thoughts I had earlier. This beast, this wolf-thing, was a mystical creature.

Where was Little Red Riding Hood when you needed her?

How many times did I pray to the moon outside my window each night to bring me the protection I needed? I didn't care if it was an animal, person, or a voice to tell me to keep surviving, to live just a little longer. I craved closeness, a deeper connection to someone or something. To get it, I tried praying to a rock in the sky. Part of me felt it was real, that *she* was real.

The wolf lowered its head, nudging my hand to do something. I had stood still for far too long, and who knew what this wolf wanted from me. He hadn't eaten me *yet*, so that was a good sign.

With the moon now higher in the sky, the moonlight burst through the fog and the small landing where we stood shone brightly. I could see all of this magnificent beast, thoughts of where Grim had gone disappearing.

Perhaps the moon brought me this creature, this gentle giant that now rubbed and licked my neck like I was familiar to him. My arms wrapped around the thick neck, the powerful tendons and muscles rippling down its body.

I let out a laugh. The wolf nudged me back to the bench, and I sat down happily, keeping my hand planted in its fur. It was a fairy tale in the making. He was a wolf of massive proportions, and no one would believe me if I told them this beast was here.

Massive paws, twice the size of my face, cradled the earth below it. That was why it was so silent, its paws cupping the earth with the pads of its toes. The teeth were large, white, and poked out from underneath the lips of the upper jaw. This wolf-creature could match any horror story of predator versus prey, but it sat so calmly.

"What are you doing out here alone?" I cooed, rubbing its ear. "Did a female run off on you like my male did?" He snorted, his head shaking until it landed with a thud in my lap.

He was so soft, and my body relaxed instantly. This wasn' t some wild animal, it felt too domesticated.

"Will you come visit me in town?" The wolf only huffed in response, irritated. "You can sneak in at the back of the tattoo shop. I'll let you in."

Right, if he can fit.

"I bet Grim will let you. He likes the outdoors, and he's got plenty of raw meat in the fridge that might fill you up." The wolf's head raised, tilting like a harmless puppy.

"Yeah, lots of raw meat." My smile faded, my hands falling from around the wolf's neck. The glow of red fur shined brightly against the moon's rays. "That...he...eats himself," I thought out loud.

We sat there in silence for the longest time. I either played with its fur or stared up at the moon which I felt had blessed me with something I'd prayed for. It wasn't just this wolf, but it was Grim, too. I got two things I wanted—a person and an animal.

Why had I not thought about that again? Was I hiding it beneath a comfortable layer of trust in a man I hardly knew? Maybe he just had some weird diet? Maybe...

A flutter from the right side of the clearing made me jump. I squealed, putting a hand over my chest seeing it was just a white dove landing feet away. It was pure white, walking out of the forest like it owned the place and no predator would dare eat it. I closed my eyes, taking a deep breath.

"Damn, that scared me." I reached out to grab the wolf's thick mane, but I stumbled on the bench with the lack of a furry wall.

He was gone. The giant beast was gone without a sound. And all that was left was the white dove walking around the edge of the cliff. It pecked the dirt, hunting for food, and my concentration fell on it instead of the continued pressure of not having Grim or the wolf by my side.

The dove, not affected by my presence at all, pecked at the ground again, this time approaching me. It turned to look at its surroundings. There was a light gray-blue symbol on its back. It was an upside-down crescent moon that expanded between both wings which were neatly folded by its sides.

"Moon?" I whispered. The dove spread its wings and lurched forward until its wings beat wildly, gaining height as it flew over the ledge. I followed, confused as hell that I would see two animals that were not right, not real. It was too fantastic for it to be a coincidence.

"Journey?" Grim stepped out of the forest. He cracked his neck to the side and rushed toward me. "I'm sorry, I was angry. Didn't want to scare you." His voice had grown soft despite his anger earlier, and I was thankful for it. I didn't enjoy seeing him upset. I was hoping to hide that part of myself from anyone and everyone forever, but Grim's persistence was too great.

Plus, he needed to know me. Just like I needed to know him.

"You didn't." I shook my head in disbelief. "Just missed you." I gave a brief smile, only for him to wrap his arm around me. The air had turned cold and despite his short-sleeve shirt with his denim club vest, he was remarkably warm.

"Let's go home." Grim grabbed me by the waist, not looking back at the forest where he had emerged.

I wanted to protest, ask him about his past, maybe tell him about the massive wolf. But tonight was enough. To hear of my past, to know that I had been used in ways I didn't want to remember again, and then telling him about an enormous wolf… He might think I was lying about everything.

Besides, digging into his past would reopen too many scars he had covered in ink. We would take this slowly. I'd wait for my answers for now. He wasn't getting rid of me. He was staying by my side, staying here for me, to build me back up to what I should have been all my life.

Happy, safe.

Really, maybe I never saw a gigantic wolf and a dove marked with a crescent moon. I mean, I just opened the floodgates of trauma. My mind was trying to soothe me, giving me the magical fairytale creatures I had dreamed of.

Grim led me into the darkened woods, my head darting behind me, waiting to see if the giant wolf was walking beside us. I held onto the sliver of hope that it was real because swore I felt the wolf alongside me while Grim was on the other. But the wolf wasn't there.

"Would you like me to carry you?" Grim's gravelly voice shook me from my thoughts.

"I'm alright." I snuggled closer into his chest. I held back a smile at the long sigh escaping him. "But if you want to carry me…"

I squealed happily, feeling his arms wrap around my legs and back.

I wrapped my arms around his neck. It gave him a perfect opportunity to pepper kisses along my neck until we reached his motorcycle. As he prepared the helmet, I peered up into the sky one more time. The moon was full, and instead of the usual white light it created, I swear the same blue-gray coloring of the moon that marked the dove's back shone down on us.

The silence between us wasn't awkward as we pulled up outside the Iron Fang Bar. It was crawling with people, and the moon still sat high above us, as I marveled at its beauty. It had been so long since I'd really looked at it, and I couldn't help but thank whatever higher power that was out there for it being so bright this night.

Grim pulled his bike into the one space left available, which had his name painted haphazardly on the pavement in white ink—a reserved spot for the right-hand man of the club.

That was why he said he was bringing me here tonight when he put on my helmet. He hadn't shown his face in quite some time and had to show the men the enforcer was still around.

He didn't like it, didn't like that I was going to be around a bunch of rough men that didn't have any companions yet. Unfortunately, he didn't have a choice because he wouldn't dare leave me at the apartment alone right now.

My eye twitched, and panic rose in my chest about going in. You could feel the bass of the music from the outside patio, where many of the club members were smoking and taking good long looks at the both of us. I felt safe even with the stares. They were staring more in curiosity, but Grim didn't see it that way.

One glowering stare from Grim and the men stiffened, turning away and shuffling themselves further away from us.

"Come here," Grim growled.

He pulled me by my waist and shoved his face into my neck, his teeth grazing my shoulder until he roughly sucked the skin. The heat of his breath traveled down the front of my top. My grip tightened around his biceps as I moaned into him.

His tongue licked passionately at my skin, which caused a squeak to come from my throat. His tongue lapped at the bruised skin, and, with one final nip, he backed away. Grim rubbed his hand through his beard, tilting my neck with the other to review his work.

My cooter was a soaking mess. My clit tingled for more while I leaned into him.

"It will do, for now."

I shook myself from my stupor, glaring. "What do you mean, for now?" I patted the skin, trying to see the reflection in the mirror of his bike. "This thing isn't supposed to be permanent!"

Grim chuckled darkly. Wrapping his hand around my waist, he guided me into the bar. "One day, it will be permanent," he muttered, opening the door into the blazing music and excited yells.

CHAPTER TWENTY

Journey

Grim opened one of the double doors to the bar before I could ask him what he meant.

From the outside, it looked uninviting, gloomy, and cold. Sandstone bricks and marble stones made up most of the building's outer structure. It was nearly impossible to see through the grimy, smudge-covered windows.

When we entered, I was ready to feel the gloom and depression radiating from the customers along with the bartender, but that was not what I was greeted with.

Servers bustled by us to serve drinks at the tables, and I watched their steady moves. They carried at least ten large glasses on top of a tray and at least one pitcher of beer in the other hand. This balancing act alone should be in a sideshow circus with how many bodies they had to dodge to serve the patrons.

Lights flashed in the bar's corner, a small area dedicated to dancing and a live band. The band was called the *Moonlight Outcasts* according to the banner that hung behind them. They must be a different breed if they liked hanging out in a biker bar.

The lot of them looked unworldly—black hair, piercings on their faces, tattoos covering their arms, ashen skin with flecks of shimmer on their jaw bones. What stood out the most were the slightly pointed ears and jaws that some had. I tilted my head, watching them play methodically through their set.

The band wasn't singing. They played an easy listening background noise. I could see their fingers fiddling with the strings and the drummer twirling his stick in his left hand.

Grim, noticing my hypnotic stare, placed his large hand on my lower back and steered me away from the musicians. Something didn't seem right about them. One of the guitarists smiled at the other and their canines were so long it looked like they could cut his lip.

A body modification of some kind, maybe?

"Journey!" Delilah's cheerful attitude took me by surprise, and I jumped back. Her eyes softened, backing away with the empty tray in her hand. "Sorry, didn't mean to startle you."

Grim grunted, setting his body on the tall stool, and pulled me closer. I stood between his legs as he ordered.

"I'm glad he brought you to the bar. It's club night, and I think people were wondering where their enforcer was," Delilah mentioned.

Delilah placed her tray on the bar and handed over the cash to the bartender. "Another round of the same thing," she yelled over the music.

"Club night?" I asked.

"Yeah, the bar is closed, so only the Iron Fangs are allowed. Every Thursday," she said. "It's one of the few days I feel actually safe in here. Those who aren't a part of the club can get a little handsy." She tucked a curl around her ear.

"And Hawke lets you work here?"

Delilah blushed, grabbing the tray. "He can't tell me what to do. He isn't like my boyfriend or anything."

"Uh huh," I raised my eyebrow. "But he doesn't like it, does he?"

"How would you know?"

I nodded my head across the bar. Hawke sat with a beer mug, completely full, and gazed intensely at Delilah. He lifted the cold mug, touching his lips and opening his throat as he gulped the entire drink down in one go. He banged the glass on the bar twice, ticking his head for Delilah to come over.

"You're right, he doesn't like it. But I'm serious. He can't tell me what to do." She stuck out her lip in a pout.

I laughed. For the first time, I laughed with someone I felt like I could be friends with.

"I'll be right back." Delilah placed her hand on mine which rested on the beat-up, wooden bar. "I'm off in ten minutes, and we can chat if Grim will let you."

As I raised my head, I could see the unfinished ceiling above me. Grim was already looking down, and I swore I could see the side-smile of the giant.

It wasn't like I was asking permission; it was more of a mutual under-standing. He hadn't told me I couldn't stay away from her, but I wanted him close. The undeniable pull toward him grew stronger by the minute, and staying away from him for too long felt like torture.

"I'd like that." I smiled.

Delilah scampered to a table, looking like an overly crazy ferret jumping from table to table to finish her orders. Her tray slowly emptied after handing out the drinks until Hawk crooked his finger for her to be at his side. I watched as they interacted until Grim pulled me on his lap.

"What do you think of this place?" Grim asked. He had turned his stool, so we gazed over the bar.

The Iron Fangs all wore denim vests with their club crests—a large one on their backs and a small one on the front. Patches on their vests ranged from the longest bike ride to the greatest dart thrower. The women who were also a part of the club had their vests fitted to work with the curve of their bodies.

"I like how there are women in your club," I mentioned. "You don't discriminate."

"Why would we? They like to feel the wind in their hair, too."

Grim picked up his beer mug and offered me some. I sniffed it, and it didn't smell appealing. I wrinkled my nose in disgust. The chuckle in his chest grew until I felt it between my legs. My body stiffened as his legs vibrated, rushing straight to my core.

I was becoming so comfortable with Grim; I was feeling things I never thought I would. I didn't want to hide away from the world or from him. I was learning that not all men were evil. Especially Grim.

Not all men wanted a woman just to sate their evil desires. I was thankful that each day I seemed to forget more and more of what had happened to me. My mind was moving on, forgetting the past.

Grim's laughter slowed, and his breath deepened. It was then the deep rumbling in his chest began, and it was not a purr, but a growl.

One arm held me close to his body while the other took the mug away. He pulled me closer, his nose trailing the top of my head and down to the base of my ear.

His hot breath moved my tangled hair from our ride, and his tongue licked behind it. "We will leave as soon as I speak to Locke."

Grim words held an auspicious promise. Words that I was looking forward to. Despite my body being used to a man, my mind was never in the moment. They felt like nightmares, and when I woke, I felt the pain left behind.

Being drugged was actually a gift.

The promise made me nervousness, but it also promised delight. Who would have thought a woman could feel that much pleasure when I was taught a woman's body was for a man's pleasure only?

Delilah tapped my shoulder, Grim's tongue sliding back into his lips.

"I will speak to Locke, and then we will leave, little one," he said as he patted by back side.

I bit my lip, excited about the endearment.

Grim slid off the stool, picked me up, and took me to the edge of the bar, sitting me in the open seat where Hawke had sat. Grim waved for the bartender and tapped the bar with his middle finger. "Whatever she wants," Grim stated. "And Delilah, too."

"Thanks, Grim!" Delilah chirped.

The bartender looked at me expectantly, not paying attention to the bar as he wiped with the old worn cloth. His shirt was tighter than most, his lanky body showing off the piercings beneath his clothes.

"I'm surprised Grim let you out of his sight." He jutted his chin toward me. "Name's Anaki, and before you ask, I'm originally from Ireland, not Scotland, so get that out of yer head." He thickened his accent while wagging his finger.

"I'll take a Lemon Drop!" Delilah said.

Anaki made Delilah her drink, swirling it between the glasses and the small steel cups. I laughed as he pretended to drop the cups in our direction, causing us to scream when we thought we would get soaked.

The members of the club threw smiles our way as we laughed, the group of rough necks laughing along with us.

Once Anaki's show was over, he poured two glasses, one for me and Delilah.

"Figured a Lemon Drop would be alright with your mister," he winked. "I can't allow you to get drunk or it will be my hide."

Delilah and I picked up the glasses, tinking them together in a toast. I felt like I had missed everything in the real world while I was hidden away. This was so normal. It was what I'd craved for so long, to have a friend, feel like I belonged and, with the banter of men and women laughing in the background, I realized I finally had it.

"So, tell me about this massive hickey on your neck," Delilah said.

I choked on my drink, coughing violently as she laughed.

I could feel Grim's eyes from the other side of the room, checking to see if I would breathe again. He took a step, Locke grabbing his shoulder to hold him back for another minute. I waved once the coughing fit was over until he spoke to Locke again.

"I can't believe you asked that," I replied.

"How could I not? It's the size of a softball!"

My face flushed red, and even the surrounding tables took a gander at the side of my neck. I pulled up the collar, trying to hide it, but who was I kidding? It was...huge.

"Yeah, Grim wanted to stake a claim, I guess." I rolled the fancy neck of the glass between my fingers. "Not that everyone doesn't know I'm his already."

"Oh yeah, it's blatantly clear. It was announced in the bar a week ago. You guys were a hot topic from what Hawke told me when he was ridiculously drunk."

"So, you two?" I waved my finger between her and Hawke, who was now in the Locke and Grim huddle.

"Like I said, don't get attached to these biker males. They don't stick around for long. Then again, you are proving everything wrong, Journey. The boys like what they see, what Grim has anyway. Now, they want it, too. I'm hoping..." Delilah paused, pursing her lips.

She was such a sweet and spunky girl. She was a ball of sunshine, the first woman that made me feel welcome in a group full of bikers. I hadn't had time to meet the other women, but it wasn't like the others were knocking at my door like Delilah had.

"I don't know you that well, but he would have to be insane not to want you," I said. Delilah perked up at that, the heat rising to her cheeks. "You are the first friend I've ever had, and you are everything I ever wanted to be growing up. You're so kind and work so hard. I don't know why you are here under their protection, but... I hope you never leave."

Delilah's head tilted. "I am planning on leaving. Not until I have enough money saved anyway, but that poses an important question for me to ask." She pushed away her glass, waving at Anaki for another.

"Are you planning on staying, like, staying staying?"

I turned my head to check on Grim. His arms were crossed, half paying attention to Locke and Hawke. His eyes were on me, and my legs tightened in response.

A life without Grim? I couldn't imagine it. I told about him my demons; I told him about my nightmares, my scars, my wounds, and he still wanted me. Would another man want me? Maybe? Possibly? But the pull to him was too strong to want to let go, and I loved his earth-shattering posses-siveness. He wanted to protect me from everything as weak as I was, still healing from years of abuse.

"Wherever Grim goes, I go," I said confidently.

Delilah gazed at me intently, assessing my words. My smile couldn't be hidden even when I lowered my head to look at the half empty glass. "I know I don't have a lot of experience in life, knowing how men are sup-posed to be, how they act, how a relationship works, especially coming into adulthood. I couldn't define a healthy relationship if you asked me. But with Grim," I sighed. "With Grim, I feel like this is where I am supposed to be. I would face my hardships again just so I could meet him."

The long pause had me longing to be close to Grim again. The burly man, the man that everyone in the bar looked at with fear and respect, made my heart flutter. He didn't sugarcoat things with the others; he didn't act affectionate with any of them. Just a curt nod and grunt, but Grim spoke whole sentences to me, despite the raspiness in his throat.

"That's really great, Journey. I'm happy for you." Delilah grabbed my hand and squeezed. "I'm glad you have that."

Hawke was no longer talking to Locke and Grim. One hand was on a hidden weapon beneath his vest, like most of the men carried in the bar. The other hand rubbed his chin thoughtfully. Delilah had feelings for Hawke, and he had them for her too.

Something told me in the pit of my stomach that would all change very soon. That Hawke would wake up when she packed her bags and left. He wouldn't know what he had until it was gone.

"He's never kissed me intentionally," Delilah said. "Not when he was sober, anyway. And I keep letting him get away with it. I can't have him abuse my emotions any longer. I have to leave, or I'll never live."

"And that is when he will wake up," I promised. "Maybe you need to do it. Have him chase you." I downed the rest of my drink, shaking my head when Anaki held out two fingers in question for another.

"I just need a thousand more, and I'll have enough. I won't have my emotions played with anymore."

Delilah had a good head on her shoulders. Who knew how long she had been here, but if this sweet woman was already claiming she was done waiting, it must have been awhile.

The double doors of the bar burst open. The coldness swept the bar, sending a chill around us. The cold front that had followed us from the valley crept inside. It wasn't that delightful cold you could feel when winter was around the corner. This was darker, more ominous.

The Moonlight Outcasts ceased the music, their eyes fixated on the group of men entering. These men were uninvited—no denim vests on their chests, no markings of any kind other than expensive, tailor-made suits, bulges in their jackets from weapons and deep chuckles.

Delilah held onto my arm, pulling me closer to her, her eyes widening in fear.

"What's going on?" I whispered while the clicking of the expensive shoes entered the establishment.

These men walked with purpose, and the leader—with a small potbelly hanging over his leather belt, a receding hairline, and forehead wrinkles—rolled the cigar in his mouth.

Taking it from his mouth, he tapped it three times, letting the ash landed on the floor in front of him, a signal that stopped the caravan behind him.

The Iron Fangs stood from their seats around the various tables, their hands rubbing the weapons hidden in their vests. They glared at the intruder.

"That's the mayor from the next town over," Delilah whispered, pulling me closer to the wall next to the bar. The door beside us was closed, a sign that said "private entrance" painted in red. "He's bad news. I've heard the guys talk about it. He smuggles women into trafficking rings. That's the word on the street, anyway. All the citizens of their town love him though, think he is some kind of hero getting rid of the homeless, thinking that he is establishing some sort of housing. Instead, he's killing the men and selling the women."

My lips parted, watching Locke step forward out of the group of men that surrounded him protectively. They were loyal to him, despite him looking younger than some of the men here.

Yet, he wasn't all bite when he was alone with Grim. He brought food several times to us and always gave a warm smile and wink before he closed the door.

But looking at him now, I saw there is something dark inside him. His pained expression, his clenched jaw, he was a biker I would never want to cross. However, he took care of his own; his club. He had protected me and other women like me, as well as given Grim time away from the brotherhood.

"Sorry to inform you," Locke said. "But it's club night. No outside customers on Thursdays. I'm afraid I'm going to have to ask you to leave."

A wave of uneasiness seeped into the room. The mayor rolled his cigar between his fingers and tossed it to the floor, without stepping on it to put out the light.

There was something oddly familiar about the man that caused me to squirm where I stood. Something dark, something evil, and it only appeared as soon as Delilah told me he was the head of a sex trafficking ring.

When he spoke, I recognized his voice, but I wasn't sure from where.

"Greetings, President," he boomed. "Just wanted to check out the establishment. My own citizens come out here to partake in your services. Had to see it for myself."

The bar wasn't anything fancy; it catered to bikers. It wasn't some uptight establishment like he was thinking, apparently. His frown deepened, watching the club members circle his group.

"Thought it would be cleaner, but obviously I was mistaken."

"Now that you had your look," Locke said. "I'd appreciate it if you left. This is a private event. Why don't you come back for karaoke night? I'm sure you'd fit in there."

I floundered, listening to Locke's firm tone. It wasn't playful. He didn't find this funny in the slightest. Maybe it was because he was being insulted on his own turf.

I waited for the reply from the Mayor, but he continued to gaze around the bar. Taking in the full scenery, committing it to memory until he laid his eyes on the back corner of the bar where Delilah and I stood. His eyes widened, and a sneer fell on his lips.

"Well now, it seems I know someone here."

My back hit the wall. His steel-blue eyes were cold as they bore into my skin. I felt dirty in his presence as he leered at me. He took slow calculated steps toward me. Grim made his anger known by grunting and pushing his friends out of the way.

"Yes, yes, I remember you." He waved his finger.

But I couldn't place him. I knew him from somewhere. The voice it was there, but...the face? I couldn't remember his face.

An older woman—maybe in her fifties or sixties—sitting in the corner at an empty table, stood. She wore no vest, but if she was in the bar, I guessed she was safe to be here.

Her steps were quick as she reached me before the mayor did and tugged on my arm to pull me lower. Her hands cradled my face, and I gasped, feeling her warm touch.

"One eye, open. Two will be too much," she muttered to herself. "Close your eyes, dear."

Despite the movement around the bar, Delilah stood in front of me to block the onlookers. I stood still, listening to this woman who was touching me.

One swipe of her thumb over my right eye zapped the inside of my brain. The sharp prick waking up a memory I had long forgotten.

It was the Mayor, but he stood above me with a gleam of lust in his eye. *"Shame she has to be so drugged up for this. I like them squirming."* The click of the belt buckle snapped me from the memory.

Just as fast as the memory appeared, it vanished, but his face remained.

This man, along with many others, had ruined my body.

"Oh my God!" I screamed, backing away from the woman. Her solemn eyes of pity turned to glare at the Mayor. He didn't make it very far into the bar. Hawke had drawn his weapon and pushed it into his side.

The bodyguards that stood near the mayor were already subdued, hands held behind their backs and their guns sitting on the bar.

My sob rattled me, my knees weakening. Hands rushed to cover my mouth as I began to collapse. But Grim was there, like he always promised to be, catching me before a fall.

"What's wrong?" He clutched me, the gentle strokes of his hand in my hair steadying me. Everything was going to be fine. Grim was here. My protector.

"He touched me," I rasped. "He raped me."

CHAPTER TWENTY-ONE

Journey

It was all I could do to stand while Grim gripped me by the shoulders. His fingers tightened, and his fierce gaze made me tremble. Fire burned in the pits of his dilating pupils.

"What?" he growled.

It wasn't his normal growl. This was laced with a fierce fire I'd never heard before. It wasn't a growl that elicited pleasure from my body. It was deep and guttural, like an animal was living inside him. On instinct, I tried to back away, the fury in his face becoming far too intense.

This wasn't Grim I was looking at. It was someone, something else entirely.

The flashing strobe lights near the band faded, with the music no longer playing, they rose from their stools in which they sat. They glared, setting their instruments into their stands. The mayor himself had been called out, by me. All eyes in the room weighed heavily on me, still processing my words.

My lungs constricted, my throat closing in on itself. The more air I tried to swallow, the more I needed.

The room darkened around me, all eyes focusing on me. I was in a crowded room with a man that had touched me in intimate ways I would have never agreed to. Whatever that woman did to me, touching me with her thumb crossing my eye, brought back what I thought was long forgotten.

"Grim, you're gonna have to stand down," Bones said as he stepped out of the private room behind me. "You're scaring your mate."

Bones reached out to pry Grim's fingers from my shoulder.

Grim snarled and snapped his teeth, saliva drooling from his lips. His canines elongated with that snap, giving way to sharp points. I pushed away from Grim to get away from the sudden morphing of his face.

Grim's eyebrows softened for a split second, but the teeth remained the same. They were pointed, too large for his mouth. And the longer he stared at me, his beard seemed to grow, stretching further up his face to cover his cheeks.

I couldn't possibly be seeing things. He was staring right at me. The hair, or fur, continued to creep up his face as I shook in horror.

"Talk to him!" Locke yelled at me as he approached.

I sputtered, too stunned to speak, barely getting enough oxygen.

The mayor and his posse were still held captive in the middle of the room.

"Talk to him!" Locke yelled again with a pleading voice. "Talk to him, Journey."

Grim snapped, pulling me to his chest. The back of my shirt ripped, and I cried. Despite his face changing, the enormous teeth that had appeared in his mouth, I still found safety in his arms.

"You can't ask her to do that!" Bones yelled. "She's going into shock!"

I was watching everything in slow motion as Locke pursed his lips, anger flaring in his eyes. The cigarette slowly fell from his mouth. I blinked, and he was gone from my line of sight.

Locke appeared in front of me again, a devilish smirk appeared.

"Grim, look over there. He touched your woman; you better get to it before someone else does," he taunted. It all came out in slow, spaced out words, and I could hardly recognize what the hell Locke was doing.

"That is not what I–" Bones couldn't even finish his sentence before Grim let go, and I stumbled to the floor.

Grim stalked toward the mayor, whose eyes widened in fear at the human wrecking ball coming at him. I blinked, watching long claws coming out of Grim's fingers, swiping the air in front of the mayor, ripping the tailored clothes off his body.

Hell broke loose in the bar. Iron Fangs dragged the mayor's guards away, raining punches onto the nicely dressed men.

A gunshot went off in the back, it ricocheted off one of the overhead lights of the pool table and turned one corner to darkness.

"Get the servers in the back!" Locke yelled, his arms flying over one of his own men as he pulled them away from a guard.

I gasped as Bones picked me up, pulling me to his side. He turned my head so I could no longer witness what Grim was doing, but the yells and cheers from the others inside the bar gave me exactly what I needed to know.

Grim was going to kill the mayor.

Grim's roar echoed in my ears when I stumbled into the back room. Bones's tight grip loosened, giving me the ability to look around the room. It was dimly lit, and the dark walls were a bright contrast from the series of computer screens. Maps littered the wall. Pictures with faces of men and women were pegged on them, red strings and post-it notes indicating the relationship between them.

I reached for the table that held hordes of computers. This wasn't just some normal biker club, just as Delilah said. They were a type of special forces search and rescue.

A switch clicked to my right, turning on a naked lightbulb that swung from the ceiling in the middle of the room.

"We're safe in here. No one will get in unless they have the right fingerprint. Are you alright, Journey?"

I nodded, my fingers entangling together. "Yeah," I whispered. As good as I could be when after meeting a man that had raped me.

That woman gave me a glimpse and only a glimpse of his face before the deed was done.

Who was she?

Delilah and the other servers sat on couches, chairs, and on the floor. Hawke was wagging his finger at Delilah, who was currently scowling at him.

"You stay, don't get up. You don't leave here until I escort you out." Hawke turned, not giving me a second glance, and opened the door.

Breaking glass, shouts, and snarls trickled into the room.

We all winced at the loud sound until Bones shut and locked the door with a click. "Sound proof room, you won't need to worry about all that," he chuckled nervously.

I glanced at the monitors to see what was going on outside, but all of them were off, except for one that was attached to a laptop. Bones was watching it intently, the sound off while we all waited for what we were to do next.

What were we to do? They shoved all of us who were not part of their club—anyone not wearing a vest—into a room filled with monitors that could show us the outside. Part of me felt it wasn't just keeping us away from the fight but hiding what kind of fight it was.

Not only did Grim go crazy, but others did as well. They weren't listening to Locke. They attacked anyone or anything that was moving.

My stomach turned into knots. It was Grim that gave me an uneasy feeling. He wasn't right, something was terribly wrong, and we were shoved in here to keep us away from him.

The raw meat, the "nest," the growls, the purrs. It was all coming together.

"Why did I not notice it before?" I whispered.

Delilah left her seat on the couch with the others and grabbed my arm. She pulled me to the wall and leaned against it, scooting me to the floor.

"Do you find anything strange with Hawke?" I asked, staring straight at the other side of the empty wall. Bone's leg was in my peripheral as I watched him sway as he looked at the monitor.

"How so?" she asked.

"Face changing, eyes weird colors," I mumbled.

"No, just that he won't commit," she chuckled nervously. "Why face changes? What do you mean?"

I shook my head, my eye twitching. It was bad, and Delilah went to touch it with her fingers, but I grabbed them before she could.

"Does he ever growl?" I said too loudly.

I turned to gauge her reaction. I didn't just catch her attention, but Bones's as well. He pushed the laptop screen down and eyed me carefully.

"Growling, purring, eating raw meat?" I panicked. "When you look into his eyes, do you see a shadow? An animal? Maybe a wolf on the other side?"

My breathing grew erratic, my hands shaking until I thrusted my fingers into my tangled hair. It was all coming together. How did I not see? There was something inside him, an animal.

How could anyone not notice?

"Honey, I think you are having a panic attack. Everything is fine. Grim will take care of that man," Delilah soothed.

"No, no, no. I'm not upset about that. It's more. Grim is so much more. Hell, maybe all of them!" My eyes widened, watching Bones pulling a syringe out of his bag.

Shit.

I grabbed my chest, feeling the unbearable pressure sitting above my heart. "He had fangs! Long, sharp fangs, his eyes glowed, his fingers had claws, Delilah!"

The room went quiet, hearing my panic. They stood from their seats, shuffling to the other side of the room. No one believed me. They looked at me with pity while I tried to stand.

"It's true! I saw it!" My voice reached an unbearable squeal. "I saw him! I did. His face grew more hair." My hands trailed up my cheeks, scratching them. "His eyes. There was an animal inside him!"

"We all know there is an animal in Grim. He kills for fun," one man said. He scoffed, sitting back in his seat.

Bones put his hand on my shoulder, the syringe in his other hand. "Let's calm down now, alright. I don't want to poke you, because Grim will have my hide, but I need you to relax."

"Please don't. I'll be quiet."

"God, you are such a jerk," Delilah scolded. Her arm went around me as I shivered. "I swear, I don't even believe you're an actual doctor. When a woman is having a panic attack, you console, not drug her!"

"I'm not great with emotions, I suppose." He looked sheepish as he put the syringe away. "Not used to females."

My lips wobbled as I kept my mouth shut. I would not be drugged, not again. God, they all thought I was crazy, but I knew what I saw. I was not hallucinating. Grim was something more. They all were. They had to be.

The door burst open, the knob smashing into the wall and getting stuck.

My head hung low, and I watched the leather boots lift from the floor. Heavy, calculated footsteps entered while everyone gasped. Fresh, deep crimson blood dripped onto the floor, banging into my head like drums. It sounded like a death march, waiting for the next victim to appear.

The few tears that dripped down my cheek grazed my collar bone, waking me from my panic. I took my heavy head and raised it to see Grim paused in the middle of the room, staring back at me. His eyes no longer held the fire, his beard was neatly trimmed the way I liked it, and no fangs hung from his mouth.

Grim was different. I know I didn't dream it. The tapestry had been unraveled, and I was now seeing him for the first time.

A fairytale is what I wanted as a child. I prayed to the moon I would get some sort of blessing, so I could live my life differently. And I had, and it's led me to him. This beast that just took down one man of the many that ruined me.

"Grim," I mouthed his name.

He stepped forward, approaching me like a wounded animal. And I was weak compared to him.

Instead of Grim picking me up off the floor, like I knew he was fighting to do. To tuck me into his side and take me away from all the prying eyes, he lowered his body, taking a knee to reach my eye level.

His body was covered in blood—his face, his hands, and even underneath his fingernails. I blinked, taking in his appearance, but it wasn't the blood that I was afraid of, it was the beast that lurked beneath.

But should I really be scared? All this time, he contained this animal beneath him and not once had he intentionally hurt me. He kept me safe from others; he nursed me back to health.

He was far better than any human I had ever encountered.

Grim raised his hand, palm up, waiting for me to take it. A shadow rushed across his eyes until they settled on me. Rising to my knees, I set my gaze deeper. The shadow inside was indeed a wolf, and the anger he displayed earlier was not at me, but for my enemy.

He'd killed for me.

As I probed deeper inside him, the deep red wolf came into view. I could see the gorgeous wolf I'd seen in the forest just hours ago inside of Grim's mind.

My body shivered as the adrenaline left it. Grim's overwhelming presence no longer made me fear him. Animal, beast, or human, he was my soul.

Without a second thought, I fell into Grim's arms. He held me close, pulling me into his embrace, purring while I gripped my arms around his neck.

"Mine," he murmured into my hair.

CHAPTER TWENTY TWO

Grim

I turned to give Journey her time with Delilah. Journey had expressed she would like to stay with me, and I knew she would have to have some female companionship. The only human I felt comfortable with was Delilah, Hawke's woman that he wouldn't claim.

Suspicions arose in me. She could be his mate. He had held onto her for nearly two years, not letting any male near her after helping in her rescue. Hawke had put her under his wing since that day, like I had with Journey. Yet he had not claimed her in the slightest.

As I walked away, I saw Locke in the corner at a standing table. He rested a leg on a stool, his elbow propped up, smoking the fifth cig of the night. That was never a good sign.

He loomed over the shifters sitting around, gambling, drinking, pissing in the wind, and telling sob stories of old times. He jerked his jaw, beckoning me over, and I greeted him with a shake to the forearm.

"Any progress?" His gaze moved to Journey, who was smiling at something Delilah said.

My wolf growled impatiently because he wanted that smile to himself, but Journey was human. She deserved to have companions of her own gender to help her flourish and grow.

"We are getting there," I grumbled, taking a cig out of Locke's pocket.

He pulled out a lighter, and I puffed a few times until I began coughing violently. He chuckled, as he sucked the fiery smoke into his body, and I threw the cig in the ashtray.

"The hell is in that?" I continued to cough, clearing my throat.

"It's just a normal one. Maybe the problem lies in your wolf."

I rubbed my chest, my wolf growling angrily. He snapped inside my mind, furious I would even attempt to harm my lungs.

Right, we had something to live for now.

Locke waved two of his fingers to Hawke, inviting him to join us. He put out the rest of his cig and popped a piece of nicotine gum in his mouth. His wolf had given up, like so many of us had. No wonder he kept seeking comfort from harmful human addictions.

"We've got some company coming in," Locke said as Hawke approached our small table.

Locke tapped the earpiece, bracing it in his ear. "Switch is off tonight, but apparently he is working from his room. We've got the mayor we saw when we rescued Journey from the warehouse. He's got some back up, too."

"How many and what species?" Hawke asked, putting his hand on his concealed weapon. His thumb thrummed over the metal to give himself comfort.

"Maybe four and species unknown. I have a feeling they are human, but they know what we are. Switch said he saw them on camera handing each other what appeared to be knives. I'm betting they're laced with silver or wolfsbane."

I growled, fist tightening. Journey laughed with Delilah, taking sips of a yellow drink.

"I don't think they're going to be a problem to deal with. They're entering the lion's den." Locke chuckled, his eyes gazing over to Morpheus—a lion shifter—at the next table. Locke groaned, shaking his head at the stupid metaphor.

"You are just going to let them in?" Hawke hissed. "We have Journey and helpless human women here; you can't be serious."

"Oh, I'm dead serious." Locke's stared at the door, waiting for their arrival. "We have been hunting him, and now he is right here on a silver platter."

Hawke groaned at another metaphor and rubbed his eyes with his fingers. "Fine, but we need to let others know of the possible hidden weapons."

Locke waved his hand indifferently. "They already know. I've got a little errand boy making the rounds. Now, I need both of you to remain cool. I'll be doing the talking, then we'll have them escorted to the basement. We have to question these fuckers, find out if there are any more parties. Our trail is running cold after the last party Grim missed."

I was usually more present in Locke's life, but after finding Journey, I had slacked on my duties. However, he wanted me to spend more time with my mate. He longed to find his own mate and wanted to see if he could truly get his hopes up if Journey and I solidified our bond.

Nothing like being the lab rat for your best friend.

My instinct to move to Journey was cut short when the frigid blast of wind came through the door, bringing in the humans. They were indeed human, defenseless humans amongst the shifters filling the bar.

The music paused, and the club members all stared at the humans. I could hear Morpheus chuckling, along with other members mumbling to themselves what idiots these humans had to be.

As Locke and the mayor talked, my wolf grew anxious. He paced inside me, ready to unleash the power that had been restored to him. Journey was here in the presence of someone who sold women into slavery.

My jaw ticked in agitation, especially when my mate gasped from the other side of the room. Her body trembled, and my wolf jumped to attention.

We pushed past Locke, Hawke, and the bystanders that stared at my mate. I pushed some so hard, they tumbled into others.

My heart raced until I had her in my arms. I wanted nothing more than to rip the bastard to pieces, but my mate needed me. She needed my touch.

As I held her in my arms, the only word that escaped her that registered was "rape." My wolf took over my body so quickly, I had no chance to hide the physical changes my body underwent.

Fear appeared in my mate's eyes. She wobbled, looking at me with her caramel eyes. My heart throbbed, but the rage I needed to expel was far too great.

Voices muffled around me, my fury overshadowing them all. I let go of my death grip on my mate's arms. My wolf's claws emerged, and I pivoted to face the mayor himself.

He paled, his enormous belly jiggled as he stumbled backward. "You," I growled, stepping forward and grabbing his collar.

Club members had already corralled the men that followed him, searching their pockets and bags for weapons. The mayor attempted to scream but stuttered, and my claws scraped over his chest.

I wanted to tear him apart piece by piece, make him suffer for touching what was mine and pay for any other females who suffered because of him.

Locke yelled, his commanding voice no longer able to control my wolf. My fangs erupted, leaking venom until I bit into the mayor's shoulder.

The yell of pain caused a chain reaction. Members who still held onto the faintest control of their animals snarled and began clawing at the intruders. This was their home, their den, their lair, their pack. Glass shattered onto the floor, men and women ripping clothes off the intruders.

The situation grew out of hand, but all I could do was watch from the inside of my mind. My wolf had become the driver, too busy wanting to seek vengeance for our mate.

"You touched her," my wolf snarled, ripping at his shoulder.

His pitiful screams filled the air, my venom making the bite that much worse. The serum helped break down bone, muscle, and skin. The burning stench of his skin filtered into the air, and satisfaction filled me as blood ran into my mouth.

My wolf groaned, lapping at the decaying flesh until Locke put his steady but firm hand on my shoulder. "He has to live. We have to find the others."

My wolf ignored him, my claws reaching around the mayor's neck, ready to slit his throat. "Think of Journey! Think of what she would want, Grim. She wants justice for all. She wants them all to die, every single one that touched her. How can we do that if you kill him now?"

What was left of an Alpha aura seeped through me. It barely touched us. We could overcome his alpha command, but his words gave us pause. We wanted all who touched our mate to pay, not just the mayor.

"That's it," he coaxed.

The room's sounds, muted from my intense rage, filtered back. The room filled with yells and snarls, softening as my rage depleted.

The mayor laid limp in my arms, his body smelling of blood and piss.

"Great job." Locke reached for the body, handing it off to Morpheus. He dragged his body and the men that accompanied the mayor to the cellar.

"I'm sorry," I choked. "I almost shifted."

"That you did," Locke mused. "But I'm glad you didn't, otherwise you would really have to explain yourself."

I already knew I would have to explain. Locke didn't see my fangs, didn't see that my face was forming into a snout, fur running up my body as my mate stared at me in horror.

Would she come to me again? Or ever feel safe again?

I turned, following her scent. The closer I came to the door, the more nervous I became. She could reject me, send me away like my first mate and all would be lost forever. I'd return to being rabid and slowly die a painful death when my wolf finally snapped and tried to kill my brothers and sisters.

I opened the door, heat radiating in my chest in anticipation. She sat by the wall, her legs pulled to her chest and her eyes gazing at the floor. My heart pounded in my ears as I approached, and the moment of truth revealed itself.

She stared up at me, but not in fear. She peered so deep into my soul, I could feel the bond thread together piece by piece to prepare for the steel cable that would tie us together for all eternity.

I lowered myself to my knees, ready to explain, but she wrapped her arms around my neck willingly.

I sighed in relief, my hand stroking her back until my wolf slipped out the traditional "mine."

Lifting my mate, who was as light as a feather, I strode to the door, the humans that worked in the bar all staring wide-eyed. I didn't even look at the doctor, who had a sedative in his hand. I growled lowly as I passed him.

My mate was in obvious distress, but even the thought of more drugs entering her system infuriated me.

Bones mouthed a "sorry," but he was already on my shit list.

Journey did not take her face away from the crook of my neck. Her soft breathing trailed down my blood-covered chest. We both smelled of blood by the time we reached the apartment.

My grip tightened around her, her fingers threading through the loose tendrils of my hair. Once I reached the bathroom, I turned on the water to the highest heat setting and sat her on the counter.

Her arms didn't leave my neck, her face staring up at me with wide eyes. "You're different," she whispered.

I could only nod as I gently removed her clothing. She didn't have any bruises or marks, for that I was thankful. I couldn't imagine holding my wolf back if something had happened in those brief moments we were separated.

Journey didn't protest. She let me peel away her undergarments, and once she was naked, I picked her up to put her in the shower. She wouldn't let go of my arm, pulling me to stay.

Toeing off my boots, I pulled off my cut and shirt. Pulling down my pants, I left the black boxer briefs on as I entered.

Journey didn't question it and allowed me to surround her with my body as we let the hot water stream down our skin.

I reached for the soap, cleaning her body. She didn't argue, didn't move. I waited for the tension in her body to appear, but it didn't.

It seemed she understood I needed to care for her, to hold her and keep her safe. For that, I was once again thankful because even my wolf calmed, laying inside me until he let out his contented purr.

Once Journey was clean, she turned to me, her body pressed against my chest, and grabbed the soap. She washed me, as I'd washed her, and my purr grew louder.

"So, it is purring," she muttered. "It isn't a humming sound I thought you were making, it's like a cat."

I growled.

"Not a cat. But...you can hear it?" I asked.

She looked up at me, blinking.

"Of course, I can hear it. I hear it when you're near me, touching me." She blushed. "I like it. It calms me, makes me feel safe."

I wrapped my arms around her, deepening the sound.

"Why does it do that? Is it because of what you are?" she asked.

"And what do you think I am?"

The water continued to pour around our bodies. Steam rose as she stood there. No fear in her eyes, no judgment or hesitation.

"I'm not sure of a name, but you are some sort of animal? One that can morph into a different person?" She tilted her head. "Like a werewolf or something?"

"It is exactly that," I told her. "I am what humans call a werewolf. Or shifter."

She rubbed her lips together, breaking eye contact and staring at my chest. Her finger traced the wolf on my skin, my cock hardening as she traced the outline.

"Are you afraid, little mate?"

Journey shifted from foot to foot. The apprehension was there. I had not been completely honest with her and had partially shifted in her presence. Of course, she could be scared, worried that harm could come to her. She knew what I could do.

"I was at first, but for some reason, I know you won't hurt me. Strange to think that, isn't it?"

"It is the bond we share." I pushed a wet tendril behind her ear. "You are destined to be mine as I am to you. That is why I call you mate, because you are my soulmate."

Her mouth dropped open.

"How do you know I'm yours, though? Is it just a claiming thing?" she asks.

"No. The goddess has paired our souls—souls that will forever be entwined once I knot you."

CHAPTER TWENTY THREE

Journey

A knot? What the hell was that?

I swallowed the lump in my throat as he explained. It was downright terrifying that this man, this shifter, was part animal, but my heart was telling me it was okay. It was crazy to think, but I felt better knowing what he was after the questions that confused me previously.

He was a shifter, a wolf shifter.

I took one long breath out and tried not to stare down at his covered appendage. He still hadn't removed his undergarments while I stood there naked in the shower with him.

"I'll explain more soon," he said.

Grim turned off the shower, his muscles dripping with clean water that washed away the blood from god knows who. He opened the door, grabbed the large towel and wrapped me in it like I was fragile. And maybe I was compared to him. He was a literal beast.

Yet, I was unafraid.

He gestured with his head toward the door, and I stepped out and kept the towel wrapped around myself, suddenly feeling more vulnerable standing in the open living room alone.

He exited the bathroom, now covering his lower half with just the towel. I bit my lip, wondering if he had removed his boxers. I didn't know why I'd became so much more fascinated with what was underneath.

Because of my history, I shouldn't be.

I was insanely attracted to him, whether or not I liked it. I knew it in the depths of my soul, and whatever this goddess thing that put us together was, I was ready to believe it.

Grim stepped over to the side table by the couch, turning on the light. The night outside was chilly, and the heater that sat below the far window of the apartment fogged the glass.

"Sit with me." It wasn't a question because it didn't need to be.

I was ready to follow him, because he had destroyed one of my nightmares tonight, at least that was what it looked like to me.

I sat beside him on the couch, but he grunted in dissatisfaction and pulled me onto his lap. He leaned back on the couch, petting my arm with one hand, and the other arm slinked around my body.

"I am a shifter, more specifically a wolf. There are many of us, Journey. Wolves, dragons, bears. And there are even fae, vampires, and demons that roam this earth."

My eyes widened with curiosity. Could all the things I imagined and wished for to be real really be true? That all these creatures roamed the earth with us?

"There are good and bad in all species, just like humans. These fantasy beings are governed by an inner circle to stay away from humans. We stay with our own kind to keep them protected and keep our worlds apart. The earth is much bigger than you realize, Journey. Witches and warlocks keep our worlds apart, but sometimes the supernatural blend into the world of the humans. Sometimes supernaturals are banished or come here willingly to hide themselves and live amongst humans. To make a different life away from their home."

"So, they live in a realm or something? Another world that is here?" I pointed downward.

Grim grinned, his finger tracing each part of my face until he gently kissed me. His beard tickled my nose, and I smiled as he pulled away.

"It's a realm called Elysian. There is a great divide the keeps us separate. I was born in that realm, as well as everyone in the club." He frowned.

I bit my cheek. The next question I wanted to ask, I already knew the answer to. He didn't come here willingly. The scars were too deep; the pain and darkness hovering around us easily told me that.

The club was nothing but suffering. You could see the darkness in their eyes. It was like they were hiding, just waiting for death. That was why they risked their lives to save others. They had nothing left to live for.

But why?

They all lived together, knowing they would die together.

"I left, unwillingly." He ran a hand through his hair. "Like everyone in the club. I had a she-wolf that was supposed to be my mate. The goddess paired us to be with one another, but she rejected me.

Anger and jealousy flooded through me. I squinted, and my hands balled into fists.

Grim chuckled, his hand covering mine to relieve the tension.

"It all worked out for the best, little mate, just listen," he cooed.

I relaxed back into his embrace, trying to stop the angry thoughts of finding this she-wolf and dealing with her myself. Even if I was jealous, I wanted to slap her silly for rejecting Grim. He lost so much.

"I was an omega, born into a family of weak wolves. But I strived to be better, stronger." He gripped his fists tightly.

"I worked hard, excelled, and became the top warrior of my pack. I wanted my mate to have someone strong to protect her. It was a great honor to go from omega to warrior."

"And a pack is like a regular animal pack. You all lived together?" I asked.

"Yes, it is a place where a group of wolves lived together, communed, and ate. We strive to socialize and to work with one another. We are very social animals and need the bond with each other."

I nodded, waiting for him to continue. He really was part animal and took on those characteristics, but was human, too.

"The alpha, our leader, was proud of me. And soon, I found out his daughter was my mate. Supernaturals can find our soul mates between the ages of eighteen and twenty and when I turned twenty, I realized it was her." Grim looked away, his brow creasing.

"My soul called to her. My wolf wanted her to complete the bond that the goddess had blessed us with.

"I felt an unbearable heat in my chest. It was a feeling I felt when I was very young, when all the children would run to their parents, and they would love and cuddle them. Bring them presents on their birthdays, tell them they loved them."

Jealousy continued to stir in my gut.

"She didn't want me," Grim gulped. "Despite my hard work to become worthy of her," he whispered.

Throwing my jealousy behind me, I cupped his cheeks to look at me. His eyes were so sad, the same sad eyes I first saw when he looked under the bed and found me completely broken.

"You were worthy, Grim. Every part of you is worthy. She was too blind to see you, too selfish to look at you and see who you really are. You have been everything to me and if she couldn't see what I see, then she is the one at fault."

Grim purred, his forehead leaned to touch mine. His hand reached around my neck to pull me closer to his forehead. I hummed back, trying to mimic his noise, but it failed horribly. This only made him chuckle and bury his nose in my neck.

My fingers threaded through his wet hair, my cheek laying against his shoulder. "So why do you think I'm your mate, then? Wasn't she meant to be yours?"

Grim kept his nose in my shoulder, sniffing my wet hair. "When we found out we were mates, I was excited. She put on a good show and acted like it, too. She told me she wanted to wait until that night and to meet her at our pack lake at midnight.

"I waited by the lake all day, too happy to see her. My wolf was tense however, he didn't like to wait and was furious with me until the moon was high in the sky. It was then I felt a horrible pain in my chest, like my heart was being ripped from my body. I screamed, howled, shifted, and my wolf drug his chest along the ground to ease the pain. I couldn't control him, and he went on a rampage."

Grim tensed, his body clutching me for support.

"I killed every animal in sight. Deer, squirrels, rabbits, and I could do nothing to stop my wolf. He wanted blood." Grim growled, his fingers digging into my skin.

He laid back on the couch, pulling me with him until I straddled his waist and my head laid on his chest. One of his legs hung over the couch, his body too large to hold both of us with my leg taking the other side of his body. He breathed in deeply while I rubbed his slightly hairy chest.

"I returned to my pack, my supposed family. They all looked at me in disgust. They knew what I'd done to the poor animals. I ripped them to shreds, none of it could be salvaged to eat. It was a crime to them, to destroy something that was a part of nature and then to waste it, so it wasn't usable.

The alpha deemed me a rogue and banished me to the human realm."

"A rogue? What does that mean?" I fluttered my lashes on his chest. "Why did your wolf lose control? What happened to your soul mate?"

Grim snarled, his body tensing. I lifted my head, my lips connecting to his until his body softened again.

"I'm sorry." He held me close. "I am happy to have you. I am just angry at the disrespect."

"What disrespect?" I asked.

"My supposed mate, she found another wolf. An alpha from another pack. They wanted to combine their packs to strengthen them. She mated and bonded with him. Breaking our connection. Leaving half of my soul broken."

I grasped Grim's shoulders. I gasped audibly at the quietness of the room.

"They laughed. The female said she never wanted an omega. 'Once an omega, always an omega.' She didn't care that I'd worked so hard for her. To give her a home, protection. Her father preferred her to be mated to a neighboring alpha anyway," he said sadly.

"What did you do?" I lifted my head and looked into his eyes.

"I took what few belongings I had and left. My parents watched me leave. They were not strong enough to leave the pack with me. Their wolves are too weak to disobey an alpha's command. They had to stay and work for the pack. They now see me as dead, because my wolf would slowly go rabid and eventually, my human self would fade away."

I shook my head. "But you're still human. You are right here!"

Grim smiled, his thumb brushing my cheek. "I am only still human because you saved me, little mate. The club was planning to put me out of my misery before you showed up. I was dying."

I reared my head back in shock. He grunted a laugh and pulled me back to his chest. "You are my second chance, Journey. My soul called for you the second my eyes met yours. The shock we felt when we first touched, the continued fire we share when our bare skin rubs against each other, the undeniable pull. All those things tell me you are mine. I don't know why the goddess gave you to me. I was about to turn rabid and die. So many before me have, but for some damn reason, you're here. The Moon Goddess that I had cursed for so long has blessed me again."

Grim went silent, and I wrapped my arms around him until my hands were pinned behind his back.

Despite my clit throbbing, feeling his heat on my body, I had to think.

Humans weren't alone. There was an entire world we didn't know about, and now I was supposed to be with this wolf. Because of a Moon Godde—

A Moon Goddess.

"Grim?" I muttered. "You said a Moon Goddess paired us together?"

He hummed an affirmative, slowly unwrapping my towel. His fingers grazed my back. Chills ran down my arms, feeling his touch.

There was no question about the fire like touches he left in his wake. My body was ready for him. Ready in ways I never thought I would be before.

My past was fading away—even the face of the man Grim very well could have destroyed.

"I prayed to the moon once," I said. Grim paused his fingers. "I prayed I would find a new life, somewhere safe, where fairy tale creatures were real and for someone to save me. To love me."

Grim pulled me to a sitting position. The towel fell from my breasts, but his eyes stayed glued to mine. "You, prayed? To the goddess?"

I nodded, my arms covering my chest. "Is this why we are together? Because I prayed to her?"

"Do humans pray to the moon normally?"

I shook my head. "No, I just ran out of people to pray to."

"Gods," he breathed. "It surely can't be that simple."

"What? What can't be that simple?"

"For a human to pray to the goddess. For happiness, for love, to find someone to take care of them."

"Did you not pray to the goddess for the same thing?" I tilted my head in question. He pursed his lips, shaking his head.

"We've all given up. You aren't supposed to be here. We aren't given second chances. If your mate rejects you and finds another to complete the bond with, you're shit out of luck. So, the whole club has rejected her, sees her as a dead."

"Maybe your club members need to pray to her again. Because I don't think humans are going to pray to the moon and ask for what they want because a lot of the time they don't know what they need."

Grim slammed his lips into me. His mouth was needy, hungry, as he slinked his tongue into my mouth. His hand gripped the back of my hair, pulling it tightly. The sharp pain in my head along with his naked body pressed up against me made my pussy roar to life, dripping for him to take me.

One hand cupped my breast, his fingers pinching, pulling. My body shivered in arousal, and my fingers tightened around his biceps.

"There is something very important I should tell you," he said between kisses.

I hummed in reply, kissing him back just as fiercely.

A fire had ignited between our bodies, and I couldn't stand another minute of him not touching me. This undying pull between us grew stronger, and the only thing that could sate it was for him to be inside me.

"Ah," I whimpered as his fingers dug into my ass. His claws lengthened and ripped the towel between us. It echoed into the room, and he pulled my chest into his.

"I am part wolf, Journey. My anatomy is different from a human's."

The haze of lust didn't care if his dick looked blue with black dots all over, I just needed it. I wanted to feel his cock inside me.

But most of all, I wanted to remember this. I wanted to know what it felt like to have his cock inside me and not just feel the aftermath.

"I have a knot," he panted. His hand reaching around and squeezing my ass. "It's at the base of my cock. It will expand and lock us in place once I release inside you."

My body didn't care. It wanted Grim.

His scent filled the air—the musk of the outdoors, the pine—and the rightness of it all soothed all my fears. Some sweet whisperings entered my ear, telling me it would be alright. That this was the gateway to something more than just Grim and I. It was opening a world for others to follow in our footsteps.

"Will it fit?" I asked breathlessly. He kissed me again, pushing me onto the couch. His hips gyrated against my core, and my pussy fluttered to life.

Wet, I was so wet I could feel it dripping down my legs.

Grim's nose flared, his eyes turning dark. The wolf behind his eyes stared at me with wanting, with lust and a desire I had never seen.

"You are my mate. It will fit." His mouth descended, kissing up my neck. My legs wrapped around his still clothed waist, and my whimpers became moans.

CHAPTER TWENTY FOUR

Grim

My lips did not want to leave the sweet taste of her skin, my carnal desires growing by the minute. The bond was pulling us deeper as Journey accepted this, accepted us.

She was taking it so well; it felt like a dream.

Humans and supernatural relationships were forbidden. It had been written in the laws of the Royal Council for thousands of years, yet here we were, our souls primed for bonding.

Those laws kept the humans safe when the supernatural ventured into the human world. If anyone found out, it would be a swift death for the supernatural and a memory wipe for the human.

It was all to keep the humans safe.

Who was to say that the mortals and supernaturals were to adhere to the laws of the land now? Especially when the goddess deemed our souls a match, and we were paired together.

Laws would be broken this night and hopefully for others just like me. No rogue would let this opportunity be spoiled by the Royal Council.

What would happen when we were bonded? Would her body accept me? Take my knot? I could only hope the goddess had it all planned out because I was uncertain how this would end. But I trusted the bond, a bond that had ruined me so many years ago.

But Journey prayed, my mate had prayed for a miracle, and here we were. A wolf and a human, defying all the odds of each of our worlds.

I was too excited, too alive to let this go. To wait and see what would become of us later by waiting for Bones to complete his research on the possibilities. My wolf wanted pups, eventually.

Only if Journey wanted them, too.

There wasn't any time. My wolf snarled for me to take her. To plant our cock inside her body, to knot her, to keep her safe. Have her smell drowned out by my own, so no other male would think of taking her from my nest.

She clawed my back, pulling my body further into her body. Her whimpers, the arousal between her legs growing by the minute.

Journey wrapped her legs around my waist, and I pulled her up to straddle me on the couch.

"Do you like our nest? Our den?" I pulled away to check her reaction. She was human, but the traditions embedded in me needed to hear her say it. That she was satisfied with the home I'd created for her, and I wanted her to be comfortable in it.

She paused, her eyes never leaving me. I waited, waiting for her to tell me she didn't understand what I was asking, but she reached up to cup my face and smiled happily. "It's a beautiful den and nest. Did you make it just for me?"

"Yes." I ran my hand up the side of her body, watching the chills erupt over her skin. "Only for you. It is my first."

We were taught as pups to create a perfect home for our mates. To make a bed soft and warm so our mates would feel comfortable. I watched my father make my mother's nest each night, so my mother would feel warm and secure.

"It's perfect, Grim. Just like you." She traced one of the many scars on my body. She didn't pity me; she cared for me.

The goddess prepared her for me. Opened her eyes to a world that she should be afraid of. But she wasn't. She really wasn't. This was far easier than I thought it would be.

Her fingers trailed down my neck, across the red wolf covering my chest. Her fingertips parted through my chest hair and moved lower between our bodies.

We were naked, our towels tossed aside. The base of my cock was touching her entrance. I could feel the heat against my knot. It was unbearable not to just slip it inside.

I watched her in earnest as she explored my body. Her delicate fingers stopped once she reached the head, her body tensing seeing my knot.

"You have a piercing?" She bit her lip, and I groaned, leaning my head on the couch.

Of course, I had to make it harder for her.

I pulled her hand closer to my dick, directing her fingers to play with the bars. "I did it when I was trying to get feeling back in my cock. I did it to punish myself." I swallowed. "But with my suffering, you can now feel pleasure."

She let out a hot, heavy breath, her pussy secreting more of her arousal down to my thigh. I groaned when she gripped my cock tighter.

"I want you, but I'm afraid," she said.

"You have nothing to be afraid of." I petted her hair. "The goddess has deemed us compatible. I will be gentle—"

"No, not that." She shook her head solemnly. "I'm not scared of that, but what if I carry a disease? I don't want you to get sick. Maybe I'm dirty.

I don't know what happened to me when–"

I growled, tightening my grip around her, burying her nose in my neck. "No human disease can hurt a shifter. You have no diseases that will impede your life. Bones took your blood while you were sick."

"But that doesn't detect everything—"

"Shifters can heal, my little mate. No human diseases have ever infected a shifter." Journey rubbed her red lips together in thought. "I will take you to a human doctor for more testing. I did not want anyone touching you without consent."

She grasped my shoulders, her hips moving against me. I tightened my hold as she tested my resolve.

"I can't get pregnant. They inserted an implant into my arm."

Bones thought as much when he checked the upper part of her arms for bruises. I wanted him to remove it, but ultimately, it was her decision.

My wolf groaned when he imagined her with a swollen belly.

"Good, then I won't feel guilty when I tell you I won't wear a condom. I must feel the walls of your pussy when you engulf my cock. The bond needs as much skin contact as possible."

Journey gasped, her nipples tightening. She relaxed her shoulders and leaned closer.

"Now, will you accept my knot, my mate? Because I cannot hold back much longer. If you wish to wait, I can take care—"

"No, I want it. I want it more than anything. To belong, to complete what this Goddess has intended for us. I can feel that it's right."

I wrapped her legs around my naked body and strode over to the bed. I planted her in the middle, the blankets and pillows all perfectly surrounding us.

The nest was laid perfectly. Her body was prepared, and my cock was a steel rod ready to sink into her. But I wanted to make her sweet cunt drenched before I squeezed my knot inside her.

I purred in my chest as I kissed her lips, tracing my lips down the column of her neck to her breasts. I nipped at the underside of her breast until my lips wrapped around her hardened nipple. Her hands threaded in my hair, pulling me close, both of our hips thrusting to gain friction against our aching lower bodies.

I trailed wet kisses down her stomach, down her navel, and to her mound. A small patch of curls decorated the entrance to her pussy, and I instantly took in a long, heavy breath through my nose.

"You smell delicious," I murmured.

My tongue parted her folds, reaching deep inside her cavity. Her breath quickened, her fingers tightening around the layers of blankets on the bed while she mumbled incoherently.

I pushed her legs further apart, baring her body to me. Her breath hitched; her eyes laced with worry.

"I will take care of you, mate." I moved my nose through her curls while my tongue flicked her clit.

"Grim!" she said breathlessly as I sucked. I gripped her ass as I feasted on her. She lowered her legs, locking me into place as I ate her delicious cunt.

I pushed my fingers into her channel, feeling the tightness of her pussy. It fluttered, suckling me inside while I added another digit. I groaned, feeling the tight walls. I paused my assault on her clit to lick the juices covering my fingers.

Her body spasmed, her legs widening so I could once again add another finger. She will needed to take me, my cock, my knot, and I wanted her well prepared to take what I wanted to give her.

I needed her utterly soaking.

Her body spasmed again, her pussy tightening around my fingers. She tightened her pale legs around my head, and a long moan filtered through the air. I pressed my cock firmly into the mattress. My hips, on their own accord, pushed into the blankets, seeking relief. My cock was achingly hard, my knot at the base of my cock swelling feverishly.

Sweet nectar filled the nest, my wolf howling inside me for a job well done. Her pussy was ready. She was going to take my body into hers.

I crawled up her stomach, my body shaking with anticipation. "I'm claiming you, Journey. As mine always. We will be paired in this life and the next. Do you accept?"

Journey's caramel eyes blinked, her reddened lips parting. "I never thought that something like this would happen to me." My nose tickled her chin, down her jawbone, planting wet kisses on her neck. "I should run away, Grim. I should shy away from all this."

"But you won't," I stated. "Because you feel it too, don't you?"

"I do." She nodded. "Someone whispers to me to trust you. I don't know if it's just my mind going crazy, but I'm going to trust it."

The goddess could present herself in many forms. It might be an animal, a gentle brush of the wind, or even mutterings of encouragement. I never believed in that, even as a pup, but I wanted to believe it more than anything right now.

She wrapped her arms around my back. My cock nuzzled her entrance, smoothing my precum across her clit. With the bond stretched tight, my body leaned into her slowly, sinking into the warmth of her pussy.

I was riding her bare, taking her in for all that she was. Her slick walls enveloped my cock, and I sighed heavily, taking in long tantalizing breaths to control my resolve.

"It's big." Journey gripped my shoulders, little half-moon circles from her nails staying embedded in my skin. "Oh, it's big."

We both panted. Her body was completely still as the length of my cock stayed buried deep.

"Journey?" I whispered. "Journey, are you okay?"

I had been selfish as a mate. I did not even consider her past. She must be terrified. Me hovering on top of her.

"Yes, now, please move," she urged.

I grinned, pulling my cock from her body, only to slip it back inside her. Her soft mewls, her hands tightening around me, urged me to continue. My wolf considered her form—a small, tiny human. We could not rut her, not now, not when it was her first time feeling pleasure from any man.

We were not each other's firsts, but we were each other's lasts.

I grunted, pushing deeper inside her. My cock was painfully hard and incredibly tight in her pussy, but that didn't deter her when she wrapped her legs around my waist.

"More," she begged.

My wolf growled, my eyes darkening. My wolf wanted this. He wanted to complete the bond before she tried to leave, not that she ever would. Journey was ours. In the short time we knew each other, she knew the connection we had. She accepted it; she accepted us despite her own pain.

Journey's back arched, and she let out a long breathy cry with my name on her lips. I gripped behind her back, pulling her up until she sat on my cock in the middle of the bed.

My hands roamed her back, her lips crashing into me. I drank her in, gripping her ass while I bounced her against me.

She gripped my shoulders, her knees firmly planted beside me as she helped guide my throbbing cock back inside her. She lowered her sweet eyes, watching the knot at the base grow.

"It's going inside you," I growled. "It's going to fill you, then I'm going to mark you."

I slammed my lips back onto her, pushing her back into the mattress. I thrusted like a wild animal, and more of her sweet come dripped from her pussy. She was drenched, the sheets below us covered in her arousal.

My wolf purred deeply, claiming the walls of her pussy until my knot slipped inside. I could feel it growing as it entered, and Journey let out a delectable moan at the tightness as it swelled near her clit. I could still move, and my wolf anxiously took over.

He growled, each thrust causing grunts and snarls of approval at the base of our throat. He became feral in his own right, rutting her into the sheets.

Journey's pussy fluttered, her moans rippling tiny bumps down her arms. "Grim!" she convulsed as she reached her orgasm.

Panic ensued, my body trembling because I could no longer control the movements to keep her safe. I yelled inside myself, watching as my mate took the thunderous thrusts to her pussy as my wolf enjoyed his takeover of our human body.

"Another. I want another," he snarled.

She cried out, her head rolling from side to side with each thrusting stroke. Her chocolate brown hair creating a halo around the pillows. She was a damned fucking goddess. Her continued screams heightened in pleasure while my wolf wrecked her soft body.

"I can't," she panted. "Goddess!"

My mate had accepted the will of the goddess. Her cries calling out to her in ecstasy as we completed the threaded bond we wove. I took back some of the control and pistoned my cock at such an angle it hit both the top of her mound and the spot deep inside her cunt.

"Come again," I begged her. I wanted her sated. I wanted to know she was happy with our endeavors.

"Ahh!" she fell from her mountain of pleasure. Her arms falling away from my body and landing in the pillows.

"Mine," my wolf and I shouted.

Our voices came out as two snarling beasts as my mate's pussy clenched around us, and my cock released spurt after spurt of seed.

My knot expanded to the fullest potential, and I was unable to move. We were locked in place, and my wolf lowered his head and pierced the skin on her shoulder.

Journey closed her eyes, her head lulling to the side while my wolf licked the blood from her wound as he clung to her, both in body and soul.

If she was a wolf, she would have bitten me in return. We would have latched our souls together as one. Since the goddess deemed us paired souls, I hoped my bite would be enough.

My wolf released her shoulder. The bite was deep, and her skin would not heal as quickly. My wolf retreated, unbothered by the bite marks on her tender skin.

While I hovered over her, locked inside her, I rose on my forearms, petting my mate's head as she stirred awake. She smiled, her hand too heavy to lift to my face.

"That was something," she said. Her eyes lowered, seeing that we were still locked together. "How long are we like this?"

"I do not know. I have never knotted before," I said honestly.

She smiled at that, nuzzling into my elbow that laid near her head.

I waited for her to ask about the obvious bite mark on her neck, but her eyes fluttered shut.

"Sleep my mate," I purred heavily.

"I like it when you do that," she whispered. "Makes me feel safe."

"You will always be safe with me, little one. We are connected in body and soul now."

Her eyes shut and I hovered over her while my knot rested in her channel.

CHAPTER TWENTY FIVE

Journey

The sunlight filtered onto the bed, the rays warming my cheeks as I turned over.

Last night was certainly magical. My mind was opened to a whole new world that I never could have dreamed of. With that, I was mated to one of those beings that I had only read about as a child.

A shifter, more like werewolf. But there were more of them. Animals, beings that defied all scientific logic in the human world. And I was mated, or soul bonded, to one of them, because their goddess deemed us worthy.

And I believed it.

It was because I wanted to believe it, wanted to believe there was some sort of higher power out there that would listen. If I had known that the goddess was real when I was just a child, I would have spent much more of my time gazing into the glowing orb in the sky.

She sent Grim to save me; she sent me to save Grim. We were two broken souls that had mended each other in ways no one else could.

I smiled, delightfully sore after our joining. We were to be together forever now, as his goddess proclaimed to his kind. Now that a human was in the mix, did that mean I should continue to pray to her? And were their other gods out there that needed to be prayed to?

I rolled onto my shoulder and winced. Deep, penetrative bite marks were embedded in my skin. I couldn't see the indentions of his teeth, but I could definitely feel them. When Grim said he would "mark" me, I wasn't sure what it would entail. He was more worried about his knot, and rightfully so, but this was something I wasn't expecting.

It didn't hurt; it was a delightful singe that reminded me of our touch when we first met. The bar bells on the underside of his dick were quite awesome, too. It rubbed me in places I never thought would feel good.

"Grim?" I rolled to my stomach. The blankets were stuffed around me, keeping me wrapped like a burrito. He loved making sure I was warm and hidden beneath the blankets, like some pup.

Grim was nowhere to be found until I heard a grunting noise in the bathroom.

I grabbed the blanket, pulling it around my naked body. Our "nest," Grim called it, was a mess, but his scent dominated it. His smell was certainly more potent. I could smell the deep woodsy scent he radiated and could sense it on my skin.

I padded to the door and heard a painful grunt on the other side. My worry intensified, my heart thrumming in my chest.

"Grim?" I knocked, and the shuffling on the other side of the bathroom door stopped. "Are you alright? What's going on?"

"Nothing," he rasped. "Everything is fine, my mate. I'm sorry I'm not in our nest."

I clutched the blanket tighter at the sound of the pain in his voice, looking back at our nest and back toward him.

"Grim, I'm worried." I pushed on the door, but it was locked. "Why won't you let me in?"

"Are you okay?" He quickly replied.

His hand thumped on the door.

I shook my head. "Of course I am, Grim. You're scaring me. What's going on?"

He sighed heavily, his feet scuffling along the bathroom floor. "Our mating caused my rut to return."

I paused, backing away from the door. A rut? What the heck was a rut?

Grim's groans came back, a slapping of skin resonating through the door.

I've heard of ruts for deer and horned animals. Surely he wasn't talking about the same thing.

Another grunt and a sigh echoed in the bathroom, and I realized it was quite possible. What wasn't possible at this point? I was mated to a wolf!

"C-can't I help you with that?" I asked bravely.

The door knob turned, and a very exhausted looking Grim stepped out.

He was naked, and his dick was hard, come spilling from the angry purple head. It continued to drip as he fisted it, and the knot at the base was tight and bulbous.

Instead of feeling appalled, I felt heartbroken for him. He was in pain, and he was taking care of it while I slept.

"Why didn't you wake me?"

"Wake you? Journey, a rut can be difficult for shifters. I can't imagine what my wolf would do if my wolf got his hands on you again. I had a hard time controlling him last night." He groaned again, gripping his shaft.

"But if we are supposed to be together, doesn't that mean I'm supposed to handle it?" I stepped forward, brushing my lips across his chest.

My desire flooded through me. I don't know if it was his vulnerability, his sweet thoughts about trying to keep me away from his animal, or not waking me to help with his pain, but it made me fall deeper into this pit of emotion I'd carved out of my heart for him.

I had fallen for this man that had saved me and, in turn, I saved him.

"Grim, I love you."

Grim still had his hand on his shaft, his lips parting and his breath ragged. The furious bulbous head of his cock was pointed straight at me.

"Me?"

"What other emotion is it then when I gave my soul to you last night?" I chuckled. "I had to love you to do it, and if we are going to make this work, I need to take all of you." I stepped forward, rubbing my hands down his stomach until I gripped his shaft.

This connection between us was powerful, and between his raging cock and my dripping core, I knew what I had to do next.

Desire pooled between my thighs, I dropped onto my knees in front of him. He rested his hand on the door, leaning against it to steady himself and shut his eyes tightly.

I licked the tip of his cock, it still leaked come from the tip as I put it into my mouth. His balls tightened, and the piercings brushed against my tongue.

"Gods!"

I could hear the splitting of wood between his fingers or claws.

My mouth widened, sucking in the smooth velvety texture. The head was swollen as it dripped down my throat. I couldn't take in the knot, so my hands cupped it gently, caressing the tightness of the bulge. I massaged it tenderly while I bobbed my head continuously.

"Fuck!" Grim reached for the back of my head, as he pulsed his hips. I followed his lead, going faster and sucking harder. The bulge tightened; my hand squeezed around it until a large load ran down the back of my throat. The bulge that I had hoped would soften to give relief only filled again.

I swallowed the rest of the load, only to be pulled up from the ground. Grim slammed his mouth on me, tasting himself on my tongue.

"If it's too much, tell me," he snarled, tossing me on the bed.

I giggled at the roughness. Grim was a puppy to me, but his desirous snarls and growls turned me on more and more. His heated gaze made me pant, and he smiled as he climbed over the top of me.

This was my Grim.

He thought his animal would be too much, but I saw those deep black eyes roaming my body last night. His wolf had taken control, and it turned my body into a heated furnace of lust. He would not be too much. I already knew that. My body was thrumming with desire, and my once torn and broken body had been forgotten.

I couldn't even pull the memory of what the man at the bar looked like after that old woman had unclouded my eyes. It was all gone, the nightmares, the memories. All forgotten.

There was only Grim.

He snarled, rolling me onto my stomach. He gripped my hips and lined up his cock at my entrance. "So wet," he growled. His heavy breath brushing over my back. I arched, wiggling my butt to taunt him further.

"You smell so good." His voice audibly changed. It was like two beings inhabiting one voice, and my pussy throbbed hearing it.

"You like me here too, don't you?" The deepened voice said. "You like knowing we both will rut you until we are satisfied. Until you are satisfied being filled with our seed."

I whimpered, his words playing my clit like a fiddle.

One thrust was all it took for me to cry out as he bottomed out. His shaft was thick and heavy, his thrusts wild while he leaned over my body, coating my skin with his.

He reached around, holding my breasts, pinching and rolling my tits with his fingers.

I cried out over and over as he continued to thrust into me. His seed continued to apply thick coats to the walls of my pussy. His knot formed at the base. But this differed from last night. It didn't lock inside me. It would spill and release for him to continue his rutting.

I could feel the piercings rubbing next to my clit. Each time he pulled out to thrust in again I could feel them rub up and down my clit.

Grim was panting after his third round. His sweat dripped down his chest and onto my back. His cock showed no signs of letting up nor his grip of loosening.

He hammered me like he was truly rabid, and I couldn't complain one bit.

"I'll ride you," I said boldly.

He paused, his muscles shaking with weakness. He let his cock fall from my body, and I turned to straddle him as he fell into the blankets. His eyes hooded, he held his cock in place.

"Journey, I'm sorry," he rasped. "It–"

"Shh." I traced his finger with my lip. "Let me take care of you now."

He closed his eyes, and I positioned myself over the head, thrusting down hard, making us both cry out. I jumped on his cock repeatedly, feeling my orgasms rising and falling. There was no end in sight. His cock continued to bulge and release.

Come dripped down my thigh; it coated us both and landed into our nest. Neither of us seemed to care that our arousal saturated each other.

Grim's hands roamed my body, holding my hip with one hand to help and my breast with the other.

I should be exhausted by now. I lost count of how many times I orgasmed. He begged me for more, but my clit was swollen, each rise and fall of my hips scraping against it.

"Come again," he would growl.

My breath was ragged, my voice sore from screaming. He and his wolf enjoyed that I was using his cock for my pleasure.

His grunts of approval, of praise each time I fell over the abyss of bliss, only encouraged me to continue.

As he released for a final time, his knot did not deflate. It widened, locking itself inside my pussy, and I stopped my movement.

Grim gracefully rolled me to the side, keeping his cock firmly planted. He cupped my face, his mouth meeting my lips.

"I'm so sorry, my mate. You do not need to do that again when my rut returns."

I paled. It's going to return? I tried to hide my worry. Or was it excitement?

I should be concerned, but I wasn't. My body was already thrumming with anticipation.

"Ah, it was nothing. I could do that again all day." I waved my hand.

He gave a brief smile, shaking his head. "My rut is not completely over. It could be days until it is."

My mouth dropped, and I gripped the sheets. "Days?" I gasped.

"I will ask Bones for more deterrent. Since we met, I've been taking it."

"More deterrent? From what? Your rut? Why?"

He sheepishly looked away, his face blushing. "My wolf has been gone for a long time before you. My rut had ceased a as he disappeared. But when you crawled from underneath that bed, you sparked life in my wolf. My rut came back, and I couldn't very well do what I needed with you." He swallowed. "You're past was enough. I would have never asked you to do that in the beginning. Never. You deserved more. So, I had Bones give me a rut deterrent to keep it at bay."

I smiled, tickling his cheek.

"But once we mated last night, it returned at full force. I've been in the bathroom since we unlocked because I could not wake you to do that to your body again."

"Grim, why didn't you just tell me? I would have woken up."

He shook his head.

"My bite weakened you." He ran his finger over the wound. It exploded with shocks of pleasure down my body. "You needed the rest."

"But now, I can help. You wake me up when we need me." I playfully tapped his shoulder. "I don't mind in the slightest that I have to orgasm over and over." I laughed.

His smile grew, and a deep chuckle reverberated in his chest. "I am glad to hear that mate. For I never want you to feel discomfort."

CHAPTER TWENTY SIX

Grim

Three days passed, my rut was persistent, especially since I'd held it back with the deterrent. My wolf was angry with me, his emotions hovering over me like a severe case of parvo for doing such a thing to him.

My wolf was vengeful, and it didn't matter that I was trying to help our mate.

It was our instinct for us to rut, and he insisted that she would have succumbed to us if I had only tried to be more forward.

This is where our personalities, our species, differed. Because I was part wolf but also part human. It would have been wrong if I had pushed for such a request when Journey and I had just met.

My wolf and I would never see eye to eye on our differences.

My mate laid in a crumpled heap in the blankets. I had swapped out many of them because they were drenched in sweat and the liquid of our bodies. I was sure to always leave at least one blanket that carried both of our scents close by. It was to deter any other shifter from coming near, but also to calm my mate.

Whether or not she knew it, her body was changing to hold our bond securely. That I knew for sure. I couldn't explain it, I'd never had a mate before, but her smell had certainly changed to a mixture of mine.

Her jasmine scent was now tainted with my wolf's, and I had to pinch myself to make sure this was reality and not a dream. Journey really was mine, she was mine forever and the indentions that lay on her shoulder had healed far quicker than I imagined.

The goddess had planned this and did so carefully. There were no records of any human and supernatural mating, so as far as I was concerned, we were the first.

Journey moaned inside the sheets. Her body was sore and mangled, wrapped beneath the blankets. I tucked them around her body again, covering every inch of her so when I left the bed she would still rest peacefully.

I didn't want to rise, but after three days of hardly any contact with the outside world, I needed to find out how Locke was doing.

I stood, stretching tight muscles. I was still naked as I walked through our den to pick up my phone from the charging station. There was a good deal of information I needed to let Locke know about.

I checked the curtains and made sure they were closed before grabbing my phone to check for messages out in the hallway so I wouldn't disturb her.

Journey was exhausted, and this was the first time in days she had slept for more than three hours at a time.

She was a saint; I wasn't sure how she survived it all. She was far stronger than she appeared because her body was always ready for me when I needed it.

Always wet, always dripping.

And now her pussy was puffy and swollen.

I puffed out my chest, proud that I had made her come so many times.

Maybe it was the bond, or just the fact she was waiting for my cock to stir, I wasn't sure, but I felt no pain in waiting for her to wake when I needed her. She rose when my cock did.

I flipped through the phone, finding messages from Sizzle and Locke.

Living above the tattoo parlor was great; he and I could stumble into the parlor right when we opened. But the unfortunate thing was that the upstairs walls were paper thin.

Sizzle could hear every thrust, every moan and every slap I made on Journey's ass while we rutted. He'd left me a message that he'd gone to stay at the bar's dormitories so he could get some sleep.

As disgruntled as the text messages were, I knew he was happy for me. We had grown a friendship bond over the years, and if I had to trust someone other than Locke, it would be him.

Every morning and evening, he placed plastic bags of takeout food by the door. I couldn't even supply my mate with proper food and nutrition during my rut. But Sizzle took it upon himself to help. I was most appreciative, but my wolf grumbled inside in dissatisfaction that we had to rely on another.

If he could keep our cock from straining and getting hard every five minutes, it would have helped the situation, but it was impossible to keep it limp.

Now that my rut was over, I would have to think of where I could move our den. We couldn't possibly stay here. My thoughts ran to the land right outside of the town. It was full of trees, caves, streams, and fresh meat to hunt for my wolf now that he had returned. I didn't remember the last time I hunted for myself or for a pack. It would be most rejuvenating for us both.

But if we built a cabin in the middle of the forest, my wolf would be lonely. Not to mention Journey would be left unprotected if I went for a run. Wolves thrived in a pack, and my wolf would eventually become restless.

As strong as I was, I carried no alpha blood. I was nothing but a warrior now, and my wolf needed to survive with a leader. We didn't have that right now. Locke could not control his wolf.

A pain stabbed my heart. My wolf needed to be commanded. He needed stability. Locke's wolf was so far gone, I knew his alpha command was lost until he found someone. With my wolf now returned, did that mean I was no longer a part of the Iron Fang? Was I no longer a rejected and lost soul that waited for his death?

Would I have to find and join another pack? What of Journey? She was human, and it would be impossible to keep that a secret.

Supernaturals and humans were forbidden to mate.

We would both be in danger.

My wolf growled at me, unhappy with the doubtful thoughts. He thought things would work out in time, that Locke would gain his wolf again someday and be able to control the entire pack. If he could gain his wolf's control again, he could even command the rogues, maybe even save them from going rabid too quickly.

The only thing I could do was put it in the goddess's hands. She had saved me—one who was almost too far gone.

Journey expressed that she had prayed to the moon many years ago. Maybe we all needed to do that. And pray for Locke to find his mate, to help save him.

But he needed to want to be saved.

My extended claw clicked on the phone's screen. There were updates on the mayor and his men. They were all mangled, witches keeping them alive so we could extract more information when I returned.

My untimely rut ruined their demise. Soon I would have to return to my job as executioner and take care of them.

Sizzle's banter about not getting into his own apartment made me chuckle. I could see the stream of emojis in each of his texts. Many of them were eggplants, fingers in the "okay" sign and fingers pointing.

My wolf purred in amusement. I didn't remember smiling or laughing as much as I had the past couple of days. My mate was surely the reason for the change.

My soul was lighter, my wolf healthier, and most of all, my heart had exploded with love for this woman. Despite her past, she was strong. She could forget her past and put me as her present, her future.

Journey shifted between the blankets, her dark hair splayed haphazardly across the pillows. Her nose twitched, sniffing, until she poked her head above the blankets.

It was like she searched for me, knowing I was gone.

"Grim?" her groggy voice shook. She licked her dry lips, and her thick lashes brushed against her cheeks. She could barely hold her eyes open. I stepped across the carpeted floor until I sat beside her.

She forced her eyes open to look at my cock. I chuckled deeply, purring with prideful admiration for this woman. "I'm fine," I stated. "The rut is over, sleep my mate. I will watch over you."

Journey groggily nodded, her head gently laying back into the pillows. I brushed her hair with my claw and tucked her tightly beneath the blankets once more.

I grabbed a pair of gray sweatpants from the floor. They were the first pair of clothing I'd put on in days. I pulled them up quickly and stepped outside of the apartment, taking one more look at my mate before shutting the heavy wooden door.

My finger hovered over the green call button to Locke. What I had to tell him would not go well.

Pressing the call button, I waited. It rang three times before he finally picked up.

"Oh, he lives," he chuckled through the line. "How is your mate? Has she been marked?" His tone turned serious. His curiosity hung in the air while I dramatically paused.

"She is marked. She is mine."

Locke drew out a long overdue breath. I could hear the scratching of his scalp and the rustling of his pants as he reached for a cig.

"That's good, that's good," his voice shook. "I knew it would work out fine."

He didn't.

He didn't know how well Journey would react to a mark, but it was there. It sat on her shoulder, bright purple and red from its healing. It healed far faster than any human should have, which brought me to the information I needed to give Locke.

"Listen," I interrupted. He was congratulating me, telling me how happy he was. But the sadness, the worry in his voice was all too familiar. He was worried that I would leave him. My wolf was fully present now, and he held no alpha command over me.

"Journey spoke to me about an old woman who approached her at the bar."

I recalled what she told me during one of our reprieves.

Locke's voice cleared, and he listened intently.

"She said she was older, gray hair, mystical looking eyes and she didn't have a cut like the rest of the members. It was member night, so no one else should have been let in besides those assholes, right?"

"Right," Locke growled. "I can have Switch look at the cameras. Did the hag do anything to her?"

I shook my head and grunted. "Journey said she came up to her, put her thumb over one of her eyes and said, 'one eye open, two will be too much,' then she felt a zap inside her head that helped her recall the mayor hovering over her." I gritted my teeth. "That was how she could pin him as her rapist."

Locke swore and threw his lighter to the other side of the room.

"But listen," I urged. "She can't remember his face anymore." Locke stilled on the other side, his breathing heavy. "She can't remember anything that happened to her for all those years she was used. Specifically, she can't remember the men using her. She was drugged, hardly coherent when they used her, but as we have spent time together, she says even those small glimpses of her memories have faded."

Locke stayed silent for a long while. His finger scratching at a wooden table. "Do you think they are connected? The bond? The old woman?" he asked.

I cleared my throat. "Journey also prayed to the goddess."

The silence between us stretched further. We could only hear each other's breathing until he swore under his breath.

"When did she do this?" Locke asked.

"Years ago. She prayed for a miracle, for our kind to exist, to belong in a fairy tale where humans didn't belong. She didn't know she was praying to the goddess, but she prayed to the moon, which is the same thing, right?"

"It is." Locke smacked his lips together. "If they are somehow connected, do you think this old woman was the goddess herself?"

My eyes widened, my arm leaning against the tattered wall. It wasn't uncommon for the goddess to present herself in various forms. I had never seen it, yet I don't think I'd ever looked.

"You really think—"

"Think about it, the letters, rescuing females, your bond between Journey. It sounds like it's her." He gritted his teeth. "Took her long enough to come to our damned rescue.”

"Locke," I growled. "You cannot curse her, not when she is coming to help now. We should begin praying again, seek her guidance, ask her to send—"

"No," Locke hissed. "I will not pray to her. I won't pray to a goddess whom I worshiped reverently until *she* rejected me. I won't."

The stubborn fool continued to curse through the phone. The padding of my mate's footsteps across the apartment and the gentle shut of the bathroom door made me want to end the conversation.

"Locke, just think about it. You'll tell the men won't you?"

Locke grumbled and swore under his breath. "Fine, I'll speak with Hawke and Sizzle. Then hold a meeting. Care to join us and explain your hypothesis? I can't tell my men to pray when I won't."

It would be the first time in years I had spoken to a crowd. In fact, it would be the first time since I tried to explain to the alpha that I was worthy of his daughter, only to be spat upon, kicked, and beaten until I left with my tail between my legs, my parents staring at me as if I had died.

I clutched my fists, reeling in the anger that wanted to spill again, but the sweet singing of my mate caught my ear.

My brothers would want what I had. They would want the heat of their mates bodies and their souls connected to their mates. They would want companionship.

I had been beyond repair, yet the goddess had chosen me, chose Journey to bring back what others had lost. It could mean all of them could be saved.

I would need to bury my torment, bury the darkness so I could bring them information they may not be ready to receive. Too many had renounced her and given up hope to find their other half. It would be a difficult speech to give, but I hoped that hearing my voice and experiencing the lightness of my soul would change their mind.

Even if it meant that Locke might never find mercy in his heart to ask for help.

CHAPTER TWENTY SEVEN

Journey

The tinkling of glasses sounded around the bar. Everyone had a pint, if not two. They patted Grim on the back, but he didn't wince or growl as they spoke to him like a long-lost friend.

Many cheered at the announcement that Grim and I were an official "couple." He was actually smiling, and it wasn't directed toward just me. He did, however, look back at me, and I blushed scarlet when the whooping noises and wild hip thrust movements from several members ensued.

"You did it!" Delilah put down a tray of empty glasses.

She threw out her arms and hugged me close. I took in her smell. I could smell a hint of her shampoo, and it smelled of cinnamon and vanilla.

"What shampoo do you use? It smells so good!" I laughed.

She eyed me, placing her hand on her hip. "You can smell my shampoo. Girl, I haven't showered since yesterday morning." She lifted her arm to take a whiff. "I feel like I stink, but heck, that makes me feel better. That means these men can't smell me."

She picked up the tray and deposited the glasses into the sink behind the bar.

"So, how did you do it?" she asked. "All the women are dying to know how you bewitched the scariest one of the them all!"

The women that had created their own cleaning services and lived in the apartment buildings across the street all eyed us in curiosity. I hadn't been able to get to know those women, but I'm sure I'd make friends with them now.

Grim brought me to the bar after I begged him. We were stuck "rutting" for days, and he'd kept me inside another two just so we could get to know each other better. Not in just the physical sense, but also in the ways of this fairy tale world I found myself in.

Rutting, scenting, what the bite mark meant, what the club meant to all these men and women that had stumbled into it. They were all a sad group, their mates rejecting them for one reason or another, and it made me hurt for them all.

He didn't explain to me just the exciting things I had already come to love, but also the danger.

A Royal Council, a group of royals of each species, had rules for everyone to follow, especially in the Earth realm. They decided the fate of supernaturals when they intermingled with humans sexually. Humans were forbidden.

But with this being a rogue commune of sorts, Locke wasn't worried about his men reporting them. They were all too hung up on the idea of getting mates of their own and besides, who would believe a rogue amongst a council of royals?

No one, at least that's what Locke thought.

Tonight, there would be a meeting held at the church at midnight. Grim was telling everyone his thoughts about the bond we shared. Locke said he couldn't do it. Locke didn't believe in the goddess anymore. He didn't believe in praying to a goddess that had ruined his life, forcing him to live alone and uncared for.

There wasn't enough evidence for him.

But why not grasp onto something to believe?

Locke took another shot of whisky and lit another smoke. He truly didn't want to believe a simple prayer asking for help or asking for someone to save him could work. He thought he could do it all on his own, despite his right-hand man getting his second chance.

Men were hardheaded. Especially the three that I'd come to know—Locke, Sizzle and Hawke. Whatever Locke was going through, though, was too painful for him to discuss, even with Grim.

He would come around when it was time. I was sure of it.

Delilah glanced across the bar, her finger wrapping around her tray. She had three more pints of beer she had to deliver.

"It just sort of happened," I replied. "Grim knew what he wanted, and I guess he fought for it."

Yes, Grim fought for it. He was more receptive to the Goddess bringing us together.

I was hoping with this new information Delilah would get her happy ending. The longing, the pining as she looked over at Hawke frequently was damned sad. But he refused to take it further—only tiny kisses he'd stolen from her. It left her more broken each time he stepped away from her, giving her the cold shoulder.

"I'm thrilled for you, Journey, I really am." She patted my hand. "And I'm sorry to tell you this, but I'll be leaving at the end of the night."

My eyebrows rose, and I frowned. "What? why?"

"I came into some money. You see, I've been working at a diner early in the mornings across town as a server. I've scrimped up enough to leave, and I'm going to do it."

"But why? You said you were going to stay longer."

She shook her head. "I can't stay here anymore. Hurts too much. But I'm gonna miss you, though."

If I had a phone, I'd tell her to call me, but she didn't have one, either.

"I'll write to you," she stated. "I'll write to you as soon as I settle down, but I need you to promise me something."

"Anything."

Of course, I would promise her anything.

"Don't tell Hawke." She narrowed her eyes. "He can't know, or he'll stop me. I'm not even doing this as a game anymore to get him to come after me. I'm really done."

"He'll come find you," I retorted. "I know he will."

Especially now that I knew he was a wolf. Grim said his wolf had been far gone, but he could still use some of his animalistic qualities to help track down anything.

I wish I could tell Delilah that.

"I doubt that. He made it very clear last night that nothing would happen between us." She scowled. "And I'm not wasting my life any longer. I deserve better, want more, and if he isn't willing to give it, then it's time I leave. Otherwise, I'll be stuck here and never get out."

My eyes watered, and I pulled her into a hug. She almost dropped her tray but caught it with her graceful hands.

"I'll miss you, Journey. I wish we could have gotten to know each other better. You're strong."

I shook my head. I didn't know if I was strong; I was just a survivor. And my past was completely behind me. No nightmares, no images of men hovering over me. It was just Grim.

Delilah left without another word, pacing around each table and dropping off drinks.

Before I could think any further, a warm arm wrapped around my waist. Grim lifted me off the bar stool and kissed my forehead.

His purr strengthened, and I leaned into him, thankful that he'd fought for me unlike what Hawke was doing to Delilah.

"It's official. You are part of the club now." He purred, wrapping his arms around my waist. "In biker terms, you're my 'old lady.'"

I snubbed my nose and patted his chest.

"I'm obviously younger than you." If I had to guess, I was at least fifteen years younger. But I guess you couldn't really tell with a shifter.

Grim hoisted me up on the bar. I squealed, laughing once my butt hit the wooden plank. His eyes twinkled with mischief, and he rubbed the sides of my legs with his hands.

He turned, grabbing the beer, and slammed it rhythmically on the table to get everyone's attention. The bar stopped their idle chatter and looked up at the both of us.

Sitting on the counter, I was taller than Grim, and I wrapped my arms around his neck when I tried to hide my face.

"This young woman here says she can't be my 'old lady,'" Grim shouted playfully.

The bar patrons moaned disgruntledly, shaking their head and banging the glasses on the table.

"She says she's too young," he droned.

"Aye, that she is," Locke interrupted. "And obviously too pretty for ya, too." Locke's scowl was gone, and he slapped Grim on the back. "I've got a better term we can give her. How about mate? Short for a soulmate?"

There were humans in the bar, ones that wore no vests, but they all raised their glasses in agreement. "Yeah, never liked it when bikers called their women 'old.' Made it seem like they had a ball and chain around their ankles," a man shouted.

"It's settled then. Mates only in this club, you hear?"

It was a statement not for the club members but for the humans that frequented the bar. There would be no question if the word was brought up now.

Locke cleared his throat when all the announcements were made. "Members to the church, we got business to attend to."

Many chairs pushed away on the wooden floor. The jukebox played, and biker's hit the balls on the pool tables, resuming their game. Grim pulled me down from the bar and tapped my butt to follow.

This was it.

Grim would give his speech, informing his friends that they could have what he had. I just hoped they listened.

Locke whispered harshly at Grim in the stage's corner. The murmurs and chuckles echoed through the once abandoned church. The stained-glass windows were broken, letting in drafts that should had made me shiver. But I didn't.

It was because I was covered in three or four layers of clothing. Grim had a weird fascination with keeping me warm.

"How are you doing, little human?" Sizzle sat next to me. His tall form hovered over me like a stone-cold statue. After gazing into his eyes, I couldn't understand how I didn't notice his slitted pupils.

He was a dragon and supposedly a large one at that.

"I'm fine." I smiled.

He nudged me with his elbow and kept his sight on the stage.

"You know," he began. "I'm moving out of the apartment next door. I think it's time that you and Grim have a bigger place."

The tattoo parlor was owned by Sizzle. He couldn't possibly want to leave the business he'd built. I went to open my mouth, but he interrupted me.

"It's already decided. I told Grim we were changing the upstairs into one giant apartment. A bear clan on the opposite side of the state has already been called in. They're bringing lumber and building supplies."

"They want to help the club?" From what Grim told me, no packs or tribes wanted to deal with any of the rogues.

"That they are. It is because we house their old clan member, Bear."

I opened and closed my mouth. "That's his name? A bear shifter named Bear? That's original." I giggled and covered my mouth.

Sizzle chuckled and put his arm around my shoulder. "That's what I told him." He nodded to the other side of the room.

Bear was everything a bear shifter human would look like—large, full beard, large torso cut into stone muscles. He had meat on him, and his torso was as thick as a tree trunk. He looked unmovable.

"But you don't tell Bear what he can call himself. Never argue with a bear."

Well, couldn't quibble with that statement.

"Anyway, you guys need some space. The tattoo shop has a basement, and I'll fix it up and stay down there. It's better for a dragon to have a cave, anyway." He turned his head, his chest rose, and I heard a muttering escape his mouth.

I should not have been able to hear that, especially what else came out of his mouth, "Because I can't stand hearing the fucking all the time."

My face grew ten times redder, and I tried to scoot down the pew. He loosened the arm that was around me, and he darted his head back to me in confusion.

"Little human, what's wrong?"

The words cut me sharper than they should have. I should have realized we were loud, but Grim liked it. He said he wanted to hear me when I came and how hard I wanted it. He was always checking on me, always wanting those reminders he was doing a good job.

"I'm sorry we were loud. I didn't mean to disturb you."

Sizzle tilted his head, blinking his golden eyes. His pupils dilated, and my eyes could only concentrate on his. I could see the speckles of red inside.

"Did you hear me?" He breathed. "You heard what I said?"

"Yeah, loud and clear." I scooted further down the pew.

I couldn't hide from my embarrassment because I was blocked in by another member at the other end of the pew.

"How the hell did you hear me? And, Journey, I'm sorry. I didn't mean to make you feel like that." He ran his hand through his hair, and a hissing noise left his throat. "I just won't ever have that."

"Since when do you hiss?" I asked, completely forgetting his pity party.

More displeasure ruffled him. He shot up from his seat, his hands pushing against the seat in front of him. The knocking of the wood against the floor hushed the crowd.

Locke hammered at the pulpit once with the gavel.

For a gentle knock it should have created, it rang in my ears. It echoed, and I held my hands over them to stop the roaring. Someone laughed in the far corner of the room, and another pound of the wooden mallet echoed again.

Once the ringing stopped, and Grim's smooth voice came over the pulpit, speaking about our bond, I pulled my hands away.

Drops of crimson red fell on my fingers.

I checked the other side of my head; more blood was coming out of my ears.

I kept silent, watching as Grim continued to speak. I pulled my hair over the red drops so Grim wouldn't give up the speech just yet. Unfortunately, it was a worthless endeavor because Sizzle and Locke had seen my blood-stained fingers.

CHAPTER TWENTY EIGHT

Grim

Locke dropped his cig on the floor. He stomped it out, his nose huffing in irritation.

"You don't have to tell them anything," Locke reminded me. "In fact, I don't know if it's such a good idea. We don't know for sure–"

"What happened to the leader that said shit whether or not we liked it?" I interrupted. "What happened to the leader that wanted what was best for his members?"

Locke growled, running his hands through his hair. "I don't think they will be very receptive to this, Grim. Don't want to get your hopes up."

"Who says they wouldn't be? Unless you give them a chance?"

We didn't know if a human had to pray for a miracle or if it was us that needed to. All I knew was that the men and women needed something to hold on to, something to believe in rather than walking in these hollow shells.

"It will do them some good to believe that hope is coming," I argued.

Locke rolled his eyes. "Since when did you become such an eloquent speaker? Doesn't your tongue hurt?"

I chuckled, slapping him on the back. "I've had nothing to say, not until she came into my life."

We both looked at her from afar. She was speaking with Sizzle, and he had his arm around her haphazardly. He hated women because he was a pussy magnet with the face he had. But he knew with my bond with Journey, she wouldn't have any interest in him.

It still didn't sit right that his arm was around my woman. I let off a low growl, ready to stomp down to the congregation, but Locke had already hit the gavel on the pulpit.

It was time.

The last time I spoke to this many souls was when my mate rejected me. My palms were clammy, sweat dripping from my brow, but the realization that I was not up here to be ridiculed and spat upon calmed me.

I was here doing a job that my leader didn't want done, and my wolf was pressing for me to continue. To take Locke's place, to make the judgment call, to tell these souls that we had a second chance. They all seemed to believe that since Journey had fallen into my life.

I began my speech with meeting Journey, the signs that she was my mate, my wolf appearing, and the mysterious old woman that was never found on the video recording. The members in the audience sat in silence, no longer speaking and jeering at one another. They were stunned to silence until I came to the last bit of information.

"Journey prayed to the goddess. She was brought to me by a single prayer. I was to save her, and I did. She's my mate. My wolf has returned, and our bond has been solidified. Not all humans will pray to the moon. Journey had a rough life growing up and prayed to anyone that would listen."

My eyes darted to her. She held her hands in her lap, her hair laid over most of her face.

Journey flashed a brilliant white smile towards me, and my confidence grew despite my shaking voice.

"So, I implore you to pray to the goddess to find your second chance."

"Pray to her? After what we've been through already?" a shout came from the corner. "All you've done is guess how you've been given a mate, Grim. You don't know if a simple prayer did it or not."

Others agreed. The murmurs grew louder, and my mate whimpered. She put her hands over her ears.

Sizzle and Locke rushed to her side to check on her, and my claws punctured the podium.

I growled into the congregation, trying to silence their noise, but they only grew louder.

"Journey was lucky. She was dropped in your lap. Be grateful for that, Grim." Bear shouted in the corner. "I'm happy for you, but this club was founded on cursing the goddess and what we've been through because of her. If we find our mates, that's great and maybe I'll forgive her. But until then, let us live our lives in peace." Bear stood, his colossal form stomping down the aisle.

"Yesss, we are happy for you," Surkash said. The naga stood almost seven feet tall and looked over everyone's heads. "We just can't trussst in something that has betrayed us once before."

I gritted my teeth. "The goddess didn't betray us. Our mates did!" The crowd was leaving; they hadn't accepted it.

Journey let out a painful cry, and my wolf immediately called to action. We jumped from the stage, leaping over each pew until I stood in front of her. Sizzle and Locke sat beside her, pulling back her hair.

"Get away!" I yelled, pulling her into my arms.

The metallic scent of copper tickled my nose, and my wolf immediately went into offensive mode.

"Who the hell touched her? Why is she bleeding?" I picked her up, pulled her away from my friends, and took her to the stage.

I sat on the stage floor while others gathered below, watching as I pulled away her hair.

Blood dripped from her ears. It wasn't actively bleeding, but it was enough to release my claws. "Why the fuck is she bleeding?!"

"Everyone get out!" Locke ordered.

Journey winced and covered her ears again. "Too loud, Grim."

I paled and pulled her closer to me.

"Where is Bones? Get him!" I whispered harshly.

"I'm coming!" he yelled.

He was fighting the crowd as they left in a hurry.

I continued to pet my mate's hair, mortified that there was nothing I could do to stop her pain.

"Grim, I'm okay." Journey touched my arm. She rubbed it several times until the tension in my shoulders wavered, and I touched her forehead with my lips.

"It doesn't hurt as bad anymore now that the bleeding has stopped. Just tender," she said.

Bones jumped onto the stage with a sharp thud, and I growled in annoyance.

"Sorry." He reached into his bag to pull out a device to look into her ears.

"This is an otoscope. It will help me see properly into her ears." He addressed me and not my mate.

Bones was wise to do so since she was the one in distress, and I would not let any male touch her unless I gave permission.

I nodded, growling in annoyance as she pulled back her hair for him to look inside. He hummed, gently tugging her ear to get a good look on either side.

"Journey, did your ears hurt before today?" Bones asked.

She shook my head. "No, it started when we came to the church. The noise was extremely loud. Just talking to you, I feel like you're yelling at me."

Sizzle stepped forward. "Yeah, she even heard me whisper under my breath. I swear I said it so low I barely heard myself say it."

Journey groaned, her face turning red.

"What did he say?" I asked.

Journey shook her head. "No, don't make me say it."

My head snapped up to Sizzle, who paled instantly. He was backing away from us, but Locke grabbed his arm to keep him close.

"What did you say that my mate heard? You obviously upset her?" I hissed.

Sizzle cleared his throat, rubbing his forehead. "I swear, I didn't mean for her to hear it. I was just telling her I was giving you guys the upstairs apartment to make your home bigger. Then... I whispered, 'so I don't have to hear you both fucking.'"

My arm shot out so fast, I punched Sizzle in his pretty little face. He groaned, his head falling backward as his back landed on the floor. The fall wasn't far enough since he was on his knees on the stage, but it would have to do for now.

"Don't speak to my mate that way, you piece of shit," I snapped.

Sizzle didn't respond. He was knocked out cold.

"Grim?" Journey tugged on my vest. "It's okay. He was trying to be funny."

I shook my head.

Bones clicked off the light of his device and put it back in his bag. "Anyway, it sounds like you had an ear infection, and the pressure became too great and your ear drum popped. Some human adults don't feel them until it's too late. Antibiotics usually cure it, but you must have been too busy to notice the pressure in your ears. You've had a stressful and physical week."

Journey groaned and thumped her head on my chest.

"Little human, you are around a bunch of shifters. We talk about mating so casually. You will just have to get used to it." Bones patted her shoulder. "I'll call in some antibiotics. Her hearing was sensitive before because the eardrum was stretched. It will be tender for a few days but heal just fine on its own. I do suggest we get her in to see a human doctor. There are some things I could be missing."

"That will be difficult. We don't know many human doctors in the community," Locke mentioned. "Would a witch do?"

Bones bobbed his head back and forth. "I think she needs to be more thoroughly looked at, considering her past. Grim won't let me near her to do a pap smear or test for any other diseases that might hurt her."

My heart grew heavy. I could feel Journey's sadness through the bond as she laid still in my arms.

Bones practiced medicine for shifters but had studied human anatomy since Journey had stumbled upon us. I still didn't want a male touching my mate, no matter how much he was devoted to the club.

"I want to get tested," Journey peeped. "Make sure I'm okay. I didn't even feel this earache coming, and I want to make sure I won't get sick later, just in case..."

"You have nothing else that makes you sick. I would have smelled it on you," I growled. "Wolves can smell cancer, diseases, drops in blood sugar, knowing if someone is hungry. I would know if you were sick since my smell has returned." My wolf grumbled in agreement.

Our sense of smell since mating had become even stronger now that we were bonded. I was sure that she had no diseases.

"Oh, like some of those specially trained dogs?" Journey quipped.

I winced. I did not need to be compared to a filthy dog.

Locke laughed, throwing his head back. His mood shifted, and it was because the club had sided with him. No one would pray to the goddess. We would remain a goddess-hating group.

"Journey, Journey, never compare a wolf to a dog. It's demeaning," he said.

"Oh, I'm sorry. I didn't mean—"

Locke shook his head. "No worries, little human. We didn't take offense. Now, why don't you head back home and have Grim take care of you?"

She nodded bashfully and stood with me on the stage.

Sizzle groaned. "You broke my nose again!" Sizzle grabbed it with both hands and popped it back into place.

Blood coated his mouth and ran down his cut. He swore under his breath and took it off.

"I hate getting blood out of denim. It takes for-fucking-ever," he moaned.

"Then don't talk shit," I growled. "Especially in front of my mate, or next time you will eat your own dick."

"Since when do you talk so much?" Sizzle laughed. "I never knew you could have such colorful language."

"There's a lot you don't know." I pulled Journey into my arms. "Now that I've got my mate, I can do anything now. If only you stubborn pieces of shit would ask for help, maybe you could get your own mate, too."

Locke and Sizzle rolled their eyes. "Too many unanswered questions, too many what ifs," Locke said. "For all we know, the council could be sending those letters and using us as free labor."

"I don't think that's true." Hawke strode into the room. He had his hand on his sidearm and a cup of coffee in the other. "Those fuckers in the basement are ready to sing. They wanna die from the sound of it. Grim, you up for a good torture?"

Journey gripped my arm, and I looked down at her. I waited for her to tell me not to go, not to kill the fuckers that had hurt her. But there wasn't any mercy in her eyes. They were filled with fire.

"Go kick their ass, Grim," she said firmly. "I may not remember them, but they hurt so many."

I didn't want to leave her after she fell ill, but if they were ready to talk, then it was time to go to work.

"I can walk her home," Hawke offered. "I'll stand by the door."

Journey nodded, pulling on my arm for a kiss. Her face was no longer pale, and the blood was nearly dried on her skin. When our lips met, fire rose in my belly, and my wolf sighed with contentment.

Her arousal filled the air, and I groaned, exercising my restraint.

"I'll be waiting." She winked and hopped down off the stage.

Her shoulders were held back, and her back was straight. She sashayed away from me, and I gripped my cock with my hand. The other men in the room knew not to look at her fleeting form. My wolf growled persistently, warning them not to look.

Damn, my cock was going to burst through my jeans. She was fucking amazing.

Locke chuckled, pulling Sizzle up by his hand to stand. "Never a dull moment. Let's get shit done then."

CHAPTER TWENTY NINE

Grim

The bar was closed by the time we arrived. The human employees had been escorted out earlier to keep them from questioning what went on in the basement. It was best they knew as little as possible.

Delilah didn't look at me as she passed. Her face was shrouded in a large, hooded sweatshirt, but I could smell the salty tears running down her face.

Even though they were hers, I could only imagine the spilled tears of countless other souls caused by the mayor.

The darkness of the basement was lightened by a flick of a switch. The clomping of leather boots was loud enough to stir the prisoners.

"Please," they shouted.

The men that once stood tall and imposing, armed with guns and knives, now cowered before us. The bars let us see inside the small cages where they were kept.

They smelled of piss and vomit, their blood the only blanket they could pull over themselves on the hard concrete floor.

Their skin hung in chunks of meat from their bodies. They were worse for wear, and to be honest, I was surprised a human could live this long after the hell we'd put them through.

"Some witches halted their death," Locke mentioned. "Stopped the bleeding, kept the infection out. We just gave them enough food and water to survive. They won't last much longer, though."

"Please, give me death!" One male reached through the bars. "Please, I can't take it any longer." His nails scratched over the stained floor.

Sizzle chuckled, kicking his iron-toed shoes into the cage. It rattled enough for my wolf's fur to bristle, and I shook my head, readying my station.

It was time to get some answers and hopefully be done with this by morning.

"Let's go to the source," Locke said as he opened the cage that held the mayor.

The mayor's clothes were tattered and tainted with his blood and his own feces. He tripped over himself, falling into a pool of unknown liquid that laid in front of the cage.

Sizzle laughed maniacally with Locke while they watched the old piece of shit try to stand.

"I don't even want to touch him. Hey, Beretta? Want to help the old man up?" Locke jeered.

Beretta stood in the corner, her yellow reflective eyes twinkling in the light of the single light bulb. She tsked, waving her hand for him to fuck off.

"If you let me pop one in the dick, maybe I'll pull him up by his collar." She glanced at the back of her hand and took one long swipe at the back of it. "But I just had a bath. Maybe I shouldn't even bother."

Switch grabbed the mayor's arm, pulling him across the floor. I went to grab my tools by the bench, but realized I didn't even need them anymore.

I had my claws, my strength.

Taking off my cut, I took a deep breath. The rattling of chains around the mayor's body sent a chill down my spine.

The executioner was here.

"Listen, Grim." Locke grabbed my shoulder. "He's said some things about Journey. He's trying to trigger us, so we'll lose control and kill him quickly. You can't do that until we have all our information. Do you understand?"

I ticked my head, my jaw tightening. "What has he said?" I asked calmly.

"Just how he took her. I can't repeat that shit. Just know that Journey doesn't remember it. That she isn't bothered by it anymore."

I grabbed Locke by his cut and pulled him to my face. "Just because she doesn't remember, doesn't mean it didn't happen. Just because you lost your mate doesn't mean you are over it. He will pay dearly, and he will suffer."

Locke raised his hands, and I pushed him away. It was stronger than intended, and he fell to the floor. No one approached me, telling me not to treat our president in such a manner. I was the leader of this interrogation. The basement had been my solace for many years.

Now, I only found my peace with Journey.

Locke returned to his feet, pulling on his cut to straighten it. His hands went to his pocket, fiddling with one of the many lighters inside.

"Let's get this shit started, then." Locke's demeanor changed. Long gone was my friend, and now the sadistic fuck approached.

"Alright, May-or," he droned. "Tell us where you've been getting the fae dust? We saw you with two she-wolves, handing them cash."

The mayor spit in Locke's direction, but he was far faster than what the Mayor could dish out. "I ain't tellin' you shit. If I tell you, he will find my soul and kill me over and over. I'd rather take it to my grave."

"And you don't think Hades himself won't torture you?" Sizzle drawled.

"Gods aren't real," the mayor muttered.

"They most certainly are," Locke said. He lowered his face next to the mayor's. "Because they know how to inflict pain and make it last a real long time."

Locke backed away, bowing mockingly and revealing my target

I cracked my knuckles, taking heavy, lumbering steps toward the fat piece of shit. I extended one claw and sliced down his inner thigh with a loud rip. He screamed straight into my ear, but my wolf didn't flinch.

We continued to swipe horizontally across his thigh and down the inner part of his leg, down his ankle. Blood poured from the wound, dripping onto the concrete.

I pushed in deeper, feeling the pull of the fat, the muscle, and the sinews of the tissues.

He continued to scream. My brothers and sister, who stood idly talking to each other about the weather, chuckled when I lifted my claw from his ankle.

"Do you want some more, Michelin man?" Locke grabbed his enormous belly from behind and shook it. "I bet Grim can give you a nice tummy tuck. What do you say, Grim? Start fileting him right here?" He poked the mayor's belly button through his torn shirt.

"No, no, wait!" Sizzle ran forward with a black marker and drew two dots on his stomach.

Sizzle squished his belly together to make his belly button look like a mouth. "Look at me! I'm gonna be the joker now! Wanna see my scars!?" He giggled and drew lines on either side of the belly button. "Here, cut here and then I can really make his belly talk!"

Locke and Sizzle slapped the stomach, the echoes of the whacks ringing in my ears.

"No! Please don't!" The mayor screamed.

"You gonna talk then?" Locke asked seriously. "Because Grim can continue with the body renovations?"

"But I wanna see his belly talk!" Sizzle whined.

Even Beretta's laughter filled the room, but Switch was vomiting in the corner, the poor soul. He always had a weak stomach.

I gripped the mayor's neck, my claws brushing around the folds of fat. "Where did you get the dust? How do you know about fantasy creatures?"

He gulped, barely. The tightness of my hold caused him to turn colors.

"I found a letter on my desk. They had photos of me cheating on my wife. I was running for my third term. The author said they wanted to meet to discuss payment to keep quiet. I had to go!"

"Ah, you were blackmailed?" Locke asked.

"In the beginning–" he choked out. "I met a man in a black mask at the docks in an abandoned warehouse. But it didn't look abandoned once I got inside. It was fully lit up, like a club. He had me sit down, offered me some drinks and told me he wanted men and women delivered to him each month. He didn't care how old or young, male or female, but he preferred young women."

"You, you worthless piece of shit, said yes, didn't you?" Locke growled.

"I had to! If I didn't run for mayor again, the debt collectors would be breathing down my back!"

"And they would have found out about you embezzling taxpayers' dollars," Switch mentioned. He wiped the vomit from his lips. "You would have been audited if you were taken out of office too soon."

"Right," the mayor nodded. "I had to stay at least one more year until I could pay it off. He offered to do that if I just continued to help him. He introduced me to other sins, however." The mayor turned away, for once feeling ashamed.

"What did you waste the money on?" Locke asked.

The mayor paled. He swallowed audibly, shaking his head.

"I can give you a guess." Switch's voice grew angry.

My grip tightened around the mayor's neck, his face turning a deep shade of red.

"Grim, wait, we need more," Locke panicked. "Not yet. Calm yourself. Do this for the other women, do this for them. We gotta find them!"

I let go briefly. "Hurry it up," I snarled.

Because I was going to end his life, as well as every other man in the room.

The mayor panted. "I took them from the battered women's shelters within a hundred mile radius. Told them I would put them up somewhere safe. They were people who wouldn't be missed."

Then how the hell did he get Journey? She lived on a damn farm for three years before she was taken, and she just somehow showed up?

"How did they get Journey?" I snapped. "How did she come to be in this life? She wasn't homeless in your city!"

"J-Journey?"

"The girl from the bar! The one you dared to touch!" My eyes turned black. They reflected into his glassy eyes as he shook.

"I-I don't know! She was the girl that was in my blackmail photos!" He cried.

My claws lengthened on each finger. My wolf roared inside me, wanting to make this bastard suffer. I shoved my hand to his crotch; his pants were already ripped, and his dick was laying limply against his bleeding leg.

So much blood covered the worm, but that didn't deter the sadistic grin my wolf flickered to me. Our claws punctured his scrotum, tearing through his package like minced meat.

The mayor's silent screams weren't enough. We wanted more.

My claws dipped into the fat folds of his neck pulling his neck upright so he could take a breath. But then he muttered words I couldn't ignore. "And she was certainly a good fuck."

"NO!" Locke leaped forward, but it was too late.

My wolf no longer needed blood; we needed to see the light leave his eyes. My wolf snarled and forced himself forward. I thrust my hand into his body, digging into his chest. I could hear the squelching of his beating heart. I pulled it from his chest, holding it in my hand. The room stood still in silence until I dropped it to the floor.

He was gone too quickly, but my resolve had been tested enough. He wanted to die, that was for certain, but his eyes continued to blink, looking at his heart on the piss-covered floor.

His body slumped over, the broken bones and guts making wet, squelching sounds.

"Damn it, Grim! I said to wait!" Locke threw his hands up. "Now we don't know who the masked fucker is or where we can find the rest of the innocent souls!"

I gritted my teeth, my eyes narrowing at the male in the corner. He blinked once, twice, until he spoke.

"I'll tell you everything! No one knows the masked man! I'll tell you everything you need to know! Just please god, don't make me suffer! Just snap my neck, please. D-don't do that to me!"

He was pulled from the cage. Locke still swore under his breath at my foolishness.

"You better know your shit, or I'll pull out your heart myself," Locke grunted to the henchmen.

"I was his right-hand man. I'm DeMarco. I'll tell you all you want." He shook. "Just please, a quick death!"

"What a pussy," Sizzle laughed. "All of them are."

I squeezed my fist in anger, I turned toward the stairs. The mayors' words still echoed in my head. His foul mouth telling me he raped my mate over and over filled me with fury. I needed to see her, to be comforted by her, and to know she was safe.

I didn't care that she didn't remember. I would always remember his filthy words and how she was used for so long.

"Grim! Where are you going?!" Locke shouted.

I strode up to the sink filled with water. At one time, I had a sick fascination with dunking our prisoners in water and drowning them. Now I used it to clean the blood from my hands.

"He needs his mate." Sizzle grabbed his arm. "You would too if you realized your mate went through the same." Sizzle's eyes thawed, nodding for me to go.

My heavy steps trailed halfway up the worn boards, and the inner circle looked up at me in sorrow. Locke sighed heavily, shaking his head.

"Go," he mouthed. "Go get your girl."

CHAPTER THIRTY

Journey

"Hold on a sec," Hawke said as he grabbed the door and poked his head outside, looking in all directions before letting me follow. He held out his arm for me to take, and I took it.

"Thanks." He nodded and led me down the sidewalk back to the apartment.

I'd spent little time with Hawke. The little I did know about him, I'd heard from Delilah. I couldn't help but have a biased attitude towards him for being the reason she was leaving. Now that I knew more about what these men had gone through, I could see understand why.

She was either not his mate, or he didn't want her to be.

Which would be a damned shame, because Delilah was everything. She ran that bar. She helped other servers when she could. She was the hardest worker I've ever met. Plus, she was a freaking ball of sunshine.

I could see the magnetic pull they had toward each other. The looks across the bar, the blush Delilah had every time she saw him staring. The stolen kisses she said he took when he had drunk too much were evidence enough that Hawke wanted her.

They both felt something. The true question was, was it just lust or was there a bond there?

When Grim and I first saw each other it was so faint, but it grew the more we were around each other.

How could he stand being away from her?

"Do you think Delilah is your mate?" I blurted.

Hawke stopped in his tracks, letting go of my arm so I could stand in front of him. I had become bolder since I'd been mated. It could have been my confidence soaring because of what Grim and I shared, that I wasn't alone anymore, or it could be the trust I now had in these men.

Grim thought of these men so highly, and I was doing the same. Especially since they were trying to find the source of the trafficking to save others like me.

I stared up at him. His short mohawk was freshly trimmed, and his dark eyes stared at me with such intensity.

It was like I ran over his cat or something.

"Why would you ask such a thing," he growled and pushed by me.

Hawke stomped down the street, taking one step for every two of mine.

"Hawke!" I ran to keep up, but he was quick. His bulky form kept me from realizing the light had changed to red, and I bumped into his back when he stopped. I fell on my ass and groaned in embarrassment.

He turned, grabbing my arm, and pulled me up.

"Considering all you guys are big bulky men, you sure act like a bunch of pussies," I snapped.

"Excuse me?" he asked astonished.

"Yeah, you heard me!" I puffed up my chest. "You act like a bunch of pussies. You guys hold grudges worse than a woman. You don't believe in anything that Grim told everyone in that meeting, do you?" I glared.

"Of course I don't. Why would the goddess listen to a human? It was just a coincidence that you guys are mates, that you 'prayed.' Trust me, we are all thrilled for you both. Grim's my brother." He paused, realizing the light had turned green.

He held out his arm again, and I took it, albeit reluctantly.

"The woman you saw, that we can't see, was just an illusion. You had just witnessed the man that had...done things to you. You were in distress, Journey. Maybe you saw someone, but hell, it wasn't the goddess."

"Why don't you think so? Why is it so unbelievable that she wouldn't come to help me?"

Hawke stopped again once we reached the other side of the street. "Because the goddess doesn't come a-runnin' when one of her children is hurt. She leaves them, lets them rot. Her children can only depend on themselves to climb out of the hole they find themselves in."

Hawke pulled on my arm and tugged me along the street. We reached the back of the tattoo shop and trudged up the stairs to the apartments.

It was far warmer up there than the first night I was brought here. All the windows on the upper floor were covered in heavy curtains, the floors covered with rugs, and even the doors had been replaced to hold in the heat.

"Fuck, he's got it sweltering in here."

"I get cold a lot," I muttered, fumbling with my fingers.

"That's good. He is taking care of you. It's his wolf's need to make sure his mate is healthy and well." He stood at the door to my apartment but didn't touch the handle.

"He's scented the entire door and everything inside. I won't be able to follow you in. I'll remain here and wait for his return." He gripped the handle of his assault rifle.

I pursed my lips, my hands fisting together. Delilah was leaving tonight, and even with the promise I gave her, I couldn't just let her go. Maybe there was a way around it. If I knew she was his mate, it would make everyone's lives that much easier.

"You didn't answer my question." I crossed my arms to look more intimidating, but he scoffed.

"Little human, you shouldn't put your nose in another shifter's business. Now prance on in there and wait for your mate before he has my head, because I didn't follow through with my orders."

"No, I will not." I stuck my finger out at him. "From what I gathered, you both are mates, whether or not you tell me. You look at each other, you secretly sniff her hair and gods knows how many times I've seen you look at her ass when she walks by you."

Hawke's clean-shaven face flushed, and his grip tightened on the handle.

"She looks at you like you hung the moon each time you walk into the bar. And shit, you do the same when she hands you a pint of beer. There's something there, I see it. And I would bet my left tit you are both mates, but you don't have the balls to pray to the goddess for your second chance. And when I bet my left tit, that means a lot because Grim likes that one!"

Hawke's mouth hung open, and a smirk appeared. "Do you kiss him with that mouth?"

"It does a lot more than kissin'. Now spit it out, or you'll be making a grave mistake that'll haunt you for the rest of your days."

Because she is gonna leave you tonight.

Hawke rolled his eyes. "I'll tell Grim to keep you out of the bar. Your language is atrocious."

"He hasn't complained yet." I bobbed my head like a southern woman judging someone for using off-brand Crisco.

He pinched his nose, his back hitting the wall. "I don't know if she is my mate or not, Journey. I care about her, but the life I live, what we all live, is complicated." Hawke grabbed the front of his belt buckle.

"I'm in more danger than most. I'm on the front line. Grim may be the tormentor, the punisher, the bringer of death, but I'm there first. I've always been that way, taking preventative actions before my brothers and sisters go into the fire. A life with me is not a happy one. What if I died?"

"But what if you live?"

He shook his head.

"What if you live once you have her, Hawke? You're breaking her heart not being a part of her life. Isn't that what a bond is about? Being together? Trusting it?"

"I've lost my trust in the bond a long time ago. No matter the status I have, no matter what I can offer, I'm not enough. I'm not enough to give her what she wants."

"Then give her what she needs!" I shouted. "It isn't about wanting, it's about needing. You will die without her, and whether or not you think so, she will die without you. For humans, the bond thingy, it isn't strong at first, but once you are connected, it's...euphoric." I dreamily looked out the window, the moon shining in the darkness.

"She will find another human, one that isn't involved in this world." He gritted his teeth.

I nodded, frustrated tears pooling in my eyes. "You know, you're right." I turned away and pushed open the door to the apartment.

"I am?" He pushed off against the wall and peered inside the warmth of Grim's home, our home.

"Yeah, let her go find someone else to take care of her. Love her, cherish her, kiss her. Have endless nights of passionate love with her, touch her in ways you are too scared to do."

Hawke growled, punching the wall beside the door.

I snickered.

"I know you're mates. The goddess needs one of you to believe in her. Do you think she will pray to a big rock in the sky when humans have their own gods to worship? It's time to eat crow, Hawke. She's trying to make it right."

I shut the door with a soft click and leaned against it. I didn't recall the last time I'd ever yelled at someone, but it felt damned good.

I kept my promise to Delilah, and I hoped Hawke woke up in time to catch her before she left. If not, then he would have to chase her, and that would probably be good for his wolf.

I showered quickly, making sure to get the dried blood out of my ears. They were already feeling much better and, sounds weren't so loud anymore.

I pulled on one of Grim's large shirts. Although he'd ordered dozens of pajamas for me, I liked how he smelled.

I blow dried my hair, brushing it with care. I'd never had the desire to look good, especially when I worked, but the idea of Grim coming home to the apartment seemed so domestic.

Sure, he was coming home after killing my rapist, but a part of me wanted to look good when he came home.

I waited thirty more minutes until I got antsy. Sitting wasn't my thing, and Grim had made me lazy over the weeks.

I trudged to the fridge, bending over to grab some eggs. I could make him a tasty omelet. Surely I wouldn't burn the apartment down with something as simple as that?

I grabbed some vegetables, pulling the knife from the drawer and began to cut, but an overwhelming deep pine scent engulfed me. I pulled up Grim's shirt to my nose, taking tantalizing breaths.

His scent was there, though faintly. This scent I was smelling was far more potent. I put down the knife, walking toward the door on my bare feet. My clit throbbed suddenly, and I raised my hand to steady myself on the counter.

Another deep breath and the pounding of feet coming from the stairs outside made my heart flutter.

Grim was coming home, and I sensed his presence.

How could I do that? I'd never heard anyone come up the stairs before? My body paused, the throbbing in my clit continuing as my wetness coated my inner thighs.

I moaned softly, picturing Grim bending me over the counter. I grabbed my breast, pinching the nipple to ease the pain of desire.

The door flung open with a bang. Grim's eyes instantly met mine.

Blood stained his clothes, and he breathed heavily.

"Journey," he said, ragged. "I need you."

CHAPTER THIRTY ONE

Journey

Grim was covered in blood, mostly on the front of his shirt and down his pants. I didn't need to know whose blood it was. I knew where it came from.

Grim's eyes burned, the deep red embers heated with not just anger but passion. The bulge in his pants grew, and he immediately gripped his length through his jeans.

"Journey," he growled.

I still stood in the same spot—right next to the fridge, with the low kitchen island behind me. I wasn't scared of this beastly man with an animal clawing at him from the inside; I was turned on.

The heat of his breath could be felt from feet away. My nipples pebbled against the worn-out t-shirt he used to lounge in. My thighs quaked with a need I had never felt before.

"Journey," he pleaded.

My knees buckled once my back reached the island. My arm held me in place as he approached. Those heavy steps, the straps of leather tightening and loosening as he walked, made the wetness pool between my thighs.

Grim took a deep breath, his nostrils flaring and his eyes darting straight between my legs.

He ripped off his blood-covered shirt. It, surprisingly, kept him clean underneath. The scent of metal and copper dissipated, and his strong musk replaced it.

"A-are you scenting?" I asked, out of curiosity.

His lips didn't move, his eyes glowing brighter than before. He pinned me against the island, a hand on each side of me, and his nose went straight to my neck.

"Yes," he purred.

His wolf let out the most beautiful sound. It was a half growl that made my knees weaken with pleasure. My clit ached. I could feel my heart beating wildly, and the wetness between my thighs trickled down my leg.

The wild thunder of his chest pressed up against mine, his hand tilting my head so I could look into the deep depth of the pools of his eyes.

"You are mine, Journey."

It was a statement I didn't need to know. I knew it already. Hell, we both did, but something had happened to him that made him need to reiterate it again.

"Your heart is mine." He skimmed his hand between the shirt that hung loosely on my body. Then his hand went between my breasts. He snarled. Using the index finger, he ripped the shirt in two.

I yelped in surprise, and the other hand went behind my neck. He slid his other hands down my body, feeling every one of my growing curves.

He hummed in approval when he reached my mound and slips his finger between my soft folds.

"No underwear?" He nipped my ear. "You are feeling brave now, aren't you?"

Was I brave?

I didn't feel brave. I felt empowered. I was letting him love me, giving him my submission. Not only in body but in heart. We balanced each other, we completed each other. And it started with a little prayer.

He threaded his claws behind my head and pulled my hair, yanking my head back and to the side. He lifted his fingers from my pussy and rubbed them over the mark he'd made on my neck, smearing it with my scent.

"Mine forever. No one can take you from me," he snarled. "No one."

"No one," I replied.

He smashed his lips against mine, his hands roaming over my body. The tightness of his leather boots groaned when he picked me up and set me on the island. He swiped all the dishes, utensils and food I'd prepared onto the floor without a concern.

Gently, he lowered me to the icy surface. My nipples grew hard as the coolness of the surface pricked my skin. He worked quickly, spreading my legs and driving his tongue into me.

He was loud in his endeavors. He was humming into my skin, licking and sinking his fingers into the depths of my cavern. I covered my mouth to suppress the sound, fearing being too loud.

My legs shook, my body reaching a high I couldn't possibly explain. My back rose from the counter, feeling the warm air between my skin and the cool surface.

Grim pulled my hand away, his mouth lifting from my pussy. "Let me hear you scream. Let them all hear you. I want them to know you are mine, Journey!"

He lowered his mouth again, suckling at my clit, and I reached my orgasm. I cried long and loud, and Grim prolonged it by pinching my nipple and thrusting his thick fingers inside me.

I tried to wiggle away, the sensation too much, but he ferociously dug his fingers into my thighs. "I need you wet," he mumbled between his lips. "Because I will not be gentle once my cock enters you."

I wheezed, his long tongue licking each of the folds until he suckled again. I reached for his hair, pulling on it. I wanted him to suffocate in my pussy.

He grumbled, his free hand now messing with his belt buckle.

My heart raced at the thought of Grim being rough. He was gentle through his rut. I knew that. He was trying to hold back even when I told him to let me have it.

The animal inside him demand he fuck me savagely now.

And I was ready.

After dealing with the mayor, and gods know what the horrible man had said to him, he wanted to make sure he fucked all the other men out of me. No scent, no touch, no part of me would be unowned by this wolf.

The clinking of the belt sent me over the blissful hill again. I screamed his name, no longer caring if Sizzle heard. Grim wanted him to hear, he wanted the whole damned town to know that he was irrevocably fucking me until my body would only know him.

Once my body lay limp on the counter, he rolled me to my stomach and spread my legs. My ass was in the air, my feet could hardly touch the ground, I could just barely feel the carpet with the grazing of my toes.

He could see everything, and he definitely took the time to look.

"Fucking perfect," he muttered to himself.

Grim pulled out his cock and the piercings of his Jacob's ladder clinked against the zipper. His pants still hadn't reached his ankles by the time he thrust deep inside my core.

My body spasmed when he bottomed out, hitting my cervix with a new heavy passion. The piercings tickled my clit each time his cock departed from my body.

"This pussy is mine." He gritted his teeth and pounded me into the table.

I laid my head to the side so I could get a view of his face.

It was stone cold, his lips parted with each thrust. I watched as he unraveled with each movement. He savored each one even if they were long and fast. His cock buried between my walls soothed him, his piercing rubbing me in ways that made me push back farther so I could push him deeper into my body.

He pushed into me so hard, the portable kitchen island moved. It continued moving until it hit the far wall and even then you could hear the utensils rattle in the cabinets beside it.

Grim repositioned his grip and used my thighs to steady me, his claws sinking into my skin.

Instead of feeling pain, I felt a rush through my body. My ears became heightened again and I could hear his sporadic heart racing like it was going to leave his chest. More of the growls, the grumbling in his chest, sounded loudly.

"Take her, make her ours." The growls formed into sentences.

The pleasure of my body was enough for me to question whose voice it was, but somehow, I knew it already. His wolf was commanding him.

"Fuck her, take her. This pussy, this soul, is ours!"

Grim grabbed my shoulder, steadying himself as he forced my body back on his cock. I screamed, more of my slick covering his shaft.

"That's it. Come all over my big dick." The voice in his chest reverberated.

I dared to close my legs, to rub my clit, but somehow he knew that was what I wanted.

He snaked his other hand around and played my clit like a fiddle.

"Ahh haaaa!" I gripped the end of the table.

"Mine. Fucking mine!"

The table rattled the cupboards; his balls slapped my thighs. The noises we were making were loud and brutal, but none of that mattered.

His thumb grazed my slick where my juices coated his cock, and I watched as he tilted my hips upward. He pulled one cheek apart, and I whimpered.

"Trust me, mate, I will take care of you."

I knew I had taken nothing beyond my pussy. I knew that was for certain.

He dipped the tip of his thumb inside, and immediately my body resisted. He cooed, pausing his thrusts. "It's alright," he said with hardly any resolve. "I need to claim all of you, I need all of this." He hissed as I relaxed my body and his thrusts continued.

His thumb reached to his knuckle, pulling in and out of my greedy body. My body spasmed while his cock and thumb rhythmically tortured me while a whole new form of pleasure took over my body.

"I'll take this ass one day," he grunted. "I'll have all of you."

I cried out again in a fit of passion. Feeling the fullness in my body and taking him in two holes was overwhelming. Stars illuminated behind my eyes, my body becoming nothing but a pile of mush.

His thumb retreated, and his body hovered over me. We were skin to skin while he continued his animistic snarls and grunts.

He had to be exhausted; he had been fucking me for what seemed like forever, but his balls continued to slap my upper thighs like they were always meant to take his beating.

"All of you is mine," he told me.

"I'm yours, Grim," I replied. "All of me."

He lost his tenacity; he pushed away from the table, his cock came free, and he jetted his come up and down my backside. His fingers rubbed it up and down my back while I panted, thankful for some relief, but relishing in his warm hands covering my back.

He hummed, his hand cupping his growing erection, his knot bulging furiously.

I licked my lips as the come dripped from the head.

"Don't look at me like that. I'll have to take you again," Grim panted. "Did I hurt you?"

Did he hurt me?

It hurt that he stopped. I wanted more.

I rolled over, my body displayed like a perfect meal. Grim's heated gaze took in my body. Claw marks riddled my hips, my shoulder, and the warm come still dripping on my back didn't feel disgusting in the slightest. His smell was on me.

I felt like I was an animal. I felt feral, like he was just moments before.

"You didn't come inside me," I whined playfully.

Grim let out a laugh that could be mistaken for relief.

"Is that what you want? My come dripping from your cunt?"

Grim had been shy before, but his wolf was showing himself now. He could talk dirty when he wanted to, and I liked it.

"Why, would it make you happy if you bred me?" I teased.

I tugged on my bottom lip with my teeth, and Grim became hard again in an instant.

He pulled off the pants that were stuck around his ankles. His growl grew louder, and he pulled my arm to sit me up.

"You bring desires out in me I never knew I had." He made me straddle his waist and led me to the couch. His cock bounced against my ass, and I giggled, holding onto him until he sat down with me in his lap.

"You mean you never thought about us having babies?" I asked.

He hummed, his hand massaging the marks on my hips. The pain had already faded, the pleasurable stings gone. His eyes narrowed, staring at my hips, and he brushed the marks away.

Along with his teeth, he must have a healing ability in his claws. That was the only explanation I could find as to why they were healing so fast. Or possibly the bond had something to do with it.

"Someday, maybe. When I know my family will be safe."

He didn't comment on my healing wounds. Instead, we talked about the first thing that popped up. His cock rubbed against my belly. The shiny barbells tickled my stomach, and my hand went to grip his length.

I sighed, happily.

"I've never thought of having pups, because I never thought it was possible. Only a bonded pair can give pups."

His hands cupped my breasts, then his teeth nipped at my nipple. We continued to explore each other, not caring that our arousal was slowly killing us.

We took our time, more so than we had when he had his rut. We explored every scar, kissing, kneading, loving every part of each other.

"Grim?" I kissed his ear.

"Yes, my pretty little mate." I felt his face widen into a smile on my shoulder.

I didn't think I'll ever get over the feeling of butterflies soaring inside me when he did that. The Grim Reaper of the club was smiling, and it was directed toward me.

I grinned into his neck, rubbing my nose into the most potent smell of him I could find. The thick, lush forest pine and the wet soil and musk had my eyes rolling. My teeth nipped him, and he rolled his head back with a pleasurable groan.

"Grim wasn't always your name, was it?"

He sighed, rubbing his hands up my back.

"It wasn't. I was called something else before I left. No one has called me by my birth name since...I left my pack."

"Is it okay if I know? I won't ever call you it if you don't like it. I was just curious."

Grim pulled me up to sitting, brushing my wild hair behind my ear. "You can call me what you want, my mate. I just see it as my past, as an unworthy wolf. Now that I have you, I feel like I've redeemed myself."

I shook my head. "Grim, you have always been worthy. That bitch didn't know what she was missing. It was all about titles. You were there for the love, she wasn't. She was not worthy!"

Grim chuckled and cradled me like a helpless baby. I wanted to protest, but his brawny arms, his soft eyes made me bite my cheek.

"My name was Andrew James," he stated.

He looked nothing like an Andrew.

Grim was all tattoos, ear piercings, and muscles. Andrew James sounded like a gentle soul, and Grim was not.

"I like Grim better," I stated.

He raised his eyebrow. "You do? Why is that?"

I tapped my finger to my lips. "Andrew James sounds like someone who has a small cock. Yours is too big and intimidating for a name like that."

Grim threw his head back and laughed, his grip tightening around my body. He leaned down to kiss my lips.

The bulge of his cock pressed between us, and his knot throbbed when I clutched it in my hand.

"Does it hurt?" I whispered.

He wanted to lie, but I shook my head, knowing what he was going to say. "A little," he cleared his throat.

"Then let's take care of it, and this time, I want you to come inside me."

"Don't tempt me to pull out your implant," he growled. "Because my wolf wouldn't think twice about putting a pup in you."

I shivered in excitement. Being swollen with Grim's baby sounded...exciting.

To make a product of our love, our bond?

Gods, what was I thinking? I'd had no family of my own for years, not since...ever really. I had no mother, no father. But making a family with Grim? That sounded...nice.

I blushed anyway, fiddling with his small patches of chest hair. "Maybe I'd like that, too."

CHAPTER THIRTY TWO

Grim

My wolf growled, pleased.

"You would?" I panted heavily.

My nose went straight to her mark. My hips rubbed against her slit, my precum coating the tip of my cock.

It has been a delightful torture for the past hour, just holding her, touching her. My knot was pleading for release—to be forced up into her tight pussy and lock it into place. To feel it pulsing was my one desire.

"Yeah, I don't know why that appeals to me so much. I've never wanted kids. I didn't want them to live a life like mine," she said shyly.

"Our pups would never live the lives we had," I promised. "Never, I would make sure of that."

Her nipples tightened, and I kissed the tightened nub and sucked hard. Her fingers pulled on my hair, my arms wrapped around her, pushing her breast further into my mouth.

"We could always practice if we aren't ready," I murmured into her skin.

Journey didn't respond. Instead, the slick of her pussy rubbed up against my cock, my knot, making the head weep with extra come.

She forced her hips up, her slick pussy dripping onto my stomach until she grabbed hold of my cock and held it steady so she could descend upon me. We both groaned, feeling the heat of her body and my hardened shaft become one.

I let her lead, but my wolf was impatient. He took the reins, using his claws to penetrate her hips and pull her up and down our shaft. She cried out in a breathy moan, and her tits bounced in my face.

"She loves it, she loves the pain," he snarled at me.

"Yes, I love it," Journey replied, and my eyes widened.

Beautiful bumps on her skin appeared and as much as I wanted to concentrate on this goddess riding my dick, there was something amiss.

"Take this cock, take this knot," my wolf snarled inside me. *"You are mine, mate, mine to fuck. No one will ever touch you."*

"Yes, I'm yours!" she screamed as we drove into her faster.

My knot, now coated in her slick, slipped inside her pussy. I wiggled my cock until it was placed firmly at her entrance and, with one swift push downward, it was forced fully inside. My knot grew, expanding until she was blissfully full.

"Ohhh, owww," she cried, gripping my arms. Her head fell to my neck, and she sank her teeth into my skin.

An euphoria exploded into my soul. My eyes blacked out despite my eyes being wide open. Explosions danced in the back of my head where my wolf hid from the world. All was light, and the darkness of my past began to fade.

The pain was gone, the betrayal long forgotten. The walk of shame leaving my only home was nothing but a distant memory.

She kept her teeth embedded in my neck. I felt the warmth of the blood dripping down my shoulder. I didn't want her to move. Her pussy engulfed my cock, and my seed took root into her womb.

This knot was harder than any other knot I had planted, and I couldn't understand why.

"Journey? Journey, are you alright?" Despite the large hole she left in my shoulder, I felt she was the one that should be in pain. My knot was fucking huge. I thought my dick was going to explode.

"Yes," she mumbled.

Her mouth retreated from my shoulder, blood coated her lower lip and down her chin. Her tongue ran across her lips, taking in the taste of my blood.

My wolf vibrated, his pride soaring that our human mate would dare try to mark us as hers.

"*Mate,*" my wolf purred.

She cocked her head, her innocent, child-like eyes staring at me in wonder. "You talked, but you didn't move your mouth."

Her finger trailed over my lips.

"Journey, do you know what you just did?" I asked.

She didn't even flinch. Her tongue was still licking the blood from the corners of her mouth.

Her hand trailed the warmth of the crimson blood around my shoulder and pulled it away to see red on her fingers. Journey's eyes widened, looking at my shoulder.

"I bit you!" She gasped.

"It's alright." I groaned, trying to keep her still. My knot was firmly in place, and it would not let her go now.

"I didn't realize I was doing it... I?" She tried to wipe it away with the back of her hand, but I grabbed her wrists.

"It's okay, little one, it's okay."

Her heart rate sped up.

"Did I hurt you? The whites of her eyes came into view and her eyes dilated and returned to normal so quickly I almost didn't notice it.

"Everything is fine. It felt fucking fantastic." I tried to soothe her, pulling her into my chest as my knot pulsed in her pussy. "You are alright, my mate, everything is just fine. It's normal. The bond led you to do it."

Fuck, at least I hope the bond led her to do it.

I took a deep breath from the top of her head. Her smell had changed. It had magnified. It was intertwined with mine, but it also had another scent that hadn't been part of her before.

I wrapped my arms around her, my worry intensifying by the moment.

"She fucking bit us," my wolf said. *"Think she will do it again?"*

As happy as I was that my wolf was returning, I didn't need the extra commentary. I needed to think.

"You want me to bite you again?"

I blinked.

"You heard that?" I pulled her from my grasp and stared down at her. "You heard my wolf talking?"

"Is that why you said, 'she bit us?'" Her head tilted like a helpless puppy.

I rolled my finger through my hair. My knot was shrinking, and come dripped out of her.

"Shove my seed back in," my wolf demanded.

Journey's nipples hardened again, and she scooped the come with her fingers and tried to push it back inside her body.

Holy fucking hell. He wasn't even using my voice, and she could hear him inside me. It was like a mind link.

Fuck!

"Journey!" I stopped her. Her eyes snapped up to mine, her face flushed with embarrassment.

"You said to put it back in," she said innocently. "And I want to."

My cock twitched, but I pulled her off me before we started fucking like damned rabbits again. I needed to get her checked out. We needed to get to Bones, to a witch, or someone. Something was happening to the both of us, because I could feel it too.

I grabbed my shoulder. My wound had already healed—much faster than any other time I'd had a wound. It was like...both sides of the bond were completed now.

Dried blood stained her lips. Her eyes furrowed in confusion, and now fear leaked from her.

"Little one, it's okay. I'm surprised," I confessed. "You are hearing my wolf. You can hear his thoughts. It means we are fully connected."

"Like real wolves? The mind-link you told me about between your pack members?"

"That's exactly it." I nodded. "I haven't been a part of a link since I left my pack. The club uses cell phones to get a hold of each other because we aren't really a pack. It's like we are creating our own mind-link."

I stood up, wrapping Journey with a blanket. She shivered as soon as I left her body, but I needed to think. I needed to pace; I needed to...run.

But she needed help first.

And I always put my mate first.

After cleaning my mate, I picked her up and raced her over to the bar. It was early in the morning; the club was quiet, and the door to the bar was locked.

"I can walk," Journey protested.

But she wasn't alright. As the minutes wore on, she tried to drift off to sleep, and I couldn't have that. Not until I had answers. This regarded her health, and I would worry until she was checked.

I pulled out my key from my pocket, fumbling with it until Switch opened the door. He wore only a pair of boxers, his thick-rimmed glasses hung crookedly on his face.

"It's four a.m., can you not wait until noon?" he complained.

I barged into the door, not paying attention to his complaints, and stormed to the back rooms of the bar. The bar was the front part of the building, but upstairs held numerous dorms, all housing the club members that preferred to stay part of a pack.

My spare room was here, but it lay empty because I felt if I went rabid I would only cause more problems.

Once we got to Bone's door, I banged on it harshly. "Get up!" I yelled.

Journey tightly wrapped her arms around my neck. "Grim, we can wait until later. We don't need to bother him. I feel fine."

She yawned again, but my wolf stirred with unease. He didn't like that she was so tired.

Her body was changing, and I needed to know what was happening. Human's mind-linking? Journey being able to hear my wolf was unfathomable. Humans just couldn't do that? Right?

Bones opened the door, his eyes had heavy bags beneath them.

"What do you need, Grim? I just got done disposing of bodies, and I need a rest."

"It's Journey. She can hear my wolf speaking," I blurted

Journey laid her head on my shoulder, letting out a precious yawn.

Bones went to close the door, but once it registered, he pulled it open again. "What?"

"You heard me. She heard my wolf, and she fucking bit me! She marked me!"

A door opened down the hall. "Hey, keep it down!" Sizzle rubbed his eyes. "I swear I can't get away from you two. Moaning, rutting, and yelling down the gods' damned hallway." He slammed the door, and the walls shook.

"I just want to sleep," Journey whined.

I clutched her body, holding her closer. I just wanted nothing to happen to her. I needed to know she was alright. If this was...*normal.*

Bones's eyes softened, seeing the turmoil running through me.

"Has she been up all night?" he asked.

I nodded, feeling the guilt eat away at me. I should have put her to sleep, but I needed her. I needed to know she was mine, and no one would touch her.

"Humans need sleep, Grim. I'm sure we can look into this in the morning. She won't be any use to me if I can't ask her questions and look her over. Take her to your old room, I'll bring some blankets so you can make a temporary nest. When she wakes, we will look at her. Any problems, I'll be just down the hall."

I bit back a growl. My wolf wanted something done now, but with Journey already asleep, there wasn't much we could do.

"She marked you?" Bones raised an eyebrow, pulling the collar of my shirt aside. "Maybe her teeth puncturing into your skin created a two-way bond against just the one. With the goddess putting a human and a shifter together, it must have been planned."

I didn't need speculation.

I wanted answers.

"I'll do some research before I go to sleep. We'll do a full workup." Bones led me down the hallway to my empty room.

All that was there was a mattress on the floor. He grabbed blankets from the closet. Luckily, they were brand new. No one liked to share used fabrics. Our scents embed into the fibers. Even a good wash would never clear our smells.

"It will be alright. I'll let Locke know the plan for tomorrow." Bones sauntered out the door, his hand clutching the side of the door.

"They got more info out of the mayor's men," he mentioned.

I sighed, relieved. I thought I'd screwed up by killing him too quickly.

"There is another party in a few weeks. Locke is planning an ambush. The masked man, who still has no name, will be there. The plan is to capture him."

I nodded, laying Journey on the clean mattress.

"I'll be a part of the ambush," I stated.

Bones shook his head. "That all depends on Journey. She may need you."

Bones's eyes lingered on my mate's body. I growled in warning when he looked for too long.

"No worries. Just want to figure out what's happening, too. She's the start of something great? Right?" His eyes lit up with hope. Maybe there was at least one of us that would pray for a miracle.

I grunted in reply, ripping open the plastic wrapping the blanket.

Bones shut the door, and I made our nest. It wasn't as comfortable as the one at home, but at least we were close to medical attention. My scent released onto my mate, the blankets, and the bed. She sighed deeply in her sleep once I wrapped my body around her.

"I'm going to figure this out," I promised her.

She buried her nose in my neck, like she knew that would bring her comfort. I rumbled a deep vibration, putting Journey into a deeper sleep.

I should be happy that my mate had marked me, but it wasn't normal for a human to bite. She deliberately bit into my skin, deep enough to grip into the muscle.

When I asked in the shower why she did it, she said something took over her body. That she'd felt an unknown force pushed her into my skin.

Since she was human and has no animal, was the goddess pushing her to complete our bond? Was it the bond itself?

More questions arose, and my wolf grunted at them. He didn't care right now; he wanted sleep now that Journey was resting peacefully.

But one thing was for certain, we had to find out what was going on with her.

CHAPTER THIRTY THREE

Grim

I pulled a thick parka coat around my mate. The snow was falling through the crisp air, and the roads would soon be dusted like confectioners' sugar on a perfectly baked cookie.

My mother used to make them around this time when I was a pup. She commented on how humans believed in some sort of large, rounded mythical creature called Santa Claus. He would leave treats and toys for the children under a tree that had been chopped from a nearby forest and placed in the middle of their home.

No one in my pack understood the tradition of it all, but we made our own holiday while the humans had theirs. Being in the realm where no humans were allowed, we weren't given the ability to ask one why or how this tradition started. We decorated our special tree in the middle of the pack and covered it with brightly colored balls and snowflakes made of paper.

One old wolf had seen these mystical trees when he visited the earth realm before he settled down in our pack. He described them in detail, and it fascinated all the pups that humans would take such an interest in the pines.

Since living in this realm, I'd come to understand this phenomenon to be Christmas. A fictitious pagan holiday mashed with several other traditions in order for humans to buy presents from big corporations. Gifts that held no meaning were purchased in exchange for friendship and the continuation of it.

Though to some, I suppose it held some meaning.

"Did your family"—I grimaced—"celebrate Christmas?"

She was bundled from head to toe. Her eyes were the only visible thing.

She mumbled and pulled down the zipper of her jacket. "Grim, I'm sweating in here," she said exasperatedly.

"It's snowing. I need to keep you warm." I zipped up her coat again.

She shook her head and pulled the zipper down again. "Not that cold. Anyway, no, I never celebrated Christmas. Where I lived, it was a devil's holiday. We didn't even exchange gifts," she said sadly. "Not that I would have had any money to give anyone anything. And there was no one who would give me one either."

I rubbed my chin. My mate looked sad and deep in thought while she tramped through the snow. She never had a Christmas, and she had never received a gift on this human holiday.

Maybe I could give her a gift.

I smiled at the thought.

"Maybe, we could get a tree," I mentioned. Bringing in a forest tree would bring more nature into our home. I didn't know about putting all the shit on it, but it would be one step closer to giving her something she might have missed from her human culture.

"I would really like that. Maybe put some lights on it?" Her eyes sparkled. "I don't want to do presents. I think you're the best present I've ever received." She batted her lashes at me.

My wolf purred deeply, nuzzling into her cheek as we walked.

"That was cheesy as fuck." Sizzle rolled his eyes. "You gonna buy that shit, Grim?"

I growled back at him, baring my fangs. He stepped back, trying to avoid another broken nose, and I pulled my mate closer to me.

"I like cheesy. You can be as cheesy as you want," I told her.

Even with Sizzle's aversion to women, he still gave Journey a playful wink and stuffed his hands in his pockets.

Dumb fuck.

Bones, Locke, and Sizzle traveled with us as we walked down our street. This side of town was usually empty at this time in the afternoon, except for humans coming to get their bikes or cars fixed at the garage.

We all looked like a bunch of roughnecks, but humans trusted our opinions on engines.

"How much farther?" my mate asked me, bundling herself in her coat.

I cursed myself, I should have borrowed the car back at the garage.

"Just up ahead," Locke answered for me. "Sorry for the walk, Journey, but with the snow and cold air, you might turn into a little human popsicle if you rode a bike."

"It's fine," Journey mumbled. "I just have seen nothing past that old church, and we have gone a few blocks past that."

"Our territory extends for most of the town. They are under our protection, I guess you could say. The sheriff pays under the table for us to take care of some scum they can never get their hands on. With that, they leave us alone and don't question the extra 'citizens' that come under our care."

"I don't know if that's a good thing or a bad thing," Journey chuckled.

"Should be a bad thing," Sizzle said. "They are lazy and incompetent. We run the town; they just turn a blind eye to it when we take on the dirty work. They only issue speeding tickets and take care of small civil disputes. We don't get paid nearly enough."

"That's enough," Locke silenced Sizzle. "If it weren't for us, this town would have died years ago with all the shit the big city throws out. We've just made this place our own when no one else wanted it."

"How long have you all been here, then?" Journey asked.

"Thirty-some years," I replied. "Locke and I came here first, and then others followed when they heard Locke, the once big alpha of our old realm, bought this side of town with his inheritance."

"Yeah," Locke bragged. "I destroyed a rival pack and took all their money. Found Grim on the way out of the other realm and bought the largest plot I could find furthest away from the portal. Best decision I ever made."

"It was," Sizzle said. "The rest of us followed when we heard of Locke's big rebellion and traveled miles to stay with him. I don't think there is a rogue out there that doesn't know about the Iron Fang. Everyone sees us as rogue felons in our world, but we are really a big family, now."

"Does that mean all rogues get into the club?" Journey leaned closer to me, seeking my warmth.

Immediately, my wolf expelled as much heat as he could to keep her warm. Apparently, she was colder than she had let on.

"No," I said gruffly. "They don't. Some deserved to be rejected and alone. That is why there is a vetting process. We find out what happened to them, no matter how painful their past is. If they have crimes that could put the club at risk, they are immediately rejected."

Journey stuffed her hands in her pocket.

"What sort of crimes?"

"Murder, cheating on a mate before a bond is completed, abuse to any of their kind, rejecting a mate bond, laws broken against the crowns of the royal council...and other things," Locke said, gripping his fists. "We're here."

Once we reached six blocks from the church, we found ourselves in front of a once abandoned shop. When we first moved here, the glass was broken, the cabinets were overturned, and the stench of rotting bodies and sulfur dominated.

Now, it was a bustling shop that had done well for itself. The inside was dark, but the illumination of red candles lighting the window gave it just the appeal that Tajah was looking for. Other witches like her, or the few humans that believed they were practicing witches themselves, made for great customers.

The Burning Sage was one of the first shops that opened before the bar and mechanic shop. She used her magic to bring an appeal to her shop by using a glamor spell. It started out as just an essential oil shop which brought in the humans rather quickly.

"This is Tajah's shop. She's a witch, an exceptionally good one that will help us find out what's going on with you," Bones said. "I'm afraid what we need to find out is more her department."

This morning, Bones did all the blood tests he could. Reading up on humans and 'hearing voices,' and came up with the conclusion that the human was psychotic if they heard voices they weren't supposed to.

Ear bleeding was only common if an eardrum had ruptured from an infection, but her eardrums were completely healed, which baffled Bones. The indentions from my claws had also healed, and she had also gained some of my healing abilities, as far as Bones could tell.

Bones deemed her healthy, but we all knew something was going on with her body. Her smell had also changed, and everyone noticed.

"Is she really old?" Journey peered up at me. "Is she scary looking?"

Sizzle snorted, rubbing his nose. "Humans." He shook his head.

Locke pushed us in the door. The bell rang abruptly, and movement came from the other side of the counter in the back.

"Who's there?" A haggard cough came from behind the counter and Tajah came up to her full height. She was nearly six feet tall and slender, but her face was distinctively paler than I remembered.

"Wow, she's beautiful," Journey commented.

"Aw, shucks, thank you, dear. I feel like shit, though."

She walked around the counter. A black shawl was draped over her shoulders, and a cane helped her walk.

"Tajah, what's going on?" Locke strode over to her, wrapped his arm around her, and helped her sit at a round table with a crystal ball in the middle.

She coughed again, dabbing with a black handkerchief. But with the blackness of the handkerchief, there was no doubt blood had landed on the threads.

"Tajah!" Beretta came from the back. Guns hung at her side. She'd brought in a device I'd used on Journey when she was first sick. "You do not run away from me. I am here to take care of you. Now take this inhaler."

Beretta held it to her mouth, and Tajah took in a ragged breath and let the medicine seep down into her lungs.

"That will not work on me. I'm still waiting on those herbs to be delivered later today, and then I'll be fine," she argued. Tajah pulled her shawl closer to her body.

Beretta stepped away, pursing her lips, but stood in the corner to watch over her. It was the same look I gave Journey, knowing that she would always be safe with me.

Locke and I shared a look.

"Now wait a minute," Tajah began. "You are here for some funny business, aren't you? You've got some strange things going on with you." She smiled at Journey and waved her over.

Journey tried to hide behind me, but I pulled her by my side. "She won't hurt you." I nuzzled into her hair.

Tajah had been with us since the beginning and not once showed disloyalty.

"Damn right I won't hurt her." Tajah slapped the table. "I've been waiting for you to come down here, but I see Grim can't keep it in his pants now that he has the use of his dick."

Sizzle snorted, turning away.

"Hey, your time is coming, Sizzle." She wagged her finger. "Once you get your dick working again and find your mate, you will be rutting, too."

Sizzle opened his mouth to argue, but Locke slapped him upside the head. "None of our dicks work you ass. Don't act like it works for you. Now, Tajah, as much as I love seeing you torment the old dragon, will you please?"

Tajah tsked, pulling a box from under the table. "Right, right. Let me see."

"She's sick. I don't want her to have to work," Journey said concerned.

Tajah shook her head and glanced in our direction as a brief smile appeared on her face. She watched as Journey's hand gripped mine, and I squeezed back.

This world was new to my mate. The customs of different species would be next on my list of things to teach her about our world.

Witches had pride and did not want people to see them as weak. I was waiting for Tajah to whip out a snarky reply with electricity zooming across the room but smiled instead.

Entering a witch's shop used to knock me to my knees, but I knew very well that my friend here was losing her magic far more quickly than she led on. She was dying yet refused to let Locke know. He was too busy taking care of the group as a whole rather than taking care of everyone individually. That was the job of the Luna he didn't have.

Tajah waved her hand. "Nah, girl. I can still help you. I still have some magic left, but it isn't as strong as it used to be. What I have planned for you won't be my doing. It will be all up to you."

Journey stepped forward to the table. I pulled out the chair for her to sit down.

As Tajah opened the box, several moths flew out of it, and she rummaged through it.

"Here it is!" She coughed again, and Beretta came back to her side. "Beretta, I'm going to peg you to the wall if you don't stop freaking out."

Beretta pursed her lips, nodding and stepping away. Again, we all looked at each other. Beretta was hovering over Tajah like Hawke looked at Delilah.

"This is a salve." Tajah pulled it from the box.

It was in an old Altoids mint tin box, and she opened it to gaze inside. The salve itself was dark, and the potency of the smell filled the room.

"Fuck, that stinks," I growled, holding my nose. Journey did the same, but no one else in the room seemed bothered by it.

"Oh good, it still works," she mused. "No one else will smell it unless you are bonded. I see that you have already bitten him, too. That's more than what I hoped for," she told Journey. "Now, hold out your finger and get a generous helping of the salve and rub it over your heart."

Journey looked to me for permission. I smiled and petted her head.

"What will it do to her?" I asked.

Witches, while helpful if they were on your side, still had the cunning of a fae. They liked to watch others suffer. It was some sadistic game they liked to play on unsuspecting receivers of magic.

"It won't hurt her, but it will force her into a hallucinogenic-like state. She's going to see things, experience things. They are going to seem real;

they might be very real."

"That makes no sense," Locke interrupted.

"It perfectly does," she countered. "It will open her mind for someone, something to enter her. Tell her the information she needs to know. What she's destined to do." Tajah shrugged.

"That is really powerful for a supernatural," Bones interjected. "Is it safe for a human?"

She eyed Journey and smiled. "Yup. Now go on and grab a bit."

I shook my head. "No, we don't know what it will do to her! Get someone else to try!"

The witch looked at Journey, and Journey returned the glare. Journey took her finger and scooped it up and smeared it over her heart.

"No, fuck! Don't!" I went to wipe it away, but Tajah's hand darted in front of her and grabbed my wrist in midair.

"Don't touch her, it's too late. She will be fine. She's no longer human anyway," Tajah cackled.

"What!?" we all screamed.

Beretta stood behind Tajah, ready to defend the witch.

"She's a wolf," Beretta said. "I could smell the canine on her as soon as she walked through the door. Don't tell me you really didn't know?"

Journey panted, her hand reaching up to grab mine. I picked her up from the chair, but before I could take her out the door, she immediately fell limp.

"What happened?!" I roared.

My eyes darkened, my sight set on Tajah. I had trusted her with my mate, and now she was asleep.

"Seems like someone has a hold of her. I can feel the overpowering spirit in the room." Tajah placed her hand over her chest. "Gods, it's strong."

"Not helping," Locke said.

I snarled, carrying my mate back to the witch, ready to tear her apart, but the soft whimper of my mate soothed me. "Grim, I'm okay," she whispered. "I'm here."

I sat down on the couch away from the crystal ball table and cradled Journey in my arms.

"She'll be fine," Tajah stated. "Journey is with someone I am sure we would all like to speak with." She pursed her lips. "Beretta, will you help me to my bed? I'm feeling a bit weak."

Beretta ran to Tajah, who stood but immediately was scooped up by Beretta. The black panther glared at all of us and took Tajah behind a beaded drape to the back of the shop.

"Now what?" Sizzle asked.

Bones got down on one knee. I growled at him when he put the stethoscope on her chest, away from the salve. As much as I wanted to rip him to pieces for touching her, I needed him. I was helpless at this moment, and I didn't want to be.

"She's fine, Grim." Bones sighed. "I can't believe we missed that she was a wolf. Our noses have really failed us. I just can't believe a human can be changed." He ran his hand through his hair. "How is that even possible?"

"It is possible." Beretta stepped from the back room. "It's a legend. My pride spoke of it, while the wolves tried to forget."

"What happened? Why haven't we heard about it?" Locke asked.

"Because the outcome was not a happy one," Beretta said solemnly.

CHAPTER THIRTY FOUR

Grim

"What do you mean, it ended badly? Why didn't we know about this?" Locke yelled before I could.

Journey whimpered in my arms and buried her head in my chest. I purred, keeping her calm. But my rage continued to build.

Why the hell did she take the salve? Right when she looked at me for permission? Did Tajah force her to move her hand and put it on her own chest?

"Tajah betrayed us," I hissed. "She forced Journey to take the salve."

The room had gone silent, and Beretta backed up to the beaded barrier. Her stance turned rigid, her hand on one of her guns.

"Is that true?" Locke demanded. "Is that why she nearly fainted, because she was forcing movement on Grim and Journey?"

Beretta laid her hand on the handle of her gun, her tongue wetting her lips. "She did what she had to do, Pres. She was ordered to do it by a higher power."

"Damnit, Beretta! I'm throwing you in the cells where you helped killed those men last night. You will sit in the same cages like the animal you are becoming!"

Sizzle lunged forward and grabbed her by the arms, pinning them behind her back. Beretta let him, and Locke pulled all the weapons from her belt.

"You will see, Locke. It was for all of us. Journey and Grim are the key, and a lot of us have little time left. The Goddess is just moving it along."

Tajah's cough echoed through the shop again. The ringing of wind chimes sang a song that sounded all too familiar to me, to all of us.

It was an old lullaby that had been handed down to the supernaturals from the beginning of time. No one knew its origin, no one knew why it had been with us for thousands of years. But it was there, playing an ominous ting, ting and echoing through the pipes of the chimes.

"If that isn't a clue for you, then I don't know what is," Beretta said. "Men think with anger. You don't listen to the hints from the gods that an atonement is coming. Journey and Grim are the doors to a new beginning for us."

"And how is there redemption coming when you just said that the last human that transitioned to a wolf died?" I yelled. "I just got my mate, my mate that I don't deserve. She deserves everything after what she's been through, and you're telling me I'm going to lose her? She's mine! I won't let her die!"

Could the goddess be that cruel and take yet another gift away from me? Dangle her in front of me like a starved animal looking for meat? I had trusted again, believed in life again because of Journey. We had come so far in such a short time; I couldn't have my soul broken again.

Sizzle loosened his hold on Beretta and nodded at her to sit in the chair.

"I'll tell you the legend, but first let me clarify—the goddess has tried to do this once before to save us. To save the souls of broken bonds. But I don't believe it will end the same way."

Locke snarled, crossing his arms and leaning back in the chair. "She's still a bitch. Don't care how you want to paint her, Beretta. I thought we were all on the same page."

"You are so blind." She shook her head. "Your members are receptive to the chance to get a mate, yet your attitude has doomed them all. They follow you, Locke, alpha or not, and they see your distrust and now they've lost the hope of gaining a mate again. That Grim was just a one and a million chance, and they have nothing."

Locke frowned but didn't reply.

"I don't think you believe that," Sizzle stated. "I don't think you believe either, you are just repeating what Tajah has said."

Beretta snarled in response. "I promised her I'd help."

"Tell us this legend," I interrupted. "I'm becoming impatient, and Tajah's life is hanging by a thread for what she's done to me and my mate."

"Fine. The shortened version since I'm in the presence of toddlers."

Sizzle scoffed and scooted his chair forward.

"Like I said before, the wolves have forgotten, hell the royal council has forgotten because even they do not speak of what happened hundreds of years ago. Panthers tend to act like human females and hold on to things that supposedly don't matter, but it actually does matter, and we bring it up at the right time when all males have forgotten," she ranted.

"Beretta!" Locke slammed his hand on the table.

Beretta glared and continued. "There was a female alpha wolf of an ancient pack. It was small, weak. Despite that, her parents told her to wait for her mate. That everything would work according to plan as long as she obeyed the mating ways of the goddess. But the neighboring pack's alpha was pressuring her secretly. Telling her he wanted her and would protect her and the pack if she would just give in. If she didn't, he would take her land by force."

"The female alpha relented to her parents and listened to their guidance. She had hoped she would be mated to a king, or another powerful alpha that would help her in this crisis. Unfortunately, that did not happen." Beretta closed her eyes and winced.

"The female stumbled upon her mate in the forest while she hunted. He never saw her, never smelled her because his abilities were not strong enough to notice. Seeing that he was weaker than her, she ran. She ran straight to the neighboring pack, to the alpha that wanted her not just for companionship, but to combine their packs to strengthen them."

"She was trying to protect the pack, her people. She didn't do it for selfish reasons," Locke argued.

Beretta smacked her lips together. "Ah, but it was for selfish reasons. She did not trust the goddess. She did not have faith it would all work out with the one she would have."

"It's easy for you to still trust the goddess. You weren't rejected. Someone killed your mate, he didn't reject you," Sizzle snapped.

"That may be true, but it didn't hurt any less." Beretta stood and walked over to me.

She sat on the couch next to me, trying to brush a hair from my mate's face, but I pulled her away from her. Beretta's hand dropped and landed on my knee.

"The rogue felt the pain a short time later. His soul shattering into a million pieces as the bond dissolved. He didn't understand at the time, but his smell changed to something rancid, and his pack mates shunned him because of his smell. He was dubbed a rogue and sent to the realm of the humans."

"He traveled to the first town he could find and eventually fell in love with a young human woman. He courted her, marked her, and knotted her. But with no pack, no alpha, his wolf was restless, and he took them both back through the veil into our realm so his wolf could be around his kind."

I rubbed my thumb against Journey's cheek, my body relaxing the more I stared at her sleeping face. She was so fucking perfect for me, so soft and sweet. She thought she was weak, a burden, but she was far from it. Journey gave me life again; she showed me love.

"On the day that the male decided to take the trek through the veil, his human became ill. The wolf decided it would be best to take her through the veil, to get her magical attention as opposed to human medical care, because she had a scar on her shoulder. He didn't want the humans to ask questions. As soon as they arrived at his pack, she had a fever, her fingers grew claws, and her teeth transformed into fangs."

My stomach churned. Journey's temperature had been spiking while she slept. Her ears had bled, and now she was dead asleep in my arms. She wouldn't fall into the same fate as this other woman, could she?

"The elders of the pack noticed she had the smell of a wolf, not a human, but the male denied it. He could not smell a wolf's scent on her, just his own scent tangled with hers." Beretta closed her eyes and let out a heavy breath.

"That night, the female died mid-shift, and the male died shortly after."

"No!" I yelled, picking up my mate. "That will not happen! Why would the goddess do that?!"

"Because she is a cold, heartless bitch, that's why!" Locke stood from his chair. "You and I both know she is, Grim. We shared the same sentiment when we first met before we crossed the veil. She is there to pick on the weak, to pick on the strong. All for fun, like a human with a magnifying glass, watching an ant burn in front of their eyes! It's all a game!"

"It is not! Surely the gods aren't that cruel!" I took fumbling steps toward the door. The wind howled outside, and I grunted in frustration. Finding a blanket hung over a nearby coat rack, I bundled my mate as best as I could.

The witch betrayed me—the goddess, my friends were no help. They were all giving up on Journey, on me.

"Grim, wait. Let's talk about this. Surely this can't be right." Bones tried to leave his chair, but Locke pushed him back into his seat.

"She will not die. I'll make sure of that," I growled at them. "She will have a successful shift. She will survive. This is not all for naught!"

I burst through the door and into the swirling wind of snow. The dryness in the air made the snow into small pieces of glitter that stung my eyes.

Surely after all that Journey and I had been through was not a ruse. No, pieces of the puzzle were coming together, things would work out. They would, right?

I'd gotten my hopes up when I was a pup, that I would have a mate to love and protect. I thought I had lost that chance, but Journey was here in my arms. I wasn't going to give up.

I pushed through the blinding wind; the snow swirling around us as I ran through the streets. I almost stumbled but caught myself on the light post near the tattoo shop. The red light of the "closed" sign dripped into the snow like blood.

I growled, pushing myself to get to the back alley and the stairs to our apartment. I would fix them, I would make sure they were sturdy enough for her to climb on her own.

Because she would not leave me, she would not die. I wouldn't let her, and I would fight death in order to keep her alive. Even if that meant I had to give my soul to keep her in this world.

Journey was too beautiful to face the harsh realities of death. She was too young to fall into the underworld without experiencing life. And life could only be beautiful because she was in it.

I kicked in the door, the knob nestling into the hole it'd made the other day. I kept her wrapped, covering her with the scent. She would be safe in the den I'd made for her. It was secure, no one would come here, and no one would take her from me.

I hurriedly shut the door and grabbed candles from the cabinet in the kitchen. I lit five of them, setting them on the coffee table, and watched them flicker in the darkness.

I rubbed my hands up and down my face as I sat beside my mate. She was laying perfectly still, bundled in all of our bedding. She wasn't sweating, her face wasn't pale, but still the ominous feeling didn't leave my gut.

What if she was taken from me?

Why did it have to be us?

A silent tear rolled down my face. I loved this woman more than my mother. It wasn't just because of a bond; it was the love that she had in her heart. She had opened up to me, to my friends, far quicker than I ever thought a woman that had been through so much could have. She was far stronger than I could ever be.

She wasn't angry about what happened to her; she didn't curse the gods. Journey prayed for a miracle. She held onto hope, and she did find it. We found it.

I leaned forward, wrapping my body around my mate. She immediately turned into my chest. She took large breaths of my scent, her body calming and nuzzling further into my embrace.

"Goddess, please don't take her from me," I begged.

A single tear welled in my eye. Gods, I didn't remember if I'd even cried the day I left my pack.

The emotion was too strong, my worry too great, so I prayed to her again. "Please let her live. I can't bear the thought of losing her."

CHAPTER THIRTY FIVE

Journey

The brisk chill on my skin woke me from a deep slumber. It felt like a deep slumber anyway, because when I tried to move my arm, it felt unbearably heavy. Instead, my eyes fluttered open. My head rested on someone's lap.

The elegant snow drifted around us. I was no longer inside the warmth of the witch's shop, but outside where I first saw Grim's wolf—the overlook near the magnificent forest.

I curled my head into my body to keep the snow away from my face. A delightful velvety feminine voice stirred me.

It wasn't Grim's lap where my head was cradled. I tried to jerk away, but a gentle hand on my cheek kept me still.

"Darling, do not fret." Her voice was serene, and my soul found comfort in it.

"Easy now. She gave you a hefty dose. I don't want you to be dizzy. Now, sit up slowly and carefully." The woman guided me, helping me sit up on the worn bench. It was the same bench where I told Grim of my past.

"There, much better. How are you feeling, Journey?"

Looking through the mess of my hair, I saw the most ethereal woman I had ever seen. She had white hair so bright it held hints of a blue sheen from the night sky. There were also tiny silver sparkles embedded between the small braids which made me instantly jealous. She was perfect, not a single flaw on her skin.

Her skin, although white, still showed hints of pink where the cold nipped at her cheeks and nose. "How are you, Journey?" she cooed. "You've been through a lot in your brief life."

I licked my lips, my eyes looking everywhere but her. I was embarrassed that I'd stared at her so boldly, a woman like this shouldn't be gawked at. There was no chastisement in her voice, yet I could feel the power radiating from her.

"Are you an angel?" I blurted. I winced at how loud it was, but something stirred inside me, telling me this woman was important.

"I am Selene. Most know me as the Moon Goddess," she chuckled.

I gasped, sliding from the bench. My knees hit the snow-padded ground. Do I bow? Curtsey? Kiss her feet? She's the one that brought me to Grim, and I was humble enough to let her know how much I wanted to thank her.

"Darling, come here. You don't need to kneel in the snow. Come sit with me."

Her words left no room for discussion, and I slid ungracefully back onto the broken bench.

Her laugh echoed into the snow falling around us. Her white robes moved along the drifting snow as wind gently blew.

"Come now, we have little time. Your mate is upset, and you need to tend to him." She patted the seat next to her like I was her best friend, so I drew closer, feeling the warmth of her body.

"Journey, I have a lot to tell you, but we have very little time." Her smile faded, and she gazed out over the cliff.

The snow fluttered onto the pine branches. Tiny movements in the forest caught my eye as I saw the small animals taking shelter in their homes. They poked their little heads out as they continued to watch the snow fall to the ground.

"You are changing, Journey. I'm sorry it is happening so quickly, but with the many dangers you and Grim may face, this was the best way to protect you."

"Changing?" I gulped.

"Yes, you are becoming a wolf. The second human that has ever attempted such a feat."

My mouth hung open in shock. The bleeding ears, the heightened smell, hearing voices—It was all because my body was changing to be like Grim? To become an enormous wolf?

"But I'm human," I argued. "How can that happen? And where is the first human to change? Can they help me?"

Selene gave a tight-lipped smile, her hand reaching for mine and pulling it into my lap.

"I will be honest with you, Journey. You deserve honesty for what you have been through. The first human did not make it through their transformation."

I slapped my hand over my mouth, and my arm trembled. Selene's hand rubbed over mine. Its warmth soothed me and calmed me instantly.

"There is a reason she did not survive. You will survive. I can promise you this," she said reverently.

"How do you know I will survive? I can't leave Grim. He needs me. We need each other."

Selene smiled and grasped my hand again.

"The last human did not survive because she had not completed the bond. It was because of my carelessness that she died." Her head dropped and wetness pooled in her eyes. "Neither of them prayed to me, but there was a pull. There was no way I could warn them. She needed to bite him to complete the bond. I was foolish. I was trying to mend two broken souls together, to give the rejected a new beginning, but I did not account for the fact that humans would not bite their partner. Their bond was not completed before her change, the threads not tight enough for her to pull the strength she needed from her mate."

A shiver ran through my body. I'd never wanted to bite anything before, that was until Grim. His scent was strong, and I went with my gut. Luckily, Grim liked it, but it scared the crap out of me. "Was it you that pushed me to bite Grim?"

She nodded. "You prayed to me, opened your soul. With that, I could give you a nudge."

We both stayed silent. The seconds turned to minutes. I was completely unsettled.

"How were you able to push me? With your magic? Can you read my mind?" I asked.

"No, I cannot read your mind. I cannot enter a human mind so easily as I can my children. But when you prayed, it gave me hope. You opened yourself to me, bringing me into your life, and you were the perfect soul to give to Grim. Out of all of my rogue children, he looked the most battered on the outside. But inside, he was worthy. I knew he would turn to mush when he found you." She grinned.

I scooted closer to her, and she leaned over to peer into my eyes. "My guilt from my first failed attempt to transform a human female terrified me and prevented me from trying again for years—not that any of the rogues prayed to me for help. They closed their souls to me. The rogues blamed me, hated me, but I cannot take a wolf's choice away. I cannot take away their agency. They must choose for themselves. It isn't all up to me. I can pair the souls, but if they do not accept..."

"You can't do anything. I understand." I gulped. "But what of the shifters, those beings that are left broken-hearted? Not given an option. Why do they have to suffer?" It wasn't fair in the slightest they had to suffer. They weren't the ones that gave up on their mates.

"I've been working with Hades to give those not paired with a soul a second chance through reincarnation," she said harshly. "I will make it up to my children, who have not been granted another chance by giving them another life. It's been a long time coming."

Selene waved her hand to the sky, the clouds parting, and the moon shone down on us. "It was when you prayed for help, Journey. When you asked for my help to save you, to take you away from all your suffering. I knew giving you a mate would make your broken soul whole again. And wouldn't you know it? You and Grim are the perfect match." She winked.

"You opened your soul, Journey. My ability to help you along the way opened the window to a new life for these broken souls."

"So, a human praying to you gives them a chance to be mated to a rogue?" I asked.

"Or the other way around. The rogue themselves can ask for a second chance. They must believe in me once again. If they close their soul to me, there isn't much I can do. If I had known that I needed a prayer from at least one of them for the first human and rogue pairing, their lives wouldn't have been lost." Her hand balled into a fist, her white nails piercing the skin. Crimson blood stained her light blue robe.

"You didn't know." I tried to soothe her. "You didn't know they had to be open to you, but now you know. It's just, I know the club, the rogues, they won't pray to you." I shook my head. "We've tried, we told them–"

"Ah, but you are trying, Journey. And that is why you are extra special. You are the first human to pray to me for help. The Fates have blessed you for it. To help me correct my mistakes."

"Grim is my gift, I know." I smiled.

"No, another gift." She shook her head.

I raised an eyebrow, and she made me stand. We walked to the edge of the cliff and stood underneath the large moon that lit up the forest below us. Snow still fell, but the moon shone over the entire valley.

"You have a giant soul. A soul so large, it's been itching to come out since you were a child."

I wrapped my arms around my body, feeling the coldness seep inside. Selene opened her robe and engulfed me inside them. She could be taller than any man I've ever met.

She was a goddess, so I shouldn't expect anything less—not in this new world.

"You are not just becoming a wolf, little one. You will become my voice. You will become the very first wolf priestess."

My mouth dropped, and I looked up at her. "A priestess? Me? I don't think I can do that!" I tried to step away, but she pulled me closer.

"Darling, you are perfect. You hold your past human life in your hands and understand how difficult a transition it is entering the world of fantasy. You can help open their souls, so I can bond them together. You and Grim are the catalyst for a new beginning."

I shook my head. How could I be that important? I had prayed to anyone, anything to help me and now that help had come, she'd asked for my help? Could I help with something so much bigger than me?

For many years, I was a toy for men. I didn't have any special power. There was nothing special about me other than Grim had saved me, and he no longer scowled when he entered a room. I could bring a smile to his face, but helping other humans, like me, could I do it?

"Do you know the twitch in your eye? How you can't sit still, how you were always different from everyone else as you grew up?"

I bit my cheek, squeezing my hands together tightly until I finally nodded.

"Because your soul was meant for great things, Journey." Selene knelt. "The Fates chose you to help me."

"Maybe they're wrong. I don't even have a high school diploma!" I said, exhausted.

"They are never wrong. They can see multiple futures, and this path is worth taking. I know you can do this. You helped your mate; you will help others."

Selene leaned forward, her forehead touching mine.

"Accept this calling, Journey. Your heart is large, and even without the powers I will give to you, you can already see the work I'm trying to pursue. With your help, these rogues can become whole again."

A goddess was pleading with me, asking me for help. Little me. But what if I failed? What if I couldn't do what she was asking?

"Did you help me forget my past? Selective memories? Those...men?" I choked, grabbing my neck. I could no longer see them, feel them, but the thought of men touching me made me emotional, nonetheless.

"Yes, you will never remember them. I'm sorry I couldn't help more. I got the help to you as soon as I could," she defended. "You were never drugged, Journey. I kept you under so they couldn't take what was left of your beautiful soul."

For the first time in a long while, I cried openly. I wrapped my arms around her neck, and she squeezed me just as fiercely.

"You were dealt a hard life, little one. And I know I'm asking much of you to become my priestess, my voice, but it will help so many of your friends."

"Like Delilah?" Her name jumped out of my mouth before I could stop it. I knew Delilah and Hawke were special. It wasn't just the attraction they had, they were magnetic.

Selene rubbed her lips together, trying to hold a smile. "Just like Delilah."

If I could help Delilah, I would. I would do anything for the first friend I'd made in this crazy world.

"I'll do it," I whispered. "I'll do the best I can."

Instead of jumping for joy, Selene pressed her forehead against mine. A blue glow lit the area surrounding us. The snowflakes reflected a blue sparkle, and my forehead was bathed in warmth.

Once she pulled her forehead away, a point down crescent moon appeared on her forehead.

"Thank you, my little priestess," she smiled.

She rose to her full height, but instead of returning to the worn bench, she covered her feet with her robes and floated over the cliff and stood over the valley.

The thought of the couple that died a horrible death because of no open connection to the goddess broke my heart. How awful it was for a human to suffer. Especially when neither of them knew what to do to fix it. Would their souls ever come together?

"Moon Goddess?" I said loud enough for her to hear. She turned to me, the blue crescent glowing brightly. "The human and her mate that perished, will they get their second chance? Soon? I feel like they shouldn't wait much longer."

Thoughts of Delilah and Hawke kept hovering in my mind. I rubbed my forehead, feeling the warmth from the Goddess's touch.

The goddess chuckled. "I'd say very soon." She swished her robes side to side. "And it is all because of you."

CHAPTER THIRTY SIX

Journey

Selene's robes twirled around her until her body molded with the sky. Her dress became the clouds covering the full moon from view. The warmth of a nearby breeze blew on my neck, and I rubbed my shoulder to find something soft and furry beneath it.

My eyes blinked once, and I found my body lying beneath soft blankets and pillows with a gigantic body on top of me.

"Why do I keep waking up covered in either blankets or bodies?" I silently huffed.

Instead of feeling Grim's beard, I felt a new texture I was unfamiliar with. It was a big, beautiful mess of dark red fur. One paw lay over my chest, the snout of the beautiful beast rested on top of my head. The heat of his breath trickled down my face and neck.

"Grim?"

The beast didn't move, not at first. All I heard was the low, deep purring of an animal resting upon me. It was Grim's wolf. I'd recognize that beautiful color anywhere.

I ran my fingers through the white fur on its chest. The deep, heavy breathing quickened, and the animal groaned.

Would his wolf still be called Grim? From the voices I'd heard, I would think he would be an entirely separate entity, but I didn't know. I knew so little about this new world save for the fact that humans weren't the only beings.

"Come on Mr. Floofers, I need to pee." I pushed his enormous paw away, but it was replaced by another, and part of his weight bared down on my chest.

"Mr. Floofers, you're heavy!" I pushed him away again, wiggling against the gigantic body suffocating me.

"Mr. Floofers? What kind of name is that?" His voice rang clear in my ears. *"Out of all the names you could have picked, you picked that one?"*

"Uh, I didn't know what to call you. You aren't obviously Grim." I pushed him again.

He huffed in annoyance and rolled away. He moved his body just enough to still be touching mine as I sat up.

"You're right I'm not. But that doesn't mean you can give me a name you would give a cat."

"Well, I didn't know your real name," I retorted. "What is it anyway?" I stared up at the beautiful dark eyes that stared down at me.

His wet nose pushed toward my neck and took a large sniff.

"Go relieve yourself, come straight back." It wasn't a request, but a command, and his body showed no signs of playfulness.

I knew he wouldn't hurt me, so I playfully scratched his head and jumped from the bed. The clicking of his claws touched the floor behind me, and I turned to watch him stretch his body, lifting his rear end in the air and his claws extending.

"Go on," he huffed.

I padded to the bathroom, took care of my business, and washed my face. I felt much lighter on my feet today than I had since I was a young child. Not to say I wasn't healthy before, but my body felt rejuvenated. I felt like a whole new person.

As I patted my face dry with the fluffy towel, I gazed up in the mirror and found out exactly why I felt so wonderful. A light tan, barely visible mark shone in the middle of my forehead. It was shaped like a crescent moon, points facing down, just like the Moon Goddess.

I touched it delicately. Tracing the small outline of the moon that graced my forehead. So, it wasn't a dream after all, it was all real.

"Of course, it was real," I mumbled to myself. "It was too magical for it not to be."

The scratching at the door paused my awe, and I opened it to find Mr. Floofers trotting back and forth impatiently.

He tilted his head, his nose bopping the mark on my head, but he said nothing. He stared at it, his fur on his back standing up on end.

"Do you need to use the restroom?" I chided, trying to break the awkward silence.

He huffed, not appreciating the joke, and pulled on the hem of my shirt. *"You are taking too long, come out."*

His maw still didn't move, and I couldn't help but smile at the freaking mind-link.

"Come." He pulled on my shirt again with his teeth and led me back to our bed. He jumped on top of it, the massive wolf taking almost the entire bed until I was fully sitting on it. He pushed my body down with nose and began pushing blankets all around my body.

"What are you doing!?" I giggled, pushing them away, but he grunted in disapproval and began again.

"Making you warm, you have been sick." He pushed a blanket over my

face, and I pulled it down to throw it at him.

"That's enough. Now tell me why are you here and not Grim?"

I didn't want to bring up the mark on my forehead, not yet anyway. It made Mr. Floofers upset. He stared at my forehead like I had grown a horn.

With that being said, were unicorns real?

His pawing and kneading the bed stopped, and his nose went to my shoulder. I petted him silently while he purred. It wasn't for my comfort; I was perfectly fine. But he continued anyway, rubbing his face on my skin.

"Do you not want me here, mate? Do I scare you? You do not smell of fear."

"Scared of you? No, I'm not scared! I just never see you; I always see Grim."

I petted the long fur behind his neck, and he settled down onto the bed. He laid across my legs, pinning me against the mattress so I wouldn't leave, and forced his nose between my breasts.

"He hogs you. It was my turn," He said reasonably.

"So, you are two different beings, right? There is Grim and there is you, his animal?"

He grunted in reply.

"And your name is what then?"

"I have no name," he stated. *"I am his animal, I am his wolf. A mate can give me a name if she so wishes, but it is not common. Animals communicate with animals, the human side to the other human side."*

"But you are communicating with me," I stated.

He kept still, silent for a long time but I waited patiently.

"You do not have a wolf, and I am lonely."

Oh my god, my heart broke.

But I would have a wolf soon, and then Floofers wouldn't be alone. He would have another animal to talk to. I smiled at that.

Floofers continued to rub his nose, his face, his ears all over my neck and shoulder. Occasionally he would nip at my shoulder, and then the most wonderful smell entered my nose. It was a concentrated version of his scent, the scent that covered him and Grim. The deep forest, the nature, the untouched portions of the earth that humans hadn't encountered. It was stronger now, like I was sticking a damned Yankee Candle up my nose.

I hummed, delighted at the newfound scent he was rubbing on me.

"I am happy you are here and that I can talk to you." I wrapped my hands around Floofer's neck. "But where is Grim? I'm worried about him."

Floofers sighed and kept his nose buried in my neck. *"He is tired. He has barely slept since I found you. Now that I am strong enough, I forced him back, and now he sleeps."*

"He's inside you, sleeping?" I asked, trying to understand. "And you found me?"

Floofer grunted, and his tail wrapped around my waist.

"It was my nose that found you. When I smelled your scent under the bed, I knew you were ours. It took time for me to regain my strength, but now that I'm here, I will never leave. You are mine, as I am yours."

"This would make such a cute romance movie," I giggled. "But why is Grim sleeping now? How long was I asleep?"

"You slept a long time, a sunset and a sunrise."

My stomach growled angrily, and I gripped it.

"You are hungry. I'm failing as your mate." He stood up on the bed, caging me in with all four legs. *"I will hunt for us. You must stay in our den. I will return shortly."* Floofers jumped off the bed, his claws clicking across the floor.

"Woah, hang on!" I jumped from the bed and ran to the fridge. It was stocked full of raw meat for Grim and Floofers, and it also had enough vegetables and fruit to sustain me as well. I could make us a meal here.

"I can cook, don't leave. Not unless you need to go use the potty?"

Floofer raised a brow, his head tilting in bewilderment.

"Pot-ty?"

"Yeah, the bathroom?" I hooked my thumb, pointing back at the bathroom. "Unless you figured out how to squat and not make a mess?"

I hid my smile.

Floofer's, on the other hand, radiated embarrassment in the link we shared. *"I am an animal. We do not use human stone seats."*

He scratched the door, and I padded over to let him out. *"Do not leave this den, mate."*

"So bossy," I muttered and put my hand on my hip, waving him off.

While Floofers was outside, doing gods know what, I pulled out hunks of meat from the fridge. Most of it was wrapped, a lot of it was still bloody, and when I put it on the counter, I looked at my hands to find them covered in blood.

Grim may have been organized and made our apartment a den, but it still needed a woman's touch. And lucky for me, I was that woman.

I picked up all the meat to remove it, found plastic to re-wrap the meat and clean off the now dirty shelves of the fridge. If Grim was that worried about me, he probably didn't have time to clean and make everything perfectly organized and sanitized.

And poor Grim? He hadn't been sleeping because of me? He was that worried? There wasn't anything to be worried about, now. I was to become a wolf, and he wouldn't have to worry as much anymore.

I wouldn't get sick or have the same ailments as a human. I'd be able to run in the forest, be more like him. And I would fit in with the club, not just as the only human that tags along. I'd actually be helping, taking care of those that would need to find their mates.

I'd be a part of something great.

Once the fridge was clean, I took the largest piece of meat and set it aside.

Floofers probably wanted it raw, but when Grim woke up, I was going to have a nice steak dinner for when he was ready. I don't think I could bear him eating raw meat in front of me while he was human. Even if he was part animal.

Did that mean I would eventually want to eat raw meat, too? My stomach churned at the thought, and I wiped the sweat from my brow. It was warm in here. For the first time, I felt really warm.

I grabbed the cloth and ran it under the water, then placed it on my forehead. As soon as I did, Floofers barged in and kicked the door shut with his back leg.

"Mate, what is wrong?" he growled.

Damn, he was so bossy.

"I'm just hot is all. What is the temperature in here?"

Floofers found the thermostat, and despite how high it was, he didn't even need to put his paws up on the wall to read it. *"It's eighty. It's been that way for weeks while you healed."*

"Good gracious, his electric bill will be atrocious," I whispered. "How are you and Grim not burning up with heat that high?"

"Wolves have heat regulation. We can thrive in almost any temperature," he said like it was the most natural thing.

I pursed my lips, taking the knife and cutting the potatoes into cubes. If that was the case, then why isn't my body regulating the temperature if I am becoming a wolf? Was I still too human for that?

I placed the potatoes in the boiling pot of water and picked up the meat and cut it into cubes for Floofers.

"I am to take care of you. I do not like you preparing a meal for me."

"Well, you kind of lack opposable thumbs there, honey. I don't think you'll be able to prepare a meal for my human stomach." I patted my belly. "Besides, Grim has fed me and you are supposedly the same person, right?

That means you have fed me, too."

Floofers tilted his head. He leaned up against me as I prepared our food.

"Do you miss speaking with other animals?" I asked. "Are animals part of a pack?" I reached around his ear, rubbing it gently.

"I miss being part of a pack, yes. But only if that pack wants me. Our last pack rejected us, even though we were not at fault," he growled.

I kneeled on the floor, and he peered down at me. I wrapped my arms around his neck, and he sighed audibly. "You are wanted, Mr. Floofers. I want you; the club wants you. And we are going to fix it all. The Moon Goddess told me so." I pointed to the crescent moon on my forehead.

His tongue fell from his mouth, and he licked my forehead. He didn't comment, but sat on his hind legs and stared at me.

He didn't believe me.

"Can I give you a name?" I asked, trying to change the subject. "Because to me, you are two separate beings, and it is driving me nuts."

"Whatever makes my mate happy," he purred.

I cut the last bit of meat into cubes and strode over to the table. His body was so large his muzzle hung over the table as he ate. I sat and watched him, entangling my fingers in his fur. I wanted to constantly touch him, let him know I was here, that I would always be here for him.

Because he was lonely, despite having Grim for company.

I wanted him to know that he was loved by me, too. That he was special, and I thought of him as separate from Grim, and that I would love to give him attention, too.

"What does Grim call you?"

Floofers licked the meat from his lips.

"Wolf or animal," he stated.

I hummed, tapping my finger on the table. "I'm going to call you Leif. It means loved."

Leif lowered his head and put it into my lap. "*Why would you give an animal such a name?*"

"Why wouldn't I?" I argued. "I love Grim, and I love you. You are a part of each other. Neither of you could live without the other, and I could never live without each of you."

CHAPTER THIRTY SEVEN

Grim

Currently sleeping, my ass.

I was awake while my wolf took over my body. The bond had strengthened him, and his will became too strong to keep him inside. So, he came out in our den, and now he was having conversations with our mate, a feat that didn't normally happen.

Animals talked to other animals, not to their mates. But this whole thing with Journey was out of the norm. Surprise was no longer in my vocabulary, however. Everything had changed since she'd stumbled into my life.

I needed to get him out of our den to run in the forest to sate his wild side, but then we also had to take care of Journey. We didn't trust anyone else to look after her. Not right now, not when she might shift into her animal.

Fuck, her animal. Her wolf.

Could what Beretta said be true? Would she die during the shift? There were too many questions and not enough answers. That was the motto that would continue to thrive in the club until we knew what course Journey would take.

I didn't like not knowing what was going to happen to my mate. I didn't like that she had already suffered so much, and now she was going to go through the pain of a shift she may or may not survive.

My stomach churned, and my heart dropped to my stomach. I'd rather be eaten alive by a dragon and sit in their stomach while the acid slowly digested my body into bones than have my mate suffer.

The goddess couldn't give her to me and then take her away. But she did once before to another couple, thousands of years ago.

I gripped the sheets tightly.

I couldn't have my mate be an experiment. Our bond couldn't break, not now.

I shifted from wolf to my human body in the bed next to my mate. She didn't stir, her body still exhausted from whatever magical salve that coated her chest. When I returned to my body, I wiped it clean from her chest so no more dreams or any other aftereffects could appear.

I worried it had been too late because now she had a crescent moon on her forehead. It was faint, barely noticeable, but any supernatural would realize the tan marking was not made by her body. The mark of the goddess was there.

When my wolf saw it on her forehead, he automatically stiffened. His anger rose immediately, thinking about Beretta's words. Now, there was no denying it. Journey will shift. Journey has been chosen to be the first and would hopefully survive.

Was it all just another experiment? To see if she would survive so others could follow in Journey's footsteps?

My nose trailed up her neck, and her eyes blinked open.

"Grim?" she muttered sleepily. "You're back. Are you feeling better?"

"Much better, my mate." I rubbed my hand up and down my arm.

"Here, I made you dinner last night. I can heat it up for you." Journey tried to leave the nest, but I pulled her back inside.

I was not hungry for food. I was hungry for her.

Journey's skin was hot, a slight sheen of sweat covering her forehead. Her skin glowed, and her scent had changed. I could smell the undertones of a wolf being born inside her body, being attached to her soul. Her nose flared when she sought me out and even her eyes would dilate when concentrating on something important.

She was changing, but did she know?

"Journey, what did you see in your vision?" I asked.

She smiled, and tiny fangs emerged.

Gods, this can't be happening.

"Oh, it was awesome! I met the Moon Goddess! She was so pretty, Grim. At first, I thought it was all a dream, but then I woke up, and this was on my forehead." She touched the symbol with her fingers. "She said I was changing, Grim, that I was going to be a wolf, just like you, because of our bond."

I gritted my teeth but forced a smile. "That's great, that's unbelievable."

Do I tell her it was attempted once before? That the other human didn't make it? Make her worry about something that was inevitable? That she might die in the process?

"Yeah, she also said I was going to help others, too. To help them find their mates. The entire club is going to find mates, Grim. We just have to get them to pray to the goddess, or at least open up their souls to allow her to help them."

I rubbed the stubble on my chin. I was still worried about us. I didn't give a fuck about anyone else.

"That's great," I said absentmindedly.

I buried my nose into her neck, pushing her back into the nest. I needed her, I needed to keep her with me. I would not share her with anyone else until I knew she could shift.

If she left me, if she died, I would die too. I couldn't handle being alone in this hell without her.

"Grim, isn't that great? I didn't get to talk to Leif about it. He was really grouchy. Are all animals grouchy? Do you think my wolf will be grouchy, too? Or are they all different?"

Journey's excitement made me smile, but I mourned for the death that might befall her. Our witch couldn't stop it. No one could stop her shift from coming.

These last moments, these last days with her, I wanted to keep to myself.

"Grim? Grim?" She shook my shoulder, and I removed myself from her hold.

"I don't speak to any other animals, just to my own," I confessed. "My wolf has always been, well, an animal."

She hummed, kissing my cheek.

"Oh, his name is Leif. You have to call him that now," she chirped. "You are two different beings. You should have given him a name."

I shook my head. "We do not give names to our animals."

"Ah, but I just gave him one. He liked it very much. He even licked my cheek afterward. You must treat him better. He was much happier after I gave him a name." She wagged her finger at me.

I chuckled, kissing her lips. "If that is what you say, then I will call him such."

"I wonder what I will call mine..." She sat up on her knees, leaning over me. Instead of wearing the sleep wear I bought her, she wore my large black shirt that went passed her thighs. Her breasts pushed against the fabric, and her nipples stood prominently, so I could see them perfectly.

"When will she come? After my shift?" she asked excitedly.

Not wanting to spoil her excitement, I leaned up, kissing her again. If she was to die during her shift, I would savor every moment I had with her until then. As much as my heart ached, I would meet her in the afterlife, find her, and mark her again.

"After your shift, during your first run," I muttered. "My wolf first spoke to me when I finished my obligatory run with my pack."

"Oh, we won't have a pack. We are each other's pack for right now. Right? You will be there with me the whole way right?"

I sat up in the bed, so she straddled my dick. She wasn't wearing any underwear, and I groaned. Did she not know what she did to me?

"You're wet," I stated.

She blushed, her hands trailing down my naked body. "I'm always wet around you." Her voice was low and sultry.

Gods, I wanted her. I wanted to feel her warm skin against me, touch her in every way.

I ran my fingers up the sides of her thighs, up to her hips, and over the front of her body. I cupped her breasts, and she leaned into my touch.

"I love it when you touch me," she said.

She leaned forward, her ass sticking further away from me, and I could see the outline of her glorious skin in a picture frame on the table.

"You drive me and my wolf crazy." I nipped at her bottom lip.

"Leif, you mean I drive you and Leif crazy."

"Whatever." I pressed my lips against hers, ripping the shirt from top to bottom. My hands roamed her body, cupping her ass, her breasts, and tweaking a nipple between my fingers.

She withered against me, the heat of her sex rubbing against the underside of my cock.

"I need you," she whispered.

Fuck, I needed her too, more than she would ever know.

She pushed me into the nest, her lips rubbing up against my cock. "Can I taste you?" she asked, her hands roaming my body until she reached my shaft. "I just really want to taste you."

Her tongue licked the head, my precum leaking onto her lips. She hummed, her body vibrating with want as I felt her pussy on my leg.

"Wait," I rasped. I turned her body, keeping her mouth close to my cock, and brought her hips to my head so her pussy sat on my face.

Now, we both could get what we wanted.

Her tongue swirled against the head of my cock, and my fingers dug into her ass as I lowered her against my mouth.

"Ah!" She let go of my dick with a pop as she squealed.

My tongue invaded her core, lapping up her arousal until I latched onto her clit with my lips, sucking vigorously while she wiggled her ass.

Her hips moved on their own, my nails digging into her skin. I could smell the metallic scent of blood from my claws scratching.

Her moans heightened, and her pussy clenched until she fell over into a blissful orgasm, moaning into my cock. Her scream was loud, long, and my cock twitched in her mouth.

"Let me fuck you, let me spill come inside that tight pussy," I snarled.

"Gods, yes, please do that."

I flipped her over, my hands resting on either side of her face. Panting heavily into her ear, I lined the tip of my cock at her entrance.

"I'm not fragile," she whined. "I want you to fuck me how you really want it."

"You always feel good," I argued. "Better than anything."

"But you hold back, Grim. Show me you really want me," she snarled.

Her teeth bared, and her fangs lengthened. The heat of her skin sparked a newly unhinged hunger inside me.

"Take her," Leif snarled. *"She wants it."*

I roared, shoving my cock into her tight pussy. She screamed, her hips pushing toward me.

Our bed sat next to the wall and my thrusts pushed her across the nest. She braced herself against the wall and waited until I thrust forth into her again.

"God, yes, Grim!" she cried. "More!"

I lifted her hips, positioning them until I was hovering on top of her, jack hammering her while she grunted with approval. The walls of her pussy swelled, sucking my cock deeper into her body.

My knot, which I could not hold back so I could fuck her again after I came, lodged itself deep into her pussy.

She screamed as she came again, and then I lifted her so her legs could wrap around my body and forced her back against the wall. I pushed up to standing on the nest as the swelling of my cock entered and retreated from her body as I fucked her relentlessly.

The smoothness of her walls, the head of my cock pushing thrusting into her cavern, called my wolf to action. Our primal urges growling, snarling, grunting at each thrust made our mate wrap her arms around our neck as she leaked more of the sweet arousal from her body.

Her hair was tangled, falling into a stream of dampened locks on my shoulder where she rested her head. "So good," she purred.

She licked my shoulder, and I felt the sharp teeth of her fangs pierce my skin. I howled at the pleasure that came over my body.

My ass clenched, and I pushed one last thrust into her body, my knot swelling so large I could no longer move. I shot ropes of my come into her, coating the walls of her pussy as she milked me dry.

"So full," she mumbled into my shoulder. "Bite me, Grim," she pleaded. "Bite me, claim me again."

I didn't wait. I let Leif take over. He took a quick bite into her shoulder, and her pussy spasmed around us.

We both sighed happily. I held her against the wall while my cock stayed inside her.

It was then I felt something graze the side of my body.

Worried that I'd knocked the drywall from the wall, I pulled my teeth from my mate's neck and looked to my left, where I felt a tiny object graze me.

It wasn't a part of the wall, but a small piece of white plastic in the shape of a stick.

I shrugged my shoulders, not caring any longer, and gently pulled my mate from the wall and laid us on the bed.

My cock continued to spurt seed inside her, her body trembling with each twitch of my cock.

"It's like it gets better every time," she giggled. "Is that how it's supposed to be?"

Her smile widened, the brightness of her eyes taking hold deep in my soul. She was so happy with me. The rejected one, the one that wasn't nearly good enough for her.

I purred and cupped her face. I stroked her cheek with my thumb and took my time memorizing every line, every freckle, every imperfection that made her perfect.

"It will always get better because I'm with you." My cock twitched, and my knot softened.

I ran my fingers down her thigh. My cock finally freed itself, and my come gradually dripped out of her cunt. Taking my fingers, I pushed it back inside, my animal demanding I keep my seed inside her longer.

Even if she couldn't get pregnant right now, the idea of her baring me a pup, one made with love, almost brought me to tears.

I never thought I would have a family, and I was excited at the prospect of it. Only to have it taken away from me again. Because she would shift, and she would...

I sniffed, trying to keep those treacherous tears away.

Still, if I had the choice to have my mate for a day or not at all, I would still choose to see her, to have her, and cherish every second with her. And that is what I would do until we both die in each other's arms.

"I love you Grim, Leif." She ran her fingers through my sweaty hair.

"And I love you, too, little mate."

CHAPTER THIRTY EIGHT

Journey

"This is so good," I said, licking my lips.

The burger was huge, dripping with barbeque sauce, mushrooms, and cheese. It was the best burger I'd ever eaten, and it was a full half pound.

I was starving. I was always starving now.

"Knew you'd like it," Grim smiled. "You will crave more meat now that you're changing." Grim took a sip of coffee.

As soon as he said that, his gaze became empty and hollow. I worried he didn't want me to be a wolf, because he rarely talked about it. As soon as I told him I would shift, that the goddess said I would, he immediately shut down the conversation.

He didn't want to talk about it, but I had questions. Like, would it hurt? I had yet to see him shift into his wolf, but I couldn't imagine contorting your body would be pleasant.

Even so, he continued to change the subject, either by enticing me with food, kissing me, or seducing me with some erotic purr that instantly made me wet.

I hadn't even told him the goddess blessed me to be a priestess.

When Locke saw the new mark on my forehead, he became grumpily silent, too. Everyone was ignoring it like it wasn't there. I knew they could see it. I knew it was significant, but not one person would comment on it.

With their hesitation and anger toward the goddess, they must see it as a curse, and they didn't want to divulge any theories, scared they would upset me. Because if Grim thought I was upset with someone, he got all growly and tried to beat people up.

I tapped the bun of my burger, looking down at the juicy, greasy meat, and my stomach decided enough was enough. My thoughts had clouded over my hunger, so I put the burger down.

Grim side-eyed me, taking the mug from his lips and tried to speak to me, but he was interrupted by a door blowing open and a blast of wind wrapping around everyone at the bar.

"Where is she?!" Hawke roared.

Everyone in the bar paused, except for the bartender on duty. He was cleaning the bar with a rag and went on with his business.

Hawke stomped straight toward Grim and I, and I backed up in my seat, my back bumping against Grim's body. He wrapped his arm around me, and he growled warningly.

"You were the last to talk to her," he grumbled to me. Hawke's eyes were dark.

He was no longer there, but an animal beneath him stirred.

I squinted, checking if I could see any movement of an animal, and there it was. It was prowling deep inside him. The wolf glared back at me, and I wanted to say I heard him whimper, but I couldn't be sure.

Grim stood up from his stool and moved in front of me. I gripped the back of his cut and put my forehead on his back.

"You do not speak to my mate that way," Grim snarled. "You treat her with respect, or I'll kick your ass out of this bar."

Hawke huffed in annoyance and backed away. "Where is she? Where is Delilah?" Hawke spoke not just to us but to the entire bar.

Everyone shrugged their shoulders. Even the bartender who was in charge of making the schedules didn't know.

"She hasn't been in, man," he said. "She's always here, and I didn't get a two-week notice or nothing. Her roommates say her room is empty, though."

Hawke slammed his fists on the bar. "They wouldn't even let me in the apartment. What else did they say?"

The bartender scoffed and put the glass on the shelf. "Well, they said she was fed up with the men around here. No one was able to commit, tired of having her heart broken. You wouldn't have anything to do with that now, would you?"

Hawke shook his head. "No, I wouldn't."

Grim

Journey coughed the word "liar." The entire bar chuckled and went about their own business. Everyone in this entire bar knew damn well Delilah was in love with Hawke, and he was too blind, too stupid, and too chicken shit to admit it.

He had feelings for her, too, no doubt about that. He held back because he couldn't be with a human. Well, things were changing, and she could very well be his mate. Question was for how long could he have her?

Now that he saw me with my second chance, maybe he was hopeful a spark would ignite, and they would be mates. But, if what Journey said was true, at least one soul needed to open up to the goddess or neither one of them would get their chance.

"Sorry, I'm allergic to denial." Journey waved her hand in her face.

The small half-moon that was centered on her forehead had darkened over the past few days. I asked if she would like to cover it so she would not be pointed out or made a spectacle, but she said no.

She wanted everyone to know that the goddess had visited her, that things were changing. Many didn't see it that way. Some didn't believe her, others were skeptical. Others thought it was a curse, and that she would die because the goddess didn't help rogues.

Journey couldn't understand why no one believed her, but so many of us had been through too much to accept miracles.

Hell, I was having a hard time believing what she said. The goddess had been quiet for hundreds of years. Why did she wait for Journey? My mate?

"Excuse me?" Hawke raised an eyebrow and slammed his hand on the bar.

"You heard me," Journey said, taking a sip of her milkshake. "You love her, and she loves you. If you would open yourself up to the goddess, she would be your mate. But you as well as everyone else in this damned club," she said it loud enough for all to hear, "are just scared."

Hawke gritted his teeth. "Me scared? Are you serious?"

Journey nodded. "Scared of your own feelings. You may not fear death, but you are scared to open your heart again. You are scared to have it broken. Can you see Delilah rejecting you? Seriously? She's the happiest person in this bar, and the way she looks at you..." Journey tsked.

Hawke stared into the amber colored glass the bartender set in front of him. He scratched his forehead, opening and closing his mouth to say something. Journey just sat in front of her food, nibbling on the meat.

She elbowed me and nodded her head to Hawke.

"Am I supposed to say something?" I thought.

"Duh," Journey replied.

I would never get used to my mate being inside my head. Her mind-link ability had grown, and now she and I could speak to one another.

"Hawke," I said, patting his shoulder. "If you want to have what I have. To have someone care and love for you, don't you think Delilah will give you that? She isn't your previous mate."

Hawke grated his teeth, his jawbone ticking. "I've been hurt—"

"We all have," I interrupted. "But look what I have now." I looked to Journey, and she waved excitedly.

I chuckled and pulled her in for a peck on the lips.

"But you don't know how long…" Hawke couldn't speak what all of us knew besides Journey. That she could very well die during the shift. He tapped his fingers on the bar and watched Journey as she finished her food.

He shook his head. "I don't want to put her through that," he gulped. "I don't want to get her only to lose her, if we are even mates."

I stepped in front of my mate, leaning on the bar to hide the words I need to tell Hawke. "To have her as my mate for any amount of time is worth it," I whispered. "I pray to the goddess each day she will survive. If she doesn't, my heart will follow her into death. That is all I can hope for."

Hawke sobered at my words. He looked around me. Journey laughed with another female server.

"She's different. She's changed a lot since she came here," Hawke mentioned. "For the good. She's a good woman for you."

"She is. And I would have died without her." And now, she may die because of me.

Journey hopped down from her stool and pushed me back so she could stand in front of me. She wrapped my arms around her body and stared up at Hawke.

"Hawke, she left. She told me she was leaving. She didn't tell me where she was going. If you want her, and I mean really want her, then you go after her. But if you go after her." Her eyes narrowed. "You better pray to the goddess and let that bond take over. Because otherwise, she can't be yours."

Hawke grunted, taking his glass and draining it. "Thank you, Journey." He patted her head and stood up to leave.

After Hawke left, letting in a cold gust, Journey sighed, leaning against my chest. "Do you think he is going to go find her?"

"I don't know, little mate. But you did the best you could."

She hummed, burying her nose deeper into my chest.

"Get a room!" one man from across the bar yelled. He laughed, slapping the table.

With the questions surrounding Journey and her future, the members were still happy she was here. They were happy because I was, because I had come out of my rogue status. It gave them hope, but also uncertainty.

Locke worried about the mark on Journey's forehead. He didn't understand it, didn't know what it meant, so he prepared for the worst.

For so long, we acted like the goddess was a cold-hearted bitch. But what had happened to me in the past month had been far from cold-hearted. She'd given me a chance, and I should trust her. But part of me was reluctant, having been broken before.

The wind would die down by tomorrow, and the snow should stop enough for us to get out and about. We both needed the fresh air, and if her wolf was to indeed come, then the smells of the pine and the spruce trees would help any anxiousness she may have.

"Little mate, would you like to go get a Christmas tree?"

Journey's eyes widened. "A tree? Like a real Christmas tree?" I nodded and rubbed my nose with hers.

"But it doesn't look like you guys celebrate Christmas. There aren't any lights in here or on the street?"

I scratched my bearded chin, looking around the bar. "We don't, it's a human holiday, but I don't see why we can't celebrate?"

"I'd like that. No presents though," she shook her head. "You've given me enough, and I just want to spend time with you and your friends."

"Our friends," I corrected her.

"Damn straight." Locke leaned against the bar. "We're all family here, so why don't we all celebrate... Wait, what holiday is it?" Locke smirked.

"Christmas," Journey chirped. "Grim said he was going to get us a tree since I've never celebrated."

Locke's eyes narrowed before showing his playful smile.

"Well, then, that means we have to celebrate then. I say we decorate the entire bar." He slapped his hand on a nearby chair.

"The fuck we do that for?" Bear yelled from a table. "Just because we have one human member now?"

Locke scoffed and stood on a chair. "Nah man, we have humans that work in this bar. We can do it for them, too."

"You are full of it," Sizzle snorted, walking out of the security room. "You are decorating to get some fresh meat in here and find your mate. He's already got flyers on the other side of town that says 'Ladies Night, come party with the Iron Fang Bikers on Christmas Eve' on it. I think it's a bad idea. Women are trouble. No offense, Journey."

Journey laughed, shaking her head. "Maybe some will find a lucky lady or gentleman and then pray for some help," she said hopefully.

I patted my mate's head, happy to see she was hopeful. Locke was doing what he could for others to find their mates, but unless the humans prayed, there wouldn't be a spark. Yet my Journey believed that Delilah and Hawke were mates, so an attraction must be there despite the bond.

"It's a great idea," I announced. "What do we need to do to get started?"

CHAPTER THIRTY NINE

Journey

For once, we left the bar in an uproar of excitement.

Locke advertising a Christmas party to the local women in the town was a first step that he believed there could be mates for them. He just didn't believe that he needed to open his soul again.

"Things will work out," Grim said, grabbing my thigh.

Grim borrowed a dingy red, rust-corroded truck from the garage. It was rarely used. It squeaked every time we hit a hole in the road, and I wasn't even sure if the tires still had any tread left. Every bump and swerve were exaggerated by the shot suspension. But it could also be because Grim wasn't used to riding on four wheels and distracted himself by keeping his large hand on my thigh.

"You could use two hands," I said.

He bobbed his head. "I could. But I won't." He winked at me and continued driving down the familiar path I'd come to know. He parked at the overlook.

Instead of a clear night sky with the moon hanging over the valley, the clouds hid the setting sun.

We spent too much of our afternoon at the bar. Locke called all the human servers and waitresses and had them pitch some ideas about creating the perfect Christmas party. They even went as far as calling their favorite band and asking if they would play Christmas music.

The band, of course, laughed in their faces and refused to play any Christmas songs on their instruments but offered to at least DJ. Something about "vampires don't do jolly shit" was said over the phone.

Vampires. Yeah, they're real. I don't know why that shocked me but still. I hadn't officially met one yet, so they still seemed like magical creatures to me.

And yet I had met the goddess of souls and was still fascinated by damned vampires.

Grim slammed the truck door shut, shaking off the remaining snow from the top of the cab. He walked around to my side, a grin plastered on his face. He said it was hard to open the rickety door, but I think he just wanted to be chivalrous like some human gentleman.

He picked me up by my waist and set me down, leading me over to the half-broken bench we had sat on once before. Grim looked out over the forest, took an enormous breath in, and put his hands on his hips.

We had a job to get a tree, a rather large tree for the bar to decorate, as well as a tree for our home. Grim was hoping for a thick spruce, but he worried about any squirrels that might be inside. Leif didn't like squirrels and didn't want Leif gnawing on one in the middle of the night and scaring me.

"Do you want to go for a ride?" Grim asked suddenly.

I blinked. "A ride?"

"Yeah, a ride." He pulled me closer, placing a kiss on my forehead.

I looked around, we weren't that far from the road, and anyone could just pull up and decide to come take a scenic look.

"I don't know if that's wise. Someone might see."

"They won't see anything." Grim shrugged his shoulders, taking his shirt off. I licked my lips at the sight of his rippling muscles, and I fumbled nervously with my jacket.

Grim tossed his shirt on the bench and gazed back at me.

"Hey, wait, what's wrong? I can feel you're nervousness?" He rubbed his hands up and down my arms and I bit my lip.

"I just don't think I feel comfortable riding you out in the open. Plus, it's kind of cold." I shivered.

Grim stared at me for a long moment until his smile grew wide, and a joyous laugh erupted. He had his hands on his knees, gasping for breath. I wasn't sure why he was laughing.

I chuckled nervously. I didn't think it was that funny. My poor tits could freeze in weather like this, and what if it started snowing again? He was all about keeping me warm, and now he wanted me to strip naked?

Grim's laughter calmed, and he leaned against a tree. "Oh, little mate, I wasn't asking you to do that."

I cocked my head, not understanding.

"I meant, ride my wolf."

"Ohhhh." I pulled my sleeves down to cover my hands.

"I'm not sure that's a good idea either."

Like... I'm just not sure about that at all.

Grim shook his head, his hand running over his face to hide a smile. "Oh, Journey come here."

He pulled me into his arms and rocked me back and forth. "I'm saying you can ride on my wolf's back and run with us in the forest."

"Ohhhhh!" I hid my face in his chest utterly embarrassed, but he didn't laugh any longer.

Instead, Grim leaned over and whispered in my ear, "Not that I wouldn't love to rut you in the forest once the weather turns warmer."

A shiver ran down my spine, and he smacked my butt which was padded with several layers.

"Let me shift, and you can climb on. We'll come back and find a tree when we're done."

Grim took off his clothes, not shy in the slightest. I could see the tattoos that crept up his back. I hadn't had time to admire him when he was naked, he usually pounced on me and had me screaming into the pillow.

I blushed, looking away but I could hear the deep chuckle from where I stood. He walked away, stepping into the forest, but I called out for him to stop.

He turned, his eyebrows furrowed.

"Can I watch?" I asked quietly. He heard me. His head perked up at the mention of it, but he shook his head.

"You don't need to see it…"

"Grim," I said more firmly. "I do need to see it. Because I'm going to be doing it, too, one day."

Grim's face fell and immediately his mood went somber.

"Why do you avoid it?" I stepped closer to his naked body, the sun hitting his chest muscles, giving his tattoos a lighter appearance. "Why won't you talk to me about it? It's going to happen, and I need to know how it will feel, what will happen. I don't want to be blindsided by it."

Grim balled his fists and didn't look at me. Instead, he looked at the setting sun and tightened his jaw.

"*He's afraid you will die.*" Leif said.

Grim groaned, rubbing his temples. "Yeah, he's going to get annoying."

"Die? Why would I die? The goddess said I am going to shift, that I am the first…"

"You will be the first if you shift fully, Journey. There was one other woman that tried to shift, but she didn't make it." Grim's voice was strangled, a deep sorrow embedded in his face.

I cupped his face. "The goddess says it will work this time. Our bond was solidified. I'll pull strength from you, and I will make it."

Grim grabbed my wrists, rubbing his beard up and down my hands. "But I worry you won't."

"We didn't come this far to give up have we? You didn't go rabid. I didn't die. We found each other and completed something so precious." I rubbed his cheek with my thumb. "I believe this will work, I believe I will shift and make it, but I'll need your help. We will get through this, I know it."

Grim closed his eyes and pressed his naked body against me. I rested my cheek on his chest. He swallowed heavily.

"She's failed me; she's failed so many others before, Journey. It's hard to open myself up like that. For all of us. You have to understand–"

"You all have reservations, I know. And for a long time, I didn't have anything to believe in, but this I believe. You, right here, with me, is a miracle. I've trusted you from the very beginning whether I knew it or not, now I'm asking you to trust me."

Grim sighed heavily, his hands squeezing my wrists tighter. "Alright. I will trust you."

With a silent thank you, I kissed his lips, and he let go of my hands. He walked backward, keeping his eyes on me.

I showed no fear, knowing that was exactly what he was looking for. I pulled my shoulders back and nodded, signaling I was ready to watch because I would not look away once he started.

First, his back hunched over, and his bones began cracking. The twisting of his body, his legs turning into the back hind legs of his wolf made me wince inwardly.

Show no fear, I told myself.

Then he grew, his naked body became larger. He no longer looked like one of those horror movie werewolves where they could stand on two legs and had opposable thumbs. The fur sprouted quickly, the thick, deep red fur covering his body entirely. With a resounding thump, his two front paws landed on the ground.

I wanted to ask if it was painful, if he could feel every break. Did he feel his skin ripping and stitching back together? Not a drop of blood was spilled during his transformation, but the intenseness of a human morphing into a larger being looked extremely painful.

Big black eyes stared back at me, his nose sniffing above him. He trotted toward me like he hadn't seen me in ages. Leif lowered his snout and licked my cheek. I laughed, feeling the softness of his fur and the way he rubbed up against me.

"I keep forgetting how big you are. You're like a horse," I joked.

"I'm going to feel like one when you climb on my shoulders," he snorted. *"Maybe we should have brought a special saddle."*

I shook my head and walked around to his side. Using the scruff of his neck along with his wolfy bow, I straddled his body.

I felt Leif's strength in his shoulders. They were bulky, massive and my legs had a hard time holding on. He was completely solid, muscle covered with glorious fur.

Leif trotted to the edge of the tree line so I could figure out my balance. I gripped his scruff, and my legs tightened around his torso.

"Hang on," Leif said as he lifted his giant head and howled at the moon as it started its ascent.

Leif raced through the trees like he was a part of the forest. Deer, drinking from a half-frozen stream, stood in confusion as he raced by. They didn't fear him while he galloped under the canopy of snow and ice. They stood watching until we were entirely out of sight.

Leif howled several more times, running up and down large hills and ravines with ease. It was easy to tell he was trying to show off. His eyes kept trailing back behind him to check on me.

I couldn't hide my smile, my laughter coming out in screams of joy when he would jump over streams and large logs.

My hair wildly flew behind me, catching on branches and waving in the falling snow. But I didn't care. I felt too alive to ask him to stop or slow down.

If this is what it was like to become like Grim, to become a wolf, to run wild and free into the wilderness, I'd take it any day. For the first time in all my life, I felt free.

I would never have thought that hiding under a bed from my nightmares would bring this angel into my life.

And now we could create a new life together, two broken souls finally mended.

CHAPTER FORTY

Grim

She loved it; she loved every nip of cold air that brushed her face. Her squeals of fear turned to joy the more I hopped over the logs and boulders that stood in our way. We ran for a good hour. My wolf, Leif, enjoyed the smells of the outdoors, the dirt between his paws, and the smell of fresh meat that could easily be devoured.

But he and I both knew we weren't on a hunting trip this time. We wanted our mate to feel what we felt, the freedom that comes with your wolf.

While we trotted back up the embankment where my clothes laid in the snow, Journey laid her head down between Leif's shoulder blades and hummed gratefully.

I couldn't wait to see her, see her in her element once she transformed.

And she would shift. She would become an animal, a wolf.

What would her wolf be like? I wondered. Would she be timid with a bite of sass that Journey so often let out when she spoke passionately? Or would she be more animal-like, like Leif, possessive, a brute, and a loner despite his deep-rooted primal urges to be in a pack?

I wasn't sure, nor did I care, because I trusted Journey, trusting her faith in the Goddess.

Journey was young, a bit naïve, but her passion for the Goddess was endearing, and I found myself believing her more and more.

The bond could do that; the strings that tied us together strengthened by the day.

Leif bristled at the thought of something happening to her, but his own drive to believe in the goddess overrode that. "*She's special*" was his mantra. And indeed, there was something special. I couldn't put my claw on it, but my mate would do great things, I just wasn't sure what.

We hunted through the trees. Journey automatically picked a large tree that stood straight as an arrow. The needles were thick, and the smell of pine wafted into our noses. We sighed in delight when we loaded the truck. It would be a fine addition to the bar where our "family" was, Journey stated.

She saw our club as her home, her pack. But soon, she would feel the tiny hole of emptiness when her wolf arrived. The need to follow, the need to be a part of a pack where we were all tied with a mind-link. A pack.

For now, I let her enjoy it. Because I wanted her to live in a moment of bliss instead of worry about what might happen later. I was strong enough to hold us together for as long as I had to. I was Locke's second, and he was my friend. However, I needed him to find his mate and complete a bond. That would be the dawn of a new pack.

I smiled, throwing the heavy tree in the back of the truck. The snow lazily fell as Journey ran back into the woods without me. Journey skipped around trees and hid among the trestles of overhanging limbs. I growled in laughter, still able to see her trying to hide from me.

She jumped from one tree to another, explosions of laughter giving her away each time.

Once I found her looking in the wrong direction, her wolf's hearing fading as it so often did while her body continued to change. I grabbed her by the waist, pulling her into the snow as we wrestled on the ground.

"Mercy, Mercy!" she cried as she laughed when I tickled her.

I pinned Journey's back in the snow. She smiled, her finger tracing my cheek, and Leif purred happily in response. I would never get over this feeling of being mated, being with someone I loved.

It wasn't about the sex or saving my soul or life. Everything was about her and how much I loved her. She completed me in ways I never thought possible, filling the empty holes in my life I felt even before I became a rogue.

"We have to get our tree," she whispered.

My tongue slipped out of my mouth, licking my lips until the cold air caressed them.

"Do we? I have a good trunk for you." I kissed her neck.

We were deep enough in the forest that no one from the road would see, but I knew she'd expressed concern about doing anything out in the open. But Leif wanted her, hell I wanted her, but I wouldn't do anything she didn't want.

"Grim," she moaned, her hips grinding against the bulge in my jeans. The gun I kept firmly placed at my side fell out of its holster, and the ax I carried had been long forgotten beneath the snow.

Journey gave a low rumble of a purr. It was the strongest I had heard yet from my mate. It beckoned me to take her beneath the trees and the moonlight.

Gods, she looked beautiful, and I didn't tell her enough.

"You're gorgeous," I blurted. My beard covered cheeks flushed with heat, and I buried my nose in her neck—not to smell her but to hide my embarrassment.

I was a brute, a killer, and this woman had brought me to my knees.

She giggled, her fingers trailing into my hair. "I love you," she whispered. "And I think you already know I find you exceedingly sexy, even when you get all embarrassed."

Journey rolled her hips, the pressure of her mound pushing against my cock. It strained heavily into my jeans, the bulbous head pushing against the cold zipper.

I hadn't bothered with undergarments since she fell into my lap. I always wanted to be ready.

"You can't do that to me," I groaned, smelling the slick of her pussy. "I can't take you..."

"Oh, you can," she pleaded. Her breasts pushed against the fluff of her coat.

I swore I could feel her nipples pebbling despite the barrier.

"I just need you. To be close to me."

I should have questioned, should have asked twice, but I didn't. I pulled off her skintight leggings, her pussy already dripping. No underwear.

My breath hitched. Leif was fully satisfied that my mate wouldn't go without.

"I'm always ready for you," she gasped, feeling the snow beneath her ass.

I couldn't very well have my mate freeze. "Wrap your legs around me," I ordered.

It was difficult to do, but she obeyed, wrapping her arms around me until I pinned her up against the tree, the coat giving her enough padding to not tear into her beautiful skin.

I took my time, taking each boot off with a pull of a string, and balancing her ass on one hand as I pulled the rest of her bottoms away. Her pussy was a bouquet of delicate aromas that could bring any alpha to his knees, but here she was, waiting for my cock, my knot.

I unbuckled my belt. The ting of the metal made Journey catch her breath. Chills erupted on her skin, and Leif immediately growled in want. Her pussy was wet, dripping down her thigh. I let out a heavy, shaky sigh when she connected her slit to my cock.

Her caramel eyes locked with mine, her breath flowing from her lips while I kissed her gently, probing her entrance with the head of my shaft. The cold made the barbells of my piercings cold, and when my cock slipped deeper into her pussy, they warmed and made my mate sigh in delight.

I eased into her pussy gently, both of us letting out contented moans. My hips pumped into her, touching her hip bones as she rode along with me.

"Grim," she said my name like a prayer.

My teeth, still elongated after my shift, scraped against her shoulder. I wanted to mark her all over again, under the moonlight, while the goddess looked down with pride.

Her work hadn't gone unnoticed. I was slowly believing again—trusting my mate that she would survive. If she didn't, I would fight the Goddess myself and then find Hades to rescue her from the Underworld. I'd fight all his armies to get to her and bring her back to me where she belonged.

My cock became greedy, my barbells rubbing her in the right places. She cried out in ecstasy and scratched my back. Claws sank into my jacket, the ripping echoing into the darkened forest. My mate clawed until she reached the skin, and she didn't stop there. Her claws sank deeper. The blood trickling down my back gave my passion a charge of excitement.

"Grim, more!" she commanded. "Fuck me harder!"

I rutted her against the tree and felt her pussy clamp against the shaft of my cock until she let out the most glorious scream.

Birds flew from the trees, my mouth finally covering hers to muffle her cries. I pumped my cock into her as it expanded until my knot was full and ready to lock her. To keep her full of my seed, to one day take root in her womb, to bring us the pups we both wanted.

I cried out my mate's name, her arms going slack while my knot stayed firmly implanted in her pussy. We both panted heavily, and her fingers tightened around my neck, her half-lidded eyes thanking me, and her sweet, pouty lips connecting to my chapped ones.

"I think I found our tree." She bit her lip.

My forehead rested on hers. "You did?" I asked, not caring.

She nodded and pointed straight behind us. It wasn't as large as the tree for the bar. The tree's height matched mine and would fit perfectly in our den.

"It's perfect," I said.

"Yeah, a new tradition for us. We do it against one tree and then the next tree over is the one we put in our den." Her excitement permeated our bond, and I nuzzled into her neck.

This was a better life than my parents ever had, and I only wished that they could see I was happy and thriving.

We took the larger tree to the bar. Locke, Sizzle, and Karma were completely wasted as they took it in. The humans they invited were also there, bringing decorations from their apartments. Locke even sang for more Christmas cheer.

Journey and I laughed, watching the crew, but I knew I needed to get my mate home because we had our own tree to set up. Not to mention my come still dripped from her sweet cunt. The cold air outside would surely make her freeze, but she didn't complain.

A primal part of me wanted to parade her around the bar and show everyone that she was mine. But they already knew that and showing her off further would only upset my brothers.

I carried the tree up to our apartment. I could hear the echoes of our footsteps through the door that used to lead to Sizzle's apartment. His apartment was already stripped bare and ready for the construction of our den.

"Over by this wall, you think?" Journey pointed to the left side of the room and the only corner that wasn't covered in either rugs, blankets, or small chairs.

"Perfect," I said, standing it in the corner.

I dusted my hands off, staring at my work. It was the perfect size for our den, and the smell of the outdoors in our little den made Leif purr in pleasure.

Maybe having a Christmas tree wasn't all that bad.

"He likes it too," Journey mused, rubbing her cheek on my arm. "It will look even better once we get lights on it. It will bring out the magic."

"The magic?"

Journey hummed happily. "Yeah, magic. But I guess it isn't really magic. Just something make-believe for children. Kinda like those old fairy tales I used to read. The lights will make it more real. I think humans are just very visual beings."

I chuckled, kissing her forehead. "Whatever you say, my mate."

I could not care less about the tree, but as long as it made her happy.

I walked to the kitchen, pulling out meat and vegetables for our next meal. Journey had worked up quite the appetite, I could hear her stomach protesting the absence of food.

While I cooked, Journey padded to the nest and put her hands on her hips. Her head tilted to the side, her hand resting on her cheek.

She studied the nest, her hand reaching out and pulling on one of the blankets. It fell to the floor, and she picked it up, sniffing it. I paused, watching her. She took another blanket and pulled it from the nest, laying it on a chair nearby.

A low growl of disapproval permeated the air, and it caused me stress watching her. Journey pulled more blankets off the bed. She hastily threw pillows to the opposite sides of the bed.

Her wolf was surfacing.

She was re-making our nest.

Leif and I had made our nest in the beginning, hoping that our mate would like it, because she didn't know how to make a proper nest. She didn't understand the importance of smells, how blankets, pillows, and even articles of worn clothing could make or break a nest.

Journey crawled into the torn nest, her nose twitching, her head tilting back and forth as she took the piles of pillows around her and placed them in distinct positions.

My mate was making our nest to her liking, and it filled me with the utmost pride and adoration. She was letting the wolf inside her take control of her body, using her primal instincts to mark the nest as hers and ours.

She would want my scent; she would want my seed.

I low growl slipped from my throat, Journey's head ticking my way. Her fingers fumbled with something in her hand.

"W-what am I doing?" she asked innocently. She gazed back at the sheets, the pillows, the blankets, and moved them again.

"You are nesting. Your wolf wants to make our nest comfortable for you, for your mate."

And then another realization struck me.

Her estrus, more commonly known as her heat, was near.

CHAPTER FORTY ONE

Journey

I stood back from the bed, my eyes widening at what I had done.

I'd stripped all the bedding and rearranged it because it felt "off." It still felt off while I gazed at it. I only paused to fiddle with the small piece of plastic I found, finding it utterly familiar. It smelled of me.

I crossed my arms, trying to listen to Grim speak. His voice was muffled, I couldn't completely hear him articulate his words. It was fuzzy as I tried to listen. Instead, I felt a presence inside me, showing me what I was supposed to be doing.

I was nesting, as Grim said, correcting the bed that he made. I felt guilty, but I had to fix it; I had to figure out how I could make our nest better.

I stuffed the small white piece in my pocket, touching the fabrics once again. I pulled a red blanket to my nose, sniffing. Nope, the smell had faded.

Not knowing what I was looking for, I walked past the couch full of blankets and closer to the bathroom. The linen basket full of dirty clothes caught my eye, and the smell instantly heightened.

I traced the rim of the basket and pulled a pair of gray joggers Grim wore the night before. I touched it, the feel of it soft, his smell transferring to my fingers.

Surely, I would not smell the soiled laundry. Not that it was soiled, it was still quite clean, just...he wore it yesterday.

I brought it to my nose, and there it was—the smell I was looking for. I grabbed it, following whatever natural instincts and pulled more from the basket and then came back to our bed, nest, and scattered the clothes once again.

"What am I doing?" I whispered again. It was a rhetorical question because Grim didn't answer, he anxiously watched as I folded blankets and reorganized the pillows until finally his smell had permeated the bed.

I sat on my knees, my shoulders slumping and sighing at my work. A low rumbling came from my chest and instantly Grim was at my side. I reached out, inviting him in, and I pulled him to me as we tumbled into the mess of fabric.

"This is nice," I murmured. "I don't know what it is, but it feels really nice."

Grim rubbed his lips together, his arms reaching around and holding me tight. "It feels very right," he replied. "It's beautiful, my mate, you did a wonderful job."

"It didn't mean that the nest you made was wrong." I sat up shaking my head. "I don't know why I changed all of it. I don't understand it!"

Grim silenced me with a kiss, his hand cupping my cheek. "A male can only make a nest so well when they first court. A female is the one who makes the final nest, adding her own touches to it."

"But I put dirty clothes in it," I squealed.

He laughed, rolling over on top of me. "You want my scent; it makes you feel safe."

I pondered that. When I'm with him, I feel safe. It only made sense that I would want my nest to always smell that way.

He ran his thumbs up and down the interior of my arm, tracing it longingly as it tickled my skin. I giggled, reaching to scratch at the inside of my bicep. It was on my left arm, where my implant sat, and when I scratched again, I realized the bump wasn't there.

My brows furrowed, and I sat up, feeling the skin. There wasn't a mark where it could escape, it couldn't escape anyway, it was in my arm.

"What's wrong?" Grim leaned on his elbow, rubbing the skin where I continued to touch.

"I don't feel my implant. The one that keeps me from getting pregnant." I gasped, reaching into the side pocket of my yoga pants and pulled out the small piece of white plastic the size of a toothpick.

Surely not.

"No," I whispered at the same time there was pounding at the door.

Grim growled and ordered me to stay. He stomped across the floor and flung the door open, finding Beretta hissing.

"Stop that now," Tajah ordered as she sidestepped Beretta, but her teeth were still bared at Grim.

I jumped from the bed, rushing to Grim, and pulled him away from the door. He reluctantly let them in. I sniffed as they passed, and a possessive snarl came from my lips.

I held my hand over my mouth to silence it, but Tajah waved her hand to dismiss it. She made herself at home, sitting at the kitchen table with a sigh, and Beretta came around, bringing a shawl to cover Tajah's shoulders.

Tajah patted Beretta's hand and smiled solemnly at her.

"What is the meaning of this?" Grim growled. "You are in our den, and you can already see that Journey is becoming territorial." Grim pushed me behind him, but I tried to peer around his body to see our guest.

"Grim, they are our friends." I walked toward the table, but Grim grabbed my hand and pulled me to his side. Neither of them looked at Grim like he was a piece of meat, in fact, they looked at each other like Grim and I did. They were utterly smitten, and a warm feeling bloomed in my chest.

Could they?

"I know, I know," Tajah said. Her hands laid on the table, ticking the hard surface with her nails. "Coming into a wolf's den is quite rude, but I needed to be here tonight. I needed to congratulate our little Priestess. From one magical being to another." She smiled widely, and the spark in her eyes flew to life. If I hadn't known who Tajah was before this night, I would say she looked downright mischievous.

"Priestess?" Grim looked from Tajah to me. "She isn't a priestess; she is turning into a wolf."

Tajah cleared her throat. "Beretta, I forgot my bag at the shop." Beretta frowned and kneeled next to her. "It has some medicine in it that Journey will need. Will you be a sweet kitten and grab it for me?"

"I'm not a kitten," she growled, but it came out more like a curious purr. "But I will fetch it for you."

Beretta walked out the door, but Grim continued to stare at me as his mouth hung open. "What do you mean priestess? What the hell is going on?" Grim let go of my hand and instantly I whimpered. He grabbed it and pulled me to him.

"I'm sorry, I didn't mean to do that. I'm shocked, Journey."

"Well, what do you expect? She tells you to trust her, she will live through the shift, and you have a hard time believing it. Would you have really believed it if she said, 'Oh yeah, by the way, I have become the Goddess's personal priestess and can communicate with her directly'?" Tajah shook her head and rubbed her eyes.

"Men really don't get it do they? And some women," she muttered. "Stupid masculinity shit."

I glanced at the door and back to Tajah. "Y-you and Beretta?"

Tajah nodded, fiddling with her fingers. "She doesn't know, yet. We have always had an attraction to each other, and she fears she isn't enough for me. She hasn't accepted it just yet, but I have. I've opened my soul to the goddess because of you. You both have given me hope, and once you shift, your power will be magnified, and instantly you will know who is to be paired. You'll know what to do once you receive your wolf after your shift."

I smiled. "Is that why you came here? To tell me that?"

She shook her head. "No, I came over because I needed to give you this–" The door opened, and Beretta came charging in with Tajah's bag in hand.

"Thank you, kitten."

Beretta purred deeply, standing behind Tajah. Beretta instantly calmed when she was close to her. While Tajah rummaged through her bag, my eyes connected with Beretta.

Oh, she knew. She definitely knew.

Her eyes said it all.

Tajah made a tsking noise and pulled out a packet of little pink pills. "Take these when your heat starts, and you won't get pregnant. You need to at least wait one cycle before you both start trying to have pups. To make sure everything is regulated and all." Tajah went to stand up, and I fell into Grim.

"H-heat? Wha?"

"I'll let your mate explain that to you." She smirked and leaned on Beretta as they walked to the door. "I hope to see you at the big Christmas party at the end of the month. I heard it was going to be a big 'to do.' We will need to write down all the matches you are going to be seeing, and we can work together on how to pair them all."

My mouth hung open as she walked out the door, laughing to herself and holding onto Beretta.

"Ah," I began until Grim led me to the same chair Tajah had sat in and directed me sit. He sat on his knees in front of me and laid his head in my lap.

"Alright, a lot of information here." He sighed, brushing his hands through his locks. "You're a priestess, is there anything else you haven't told me?"

I shook my head, feeling guilty. He kissed me to stop the abrupt shaking and gripped the back of my hair with his fist. The tightness brought a pulsing desire to my core, and my lips parted.

"No more hiding stuff, even if I won't believe it okay? I need to know everything, little mate."

I tried to nod, but the grip on the back of my head prevented that. "I understand." My legs tightened together, and the wolf smirked like he knew exactly what he was doing to me.

My pussy was already wet, ready to take him again. I purred, and Grim dropped his head to my lap once again, taking in the deep aroma of my arousal. I threaded my fingers through his hair, working the knots away.

As he lay in my lap, he explained what a heat—or estrus, more scientifically speaking—was and how female shifters felt during their first cycle. It wouldn't be the worst, but it would definitely be a wakeup to becoming more of a wolf once I experience it.

The worst part was it could hit at any time. Once we both understood my cycle, we could plan. But if it started while we were in public and other shifters were around, it would definitely cause some problems for them. Grim would become completely territorial, and I would feel pain in my stomach and pussy until he soothed it with his cock.

That part didn't seem so bad, but until my first heat, it would be something I worried about.

"So, I can't get pregnant right now, even with this out?" I pulled the implant from my pocket, looking it over.

There was not a speck of blood and no scar from where it 'fell out.'

"Your body has changed enough where you are no longer on a human cycle. Working on your nest proved that. I also smell nothing different about you, so you can't possibly be pregnant yet."

There was a longing in his voice that I could decipher. He wanted a family, while all my life, I never thought to have one. I didn't want my child to ever experience anything I had gone through.

But they wouldn't, Grim wouldn't allow it—not with him and all his friends who stuck together through thick and thin. I knew that. I knew this band of rogues was tighter than any human family I'd ever seen, yet they were all still so broken.

Once we started getting everyone mated, we could turn this band of rogues into a pack of unstoppable supernaturals.

CHAPTER FORTY TWO

Grim

Locke struck the pulpit with the gavel. The banging rang through the church to silence the haughty laughs and jeers. They all had been excited for weeks, waiting for the opportunity to visit with women and men that had not dared come to this side of town before.

The bikers drove into the human part of town, helping old ladies cross the street and donating food to the shelters. They no longer hid away from the women, hoping to catch a whiff, have their animal stir, anything that might indicate that their second chance human would arrive.

No one had brought anyone back, not that they would. At least one of the bonded souls had to open their hearts, and Journey was, of course, a special case.

However, with the upcoming party at the end of the month and the hope that finding a mate was heavily on their minds, they wanted this to work. And Journey was all too excited to help.

Leif had begun to be more territorial with her since she had completed our nest. Each morning and night, Journey rearranged our nest, adjusting it to her liking. Each time she did it, Leif and I were invited inside to fill it with our scent and our seed.

That was his favorite, and I had to admit that it was mine as well.

I kept hoping that her heat would come soon. I didn't like her out around other males. I was insanely jealous of anyone smelling my woman. I knew they would never dare to touch her, but if there were any wolves close to going rabid, it may pose a problem.

One that I would eradicate if they came near my mate.

I smiled down at her, keeping my arm around her shoulders. She now stood with me at the front of all the members of the club, as Locke's second. Now that I had my mate, she was second as well.

"Settle down." Locke smiled and waved his hands for his members to calm down. They all sat, their murmurs trickling to silence.

Two weeks had passed, and it was now time to take down the human traffickers at their next party. Journey was worried, because I was attending, and I would not bring her with me. I had to keep my head on my shoulders for this mission. Having her there would distract me.

Even sitting on the rooftop with Beretta was out of the question. I would not have her near any of the violence.

"Alright, we are going to follow the same plan and pattern, except Beretta is going to be the sniper team lead. It's the same warehouse, same layout as far as we know. Switch has gathered the blueprints, and of course I'm sure they have used a glamour spell to change some other shit around. So, when we enter, make sure you're paying attention," Locke said as his gaze ran across the congregation of overly excited bikers.

Switch held a tablet in his hand, his finger pushing up the glasses on his nose. I frowned, watching him, still squinting, to look at the screen. It seemed his sight was going, and his time might be short as well.

Journey grabbed my hand, instantly knowing what I was thinking. Her heavy sigh reminded me of the heavy burden she carried for the club now that she was a priestess. But no one really knew. They still looked on her with pity, waiting for her to die and I along with her.

"Where's Hawke?" Karma asked from the back.

"Hawke is MIA. He cannot be contacted, and Switch can't even get a location on him." The room went quiet, listening to Locke's furious taps on the pulpit.

"Beretta will head the sniper team, as I said, same positions as last time, taking anyone out that tries to get in. She is already stationed with her men, ready to go. Right now, we are in the clear."

The men rose with their guns, knives, and brass knuckles. I reached to my hip and grabbed the several knives that dangled from my belt.

"Please be careful," Journey whispered. I pulled her in for a kiss, and she melted into me. "Do you really have to go?"

"I am the Grim Reaper; it's my job. But I promise you, it takes a lot for anyone to bring me down, little mate. Now that we are bonded, wolfsbane and silver have no effect on me. They would have to pull out my beating heart."

Journey gasped, shaking her head.

"Sorry." I kissed her forehead and put my hand on her lower back.

Locke continued to speak to the crowd, but I needed to get my mate back to the bar. All the humans were congregating along with some of the less trained members and would be protected while we executed our raid.

"It's just routine, Journey. You have nothing to worry about. I've done this hundreds of times."

Journey kept her lips pressed into a thin line and nodded. She didn't like it, but she didn't have a choice. I had to keep her and other humans safe.

We knew that a fae was holding humans hostage, and it wasn't like the royal council would do anything, anyway. Especially if a bunch of rogues reported it.

As we entered the bar, it was a pre-celebration party. Only members and those that worked here were eating, drinking, and playing cards.

Bear strode up—the senior member that would stay behind.

"Journey." He nodded his head to her. "I'm your personal bodyguard, so I ask you to stay close."

Journey blew an exaggerated breath. "Grim?"

I chuckled, squeezing her ass, and pushed her forward. "Be a good little mate and stay put. We will be back in a few hours. I trust Bear. He's the muscle despite all that hair."

Bear was indeed a bear, even by human standards. He was twice my size, hairy all over, and had a thick, trimmed beard that scared our human staff. The only people that seemed not so scared of the big fuzz ball were my mate and Delilah.

Now that my mate was almost a wolf, I didn't worry so much about other species of shifters. A wolf and a bear just weren't compatible, so Bear was the right choice to look over my mate.

"Do you think the man you are after is a fae, too?" Journey asked.

"Fae work solely with each other. I wouldn't doubt it," Bear answered. "They are like fucking bees. They follow a female, like a queen bee, but since this is a male, I worry that there is more to this."

I nodded, wrapping my arm around Journey. "It will be alright. With the goddess helping us, and the plans she has. I'll come back to you safe." I kissed her forehead and let her go before she could argue.

"Come on." Bear motioned for Journey to follow. He kept his arms to himself as he led her to the table where Tajah sat.

She waved, shooing me out the door.

Leif whimpered as we backed toward the door, watching her as she hugged the witch. My jaw tensed, not enjoying leaving her one bit. But the bar was far more secure than our den. Switch would remain here, bars would cover the windows once activated, and the glass was bulletproof, leaving her here would be for the best.

"She's safe," I whispered.

"Bye, mate!" Journey called through the link. *"We can do some butt stuff when you come back!"*

My eyebrows rose, and my face reddened. Tajah was laughing, slapping the table with her hand. Witches could infiltrate a link, but only if they were healthy enough after turning rogue. She indeed looked healthier, and a sparkle in her eye had returned.

"Behave, little mate," I growled sensually. I turned to walk out the door and take care of the bastards who'd touched my mate.

We traveled swiftly to the same warehouse where we found Journey. They were either unexplainably stupid to choose the same spot or insanely smart, thinking no one would return here. Either way, we were ready.

Beretta flashed a small red dot on the door, signaling the surrounding area was clear. Locke waved her off, throwing up a hand gesture to ask her to keep us posted. He tapped his head piece three times and waved us all to follow.

Locke, normally in a joking mood on a raid, was not all smiles today. Since I'd found Journey, since I'd found a mate, his mood was more dangerous.

He feared death, instead of welcoming it.

I gripped the knives on my belt. They were there as a constant reminder of how I used to be. Once helpless, wolfless, like a human that could be killed in an instant—scarred with silver and poisoned with wolfsbane.

Now, I was unstoppable. That was why I needed to come. I needed to protect my brothers, the rogues that were rejected for the wrong reasons and who deserved a second chance. That was my calling, to be the warrior to a priestess.

As we entered the warehouse, the fae greeter didn't stop us. Which signaled to us this was indeed a trap and our plans had changed.

The members spread out, some taking stairs, while others crept forward into the darkened room. The dark was intentional, because none of the members should be able to see the creeping faes in the darkness. Only they didn't think of the night vision goggles that Switch had supplied.

As we entered, enemies were knocked out swiftly by snipers from the outside. Their vision enhanced by their scopes. You could hear thumps along the rafters as more of the enemy filtered in. Small gasps of surprise continued as more of our men entered open windows from the outside.

The only beam of light fell on a lone red chair in the middle of the warehouse with a table beside it with a glass and a bottle of scotch on it.

Locke gripped his fists, the leather gloves tightening around his knuckles. "Get ready," he spoke into his mouthpiece.

All of our backs stiffened as the low clap of dainty hands echoed into the darkness.

Locke squinted to get a better look. He was the only one that refused to wear the bug-like goggles. He said he would rather face his enemy with his own eyes than rely on a human contraption.

"Well, you came prepared. I'm impressed." The deep voice didn't match the delicate hand that placed itself on the red velvet chair.

The enemy's body came into the light. The broad shoulders, narrow waist, and long dark fingernails indicated he was in fact a fae. The fuckers were tall, and even the males had a feline looking eyes.

We couldn't see his face, just a plain black ski mask of quite inferior quality, considering the suit he wore.

"Come now, I won't bite." He lifted the scotch bottle and poured himself a glass.

Locke approached, his hand on his weapon, but his movement was graceful. He showed no fear as the rest of us waited for the inevitable to happen.

Because we already knew we were surrounded, Beretta had already tapped her comm to let us know. There was no way out of this except through bloodshed. This fae had the warehouse completely stocked full of his men.

Vampires, witches, even rogue wolves were creeping in as Beretta and her team tried to pick them off one by one.

"Free beer if all of you make it," Locke murmured into the mouthpiece. "And hopefully, a mate in your future."

As much as I didn't want my brothers and sisters to fall in this battle, I knew I would survive. My strength from the bond would see me through. My mate and I were meant to be. And I'd fight until I won my way back to her, one damn fae at a time.

CHAPTER FORTY THREE

Journey

The bar was filled with laughter and overflowing drinks. But the humans didn't know that their friends were in danger of fantasy-like proportions.

I wrung my hands together, trying to keep the overwhelming dread at bay. Grim was well supplied with his wolf. His healing abilities would take care of him, or at least I hope they did. I still didn't understand a shifter's anatomy or the tiny details that went along with it. I mean, I'm supposed to go into a heat soon, and I didn't even know what that fully entailed.

"Don't worry." Tajah took a sip of white wine. "They will be fine. Locke and his crew have done this so many times, I'm sure they could do it blindfolded."

Bear huffed, his arms crossed over his enormous body. "Hell, with fae, you never know, though. Those are some tricky fuckers."

Tajah slapped Bear on the arm, who didn't even flinch. He glared at her and picked up his bucket sized glass of cold beer and drank it in one gulp.

An hour passed, and I slowly became familiar with all the humans in the bar. They were all sweet and kind; most of them were women. They were all very fond of Delilah, who they hadn't heard from in the slightest, but the buzz from another table caught my ear.

"They're surrounded. I'm heading back to the control room." Switch tapped his earpiece and swore under his breath. "I'm getting static."

I stood up from the table, the chair falling behind me. But I didn't care. I ran after Switch, trying to listen to the static which I could hear as well.

"They're surrounded. More are trying to get in a side entrance, but we have popped several off. I don't know if there is an underground tunnel. But they keep disappearing; don't know where they're going," Beretta hissed through the earpiece. You could hear another crack in the communication, static rumbling through the ear piece. Then there was a pop of a gun firing through a silencer.

Tajah stood from another table. Her movements were quick as she ran across the bar to catch up. "What's going on?"

Startled at her quick movements despite her cane usage just weeks ago, I pulled her along with me until we reached the private room beside the bar. "Something is happening. They're surrounded."

Bones was already inside the room filled with computer monitors. He leaned on the table with his fists, pointing to several corners of the screen. "Here and here," he spoke into an earpiece. "They're portal jumping now. They're using all their magic reserves; they won't be able to escape once inside. I don't think they have enough gateway runes to get out with how far they are having to jump."

Gateway runes?

"Magic," Tajah said, standing behind me as I stared at the screens. "Magic isn't done with wands like humans believe. It's all inside the being. However, enchantments can be written on special pieces of parchment and thrown into the wind with a gentle whisper of a non-magical caster. For them to have so many is quite astonishing."

"Why would that be astonishing?" I asked, still staring at the screens.

"A witch or warlock can only put their spells on three pieces of parchment at any given time. It means more magical beings are working with the fae than we all realized."

"Shit!" One screen went black. Then another and another.

The middle screen was Grim standing beside Locke, in front of them was a man sitting in an overly ornate velvet red chair. He had a ski mask on, and upon further inspection I recognized his...well, the mask anyway.

The black, worn ski mask only showed his eyes, which I could see were deep black. No soul was evident in his eyes as we tried to study his face, trying to find some sort of familiarity to him.

The rest of the screens were all black now, except for the camera pinned on the masked figure. And unfortunately no sound to detect what they were saying.

"Get them back up! We have no way to know if they need help! The earpiece is dead!" Bones roared and began picking up an old-fashioned corded black phone on the corner of the desk, dialing a number.

"I'm trying. Stressing me out isn't helping!" Switch yelled in reply as he beat on the keyboard.

Panic rose inside me, bile reaching my throat when Grim stood in front of Locke with a snarl on his face. He was standing right in front of him, not three feet away from the enemy. That was when Grim pulled off his jacket, his body growing thick body hair and ripping through the rest of his clothes.

Grim's eyes turned red, looking around the room until they settled back on the man in the chair.

"Fuck, he's pissed off, he can't control his wolf," Bones muttered in horror. "That's what the fucker wants. He wants chaos."

Within seconds, Grim shifted faster than I have ever seen. His large red wolf breathed heavily and lunged forward to capture the male in front of him, only to hit an invisible wall.

Leif shook his head, ready to lunge again.

The long, elegant fingers of the man in the ski mask rose and peeled his mask away slowly. Once the mask was completely off, it showed not someone ugly or hideous but something ominously beautiful, but certainly deadly. Sharp features decorated his face. His cheekbones were pointed with black sparkles scattered over them. His lashes were long and thick enough to rival any woman, and his lips were the color of black onyx.

He smiled, fangs protruding from his lips.

"Holy mother Gaia," Bones rasped.

"Hecate, save them," Tajah cried, dropping to her knees.

"What the hell is going on?" I cried. I pulled my hair in frustration, watching every shifter on the screen.

My body grew hot, the suspense killing me.

Bones cleared his throat, not looking away from the screen. His hands shook as he ran them through his hair.

Why the hell would just one face strike fear into those around me? These same people that told me not to worry about these bikers going into an ambush, that they do this all the time, were trembling with fear.

They created their own world. They had survived. They had come this far, and now they feared the face of one man...being? What power could a being like him hold?

"It's the Duke Idris, dark fae of the Stone Court," Bones said.

Tajah rose to her feet, her head still bowed. "Former duke. He was banished from the Stone Court centuries ago. No one has seen or heard from him since."

Everyone in the room was stunned into silence, while my heart rose into my throat. A bead of sweat fell from my brow and another wave of heat washed over my skin.

My body trembled. "And what was he banned for?"

My mouth had gone dry, my tongue feeling thick in my mouth. I needed water, I needed sustenance. I feared for my family, for Grim, but my body was also craving too many things at once. It craved blood; it craved to rip someone or something to pieces. Such violence had never come across my mind. The thought of blood being spilt by my own hands would have repulsed me before this moment.

Now, I wanted it. I wanted to feel the enemy's blood beneath my fingernails, let it run between my fingers. I wanted to eat their heart.

Which enemy?

The one that was laughing hysterically at my mate, at my friend.

"He used forbidden magic to try and raise the dead, to torture, to humiliate, and to reverse time."

"Reverse time?" I growled, then cleared my throat.

Switch looked me up and down, his eyebrow raised.

"To find his dead mate. He was almost successful." Bones fisted his hands together. "She killed herself, seeing how evil he was. She chose death rather than to supply a bond that would give him more power."

Then why was he still living? Why was he alive?

His mate was dead, he couldn't possibly live for hundreds of years without a mate, right? That's how rogues going rabid worked?

My back popped, and I yipped in pain. My hand wrapped around my ribcage, it shuddered under my touch, and my stomach rolled as I retched my dinner.

I wiped the filth away from my lips. "God, I'm sorry." I winced, my voice hurting my ears.

Tajah, Bones, and Switch talked frantically among themselves. The looks of concern and their helplessness made me feel guilty and sorrowful they had to watch this.

My knees hit the floor, and I cried out. I could feel my bones moving and cracking. And a terrible ringing in my ears took over my hearing. It was me and my body, hearing the bones crush and move.

I knew exactly what was happening as my body heated. Sweat dripped into my eyes and I finally fell to the cool floor.

I was shifting.

Time slowed.

Grim isn't here; he isn't here to help me.

The bodies around the room were slow compared to my movements. I rolled to my side, clutching my stomach, throwing up yet again, releasing all the food from my stomach.

Bones knelt beside me, his hand brushing my hair from my face, sympathy radiating from his eyes.

The cold cloth wiping down my face warmed instantly. Too hot, I was way too hot.

My fingers pulled at my sweater, the strands unraveling. My pants came next. I couldn't understand my body movements, but I knew one thing, my fingers no longer had blunted nails.

My nails grew long, black, and were tainted with my blood. My body arched while I let out a blood-curdling scream that made the entire room wince in pain. The scream turned to howls and the howls into snarls.

The lights flickered in the room until we were covered in darkness.

Tiny pinpricks echoed painfully across my heated body until thick layers of fur rippled over my skin. I no longer had alabaster skin, it was tinged red with my blood from ripping through my clothes.

My mouth lengthened, which was by far the most painful part. My longer teeth, now fangs, pierced my bottom lip as my lower jaw tried to keep up with the upper.

My voice came out as a strangled cry, no longer able to speak in my human voice. Only whimpers, whines, and yips.

I was no longer a human, a being on two legs. My hands, now paws, told me that much.

My legs and paws were black. Sheens of blue were highlighted by the lone computer screen radiating its light. I blinked my enormous eyes. I could now see the tiniest particles of dust floating by.

My urge to move, to get to Grim becoming more urgent. I put one paw in front of the other, growling.

I wasn't in control of this body, this enormous animal that was now a part of me. It was in charge, this other soul inhabiting me. I was in the passenger seat, yet I could feel every emotion that went through my wolf. I could feel the cold concrete beneath me, the anger radiating that our mate was trapped in a warehouse not too far from here.

A throaty grunt left our throat. I was in the passenger seat, but my thoughts were clear.

We needed to get to our mate. And fast.

Our lips lifted in a snarl, our colossal head swinging to the door.

Bones shook his head, his hand reaching for the handle.

My wolf didn't like that.

I didn't either.

"Easy there," Bones said, taking slow and steady movements. "You just shifted. We don't know what's going to happen. Any normal young-shifter will last ten minutes and need to shift back. We got to think about this."

Yeah, that wasn't happening.

My wolf snapped her fangs, her teeth bared, until we lunged to the door. Bones fell away, landing on his ass. The force from our body was so strong we pushed the door off the hinges and pounced into the bar full of people.

The members, mixed in with the humans, all stood from their seats in astonishment.

I didn't care about the ramifications of humans seeing me; I didn't care that they could be put in danger, because right now, the members trying to defend the helpless were in their own damn mess. Without them, this haven would no longer be safe.

Instead of charging the room, knocking over tables and the adoptive family, we took one agile jump to the bar. Our sleek body, trotting down the wooden runway, knocking over a few pints of beer along the way, until we reached the door.

Bear, with his mouth agape, opened the door, letting the cold blast in.

And once we reached the outside, with the crowd behind us, we let out a thunderous howl that would let everyone know someone would die tonight.

CHAPTER FORTY FOUR

Grim

My fur bristled.

"He knows where our mate is," Leif snarled. *"He knows where we live. Idris must die."*

Our club, the bar, the church. It was our refuge. The only stronghold that protected us from the humans. Where we could be ourselves. He knows exactly where we are, it was all planned from the very beginning.

"You honestly think I left one little slave behind? You really think I would have left a loose end so carelessly?" He shook his head, a deep chuckle echoing in his chest.

Idris scoffed, twirling his finger inside the amber liquid in his glass. He tinked the glass with a lengthy, black nail and dripped the excess into his lips. "You wound me."

"How did you find out about the club?" Locke stepped forward.

With each step he took, I took one alongside him. He was our leader, he was our stand-in alpha. Without him, the club would fall. He was so powerful in his past life, behind the veil that separated Earth and our realm, he was the only one able to create order.

It was my duty to protect him.

My steps matched his as we drew closer, Idris laughing along with the men in the background.

They were all closing in, our earpieces only rendering static. There was no contact with the club. We didn't know if the security cameras still worked. We couldn't contact Beretta for back up. We were going in blind. As much as we thought we were prepared, losing contact with the outside would maim us. And Idris knew that.

"Your little pathetic rescues have become quite the talk in our world. The smaller human rings you've eradicated, and I thank you for that." He nodded. "You've made me a monopoly. But as I watched your pathetic little band of rogues from the shadows, I realized you were getting out of hand. I have men everywhere, don't you know? Humans, fae, vampires, shifters, there are a lot of rogues out there, but none like your little, club," he spat.

"I quickly realized I would need to dispose of all of you, or you would be a thorn in my side. So, I implanted a little device into your little pet human that not only kept her womb empty but also relayed your location. I knew her every move, every place she's been. It's really amazing what technology can accomplish. We all know how tender little human lives are."

I snarled, Leif ruffling inside me. He wanted blood on his teeth, to sink his claws into his abdomen. We wanted to take his life, but most of all, he needed to make him suffer. Idris should have died years ago. His mate committed suicide, so why is he still here? He'd grown insane.

He'd somehow broken all the laws of a mateless life—a curiosity that would need to be solved in all due time.

"It's a shame I wasn't able to partake in her flesh. I heard her cunt was tight compared to a supernatural being." He giggled. "Maybe I will still get my share when my men rip your home to pieces to bring her here."

Our den, our nest, our mate was in danger.

And then we shifted. Leif could no longer contain his rage as he ripped the clothes off our body. They laid in shreds on the floor, the knives fell along with them. Now, we stood in our animalistic form in front of the magical barrier that separated us from our target.

"Remove the barrier and fight like a fae," Locke ordered. "It only shows your cowardice that you can't face a wolf that you look down upon."

Fae hated shifters, almost as much as humans. They wanted the power to control, to hold the high table of the Royal Council and decide the fate of them all. They wanted anyone that was not of their race to serve them indefinitely. Fortunately, the Royal Council, composed of representatives from all supernatural races, saw to it this wouldn't happen. No species had more power than the others.

The Faes would never get their way unless they wanted a war.

And that is why Idris was here. He was powerful. He wanted to overthrow the laws our forefathers had set. No race was above another, but it was well known that if he'd bonded with his mate, he would have become too powerful for even the royals of the council.

And that was why his mate killed herself. Her sacrifice saved us all.

Until now.

He was still alive after all these years.

How?

Another deep chuckle reverberated against the walls of the warehouse. The lights flipped on and fae, vampires, and those we rejected to join our club stood in the corners. They wanted our blood; they wanted revenge. But they had blackened hearts when we first met them. We knew they would never bow to Locke.

And now they were here, bowing to an evil master and daring to defy the council.

"I'm getting a bit bored." Idris frowned and stood from his chair. He buttoned his suit and walked to the barrier, near my wolf.

Leif snarled, snapping his jaws.

Idris only chuckled, his fangs lengthening and the black sparkle on his cheeks twinkling in the new illumination of light. "As you can see, you are surrounded, little pup."

Locke growled in annoyance that he was being ignored, a tactic a fae would use against a leader.

"And while you are fighting," Idris rose to full height, "I'll be out the door, untouchable. Going to pick up my new little fuck toy."

Leif snarled and lunged forward, crashing into the barrier. Idris threw his head back with an evil cackle, the impenetrable wall following him as he walked away.

"Idris, I suggest you get back here and stop running like a little pixie," Locke said coldly.

Idris's eyes narrowed as he stopped in his tracks. "A pixie, eh? You find me to be a pixie? Tell me, Locke, President of the Iron Fang, how does it feel to be running the largest sect of rogues, soon to be rabids, in all the world?"

Idris's finger spun, bringing forth a crystal ball displaying images inside it. Inside were the faces of members, our friends, laughing and drinking. Until they weren't.

Howls of pain, their bodies forced, shifting themselves into feral beings. They were rabid, tearing each other apart. There was no human life left in them. They were savage.

As we watched, Idris smiled while Locke gripped his fists in anger. This was the worst that Idris could show him. Locke's future if he failed.

But we would not fail. Not with all the hope that my mate would bring.

The goddess was on our side, a deity that could sway other gods to help the pathetic souls that relied on them.

Inside the orb, they continued to pull and rip flesh from the bone. Bear destroyed everything in sight and then, at the very end, a human woman none of us recognized appeared. Locke's jaw dropped, his fingers unclenched from his fists.

An enormous wolf appeared, Leif instantly knew it was Locke. The wolf snarled and charged the woman, who screamed as his fangs bit into her neck. She was being eaten alive by a wolf as black as night with emerald green eyes.

Locke's eyes widened, his body trembling at the sight.

"This is your future. You know, I harbor premonitions. Everyone in this room knows it. Now, I suggest you take your death now before you destroy a woman you don't even know. A woman you don't deserve to know."

Locke snarled.

"I need you out of my hair. I don't need you interfering with my work. If you dare to leave this warehouse, I'll find her," Idris nodded to the woman, screaming for mercy in the orb. "And I'll destroy her."

"His mate, that is his mate," Leif argued. *"Our lives for hers. He will choose her."*

With us still in our wolf form, we could not communicate with Locke. We couldn't express how Idris would kill her anyway, that he would take her away once we were all dead. Locke's mind would be clouded.

Before I could nudge him, push him into the decision, we heard the doors to the front of the warehouse burst open. The frigid chill of the wind rushed around us.

A large, black wolf with a blue sheen on their fur entered. A light blue crescent moon decorated her forehead. Long, white fangs shone brightly against the darkness. Their growl was so deep, we all felt the undeniable power escaping them.

Mate.

She'd shifted on her own. Without me.

A pang of guilt washed through me. Shifting was held as a sacred change among a pack. When a pup reached adulthood, we all celebrated to embrace the wolf. Not to mention, it was painful as hell the first time.

But here she was, standing on all fours, looking damned elegant. She held her form like she'd done this hundreds of times. There was no shaking, no painful steps as she got used to four legs.

She was made for this.

My brothers were brought to their knees by the stifling power and lowered their heads. The enemy backed away slowly.

It was the unspoken force that empowered our members when her howl permeated the room—the sheer weight radiating so strongly, even my throat closed.

Her two front paws clacked against the surface of the concrete. She dipped her head until she reared back and let out the loudest, ear-piercing roar that silenced the room.

Beretta walked to my mate's side. Her body was tiny compared to my mate. The heavy breathing coming from Journey blasted streams of hot breath against the darkness trying to stifle the light.

She was fucking magnificent.

Journey stood regally, in all her glory as her gaze filtrated over the vast room, until it landed on Leif and me. An instant purr came from her chest, and her padded feet pounded the floor, charging straight toward me.

Locke's decision was made for him in an instant. We were going to fight, and we would not let Locke make the wrong choice.

Backup arrived behind Beretta, as she fired her gun into the chaos. The whole warehouse was turned upside down. The enemy was dwindling, and our numbers were increasing.

How did they get here in time? How did they know without the cameras and the comm?

Journey charged toward me. I waited for her to nuzzle beside me, but she burst through the small group surrounding Idris.

"*No!*" Leif yelled to her wolf, but it was already too late. Journey and her wolf broke through Idris's barrier, and she sank her teeth into his shoulder, ravaging it.

They fell to the ground. Journey wrestled on top of the dark fae while Locke and I stood astonished.

Gargles of blood ripped through Idris's throat.

"Don't just stand there," Locke said, motioning me to go forward. "Help her finish him off!"

Locke pulled out an assortment of baggies, pulling the string and throwing the sand-like substance in the air until it caught fire once it reached the ground.

The fire circled around Journey and Idris, and I backed up and took a roaring leap through the blaze. I landed next to Journey who was still latched onto Idris.

Idris's screams pierced my ears, his fae voice trying to rupture our eardrums.

"*I can't control my wolf! What do I do!?*" Journey's panicked voice wailed.

I growled, looking for submission from her wolf, but she continued to shake Idris like a rag doll. His hair came untucked from his sleek ponytail, his dark eyes glowing red. He was going to expel some sort of magic if I didn't get her off of him soon.

Leif grabbed Idris' foot, pulling him away from my mate. She growled frustratedly, prowling forward to take another shot. We needed to kill or subdue him before it was too late.

"You won't be able to control her, but explain to her she needs to sto–"

A blast of darkness came from Idris. The shadows curled around the both of us like long tentacles wrapped around our necks. It shook us both as we whimpered and grunted to fight against them, but it proved far too strong. Seconds later, we were both slammed to the floor.

Journey whimpered, and I bolted as soon as the tendrils left my body. I hovered over her to protect her. That was my purpose. To make sure she was safe, especially when her wolf had just surfaced.

She looked up at me with those caramel-colored eyes in thanks, her moon shining brightly until it faded. I cocked my head in curiosity and another boom came from the middle of the room.

The red velvet chair laid backwards, the scotch spilled across the floor, the fire consuming the masses.

Idris stood, holding his shoulder, his black eyes blazing red.

He was wounded, but I wasn't sure if it was mortal, but a fae couldn't heal like we could. Especially after the bite that Journey gave him. It bled silver, not the black that his dark fae would typically bleed.

Her venom.

"You fucking bitch!" he shrieked. Journey winced, his voice too high for our wolves. "How in the ever living shit, did you...?" His mouth dropped, and he pointed to the top of my mate's head and snarled. "A priestess? Fuck this, I'm going to fucking end you rogues. And best of all no one will even care."

Journey skittered passed me, her claws clacking against the cement. Leif lunged forward, running toward the fae. My heart pounded, the adrenaline racing through my veins as we braced for impact.

Unfortunately, we fell to the ground. The fae had vanished into thin air, leaving wisps of smoke.

"It will take more than two wolves to stop me," he cackled, appearing behind us.

Journey growled beside me, her head lowering to cover my neck. A wolf's most vulnerable spot. I wanted to swell with pride that my Journey had come here to save me. Her wolf had forced a shift because of the fear that raced through my body.

"He was going to find you. I'm glad you are here where I can see you, but I need you to stay back. I need to keep you safe," I ordered.

"Not happening." Journey stood to full height to meet my gaze. "We *do this together. Besides, my bite can rip through magic."*

"What how?"

Journey huffed. *"Do you want a history lesson, or do you want to get rid of the prick?"*

I snarled in agreement. We both circled. *"Your ass is mine after this."*

"Are you trying to turn me on?" she giggled.

Tendrils of smoke shadows dripped from Idris's fingertips, his eyes concentrating on the two of us as we circled. If we had a third wolf, this would be easier, but with just the two of us, it would have to do.

The walls of the warehouse were burning. Enemy bodies littered the floor. Beams from the ceiling cracked, and debris fell around us, but neither of our wolves found the situation to be as dangerous as the fae before us.

We could survive a fire and a beam landing on us. Our family couldn't.

Journey lifted her paw, ready to slam it to the surface of the floor to get a better footing. Idris concentrated on her. He knew Journey was important and could inflict the most damage. Like he said, she was a priestess, but even I did not know what power she wielded.

My jaws opened, my lunge quick and precise. I sunk my fangs into the back of his neck, only for it to burn my tongue.

He was coated in wolfsbane.

Leif gagged, our puncture wounds on his neck healing faster than that of a shifter.

Journey, feeling my distress through the bond, padded forward, stalking him.

Idris grabbed his neck, pulling the blood that dripped down to the front of his chest. His claws extended when Journey tried to fake a left, but his nails stabbed into her fur.

The thickness of her hide kept the nails from digging in too deep, but her yelp didn't help me or my wolf. Rage built inside us like never before. Our hair stood on end.

He was hurting our mate. He was going to kill her.

My bite may not kill the bastard, but I was going to make him fucking hurt.

Idris kept his nails embedded in her skin. I scratched the bastard in the head with my paw. The pointed tip of his ear was ripped and hung by a single thread.

Idris's claws dislodged, and he fell to the floor with a thud as Journey fell limply to the ground. I snarled as I hovered over him, my claws raking his body. Each scratch drew his black blood. It would dribble to the surface like black tar but would disappear as quick as it came as he healed himself.

He wailed in pain and shuffled through his robes, trying to search for something. My teeth pulled on his cloak and runes fell from the pockets.

Idris would not escape; he would not live. I would do this throughout eternity if it meant keeping my mate safe.

She shook her fur as she rose from the ground, her body was becoming tired and the adrenaline from her wolf's shift was wearing off. I wasn't sure how much longer she would last in her wolf form.

I moved my claws up to his face, watching the black speckled dust fall to the ground. I gouged his eyes out, but as soon as one was scratched, it healed once again.

Frustrated, I gripped his neck with my teeth, breaking his neck. I wrung him like a doll, shaking him violently. I let go, and he flew, striking the support beam across the room.

The fire roared around us. Our men were long gone besides Locke. He stood in the corner, covered in blood from the carnage. I didn't have time to check for my brothers. Leif's concentration was pinned on the fae and my mate.

We leaped to the other side of the room before he could stand. His back hit the burning beam—one of the last beams able to support the enormous warehouse.

Journey opened her maw. A silver-like substance dripped from her fangs. A venom, but like no venom I had ever seen before.

Idris chuckled, his hand wiping his brow. His black suit was ripped to shreds, his white shirt covered with the black blood tainted with venom from Journey's previous bite. She would have to end him.

My heavy breathing was no match for the scorching flames. I looked back to check on Locke. He saluted with two fingers, pointing to the doorway. This was where he said goodbye, his body, his wolf too far gone to save him from the flames.

I wanted to make Idris suffer more for all the lives he had destroyed. Shifters, humans, and anyone else that suffered at Idris's hands. He was cruel and unjust, even his own kind rejected him, even his own mate.

He threatened to take what was mine. He wanted to take her, use her, dispose of her. What kind of heartless fool would make anyone less than him suffer?

A monster.

No male would dare take my mate, my love, from me. Over my dead, fucking body.

I leaped forward, my fangs bared millimeters from his face. He couldn't do anything to me. His runes were gone, his magic was being sucked from his body by whatever venom Journey had previously inflicted. She saved our asses, all of us.

My mate.

The fae's head tilted back against the burning beam, his hair instantly catching fire. It slowly crept up his hair and onto his scalp. Idris ticked his jaw in annoyance and watched as my mate slowly padded forward.

Her eyes gleamed with excitement, her wolf not blinking once as she approached. The blue moon on her fur shone brightly, and she lowered her head for him to look.

"It's been a long time since I've seen that symbol," he gasped for breath. "I thought the rejected were to be all forgotten."

"*They are not forgotten. They will have a second chance,*" Journey spoke to me. "*Every one of them will be reborn to find the other half of their soul.*"

Idris coughed, his mouth dripping silver droplets on his burning lapel. "If that's the case, then I too, will get my second chance."

My eyes widened. He could hear her.

"*If Hades permits you to be reborn,*" Journey snapped. "*Which I doubt you will be.*"

"*My mate will need a soul that matches hers. Who else would she be bonded to? Did your precious goddess tell you that? My mate was already destined to be mine!*"

My mate's heart fluttered, her bravado shrinking rapidly. I snapped my jaw around his head, cracking the bones that held his brain. The liquid tainted my mouth, and Leif gagged at the taste.

I could feel Idris's body trying to heal, trying to survive as long as he could. Journey tore into his chest with her claws and fangs until her muzzle was coated in his black blood.

The silver of her venom intertwined with the onyx liquid, as the marbled liquid pooled on the floor.

Beams around us fell faster, the walkways of the warehouse falling forward. The glass windows burst, and the smell of burning flesh caught my nose.

By the time I looked back, Idris was nothing but a large pool of tar. Journey dropped the heart of the beast that held her and so many captive for years and kicked it into the flames.

My chest swelled, my nose nuzzling her dampened fur. Even with the fae blood, Leif and I could smell her strong musk.

I was so fucking proud of her, so damned proud. She'd gone from a human with a body so frail and sensitive to a damned warrior. All on her own, she completed the task all by herself—a feat I would still be upset about missing for years to come.

The beam where Idris laid, cracked. My senses told me it was time to go. The flames grew hot as I pulled on my mate's scruff as she continued to look at the death she helped to bring about.

She'd never killed, never done something so violent in all her life. I couldn't imagine the thoughts that were swirling in her head.

But as her guardian, her mate, I would take care of her, bring her back from the darkest parts of her mind, and lead her to the light. Because she was my light, and I would not have her feeling guilty for taking such an evil soul.

After a few moments, she trotted alongside me as we jumped over the beams, chairs, and bodies. We burst through the open doors to be greeted by the members—our family.

Journey stayed beside me, her body leaning against mine. Leif purred appreciatively, loving the show of affection from her wolf.

My mate was a survivor, a damned warrior. Journey had taken everything thrown at her and flourished. She was made for this world.

She didn't fear me when I nearly shifted; she didn't fear me when I told her what we all were. She accepted, embraced, and now had been rewarded with a gift that would bring redemption to the entire club.

Gods, she was strong. And now she was the strongest in the club.

My mate. She was mine.

We both came forward, Locke with his arms crossed, along with the rest of the crew. Locke looked her up and down, and I bolted in front of her. He looked too long.

She was mine, and his unmated soul was enough to piss Leif off.

I snarled, snapping my maw at my friend.

"She saved our asses today," Locke announced, turning to the crowd. "A human turned wolf shifter and fucking survived." He wiped away the blood that dripped from his hairline. "I never thought I would see it."

Beretta shuffled to the front of the crowd. Her top torn, a scratch crossing over her eye and down her neck. "Does this mean all she said was true? We must believe? Open our broken souls again?" Beretta gripped her handgun on her hip.

The crowd stayed silent, waiting for Locke to respond.

"Because, I do," Beretta said. "I will open my soul again."

"Tajah," Journey said tiredly. *"Tajah is her mate, I feel it."* All four of my mate's legs gave way, and she fell to the ground. Her pants turned to a small whine.

Leif circled her until we rested around her body and licked the side of her head.

"It's alright, just rest." I buried my nose in her scruff.

I needed to get her home. Clean her, bathe her, heal her from any magical wounds. Hell, she needed to sleep, I couldn't understand how she was still moving. Any normal shifter would have shifted back by now.

Her wolf growled.

Right, she was no normal wolf.

The crowd stayed silent as the warehouse continued to burn. The sirens in the distance, becoming increasingly loud.

Locke shook his head, tapping the comm in his ear. "We will talk about this in debriefing. Now we need to leave. Grim?" He nodded his head to me and then to Journey. "Priestess," he winked.

CHAPTER FORTY FIVE

Grim

Shortly after Locke's announcement to leave, Journey's wolf laid her head on the gravel, her eyes closed, and her transformation back into a human was instant. We were all shocked that she made it this far, holding her form for well over an hour as well as fighting an enemy she knew nothing about.

I wrapped her in a blanket and took her home on my bike, cradling her in my arms. Luckily for me, I had at least a spare pair of jeans, so a human didn't get an eye full.

Locke stayed behind to talk to the police. They were more than happy to know that the secret sex-trafficking ring was shut down, and no news of it would spread. Humans preferred living by the adage "no news is good news." It was abhorrent that humans would rather not save their own.

But the police looked at it in an unusual way.

Job security.

If word got out that this tiny town harbored a trafficking ring, it would strike fear into the community, and they would leave.

With the warehouse going up in flames and the enemy properly disposed of, the town's law enforcement let the entire wooden building burn until it was nothing but ashes. No traces were left behind—no bodies, no cameras or evidence for anyone. It was like nothing had happened in the old, worn building that would have eventually been torn down, anyway.

One could arguably say that the police in this town were just as evil as Idris and his men, turning a blind eye to the matter and reaping in the benefits while we took care of the town. But we needed it that way. We needed to be in control, and they all knew we could overpower them.

Our men scouted the whole warehouse before fleeing the flames, and no innocents were found. The building was deserted except for Idris and his men, which posed another problem. We didn't have the rest of the missing women.

These women were nobodies. That was the appeal of taking the homeless or those with no families. No one was looking for them, and no one cared. The local police would do nothing about it, so it would be our job to find them and bring them back here to help them start over.

Because that was our job, our purpose. To help those who'd been rejected like we had been.

Like I used to be.

Three days after the fire died, Switch scoured the internet. Idris was dead in the supernatural world, but not in the human world. He thought he was so invincible that he didn't even need to change his name. Instead, he went by Adam Idris, businessman and entrepreneur. He had his hands in the pockets of the many politicians around the country—stealing, blackmailing, human trafficking, gambling, you name it.

Since Switch had found the fucker's name, he was dragging apart his entire empire via the internet. He was also working on hacking into Idris's home computer, which had proven a challenge. Once he was inside, we hoped to find the women and any other scumbags that had worked under him.

Soon, we would have pages and pages of assholes we could go after and an abundance of places where we could find the innocents. It would take time to go through the information, but everyone in the club was more than willing to pitch in.

Journey slept for four days. I brought her home, and I immediately took her to the shower. I cradled her in my arms as I bathed her, washed away the blood and the dirt that covered her body. The only sounds that came from her were the gentle purr of contentment. She frequently nuzzled me, trying to find my neck for comfort.

She looked so frail when I held her beneath the water. Her hair was dark and damp from the constant flow of raining water, but I had to remember. My mate was a warrior.

Journey might have thought of herself as weak when I first brought her here, but she was far from it. The moment I laid my eyes on her, I knew she was strong. Despite finding her under the bed, shaking, she was a warrior. She survived.

Now my mate had blossomed into something new, my wilted flower had now come to full boom. She'd grown into what she was destined to be—a wolf, a priestess, full of hope and light that brought every one of my brothers and sisters a second chance. Because of her, they would live.

I kept her in our nest for days as she slept—cleaning her, bathing her, wrapping her into our blankets. She hardly moved as I kept watch over her, watching each breath escape her. It was the most rewarding feeling, having her by my side.

She was mine; she was everything I ever could have hoped for. I didn't think I would ever be able to get my head around that.

Locke, Sizzle, and Bones kept frequent tabs on the both of us. It could be a delicate time when a wolf first shifted. It was a shock to the body, even for a shifter. I can't imagine how it was for Journey. So, I wanted them to stay away. Let Leif comfort the beast inside my mate, that way she would be more receptive to waking up.

Bones offered to do an exam to see how she was healing and progressing. In reality, the bastard just wanted to monitor her so he would have a better idea of how future humans would take the shift.

I was a selfish bastard. I was going to keep my mate away from all the poking and prodding. She wasn't a damned science experiment. So, I selfishly took the meals they left at the door and kept them away.

And I was left completely alone in my thoughts.

As the minutes ticked by, I only worried she wouldn't wake, but Leif reminded me how much energy she had to put into becoming what we were. Journey had every right to sleep as much as she wanted. She was a damned hero to everyone, and her new priestess status only added to the legacy she was creating.

Leif continued to listen for Journey's wolf. We could feel her wonder, her curiosity about the new world around her. Despite the outburst and taking immediate action when she saw us in danger, she would have trouble trusting anyone around us.

A jealous wolf. I liked the idea.

Leif purred, soothing the beast inside my mate. She was already perfect, Leif especially thought so. Most men would take it as a stab at their masculinity that they could not protect themself and their mate had to save them, but my heart swelled with pride.

She fought for me. She fought for us. She fought for all the souls waiting for a mate.

It was as if she didn't need me.

Leif growled as I frowned. My finger traced her cheek as the doubts of inadequacy filled me.

She purred continually beneath me as I hovered over her. I'd like to think she was trying to comfort me, because all these thoughts running through my head were becoming worse. I rested my cheek on top of her head.

I took long, deep breaths until a spike of the most intoxicating smell enticed my lungs.

My eyes darted open, and a growl rumbled in my chest. I held her from behind as my dick pressed against her ass. I cupped her breast and squeezed it gently while my dick pushes into her body.

Fuck, she smells good.

My nostrils blazed as I ran my nose up her neck.

"What is this?" I murmured to Leif. "She smells so good." Her scent heightened, tinged with something sweet and savory. My mouth unconsciously watered, my teeth biting back the tongue that wanted to lick every square inch of her.

Because, hell, she smelled delicious.

My fangs lengthened, my nose running down her body, trying to find the pungent smell. The scent ran across each breast, my lips capturing her nipple, and I sucked the sweet tasting peak.

"Gods, she tastes so good," I murmured. Leif growled in reply, the smell enticing us to travel lower.

My tongue licked down the middle of her stomach until I reached her mound. I parted my lips, my mouth barely able to contain the pooling saliva.

Shaking, my hands were shaking. I felt like a damned teenager getting ready to blow my first load.

My cock was hard, my muscles tensing at the thought of just touching her. It was like the first time all over again. I touched her scorching skin, licking her up and down her body to cool the heat that continued to radiate from her cunt.

I blinked, taking large breaths to calm my racing heart.

This surely couldn't be it, could it? Had her heat finally arrived?

Journey stretched her back, her arms raising above her head. Her breast arched into the air, and her hands delicately landed back on the pillows. She was finally waking up, and my dick was done waiting.

"I think she is saying yes," Leif chuckled.

I shook my head. "She needs to be awake," I mumbled.

"She is our mate, which is consent enough. You don't want her to wake with pain, do you?" he taunted.

He truly was the devil, sitting on my shoulder.

I spread my mate's thighs apart, ready to see the temptation before me. The aroma was stifling once her lips parted. Her slit was glistening and drenched in the sweet ambrosia that only a god could say no to.

And I was no god.

"Thank you, goddess," I whispered to myself.

Her slit dripped with her own lubrication. I watched as one lone drip leaked down the apex between her thighs and fell onto the fabric. I licked my lips, and I no longer listened to my human side.

The human in me would stop, the human in me would at least wake her and ask for permission, but we weren't in the state of asking. No, now we were in the state of taking.

Because I needed her. I needed her more than the goddess needed the wolves that prayed to her.

I let out a slow, shuddering breath, my tongue parting her folds. A sweet moan came from her mouth as I pushed my tongue further into her body.

I tongue fucked her and felt the walls of her cavern tightening around me. I was doing this to make sure she was fully wet, ready to take my cock, but obviously she was already ready. She was willing. Her body was telling me this by the way her slit was drenched in her own juices.

I would let her come this way, just once.

My lips surrounded her clit. I sucked while I inserted two of my fingers into her body. I rubbed her g-spot, and her body convulsed while she squirted onto my fingers. I halted the gyrations of my hips against the bed, my tongue lapping her juices.

She fucking squirted in my damn mouth.

I groaned, tasting her. It wasn't just her smell I craved now; it was her cunt, her slick, I wanted to paint it onto my beard so I could smell it as I fucked her.

I growled and gripped her thighs, pulling her closer. A beautiful moan escaped her, her fingers gripping my hair and pulling me closer.

"Grim," she said breathlessly, her hips moving against my face. "Fuck me, please!"

My head perked up from her pussy, my smile widening as I saw my mate staring down at me with heated eyes.

"You're awake," I growled.

I crawled over her body, my mouth slamming into hers. Her moans of delight were swallowed by my lust when I forced my tongue into her mouth. My fingers entangled in her hair, and I pulled her head to the side so I could trace my fangs along her neck.

"Yeah," she panted. "You woke me up like sleeping beauty, except you were kissing the wrong end."

I cupped her breast, squeezing it tightly while I ground my cock into her mound.

Her fingers raked down my back, pulling my body closer. I shuddered once I grabbed my cock, giving it two good tugs before I lined it up with her entrance.

"Grim, please! I need you!"

And fuck, I needed her. I'd never heard such a beautiful plea, one that needed me, ready for me to fuck into the next realm.

"Say it again," I growled, only inserting the tip. "Tell me how much you want me."

Journey grunted, her hips trying to engulf my cock.

"Now, Journey, tell me you need me." Because deep down, I felt like she didn't need me anymore. She was a wolf now; she'd killed a damned magical fae. I hadn't done shit to protect her.

I hadn't done enough for her.

I ran my lips up her neck, my body shaking above her. "Tell me," I growled.

She placed her hands on my chest, pushing me away from her body. My sweat beaded on my forehead, my cock weeping with my precum as I waited.

"I'll always need you." She'd read my mind.

Her eyes softened until they hardened again. She tilted her head, her jaw clenched in anger. "I'll always need you. Now fuck me like you mean it."

I roared, shoving my cock into her cunt. My hips thrusted violently while her arms wrapped around my neck. I kissed her with everything I had. I wanted her to feel my dick all the way in her throat while she screamed.

Her nipples rubbed against my chest as I took her. The warmth of her body radiated onto me, and my body shook violently, wanting to do nothing more than to make her feel this. Feel my cock stroking the walls of her cunt.

We had talked a little about having pups, but fuck, I wanted them. Leif wanted them more than I did. It was a wolf's purpose to procreate. He wanted our seed to take root, to grow a baby inside her, to create a life out of love and give that child everything we never had.

A life, a den, a family.

"I want to fill you with my come, I want to plant a pup inside you," I confessed, panting.

Journey's eyes dilated, her grip becoming stronger.

"I'm going to pump you full of my seed until it takes root. I want a family Journey; I want that with you."

Her eyes were half closed, her breasts bouncing at the force of my thrusts. My lips descended, kissing her passionately. "A family," I whispered. "I want our love to grow."

She purred, fingers running through my hair.

Leif snarled, wanting us to take what we wanted, but we couldn't do that. Journey had been robbed of choices for most of her life.

I continued to pump in and out of her, my cock still being too selfish to pull out. She felt so damn good, my dick continuing to massage the walls of her fluttering pussy.

"You like that? Being filled with my seed?"

Journey nodded frantically, her moans becoming louder.

"You want to bare my pups. I want to see your stomach round and swollen, Journey. Your breasts filled with milk, your pussy swollen from being recently fucked. That would be the greatest treasure."

"Yes!" she screamed as she came.

I pumped into her three more times before I pushed my cock so deep, my balls feeling empty, and I gave her everything I had.

We stayed in each other's arms in a state of bliss. Her hair was a tangled mess despite me brushing it every day, her skin flushed red, and her lips parted, seeking extra air.

She looked absolutely spellbinding.

I touched her forehead with mine, a deep resounding purr echoing in my chest.

Except now, panic filled me.

"I'm sorry, I shouldn't have said those things... Leif is just, well, he's an asshole." I panted, my eyes trained on Journey while she continued to hold my waist with her legs, to keep my knot fully locked into her cunt.

We had things to do for the club, to help save everyone else before we could think about us.

I was being fucking selfish. I couldn't just breed with her, not now. Not in a club. We needed a pack.

"Yes," she whispered. "Yes, let's make a baby."

My head turned so fast from trying to pull the packet of pills from the ledge, I almost cracked my neck. "What?" I said breathlessly.

"Maybe not now. Maybe next cycle?" She fluttered her lashes and my cock almost exploded again. "Just wanna make sure my wolf talks to me first."

I pulled a pill from the bag that sat on the windowsill and handed it to her. She popped it in her mouth, and I lay beside her. Keeping my cock fully planted, I brushed the stray hairs from her face.

I shook my head. "No, it's too soon. We need a pack to raise a pup, Journey. It needs guidance, other pups and..."

"Aren't we on our way to having that?" She smiled. "It's happening. More and more of the club will be mated. Wolves, bears, panthers, we will have a mixed group, but soon, they will want to have little animals running around too, right?"

I sighed. After Journey passed out, there were very few that were convinced. Many held too much pain to believe. But there were some who believed.

"Tajah and Beretta are mated now," she whispered.

My mouth parted, unable to speak.

"While I was sleeping, I felt it here." Journey grasped her heart. "I felt them. It was weird. I don't know how it all works, but I just knew. I felt them, I felt them both accept it, opened their souls and just, 'boom.'" Journey wiggled her fingers in front of me. "And there will be more. Much more. You may not think many are open to it, but they are."

My knot released her, and I pulled her on top of my body. I wrapped my arms around her and pulled her close.

"Are you okay?" I asked. "You worry about everyone else except yourself. I don't like it. I need you healthy. Be selfish for once and think about us."

Journey scoffed. "I'm more than okay. Except I might be a little horny, a little thirsty, hungry, and did I mention horny?" She giggled, and my heart damn near exploded.

I gripped my mate's ass and rubbed it against my cock. She shivered, and her nipples hardened against my chest.

"Oh yeah, still horny," she moaned. "This heat is no joke."

She straddled my waist, rising above me. Her dark hair cascaded down her chest, covering each nipple. Her pouty lips looked too delicious not to kiss.

I took them feverishly, gripping the hair on the back of her head to keep her close. "Then let me feed you so we can prepare for your heat. This is only the beginning." Her eyes widened, and then a mischievous grin played on her lips.

She panted, goose bumps running down her arms. "I could think of something that could sate my hunger." Journey bit her lip, gently letting it go until it fell from her teeth. She rolled off my body, taking my already erect cock in one hand and putting her lips against the tip.

"Fuck, little mate, I need to feed you actual food."

But it was too late. Her mouth already engulfed my shaft. She reached out and took my hand, pulling it to the back of her head, urging me to push her lower.

Fuck, what a beautiful mate I had.

My selfless, gorgeous warrior.

CHAPTER FORTY SIX

Journey

My legs were spread on the kitchen table with Grim hovering over me. He sucked on my hardened nipple while he pushed his come back into my body with two of his fingers. He was relentless. He couldn't get enough of rubbing those special spots that made my body turn to jelly.

"Not a drop, don't waste a drop," he muttered to himself as he bit down on the side of my breast. My back arched, feeling him rub the inside of my cavern.

Even with the pills keeping me from getting pregnant, Grim had a new fascination.

A breeding kink.

As much as I wanted to find it weird, I found it incredibly sexy. My heat drove him wild. His cock was constantly weeping come. A new confidence radiated from him every time he talked dirty to me and caused my pussy to weep for him when he spoke forbidden words.

We were exploring things I never thought I would.

The last few days had been spent like this. Whether it be on the bed, the kitchen table, the floor, or even in the shower. My heat was finally fading thanks to the pills. While we ultimately rode out this heat and tried not to get pregnant, Grim said it would last much longer without the pills.

Not complaining.

His deep growl made my pussy flutter again. His warm breath fanned my neck, and I wrapped around his sweaty body. Once my heat subsided, I didn't think I would ever get used to this. Not just the sex, even though that had been fantastic. I would never get used to the intimacy after.

He cared for me like I was some magical unicorn that would disappear from his sight. I kept reminding him we were mated and bonded, but part of him still worried. He had his insecurities. He was still branded with those memories of rejection. But it was my job to make sure he forget them. I'll make sure he always feels cherished.

Just like he always strove to make me feel loved and treasured.

He may not have expressed it out loud, but I felt the conflicting emotions through our bond. For the longest time, he was the warrior, and no one rivaled his brutality during a fight.

But this time, instead of fighting a battle by himself, I was there with him.

And that is how it should be from now on.

He told me it didn't bother him that I'd stepped in, but I knew it did. He protected me when I was a fragile human, and he took pride in that. And he still should because, I was already used to the doting and the constant care he gave me.

And I couldn't give that up. Not by a long shot.

My wolf was submissive enough for that, that was for sure. The tiny purrs she radiated when he cuddled us, fed us, and wrapped us in warm blankets were enough to tell me she enjoyed it.

My wolf had remained silent. I hadn't heard her speak to me or to Leif. But I could see her, I could feel her and the emotions she radiated when I tried to coax her out of the corner of my mind. She was a fragile thing, just like I used to be, not sure who to trust. Except for Grim and Leif, she knew they were ours and would do anything to protect them.

Grim said her voice would come in time. Sometimes it took up to six months if a wolf came out during drastic circumstances. However, with the traumatic way she surfaced over my body, it could be longer. Not to mention that she was a magical being. She didn't fit the mold that most wolves did. Bones theorized that the reason I could hold the form as long as I had was because she was blessed by the goddess.

And by George, the Goddess wanted everyone to survive.

And they did. No one died. A lot were severely wounded, but they were all accounted for.

When my wolf surfaced, it was like I already knew her. Knew what powers she held, one of which was the bite that could power through any magical concoction. My saliva, my venom, was deadly to any magical being.

So, I bit the douche.

But other than feeling my wolf, understanding she needed time, and automatically just "knowing" what I could get from her, she had been radio silent, which disappointed me. I was excited to have an automatic friend.

She got antsy when it came to our mate. When Grim left our side for a moment, she perked her head up and urged me to follow his every move. Which I did, of course, because we had been naked for days and watching his muscular butt had been the highlight of my week.

Besides the orgasms, anyway.

I wasn't sure how it was going to work with him having a rut and then having a heat at another time, but he gently explained we would be on the same cycle now that we were mated. Though I wasn't sure if I was happy or displeased about that.

Who wouldn't want to stay locked up in your home for a couple of weeks out of the year to have copious amounts of sex? I can't think of anyone.

Gods, I'd turned into a sex crazed lunatic.

Once my blinding orgasm subsided, I reached for Grim, and he covered my body with his. The poor table had seen things it shouldn't have.

Grim lifted his fingers, opening his mouth, and swallowed not just my juices but his. My pussy was dripping with both of our arousals, and I found it insanely hot that he would just stick all of it into his mouth.

"Mine," he muttered.

I snickered and sat up on the table. His eyes looked over my body, and his cock hardened again in an instant.

"I just can't get enough of you," he purred. "I'm ready to take you all over again."

I scooted to the edge of the table, and he helped lower me to the floor. Then I reached for his cock, tugging on it, and his groan of appreciation made me tingle with approval.

I stood on my toes, trying to kiss him with a simple peck, but he ravenously took my mouth. Teeth bit down on my lip, and my fingers ran through his hair.

"As much as I want to take you again–" He pushed his cock against my stomach. "We are going to be late."

After being stuck in our den for almost a week, we really needed to get out. It smelled of nothing but hot steamy sex and even with my newly enhanced healing abilities, my body was achingly sore.

Opening a window would be wise. Our scents had permeated to the walls, the curtains, and the cushions of the couch. It wasn't like anyone would come into our den now.

I kissed him one more time before he followed me into the shower, and no matter how much we both wanted to rake our hands over each other's bodies, we kept it clean.

Tonight, we would enter the bar for the first time since the warehouse incident. Everyone was excited for us both to be there, and my new closest friends texted Grim they had a wonderful surprise for me.

We walked to the bar hand in hand. The snow gently fell around us, and the lights of the bar illuminated the entire street. Christmas music could be heard from the outside blocks away, and my face brightened all the more.

Just two weeks until Christmas, and for the first time in my life, I could feel the Christmas spirit.

My smile widened seeing the two giant Christmas trees that stood on either side of the entrance to the bar. They were hung with bright, colorful lights and silver bells.

When the wind blew, they let out a beautiful song, inviting us into the once rough biker bar.

"Ready?" Grim's lips touched my ear as his hand guided me in.

Once we entered, the bar was filled with warmth and color instead of the sparsely decorated cold facade it usually had. Music played by the band members that have stayed despite their traveling tendencies. Maybe they were looking for mates too?

Instead of using the DJ equipment, they opted for live music, getting into the spirit of Christmas.

Tajah's cackle rang across the bar, and her beautiful profile showed the liveliest of smiles.

"Tajah!" I waved, bolting towards her.

She stood from the table, her arms spread wide, like she was waiting for me all along.

There was no cane to be seen, her face full of color instead of the gray sickness that hovered over her weeks ago. She stood tall, her dress a low cut and deep crimson red. Her curled hair bounced effortlessly as she wrapped me in her arms.

"You look amazing," I muttered into her chest.

She snickered, pulling me away and brushing my hair from my face. "All thanks to you, little human."

"I don't know about that. If we need to thank anyone, it's Grim." I looked up to see Grim looking down at me. "He's the one that found me. Without him saving me, I don't think any of this would be possible."

A loud bang hit the table where our group stood. Locke groaned dramatically and watched his beer spill on the table.

"Enough with the sappy shit. We're all happy you and Grim found each other, glad you came into our lives, bla, bla, bla." He waved his hands around dramatically.

But his barely visible wink told me he truly was happy. He smirked and pulled Tajah into a hug. "I'm glad you're doing better. This place wouldn't run without your help," Locke snorted.

"Blah, blah, blah," Tajah mocked.

Tajah swayed her head, patting his back. "Without you Locke, a lot of innocent rogues would have died, including me." She pulled away from him. "And the Iron Fang will have its own pack soon enough. The broken shall be mended."

Locke's playful smirk fell, his eyes filled with understanding.

"Back off, Locke," Beretta snarled, pulling Tajah away from him. Beretta's nose traced Tajah's neck and pulled the skintight dress away from her shoulder. A bright red mark shone beneath and instantly I knew what it was.

"It's true, you really are marked?" I gasped, watching Beretta smile. "Is that my surprise!?" I jumped up and grabbed Grim. He choked a laugh at my unexpected jump.

I already knew of their pairing, but I wanted to join in on the excitement.

"Part of it, yes," Grim said, and led me to the middle of the room. We gazed at the party.

Humans mingled with the club, some serving, some just enjoying the company with others. Some danced with each other, some shared flirty glances, and my heart grew.

The members were really trying to get to know the humans that could be mates.

"Do they know yet? The humans?" I asked.

"None of the humans know what we are. It will be up to their mate to tell them. It's a need-to-know to keep everyone safe, and no secrets spilled amongst the community."

My chest warmed, watching the lively chatter. As I stared at each one, I could feel the openness in their soul. It was a strange feeling looking from person to person knowing who had invited back the goddess.

My thoughts turned to Hawke and Delilah. Did he go after her? Did he open his soul to her?

"Grim?"

Knowing my thoughts, he shook his head. "Hawke is off grid. We don't know where he or Delilah are. Hawke is a very efficient wolf; he's done this before. I believe he will return to us and bring Delilah with him."

I hoped so. Because that was a couple I had been rooting for from the start.

I nodded, watching the crowd. Locke and Sizzle stood in the room's corner, drinking and talking to themselves.

"What of them? Are they happy with everything happening?"

Grim pursed his lips and sighed. "Locke's heart remains guarded. But he is happy for the rest of us. He's still angry at the goddess for letting him go through the pain he's been through. I'm sure you can feel it. But I believe once he sees his mate in person, he will change his mind. Sizzle, I am not so sure about. He doesn't trust women. He barely trusts you."

I hummed in understanding. "They will see. Once mates are being paired, they will see," I chanted to myself.

Grim's lips grazed my mark. I tilted my head so he could nip at my shoulder. My body shuddered and leaned into his body with his arms wrapped around me.

"I believe anything you say, little mate. If you say they will have a second chance, they will."

"They will. They are bound to get jealous once they see everyone else with someone. Then maybe their stubborn butts will try."

Grim cupped my cheeks, his stare intense with the same passion he had right after he had come inside my body. "I love you," he declared in his gravelly voice. He lowered his lips to my forehead, caressing the moon on my forehead. "So much."

"I love you too." I nuzzled into his embrace.

The surrounding laughter caught my ear. Men on the floor flung their dates in a swing-style dance. I smiled, watching hope light the faces of those who'd been sad and dejected.

The song faded and a new, slower one replaced it. "Will you come and dance with me?" I pulled on his hand to lead him to the dance floor.

Grim shook his head and watched others on the dance floor. "I don't dance. How about I just hold you here?" He wrapped his arms around my waist.

"Aw, are you chicken?" I raised an eyebrow.

He scowled. "I am a warrior. I'm not a chicken," he growled.

"Mhmm. Sure." I tried to walk away until he grabbed my wrist and turned me to throw me over his shoulder.

I screamed excitedly and gripped the back of his shirt as he carried me to the dance floor.

The surrounding people pounded the table with their fists. The guys cheered and yelled obscenities at Grim, saying to take me to the back and fuck me thoroughly. My cheeks reddened, but my laughter couldn't be contained.

He unceremoniously dropped me to the floor, his hands staying around my waist. "Now teach me," he demanded.

We took it slow, because hell, I didn't know how to do it either. Taking a quick look at my surroundings, we mimicked the couple next to us. My arms went around his neck and his hands wrapped around my waist. Grim became comfortable too quickly and pulled me against him so tightly, I could feel his cock on my stomach.

I laid my head on his chest, watching the people go by as he gently rocked me while we danced. Everyone was here, everyone was going to be happy, just like Grim and I were.

My arms tightened around him as my heart felt so full it almost burst.

I'd grown up with a family who didn't love me. I had no friends to chase away my nightmares, because I was deemed too different.

They were correct in a way. I was different because I was destined for bigger and better things. And all it took was a gravelly voice that told me to "come out" from under the bed and straight into his arms.

EPILOGUE

Grim

I pulled Journey out of bed early this morning. Her reluctance was palpable when she groaned in protest. She had become accustomed to my work schedule in the tattoo shop, and now her biological clock was arguing with her.

The shop didn't open until noon. Those who wanted to get tattoos preferred not to get stuck so early in the morning. Which suited Sizzle and me just fine because we weren't morning people either. Just meant we were always in for a later night.

Journey was our official front desk receptionist. It was her idea to work the desk, but a selfish part of me wanted to keep her up in our den so no one would see her. She was my secret treasure I didn't want to share.

I didn't like the idea of males around her, near her, breathing the same precious air as her.

Of course, she argued she could go work at the bar or with the females that started a cleaning service. She didn't want to sit around our den and lay about. She wanted to work.

Nope.

Working away from me wasn't happening. She needed to be in my sight always.

Sizzle was apprehensive about having a female around, but this was Journey, and he thought her priestess calling was a good omen. He still didn't take female clients, not that we had many anyway on this side of town, but at least his willingness to have Journey take over and organize our mess of appointments was helpful.

And she truly was helpful. Sizzle and I both had more time to attend to clients. The chairs were constantly full, and she took over the social media for advertising our little shop. We'd talked about expanding so we could add two more chairs to the shop. We had exploded overnight because of her.

I peeled back the sheets. Journey's bare back was a perfect porcelain, her dark hair covering her latest ink.

I smiled, looking at the two wolves—one red, one black—that were in the shape of a yin-yang. As much as I protested against marring her skin and causing her pain, she wanted the upper back tattoo so much I couldn't deny her.

Because I would give her everything.

When asked I her who she wanted as an artist, she looked at me with a flabbergasted face; it made me throw my head back in a laugh. I wouldn't let anyone touch her, anyway. If she wanted some ink, it would be me. No one else could come near her.

Now she carried not just her wolf, but mine as well. It brought me such happiness to see both of our wolves surrounding each other.

I kissed the now healed art. It was a brand that humans would see in the summertime when she wore more appropriate attire for the weather.

"Come on, mate. We need to go." I kissed her nape, and she delightfully moaned.

Her ass pushed into my cock, but I needed to restrain myself. It wasn't the time to take her again like I had three hours before, it was time to bring her wolf to the surface again.

I could feel her restlessness.

The snow covered the flora, the benches, and the elevated surfaces, but not the road. It was well treated with salt by the humans, and with Journey's wolf radiating heat, we went with the bike for transportation.

Having my wolf return didn't mean my love of the bike faded. The roar of the engine, the wind blowing in my hair—It was a way to stay close to the surrounding nature when we could not shift as much in town. It was enough to sate my wolf, but now that Journey's wolf wanted to surface more, she was going to want to be in the forest. The bike wouldn't satisfy her young wild wolf.

Instead of riding to our usual spot, the cliff that overlooked the valley below, we drove deeper into the woods. I could feel Journey's confusion through the bond, her fingers gripping my cut as we traveled deeper into the lush pines.

Once we hit the gravel road, she became vocal, wondering where I was taking her.

"It's a surprise," I yelled over the roar of the engine. Leif was too damned excited to speak to our mate. He was prancing like a small pup ready for their mother to come play.

We came to a clearing at the end of the freshly made gravel road. Trees had been torn down and stacked around a large area that extended five hundred yards in a perfect circle. The foundation of concrete was already poured in the far corner of the lot. Logs were piled high, ready to be stacked and mounted to make the frame of the log cabin.

Our cabin.

"What is this?" Journey gaped with awe as she slung her leg over the bike to dismount.

I parked the bike, throwing the kickstand out, and smiled widely at the site.

Our new home.

I placed my hand on her lower back, leading her to the foundation that would soon be our den. She looked between me and the piles of timber, still not understanding.

The entire upstairs of the tattoo shop apartment was completed. We had an actual bedroom, bathroom, large kitchen and additional bedroom for any pups we may have in the future. It had been completed in the span of a month and a half, and it would be the perfect home away from home when the time came.

But things were changing within the club, and once a certain someone woke up from their foolishness, we would all need to return to the sanctuary of the forest where our animals would have a place to roam.

"Is this?"

I nodded. "It's our future home."

Journey took a deep breath, her breasts rising and falling. My lustful eyes couldn't help but stare at her. It was as if I was seeing her for the first time all over again.

"How long will it take to build?" she asked. "I'm rather excited." She laid her head on my chest.

"Longer than our apartment, and that's okay. They also are working on the future pack house." I tilted my head to the extensive area plotted out with orange flags. "We won't live here permanently, maybe on the weekends, until we get enough members willing to move into it. But it is important for your wolf to spend as much time in nature as possible. Especially in the early years."

Journey beamed, holding onto my arm. "I think Cassandra would like that."

Journey has coaxed her wolf out slowly over the months. But she did not talk as freely as Leif and I did. Journey felt the name Cassandra was perfect. She was elegant, graceful and every bit like Journey from the feeling I got from her. She was conscious of her surroundings, not just for safety but empathy toward the souls around her.

"Are we here to run, too?" Journey asked.

I chuckled, rubbing her head with the top of my hand. She scoffed, pushing it away to fix her hair. "No, I thought we would go back."

Journey gasped, slapping me on the arm and stripped. "Well, I'm running. If you want to go back, you just go right ahead!"

I growled playfully, pulling off my clothes as quickly as I could. Journey was already shifting, her bones popping and whines of pain wrapping around my throat. I fucking hated that it still hurt her, but it would be years before the pain would be nothing but a distant memory.

By the time I shifted, she completed hers, and she dashed into the lush forest.

Our paws synchronized, hitting the soil beneath us. The dead leaves that refused to fall the past winter fell to the ground as we raced by. Journey was free, Cassandra panting happily as we dashed through the thawing streams and the flora sprouting for spring.

"Ready for our wolves to take over?" I linked.

Journey laughed, her head shaking playfully.

"Totally, I'm ready to not have to think for a while."

We let our wolves emerge, their fearless howls penetrating the forest.

If I was told six months ago, I would soon meet my second chance, I would have instantly tied them to a chair and brutally tortured them until I was satisfied. I would have done everything in my power so they would not speak of mates, because I was so sacred.

But now I had her, I truly had my second chance. A woman that had changed me for the better. I'd found my heart, my wolf, my place within the pack that would continue to grow into something so ordinary that we had craved all our lives.

Only this time, we had the goddess on our side. She was rectifying everything the rejected had lost and was bringing those that had missed their chance back to the plane of the living to sync their souls with another.

"You're thinking too hard," Journey taunted as our wolves spotted a deer in the clearing.

Our wolves were readying themselves for a kill, but I still couldn't clear my mind, thinking about how grateful I was for this moment.

A mate at my side, my soul ever intertwined with hers, and a family with the Iron Fang I never knew I needed.

"I love you," I muttered to her.

Our wolves took no notice as they surrounded their prey.

"And I love you too, my big and scary Grim Reaper."

BOOKS BY VERA

<u>Under the Moon Series</u>

Under the Moon
Clara and Kane's Story

The Alpha's Kitten
Charlotte and Wesley's Story

Finding Love with the Fae King
Osirus and Melina's Story

The Exiled Dragon
Creed and Odessa's Story

Under the Moon: The Dark War
Clara, Kane, Jasper and Taliyah's story

His True Beloved: A Vampire's Second Chance
Sebastian and Christine's Story

Alpha of her Dreams

Evelyn and Kit's Story

The Broken Alpha's Princess

Melody and Marcus' Story

Twinning and Sinning From Mutts to Mates

Dax, Dimitri, and Seraphina's Story

<u>Under the Moon: God Series</u>

Seeking Hades' Ember

Hades and Ember's Story

Lucifer's Redemption

Lucifer and Uriel's Story

Poseidon's Island Flower

Poseidon and Lani's Story (Coming Soon)

<u>Under the Moon: Monster Series</u>

(Coming Soon)

Visit authorverafoxx.com for updates and future books!

Be sure to subscribe to get naughty new books to your inbox!

Vera Foxx | Facebook